ORPHAN OF THE STATE

BY

DAVID J ROBINSON

To Stephen

Hope You Enjoy My Book!

David Robinson

X

Also by David J Robinson

APOTHEOSIS ebook available on Amazon.co.uk

drobinson321@btinternet.com

ORPHAN OF THE STATE

His only crime was to tell the truth...

BY

DAVID J ROBINSON

ORPHAN OF THE STATE

MOSCOW-BERLIN-LONDON-PARIS

A MatoTope Publication 2020

COVER DESIGN BY KATIE BIRKS
www.katiebirks.co.uk

For Victoria

Moya Lyubov

Orphan of the State

"His only crime was to tell the truth..."

Berlin 1945.

As the Red Army raises the Soviet flag above the Reichstag it signals the dawn of peace over Europe. But for the daughters of the Fatherland the darkest hour of the war has only just begun. In the coming days thousands of German women will be raped by drunken Russian soldiers. Orphan Dimitri Petrov is a naive Russian soldier fighting on the eastern-front during the Second World War. His parents died in a car accident when he was only nine years old. In pre-war Moscow he fell in love with the freethinking ballerina, Ava. Her probing questions into the death of his parents make him begin to question everything. And now having lived through the brutality of warfare he's seen the depths to which mankind can plunge. But will Dimitri succumb to the urgings of his comrades or can the Pole star of true love guide him back to his humanity? A tale of betrayal, heroism and espionage. Orphan of the State follows Dimitri Petrov through a war that destroys all his cherished beliefs and into a time of peace where redemption, truth and love seem forever out of reach. Confined to a sanatorium, suffering shell-shock, amnesia and with his reputation in tatters, Dimitri learns that when a man loses everything, nothing can stand in his way.

ORPHAN OF THE STATE

Prologue

First-floor apartment in a suburb of Berlin, 1945.

A drunken cry, "Make way for the virgin!" and I am pushed into a room where my comrades are gathered. Head to toe we are all caked in grey dust, a mixture of plaster, soot and ash. Like ghost soldiers, it's hard to see where our skin ends and our uniforms begin. The huge dust clouds we kicked up crossing the endless Russian plains seem to have followed us here, casting a Biblical cloud of doom across all of Berlin.

We are in a stranger's bedroom, once a place of sanctity for a married couple. But for us, nothing is sacred anymore and only the profane remains. The room is filled with the acrid fog of war. As though seeing through a shroud, we now occupy a murky underworld devoid of light and love.

There is a feeling of dread in the pit of my stomach, a slow churning of anxiety and fear. I don't notice the gaping shell-holes in the walls, the snatched glimpses of a city in its death throes. I am oblivious to the flashes of bombardment and the distant glow of blazing buildings through shattered windows. I have become a zombie soldier, unaware of the bullet-holed walls and the shards of glass being crushed under every footstep.

The men part and there, face down, tied and spread-eagled on the bed with a pillow under her hips, is my sacrificial victim. This is my first sight of a real naked woman. A woman I'm expected to rape. The men jeer as my belt is ripped off and my trousers dragged down to my ankles.

Sirens wail in the distance.

"We've warmed her up for you, Petrov." Oleg raises an empty bottle in the air, followed by the sadistic hint of a smile.

"She's fucked many SS Officers, Petrov." Cerenkov shouts over the din of artillery. His dark hooded eyes penetrate deep into mine. "Don't you dare let the Motherland down."

My mind is in torment. Is this what we've become? Sons of the Motherland avenging the sins of the Fatherland?

Orphan of the State

How will the history books remember us? Liberators, rapists, heroes or villains? Right now, we are a mixture of them all.

Discipline has broken down. Commanders allow our men to roam the streets unsupervised. Moral codes are non-existent. No women are safe. From as young as twelve to eighty, some of our men think it is acceptable to gang-rape them. Not only is it acceptable, it is practically encouraged through propaganda which places the blame for the war at the door of every German civilian for not resisting the Nazis.

I feel both shame and pride. Shame for what I am about to do, yet proud my impulses can still respond to a sight so cruelly erotic. I'm embarrassed to say the more she squirms and thrashes about, the more aroused I become.

For a brief moment I think of Ava. What if she could see me now?

How far I've fallen from her standards.

How far from my ideals.

Goaded on by the war-weary veterans, I now feel compelled to rape just to fit in. War-weary, battle-hardened and life-destroying; we are all these and more. A gallows humoured, cold-blooded army of the damned.

I am drunk, but not too much. My longing for sex competes with revulsion for what I am about to do. Then the bombing starts again and the building shakes. Some of the men run out. My instincts take over. Kicking off my boots, I step out of my trousers and grab the woman by the hips. She screams and curses in German.

"Get on with it!" Cerenkov shouts.

A nearby explosion shatters the remaining windows. Colonel Marchenko barks orders from the street below and the rest of my comrades hurry out of the bedroom and down the stairs.

The woman struggles valiantly against the ropes tying her wrists. I freeze as another huge blast close-by sends glass, furniture and masonry crashing to the floor.

Cerenkov is the only person left and he is losing patience. He grabs the woman by her long blonde hair, places his gun in her mouth and looks at me.

"Now, fuck her!"

CHAPTER 1

Russia, St. Petersburg, 2001

S teady rain pours down upon the crowded cemetery of St Lazarus where row upon row of granite tombstones glisten above plots of freshly-dug soil. Beside the graves, Red Flags of the Soviet Union are draped loosely over numerous coffins.

In the distance, nine year-old Julia Stirling watches from under a black umbrella as a Russian Orthodox Priest in a purple wind-swept cassock performs the ceremonial rites. With the Church of St Lazarus towering behind him, his Latin prayers rise and fall on the billowing gusts. Around the graves a crowd of black-clad mourners huddle together in defiance of the elements.

At the other end of the cemetery, surrounded by a thick forest of silver birch and black pine, Julia and her mother stand before a lone grey headstone inscribed with the epitaph,

Dimitri Petrov
1925-1947
Coward, Deserter and Traitor to the Motherland
Only God Can Forgive

Over the top, someone has graffitied the words The Unknown Rapist. On the ground a shrivelled floral wreath shows at least someone had once cared for him. Barely visible through the wreath and dead leaves, Julia notices a small stone plaque on which is engraved,

Matthew 10/26
"there is nothing covered, that shall not be revealed;
and hid that shall not be known."

Maria Stirling, in a black rain-soaked headscarf and grey woollen coat, curses as she kneels to pull out the dripping weeds sprouting from the grave.

"Who says only God can forgive?" she mutters, "those hypocrites at the church?"

Julia, her long dark-brown hair blowing freely in the wind, holds the umbrella in one hand and crouches beside her mother.

"Why are we here, Mum? Who was this man?"

"Your grandmother," she huffs, "my mother, asked me to find him."

"Grandma Violetta?"

Maria nods and Julia sees droplets of rain drip from the tip of her nose onto the withered floral wreath.

"She asked me to forgive him for what happened at the end of the war."

Standing up, Maria shakes the wetness from her hands. Julia, despite being wrapped up in a scarf and navy-blue duffel coat, shivers with the cold.

Maria roots around in her handbag.

"Damn, I must have left the camera in the car," she mumbles to herself.

"But... Grandma was German." Julia frowns, "this man is a Russian, yes?"

"Yes," Maria continues to rummage in her bag, "but some of the Russian soldiers did awful things to the German people."

"I don't understand," Julia replies.

Pulling out a silk handkerchief, Maria wipes the rain from her horn-rimmed glasses and turns away. "No. Neither do I."

Julia follows her mother's gaze back towards the priest and reaches out to hold her hand. Beneath clouds as grey as undyed wool, the priest now defies the wind with an incense burner. He chants more prayers between the rows of coffins. Some of the mourners are sobbing quietly.

"We'll talk about it another day." Maria straightens herself up and lets go of Julia's hand.

As they are about to leave, an elderly couple huddled together beneath a green umbrella break away from the main ceremony. They begin walking down the cinder path towards the car park.

"Excuse me," Maria asks as they are passing, "could you please tell me what's going on over there?" She signals towards the mass burials.

They stop and the old man, dressed in a black overcoat carrying a wood handled walking stick, slowly turns around.

"That," he gestures with his stick, "is Russia's long overdue remembrance of fallen soldiers." His voice falters as he turns to face Maria and Julia.

"A forgotten army of men from World War Two," he swallows slowly, "millions of them were left to rot where they fell, and then covered by years of leaves and moss and mud."

His wife, with silver hair swept sleekly up into a French pleat, grips his arm.

Casting a glance at the neglected grave of Dimitri Petrov, he continues,

"They were men who died defending their families, their land and a Communist system that betrayed them all."

Julia wonders if this old man is a war veteran. She wonders if flying shrapnel had caused the scar above his right eye.

"This man..." he nods to the headstone, "was he a relative of yours?"

"No," Maria shakes her head, "it's a long story, but no, we're not related."

The old man gives a grim smile and produces a crumpled white handkerchief from his pocket.

"With an epitaph like that," he blows his nose, "I wouldn't want to be related to him either."

The rain eases slightly as the church bell rings the hour.

"But," he puts away his handkerchief, "if God can forgive, then why can't we?"

Julia is touched by the old man's sentiments.

"Yes," Maria agrees, "forgiveness is the best of our virtues."

The old man reaches for his wife's hand.

"Second only to love."

He looks at his wife then at Julia.

"If it wasn't for love, I could have ended up in a grave like that."

Julia smiles politely.

"Have you come far?" Maria asks.

"We've come from France to honour these men," he replies.

"Every country involved in that war should honour the dead," his wife speaks for the first time. The umbrella she holds shakes slightly as she shivers inside her cream moleskin jacket. "Everyone should realise that living life is not like crossing a meadow."

As Maria continues the conversation, Julia again becomes preoccupied with the ceremony taking place in the distance.

Beyond the hallowed ground of tombstones, sarcophagi, and mausoleums, a small church choir has assembled by the soldiers' graves. Dressed all in black, with a thick grey beard, the lead chorister begins to sing. Even from a distance his voice sounds incredibly deep. His guttural chanting traverses the depths of Russia's collective sorrow, evoking the struggles and forlorn hopes of generations past. A solitary church bell punctuates his requiem like an eternal heartbeat. A balalaika player and accordionist quietly accompany him. The rest of the choir join in. Their vocal blend of bass, baritone and tenor merge into soaring Byzantine harmonies.

Mesmerised, Julia gazes upon the crimson flags. They are now so drenched that every facet, every carved edge and corner of the coffins are seen in sharp relief.

"Remember us!" the caskets seem to cry out through those blood-red banners.

The colours of a country whose entire history is steeped in blood.

The autumn sun begins to set behind gloomy black clouds. On the cinder pathway leading to the car park, Julia breaks her silence.

"It seems a bit late to be burying soldiers from the Second World War, mum."

"I agree." Maria answers, "but those men were left where they fell." Julia struggles to keep up with her mother on the winding path lined with hundreds of herbaceous plants and well-kept shrubs. "After the war many battlefields were bulldozed over then built upon or farmed. Apparently the authorities wanted to cover up their enormous losses and forget they even existed."

Julia takes a last look across at the cemetery's ponds and woodland.

"The old couple told me that four million Russian soldiers are still classed as missing in action," her mother adds.

When they reach their hire car in the far corner of the car-park, Maria retrieves her camera and tells Julia to wait inside while she goes back to take pictures of the church and gravestone.

As she waits in the passenger seat, Julia becomes aware of the roar of the wind sweeping through the forest. It is now getting dark and she wishes her mother would hurry up. Shuddering with the cold, she wraps her coat tight around her body. Thoughts of hot pancakes and the hotel's roaring fire flash through her mind. With heavy eyes she relaxes further into her seat. It is really gusting outside. She locks her door, winds the window down a fraction and listens to the white noise of the forest.

Wraithlike clouds flee beneath the early evening stars. Julia imagines them to be evil spirits flying away from the sacredness of St Lazarus.

Lazarus was raised from the dead, Julia remembers. How fitting it is to be the final resting place of those poor soldiers. Men who had been raised from anonymous graves could now finally be honoured and mourned by their families' descendents.

Four million still classed as missing in action.

Julia can't visualise such a large number. She tries to imagine them still out there, in shallow graves around which no prayers are ever uttered, no candles lit. The lonely silence. Their blood and bones left to enrich the dirt of a land that had turned its back on them.

Twilight deepens. Something fast and dark suddenly plunges through the high trees, flapping wildly. Is it an owl? A bat? Whatever it is unnerves Julia. She sits bolt upright and squints through the gloom desperate to see her mother. By the foyer of St Lazarus, Maria is stood talking to the priest who'd presided over the ceremony. Their silhouettes are lit by the votive lamps beside the church entrance.

Julia jumps again. A shrieking animal-cry from the ancient forest sends a chill through her body. She struggles to see anything, but the impenetrable wall of oak, lime, birch and pine trees sets off her imagination once more.

Now the wind howling through the foliage becomes the baleful cries of ghost soldiers. It becomes the wailing of lost souls echoing down the decades, pleading to be found, begging to be brought home.

Julia shivers and closes her eyes.

CHAPTER 2

Eastern Front 1944

D imitri Petrov hunkered down in his fox-hole as the icy wind blasted the land all around. It felt as though he'd been away from the Motherland for years. Yet, even if he was fortunate to survive the battles still to come, his hometown of Peredelkino would see only a ghost of his former self return.

Dimitri was sixteen years old when he joined the Red Army and the Great Patriotic War was well under way by the time he first saw action.

The Wehrmacht - the unified armed forces of Nazi Germany - having rapidly advanced into Russia had ground to a halt during the harsh winter of 1941. But first the autumn quagmires had struck. This was a season known as *rasputitsa* when all roads to Moscow dissolved into thick mud and slush. Their fuel supplies had been cut off along with provisions of food and ammunition starving their military force.

The Red Army, by sheer weight of numbers, had surrounded these platoons and crushed them mercilessly. They were fired up with revenge for what had happened to the people living in the first Russian villages to fall into the hands of the Reich. Rape, torture and outright slaughter. Barbaric was too kind a word for what the German troops did to those Slavic peasants. Hitler's men had plumbed the depths of inhumanity guided by the belief that Russian people were sub-human.

Dimitri peered through his balaclava onto the desolate landscape. He saw ruined buildings, mountains of rubble, barbed wire and random objects; an armchair, typewriter and children's toys. Seeing the innards of normal society blasted out onto barely discernible streets, Dimitri felt that nothing would ever be normal again.

Shelling began in the distance along with the rat-a-tat of sporadic gun-fire from the frontline. He lit a cigarette, shielding it with his trembling gloved hands. He never smoked when he joined up. He never understood why professional soldiers would do anything to damage themselves when service to Stalin, the Motherland and its people demanded fit and healthy bodies to defend it.

He was amazed how much the war had transformed him and how much idealism it had beaten out of him. War, where every ideal is stripped away to reveal an animal instinct for survival. And if the Nazis thought them sub-human before, they would be shocked to feel the wrath of the feral beasts they had now become.

It was only the discipline of the training that kept things going. Despite the freezing cold, lack of sleep, aching limbs and sheer exhaustion, here in the crucible of war, the training kicked-in and the soldiers could perform the most arduous of tasks on auto-pilot.

Now, here huddled in his fox-hole, was a moment of respite. The worst of times as this was when thoughts of food and thoughts of home ran amok in his brain. Some said thoughts of home gave them strength to carry on. But they saddened Dimitri. Convinced that even if he could go back home and nothing had changed, everything would be different because of how much he had changed.

Dimitri's parents had died in a car accident when he was nine years old. The ensuing years of being raised in a Moscow state orphanage were relieved by brief periods of living with his uncle Leon in Peredelkino. Uncle Leon was a writer of short stories and writers were the cultural icons of the USSR. Stalin had set up a writer's colony in Peredelkino, outside Moscow, where the NKVD, Soviet Secret Police, could keep an eye on them all. Any work which failed to adhere to Stalinist ideology was banned; their author censured, exiled or, at worst, simply disappeared. Uncle Leon told his nephew of one such man.

"There was a writer who lived near the wooded path by the train tracks. Andrei Yudenovich was his name. He was a good writer. He wrote fairytales and children's stories. They

said his tales contained too much Christian symbolism. They shot him in 1938. He had a lovely garden."

Dimitri recalled Leon sat at his humble desk in his monastic study staring out beyond the birches and verandas. He never seemed to do much writing, but he certainly did a lot of thinking. *"Incubating ideas,"* Leon had said when asked about his lack of output, *"the best writers work best when not writing."*

Leon Petrov, with fair cropped hair framing his narrow face and hawk-like features, was a man of rare intelligence. Dimitri could see it in his deep-set eyes, as his brain fixated upon any subject with laser-like attention. He had such a brilliant mind that Dimitri could never understand why, after weeks of abstinence, he would again take to the vodka. Helplessly he would watch his uncle stupefy himself into incoherent speech and thought, drowning out his God-given talent. It saddened Dimitri even more because, when sober, Leon was the closest thing he now had to a father figure.

At that time Dimitri was a model citizen of the USSR. Handsome and lean, he held himself well in the regimented way of the Komsomol. Beneath his shock of unruly dark hair lay a brain steeped in the tenets of communism. Behind his clear blue eyes was a worldview filtered through a lens of red.

Leon tried to fill his nephew's head with an alternative view of Russian history and her present masters in the Kremlin. He encouraged Dimitri to read illegally imported books by Rumi, Hemingway and other banned authors to stretch his mind.

Orphan of the State

Leon's political views chafed with the party propaganda Dimitri had been drip-fed at the orphanage. Like an icicle in his brain, this clash of ideals pained Dimitri. But he would never denounce his uncle for his anti-Soviet rants. He reasoned that Leon came from a generation who couldn't adapt and see the glories of communism. A generation deep-dyed with deference to the Tsars.

And yet, when the vodka got the better of Leon, which it always did, the ties of blood dissolved. Leon's temper veered from ridiculing Tsarist nostalgia to outright damnation of Stalin's Russia. And, as Dimitri embodied all the traits of the new Soviet man, he directed all his anger onto him. The neighbours would then rally round to help Leon and eventually Dimitri was sent packing back to the orphanage.

Back to hell.

Alone in his fox-hole, Dimitri took out his photograph of Ava. She was beautiful. Her perfect skin, emerald eyes and hair as fair as the corn on the southern steppes had captivated him from the moment he first saw her. The moment his life changed forever.

Dimitri recalled that cold December night when a troupe of amateur ballerinas had come from Moscow to Peredelkino Communal Hall for a choreographed lecture on the history of dance. Outside, urged on by his friends and with courage imbibed from a hip-flask of Armenian brandy, Dimitri climbed the walls of the building. The glacial light of the moon and stars guided his ascent. Balancing precariously on the tiles of snow and ice he made his way to the glow of the skylight. Lying down, with frost-numbed fingers, he gently scraped the snow off the glass and peered into a brightly lit room full of young ballerinas.

After a while the lights dimmed and a spotlight fell upon the glittering figure of Ava Antonova. She glided into view performing a solo routine right beneath him. Although Dimitri was then yet to know her name he was instantly transfixed by her beauty. Her body flowed effortlessly yet purposefully across the floor. Her movements were delicate and finely measured. He would, much later, discover the perfect description for such feminine grace, savoir faire.

The booming refrain of Mussorgsky's The Gates of Kiev vibrated through the iced glass, into his ears and deep down into his soul. The cold night air, the rousing martial music and the sight of Ava spinning and pirouetting below him raised his soul up to the heavens. He was sure her eyes met his for an instant and for the first time in his life Dimitri Petrov felt fully alive.

Rurik the Rus is in my blood!

Although he had never felt more alive, there in that moment, he had also found the soul of a Russia worth dying for. He considered a nation bearing such cultural fruit as Mussorgsky, Pushkin, the marvels of St Petersburg, vodka and the beautiful Ava, must surely be the light of the world! Dimitri felt the surge of patriotism course through his veins as far as his freezing fingers and toes. And, he remembered thinking excitedly, though not perfect yet, Russia would be made perfect through the creed of communism. And though his life was far from perfect it too could be transformed if he could share it with one such as the beautiful girl he'd just seen.

He had to meet her.

David J Robinson

CHAPTER 3

Winter had been and gone by the time Dimitri found out her name. A fortuitous coincidence, it happened one overcast Friday afternoon in April 1941. Dimitri was on his way back to the orphanage from the Soviet Youth organisation known as the Komsomol, a place where they forged young men into future members of the Communist party.

Moscow at this time was a place of squalor and splendour peopled with anxious peasants and arrogant officials. It was a city where desperate men and women rubbed shoulders with high-minded dignitaries. Yet neither bureaucrat nor pauper could escape the soot and filth pouring out of the factories and warehouses as Russia forged ahead into a brave new industrial era. This pollution was considered a small price to pay in the scramble to catch up with the countries of the West.

The old quarters were being demolished and in their place new concrete skyscrapers were being erected at a frantic pace. Russia was in the midst of constructing its post-Lenin utopia. The sheer power and will exerted in the architecture heralded the dawn of the Soviet age and Citizen Dimitri Petrov felt proud to be a part of it all. He was one of the youth of the century, a revolutionary child of the October Rebellion. In those days the words of the *Children's Internationale* were never far from his lips.

"Arise ye children of the future. The builders of a brighter world!"

Cars were still sparse on the now widened and asphalted roads but their numbers grew weekly. Trams remained a popular mode of transport but the number one attraction was the gleaming new Metro station. It was a palace for the people of Moscow. To Dimitri, this was the dream of Communism made flesh. Vast marble corridors flanked by a procession of grand uniform archways exiting out onto the platforms. Pilgrims from all across Russia surged up and down the escalators paying homage to this shrine of socialism. The grandeur of the design was awe-inspiring with its vaulted high ceilings and widely spaced columns. It felt like an underground metropolis adorned with statues, mosaics and stained glass windows. A jewel amidst the capital's shabbier buildings, it was a hint of the perfect world to come.

Orphan of the State

Some older Muscovites quietly cursed the opulence of such constructions but Dimitri saw it as proof that the revolution was working. He saw the gleam of pride in the workers eyes as they lifted their gaze from the gutter. It was buildings such as these, he thought, that would raise their sights to the stars, tempting them to dream a bigger dream.

"Yes, there was still corruption." Dimitri reflected. *"And no, a new Metro was not the most needed of civic amenities."* But after a tumultuous century in which the primitive ways of the Mongols were only to be replaced by the stagnant traditions of the Tsars, the empire was finally stirring. Stalin carried the torch of Socialism, lit by the flame of Marxism and fanned into life by the genius of Lenin. As long as the Soviet-German Pact continued, it appeared to Dimitri, Mother Russia could at last find her feet.

But now the people's gossip and rumour of impending war had led to lengthening queues for salt, matches, sugar and tinned food. From the west a trickle of refugees had started to arrive, driving their flocks of sheep, cows and pigs through the city. Bakers were already being conscripted and Dimitri marvelled to see hundreds of people queuing just for a loaf of bread. From huge billboards above the streets, the eyes of Lenin followed everybody, whilst solemn-looking men from the NKVD seemed to be everywhere.

Outside the Alexandrovsky Gardens, Dimitri had spotted a man in a grey coat and black hat standing by the entrance wall. The man was wearing dark glasses, which was odd in itself on such a cloudy day. Yet stranger still, he appeared to be reading an upside-down newspaper. He also kept looking up and glancing both left and right. Something was wrong about him. Dimitri carefully watched as the man held the folded newspaper in one hand and with the other furtively traced the mortar between the red bricks behind him. From a tiny cavity in the cement he retrieved what looked like a small capsule. Was it a cigarette? Dimitri mused, or some kind of coded message? Plunging it inside his coat pocket the man placed his newspaper under his arm and began to walk away.

Dimitri followed him without hesitation.

From day one at the Komsomol, Dimitri had it drummed into him there were *'enemies of the state'* everywhere, sabotaging industry, blowing up factories and derailing trains. Now if he saw a suspicious character on the street he was duty-bound to follow and report him.

No-one was free of suspicion. People everywhere were wary of eavesdroppers or informers. They knew every thought and every emotion had to be filtered before it could be given expression. A careless word or an inappropriate sentiment could be collated and used against oneself. Many suspected their houses were bugged, their mail censored or their phones tapped. It was a strange kind of reality.

To live and work and play in such a guarded manner was exhausting. Dimitri saw it in the faces of men murmuring to each other on street corners. He saw it in the faces of women whispering in cafes, and the agents patrolling the highways in their ominous black cars. In the world of the secret service it was dog-eat-dog too as they had to prove daily their loyalty to the regime.

Dimitri tailed this potential spy all the way to Kievsky station. The train station was busy but he kept close to the black-hatted suspect as he queued at the ticket booth. His heart beating fast, Dimitri was unsure what to do next. Follow him onto a train? Inform one of the porters?

Inside the station, from a central hoarding, the unswerving gaze of Karl Marx swept over everybody like an omniscient god. The atmosphere of oppression was inescapable. Who would be a spy? Dimitri thought, convinced those piercing looks could penetrate into anyone's soul.

A group of laughing schoolgirls suddenly ran in front of Dimitri.

"Bye Ava!" a red-haired girl shouted loudly as she joined the adjacent queue. When he looked up again the man in the black hat had disappeared. Dimitri cursed and turned to get the attention of a station attendant. As he did he caught sight of 'Ava' the ballerina, waving goodbye to her red-haired friend. She was heading towards the platform he regularly used to go to Uncle Leon's.

Seeing Ava proved to be the antidote to the all-pervasive propaganda which, like snake venom, had held him in paralysis. In that split second Dimitri forgot about the suspect and became a spy himself. Buying a ticket for the twenty-minute journey to Peredelkino, he secretly followed Ava onto the platform and then all the way to her home.

Dimitri was amazed to discover she lived at the far end of the same village as his uncle. He was amazed too that he'd never seen her there before. It was only half a mile away from Uncle Leon's home and the following day he summoned all his courage and went to call on her.

The dark green and white trimmed dacha where Ava lived was surrounded by a wooden fence. In the near corner stood a cherry tree and farther on a small apple orchard.

That first time Dimitri called at Ava's house, her mother, Katryn, a thin sour-faced woman, answered the door. She took one look at him, standing there awkwardly in his broad flat-cap, black woollen jacket and well-worn boots, and slammed the door in his face.

On the second occasion, a week later, Ava's father, Stepan, a heavily built, balding man with fierce looking eyebrows told him he'd come to the wrong house. He insisted that no-one called Ava lived there and if Dimitri called again he would inform the authorities.

As Dimitri dispiritedly trudged away down the garden path he sensed he was being watched. He glanced back and, at the upstairs window, saw a figure suddenly retreat away from the swaying net curtain. He knew it was Ava.

At that same moment Ava was wondering what spell she had cast on this boy. She recognised his face from the skylight and from the crowded railway platform in Moscow. And now he was turning up at her home. Ava's parents had always shielded her from male company. But this young man's persistence had quietly intrigued Ava. She thought he was handsome but from the state of his clothing could tell he was from a poor background. Yet hadn't her grandmother taught her the old Russian proverb, *'one is met according to his clothes, but seen off according to his intellect?'* Her wise old grandmother was from Siberia and she memorably foretold Ava that she would marry the man who gave her flowers on their first date.

Orphan of the State

As she watched him walk away he'd glanced back at her window and in that moment she sensed it might be the last she would see of him. For the next hour she tried to ignore the stirrings of her heart and concentrated hard on her book by Boris Pasternak. His poetry spoke of passion and unrequited love and it cried out to Ava that beyond the fairytale tranquillity of Peredelkino there was a world of romance and danger. It made her all the more long to be free of her parent's restrictions. Yet she also knew beyond the wild lupins and pine-shaded graveyard there lurked NKVD agents guardedly watching over their fragile world.

A few days later Dimitri saw Ava's father, Stepan, walking hand in hand with a plump, red-haired woman in Manezhnaya Square.

It wasn't Ava's mother.

Emboldened, Dimitri decided to try one last time. This time Ava answered the door. He nervously introduced himself. She looked shocked to see him and yet Dimitri thought he saw some flicker of recognition in her eyes. A woman's voice cried out from the back of the house and Ava, with a poignant look of discomfort on her face, quickly closed the door. Dimitri was devastated and traipsed forlornly back towards the grove of pine trees leading towards the station.

Waiting on the platform's wooden bench, he resigned himself to the fact Ava obviously wanted nothing to do with him. His heart was full to bursting with the emotions welling up inside. He felt his inability to quell these feelings was a weakness. After growing up in a place where he had been beaten up by warders, practically starved and subjected to daily squalor, Dimitri thought he was stronger than that.

Above the platform a placard of Stalin's face projected absolute authority to all within its orbit. Trapped in the great leaders gaze, Dimitri became riddled with guilt. He felt ashamed for allowing his own selfish desire override his one true aim of serving the Party.

The train arrived. The train which would take him back to the institution where Stalin was venerated as the 'little father' raising the next generation of Soviet men and women. Back to the orphanage where he was taught to believe Russia was the best place to live in the whole world.

With his mind now a whirl of conflicting ideas, Dimitri vowed that from this moment on he would cling to the surety of Communism.

Then, through the haze of steam billowing onto the platform, he saw her...

CHAPTER 4

A t the time, those last idyllic days of peace seemed to unfurl at a snail's pace. But to Dimitri now, on the Eastern front, it felt like they'd passed by in the blink of an eye.

The late afternoon sun was beating down as he followed Ava along a well-trodden path that took them into the birch and pine woods surrounding Peredelkino. The ochre leaves of the towering trees fluttered gently in the warm breeze.

"How did you find me?" she asked.

"I did some investigating."

Dimitri still couldn't believe she was right here beside him, breathing the same forest air.

"You'd make a good spy. You're not one, are you?" she snapped, "a spy I mean?"

"Would I tell you if I was?" Dimitri answered, cleverly he thought, "I do want to become a journalist one day though," he added, "I suppose they're nosy by nature."

"Nosy and reckless! I saw you that night," she shot him a stern glance, "spying on us through the skylight."

"Us?" Dimitri raised his eyebrows, "I only had eyes for one."

"You could have got yourself killed up there, or arrested."

"Well, you know what they say. To eat the fruit you must climb the tree."

He noticed a slight smile appear at the corners of her lips. Ava was wearing a military-style green jacket and matching skirt that fell just below her knees. On her feet she wore suede walking shoes.

With his senses heightened by her mere physical presence, Dimitri grew receptive to all around him. The forest became a symphony of chirping crickets and birdsong underscored by the cooing of a distant wood pigeon.

The path narrowed, overgrown with scrub, and Ava walked in front of him. She negotiated her way over the gnarled roots spreading across the path and under the low hanging branches. Dimitri could see the discipline of the ballerina in all her movements, lending her body a feline suppleness and childlike grace.

"Why did you want to become a dancer?" he asked.

"Why?" her brow knitted in astonishment, "I never thought why. I've always danced, for as long I can remember. It's the only time I feel free."

"And what makes you feel not free?"

"My parents... this country..." she tailed off.

"Russia? Why it's the best place to live in the world."

Ava looked back at him, bemused.

"Pasternak was right," she reached out and tugged his workers cap down over his eyes, "men who are not free...always idealise their bondage."

"But we are free!" Dimitri answered, pushing his cap back, "free from the bonds of the Tsars," he spoke defiantly, somewhat offended by her tone, "other nations are still slaves to imperialism."

"How do you know?" she answered sharply, "have you ever been beyond our borders?"

"No," the path widened again and Dimitri hurried up alongside her, "but I hear the rest of the world envies our socialist system and how we liberated ourselves from the Romanovs."

Ava shook her head.

"That's not a good start for a journalist, believing hearsay without examining the facts."

"I know things aren't perfect, but we must give it time, Ava," he halted, "may I call you Ava?"

She shrugged in an offhand way.

"The world outside needs our revolution too." After a brief pause he went on, "Karl Marx said the workers of the world must unite..."

"You're a Marxist?" Ava slightly screwed up her eyes.

"Unashamedly."

"Well maybe we should part ways right now, Dimitri Petrov."

"Why?"

Ava paused to compose her thoughts.

"Although I do... admire the spirit of Communism," she began falteringly, "I hate the form it takes. It doesn't allow for human nature, our frailties... our passions."

"We have to be patient," he spoke gravely, "some people want to undermine Communism but I truly believe in its aims." Dimitri looked ahead to the far horizon where the treetops disappeared into a boundless blue sky. "Utopia will not be built overnight."

"Utopia!" Ava laughed aloud. "My Grandmother told me the word Utopia is a joke. It's a pun on two words, *Eutopos* and *Outopos.*" The words slipped seductively off her tongue. "Eutopos means a good place. Outopos means nowhere. So Utopia is a good place which is nowhere to be found! Good luck building that."

Dimitri didn't know how to reply. The path became grassier and led them through a coppice and out onto an open glade.

"Life is to be lived, Petrov," she looked attentively at him, "not postponed until the conditions are right. Besides, how can there be a Utopia under a system that demands blind obedience and deadens the soul?"

Dimitri couldn't understand her reasoning.

"Have you actually read Marx?"

"Of course." she retorted, "*from each according to his abilities, to each according to his needs.* It might as well say, "work as little as you can get away with and grab all you can get!"

"I can tell you are well read Ava, but I fear for what you read if it makes you so cynical."

"Cynical? I'm a Tolstoyan!" she said, briefly losing her composure. "It's Tolstoy who inspires me to think for myself."

Dimitri felt outfoxed by her quick answers, outwitted by her ability to lob his own verbal grenades straight back at him.

"I doubt Lenin would have agreed," he said quietly.

She looked at him pitifully.

"Are they your own thoughts, or those of your parents?"

Dimitri looked down in confusion and kicked a small rock into the bushes.

"I barely knew my parents," he began after a short pause, "they died in a car accident when I was a child."

Ava suddenly recalled her father referring to Dimitri after turning him away;

"He'll be trouble, that one. The apple never falls far from the tree."

"I'm sorry," she said with genuine concern.

"No, it's fine. It was a long time ago."

The path wound on, and in the brilliant sunshine the colours of the forest ran deep. Dimitri would never forget these blissful moments. The shadows and shade contrasted with intense beams of sunlight illuminating red berries, hordes of wild orchids and vibrant butterfly wings.

"So you are an orphan?" she said, looking curiously at him, "raised by the state?"

Dimitri's pale face flushed and a shudder passed over him.

"In part," he answered, "I live here in Peredelkino with my uncle Leon from time to time."

"Leon Petrov's your uncle?"

"You know him?"

"Yes, who doesn't? I consider him Peredelkino's foremost..."

"Alcoholic?"

"I was going to say 'freethinker'. In that respect he's nothing like his nephew," she scorned, "I'm surprised you haven't denounced him yet."

"Don't think I haven't been tempted!" Dimitri joked but Ava didn't laugh. "He must be careful though," he became serious, "like you he sees our Imperial past as some bygone golden age."

"I'm no imperialist and I'm no communist," she replied, "I simply believe we should treat each other as we'd like to be treated ourselves."

"Aha, you're an idealist, Ava."

"Aha, no," she mimicked him, "I'm a Christian, orphan boy."

As if on cue, the 15th century Church of the Transfiguration came into view, towering over the sweeping fields of grass beyond the forest. The sun, gleaming off the golden cupola and gilded turrets, momentarily blinded Dimitri.

The conversation wasn't going as Dimitri expected. He didn't know exactly what he'd expected only that there would be more laughter and light-hearted discussion. But this young woman, this force of nature, had an intelligence to match her beauty. And anyway, the conversation fascinated him. He was always intrigued, and slightly disturbed, by anyone who challenged the orthodoxy of Communism. There was a tiny flicker of rebellion within him that delighted in the thrill of new ideas and new ways of thinking. But this subversive spark was always smothered by the conventional Dimitri, the orphan who had allowed the state to do his thinking for him.

As though sensing his inner turmoil, Ava added,

"I think you've been indoctrinated, Petrov," she regarded him thoughtfully. "I wonder... are you too far gone to think for yourself?"

"I do think for myself, and I happen to think Tolstoy was a troublemaker."

"You really believe that?"

"Yes. I agree he was a great writer, but his ideals?" Dimitri shook his head, "in politics he was out of his depth."

"Well, I judge a man by the status of his enemies. The Tsars hated him and the Bolsheviks despised him. That tells me he was doing something right." Ava answered firmly.

Near to the edge of the forest, the pine trees gave way to oaks and beeches. They rested on the wall of a stone bridge. With eyes closed, Ava tilted her face to the sun. Her pale skin had reddened slightly from the heat. Dimitri noticed a trace of perspiration on her slender neck and his gaze followed the delicate contours of her profile all around to the golden tresses trailing down the curve of her back.

"If you are to make a good journalist, Petrov," Ava spoke without opening her eyes, "and not just a Pravda mouthpiece, you must only be concerned with the truth."

"But communism is the truth!" he thought to himself. And, not for the first time, Dimitri felt the discomfort of holding two opposing ideas in his head. He turned his gaze away from Ava and lost himself in the sunlight dappling the surface of the silver-white stream gushing beneath them.

Ava spread out her arms and accidently brushed his hand. Dimitri's heart beat faster. She turned to look at him, his handsome face framed by the pale blue sky.

"All that Tolstoy believed was true," there was steeliness in her voice, "that love is all, that evil begets evil, and that no-one should exert control over another. But," she rose to her feet and slowly stretched her shoulders clasping her hands behind her back, "you can't express that today." She hitched up her skirt. Then with straight back, twisted hip and arched foot she began to perform ballet exercises on the bridge wall.

"No... you can't." Dimitri stammered, entranced by her toned, slim legs, "the forest... has ears."

"Exactly! And I suppose that is why I dance, Dimitri," she lowered her voice as she clasped her taut calf muscle, "I dance to express through my body those emotions my soul dare not speak."

With that she straightened up, rearranged her skirt, took a deep breath and said flatly, "We should be heading back."

The late afternoon air carried a sweet earthy smell which Dimtri inhaled deeply as they retraced their steps. They fell silent again as the breeze whispered through the tall grasses. Only the croaking of frogs and the sounds of small animals disturbed the peace.

Dimitri was sure she despised everything he had said. For all her outward beauty he was convinced that inwardly she saw him as a simple proletariat, provincial and untrustworthy.

While she, he reasoned, was too headstrong and too opinionated for him anyway. She had been insulated from the realities of life by over-protective parents. And, although the world of ballerinas was undeniably tough, he told himself it was a blinkered and selfish one, glitteringly artificial and ultimately vain.

As they walked back she asked him what happened to his parents.

"It was an accident." Dimitri's tone was cold, detached. "They were driving somewhere, I forget where, I was only a child. It was in the depths of winter though, Moscow River was frozen over. I do remember that. Apparently as they approached Borodinsky Bridge my father took a bend too fast, skidded on some ice and smashed through the barriers."

Dimitri cleared his throat.

"They plummeted hundreds of feet and crashed through the river's frozen surface so hard they died on impact. So I was told. Whether I was told that to make me feel better or they drowned in the freezing cold water, it makes no difference now."

"I'm sorry to hear that." Ava slowly shook her head and grimaced at his recollections. "It must have been terrible for you."

"I was so young, you know. It didn't seem real. For a long time I thought there'd been a huge mistake. I couldn't imagine them dead. I refused to believe it, I suppose."

37

Ava shivered. It was getting cooler as they continued their route back through the trees. A gentle gust of wind rustled the leaves of the upper branches.

"But it became a nightmare. There was a physical pain right in my chest and stomach. I couldn't eat, didn't want to get out of bed in the morning," he huffed, "no wonder Uncle Leon lost patience with me."

"What about the rest of your family? Your friends?"

Dimitri frowned.

"Uncle Leon was the only family I had left. I don't recall my friends coming to play with me after that. Uncle Leon said they probably felt awkward and wouldn't know what to say." He paused briefly. "The man from the Cheka called round a few times."

"Who?"

"Oh, sorry, that was just a nickname, *'the man from the Cheka'*. I never knew his real name but I was sure he worked for the NKVD. Leon always called them by their old name, 'Cheka' and it rubbed off on me I suppose. He lived alone in the apartment above ours."

"Had he always called round?"

"Come to think of it, no. Not before my parents died. He would sit and drink in the kitchen for hours with Uncle Leon."

"Did you ever hear what they spoke about?"

"No." Dimitri shook his head briskly, "I wasn't interested in adult conversations. I lost myself in my imagination, reading books or setting up wooden soldiers in battle formations all over the living room floor," he tried to sound brighter but there was a wistfulness in his voice.

"Hmm." Ava looked thoughtful. In the distance her parent's dacha now came into view through the thinning pine trees.

"I think now, they must have been preparing for me to go into care. It made sense. Uncle Leon had no children and didn't know how to handle me."

"Surely your uncle could have found a way to make it work? You were his only nephew after all."

"He told me he had to leave Moscow. He'd been commissioned to write a book for the Government. After which he'd be moving to Peredelkino, joining the writer's colony. He said I could visit anytime, but for now, for my sake, I'd be better off at the orphanage."

Dimitri could still hear his words. *"It will be good for you, Dimitri. People your own age, you'll love it!"*

Ava glanced at her watch as she sat down on a fallen tree trunk surrounded by a cluster of wild mushrooms.

"I'll have to be back soon."

Dimitri nodded and sat next to her noticing a scattering of violet-blue *Iris sibirica* near the base of the levelled birch tree. Above their heads billowing white clouds moved slowly across the sky from the west.

"So what do you remember about your parents?" she asked.

Dimitri frowned. No-one had ever asked him that before and yet he soon found talking about them to be oddly cathartic.

"I remember them through smells," he smiled vaguely, "it sounds strange but whenever I smell fresh bread I remember my mother who always seemed to be baking. And when I smell oil or petrol fumes I can see my father in dirty work overalls sitting me on his knee, talking about trams and the engines he'd been working on."

Dimitri suddenly realised he was speaking with surprising rapidity and liveliness and became conscious of boring Ava.

"Go on, don't stop," Ava urged him.

"I remember him carrying me on his shoulders and pointing out the ice-breakers on the Volga," Dimitri half-laughed, "and shouting at me for playing his radio at full volume in our apartment."

Other memories slowly surfaced.

"I vaguely recollect my Mother saying we were going to meet someone famous called Pushkin, and my disappointment when it turned out to be just a statue at the end of Strastnoi Boulevard. I remember her talking to the statue as well," he stared into the mid-distance, "though she was probably just praying. And that's it," Dimitri shrugged. "Oh, apart from my eighth birthday when they both took me to the zoological gardens. I didn't like the menagerie, all those caged birds with no freedom. I didn't know at the time that's what fate had in store for me."

"The orphanage can't have been that bad, surely?" Ava said.

Dimitri stared ahead as though in a trance.

"Uncle Leon told me, *God takes care of drunks and little babies,* but not both at the same time. It was another excuse for sending me away. To be fair, I realise he could barely look after himself never mind me. He showed me the publicity leaflet for the orphanage, spotless dormitories, pictures of a chapel and well-fed children in white smocks playing outside."

"Sounds fine."

"The truth was different. On my first day they scrubbed me down with carbolic and water. But the first sight that stood out to me was in the dining room. Row after row of children sitting there with shaved heads, all soiled and unwashed. The walls were pockmarked and peeling. The window frames rotten with condensation. We slept in damp bedclothes. I was given my own cup for drinking from. A dirty tin mug with rust spots all over it. No wonder tuberculosis was rife along with malnutrition and anaemia."

Dimitri took a deep breath.

"Sometimes we were only allowed a bath once a week in an old horse trough. Other times, as a result of an epidemic or civil unrest we were overrun with new-born babies. What with the over-crowding, central heating that never worked and freezing rooms in winter the death rate was appalling. The babies were neglected due to a lack of wet nurses and, with their constant crying at night, I wrote many times to Uncle Leon, begging to let me live with him."

They were interrupted by a woman's voice, not far away, shouting out Ava's name. It echoed dully through the woods.

"That's my step-mother," Ava stood up abruptly, "I best get back." As she stole a wary glance through the trees, Dimitri bent down and picked up one of the flowers.

"Can I see you again?" Dimitri asked, holding out the Iris to Ava.

She paused as though reflecting, dipping her eyes to the forest floor.

"I don't know." She looked up at him and, smiling faintly, reached out for the flower.

"Don't ever call at my house again, whatever you do."

"Don't worry. I won't." Dimitri scrutinised her with puzzlement.

Ava looked thoughtful whilst gazing back down the wooded path. *She was thinking about her Siberian grandmother. Iris sibirica, known as the Siberian flag, what could be more portentous?*

"We're going to an open air dance next weekend," she suddenly blurted, "in the park near to Red Square." She turned to Dimitri. "It costs five kopeks to get in."

Dimitri went pale, but knew he would get the money somehow.

Ava seemed to notice his discomfort. "But we never pay," she added mischievously, "we usually squeeze through a hole in the fence round the back."

Dimitri laughed aloud and felt relieved. Ava started to walk backwards slowly towards her home.

"With the money saved," she gently twirled the Iris in her hands, "you could then take me to the cinema." She brought the flower up to her nose and breathed in its creamy floral aroma. A gleam of joy came to her eyes. For a moment she seemed to lose herself in the intense blue petals in front of her face, before adding dreamily, "There's a musical called Moya Lyubov (My Love) *I'm dying* to see!"

CHAPTER 5

Eastern Front 1944

Now all Dimitri had of Ava's vivacious personality was a flimsy image frozen in time, frozen, as he would be if he didn't get to a fire sometime soon. He replaced the photograph, which had got him in trouble when he'd first joined up, back in his cigarette tin.

It now seemed a lifetime ago when comrade Boris, had snatched the photo from him and goaded Dimitri by saying she'd be getting plenty of action back home. Boris, the bastard son of a mountain troll. Dimitri had punched him and knocked Boris sprawling onto the wooden floor of the gymnasium they had billeted. Comrades Vasily and Ivan jumped between them to break it up. The other soldiers cheered them on.

"You fucking virgin!" Boris spat on the floor whilst being restrained.

The gymnasium went quiet.

"What if I am?" Dimitri blurted. "Some of us wish to be married first."

As soon as the words left his lips there were snorts of derision all around. *A weakness found. A victim to taunt.*

"We have an idealist in our ranks, comrades. A naive, wet behind the ears, holier-than-thou, novice of the world!"

This was Cerenkov talking. His deep growling voice cut through the air. Cerenkov was the hardest and bolshiest of the lot, at least when no superiors were present. The words stung Dimitri. Even Boris was laughing at him now, his embarrassment of being floored replaced by glee at having rooted out a virgin soldier.

Cerenkov walked slowly towards Dimitri, stroking his beard like a wizened professor pondering a puzzle.

"Take my advice, virgin," his cold eyes penetrated deep into Dimitri's, "fuck all the women you can, because you'll never fuck all the women you want!"

Laughter reverberated around the gym.

Boris shook free of the men holding him and stepped forward sneering at Dimitri.

"I don't think he has it in him. He's a little boy in a man's war. He'll be lucky to survive...

Cerenkov spun round in a flash pointing a knife at Boris's throat.

"Floored you with one punch, Boris," Cerenkov cocked his head and frowned, "that not man enough for you?"

This was classic Cerenkov, never taking sides but revelling in any confrontation. His erratic behaviour kept everyone on edge.

"I slipped," Boris whimpered pathetically. Cerenkov snatched the knife away and roared with laughter. The others shook their heads and went about their business.

Boris wouldn't let it go.

"There!" He pointed to the floor, "that shiny bit, slippery as ice."

By now no-one was listening. From the corner of the gym a gramophone started playing a slow crackling polka.

Diary of Dimitri

News of our altercation soon reached the ears of Colonel Marchenko who never missed an opportunity to enforce discipline or boost morale. It was decided a boxing match between Boris and I would be staged the following day.

As I dined alone in our temporary mess-room Oleg approached me. With his shaved head, bull-neck and squat physique he looks like a prize weightlifter. Vasily calls him the *'muscleman from Astrakhan'*. He pulled up a chair and sat facing me. Arms folded emphasising his huge biceps. Things could be worse, I thought as I gulped my food down. I could be wrestling him tomorrow.

"Boris will kill you in the ring." Oleg said matter-of-factly whilst nodding to himself.

I don't know about his upbringing in Astrakhan but I've never seen Oleg smile or crack a joke. He seems to be a humourless bastard with a sadistic streak.

"You got lucky today but tomorrow he'll be ready for you. Believe me, I've sparred with Boris, he's been round the block."

'Been round the block'? I always wondered what that was supposed to mean.

"By the way," Oleg stood up, "ignore what Cerenkov said about you being a virgin."

"I will, Oleg, thanks." I said, surprised.

"When Boris has finished rearranging your face," Oleg narrowed his eyes, "no woman will want to fuck you anyway!"

CHAPTER 6

Diary of Dimitri

So, as if having my body pushed to its physical limits weren't enough, I, Dimitri Petrov, now had my manhood mocked. I see it in the eyes of my fellow soldiers, pity mixed with dismay. As though carnal knowledge takes you higher up the ranks of manliness than honesty and ideals ever can.

The next day I found myself seated in a corner of a boxing ring inside our dilapidated gymnasium surrounded by soldiers sat on hay bales and old tractor tyres. I was wearing crumpled shorts and vest with musty leather gloves on my hands, staring across at Boris in the opposite corner. A grudge match if ever there was one. Cerenkov had stoked the atmosphere by describing it as the ultimate showdown.

Boris, the Chechen Rebel versus Dimitri, the Soviet Acolyte. Hundreds of years of cultural enmity were about to be played out in a boxing ring. It had caught the troop's imagination and the whole gym resounded with a vodka and testosterone fuelled roar.

Vasily was the only person to volunteer to be my corner man. Slim and bespectacled with an aristocrat's bearing, Vasily is very much the gentleman of our unit. Courteous with impeccable manners he also has a first class analytical mind. Yet he swears liberally and I feel he is more loyal to the church than the state.

Vasily had to shout in my ear to be heard.

"Okay, he's much bigger than you, but that just means there's more to hit. Keep moving and imagine he fucked your mother."

The bell rang. Seconds out. The crowd roared. The sound gave me extra energy. We circled each other, feigning jabs, bobbing and weaving like we knew what we were doing.

I did.

And although I didn't want to show it, I was more confident than any man in that gym could have guessed.

From the age of ten I had learned to box. One-too-many losses to the orphanage bullies had Uncle Leon dragging me across town to the amateur boxing club. After that first session he never had to drag me again. I was hooked. I loved the training, the discipline and most of all the sparring. Out of the ring I remained as I'd always appeared, shy and introverted. But my baggy, second-hand clothes masked an ever improving physique. I never saw the appeal of boasting or bragging. I never told anyone in my orphanage I boxed.

But the bullies soon moved onto someone else when they found I was no longer a push-over.

A lot of my comrades had lean and wiry physiques so no-one seemed surprised at my modest welterweight muscles, their definition all but lost with lack of regular training.

Bam! Boris' left-hook came from nowhere and had me staggering into the ropes. He took this opportunity to unleash a barrage of body punches. I'd taken my eye off the ball. My worst habit. "*Focus, focus, focus!*" I could hear my old trainer scream at me.

Although sluggish, Boris' body shots had knocked all complacency out of me. It took some deft footwork to get away from the ropes and out of his range. He was gasping for breath already. I kept moving, giving myself time to recover. Boris was crude but no novice. One good punch from him and all my years of training would count for nothing. His left-hand had definitely dazed me. I finished the round better but, wary of his sheer brawn, was probably over-cautious. I surprised him with a couple of one-two's but never really shook him. The bell went. My longest three minutes ever.

I dropped onto my corner stool. Vasily poured water over my head and crouched in front of me.

"You dark horse!"

"What?" I gasped.

"You're a boxer, I can tell. So why the fuck you let him boss you like that?"

He chucked more icy water into my face, it shocked me awake.

"Stop fooling around. Use your speed. Speed beats power every day."

The bell went.

"You want respect from the men? Knock him out this round."

Boris was stronger than he looked. He appeared slow and cumbersome but the way he approached me showed, as Oleg said, he too had boxed before. He was sparing in his movements knowing how much energy it took just to move his heavy limbs around the ring.

I was light on my feet. I felt like a mosquito trying to sting a giant. His slow reflexes were no match for my quick-fire forays. But just one sucker-punch, one mistimed lunge and I would be a goner, down and out for the count.

I realised Boris was a journeyman boxer. He'd learned the trade but never mastered it. I think Oleg and everyone else knew this and expected me to be no more than a stooge out there. The old slugger stalked me around the ring with commendable patience. He never got rattled as I unleashed counter punches and lightning combinations which easily penetrated his rigid defence. But every now and then, *bam!* He hit me hard. A heavy blow to my left ribs hurt and winded me badly. Hard not to show you're in pain when you instinctively recoil and struggle to catch your breath.

He knew when he'd hurt me. A glint of iron determination shone in his eyes. Yet, alongside his dirty trick of standing on my toes to pin me down, there's a hint of desperation about Boris. He wants this fight over quickly. My chopping left jab has opened up a cut over his left eye and I notice he struggles when I change to south-paw. I begin to dominate the centre of the ring, dazzling him with a flash of hand speed. He's dazed and when I hit him hard with a straight left-right he staggers backward into my corner. I close him down.

Boxing, as ever, proves an uncanny metaphor for life. I am the Red Army. Boris is Hitler. I have him cornered, on the ropes. Barring a catastrophe I should beat him. But even when I'm sure he's on the verge of defeat, he finds reserves of strength and rallies round, swinging wildly, desperate to pull something out of the fire. You learn never to switch off in boxing, never to let smugness creep in. Boris's wounded-animal trick has been used many times in warfare. Pretend you've got nothing left to give, let your opponent wear himself out. Although it looks like you're taking a beating you're actually using the ropes, not your legs, to absorb most of the shots. Also it gives you a rest from punching. And when he's spent all his energy you counter attack and catch him off guard. Then, with just one sweet punch or the luckiest of haymakers you've snatched victory from the jaws of defeat.

Boxing is more than sport. It gives strength to the weak, courage to the coward and discipline to the lazy. My trainer back in Moscow said it's not your opponent you face in the ring, it's yourself. In the ring you find out about yourself. How to transform fear into energy, how to handle pain, how to dig deep when you feel you have nothing left to give.

He also said, *"It matters not how many times you hit the deck but how often you get back up again."*

The crowd's bloodlust was up. I finished Boris off with a right hook which almost spun his head off his neck, sending a shower of blood and sweat arcing across the ringside. He swayed sideways. The crowd roared as he hit the floor. Boris stayed down for some time.

To the victor the spoils! I lay exhausted on my mattress of smelly, rubber sports mats. I replay the fight in my head. I have found a respect for Boris' courage and resolute spirit. We may never be friends but I am glad the Motherland has men of such hardiness to call upon in her hour of need. And, although my virgin status is now known all over the eastern front, I feel my prowess in the ring has earned me the respect of the men who matter.

"You didn't knock him out you know," Cerenkov had said in front of the men, "he slipped." The ensuing laughter, at Boris's expense, was the sweetest music to my ears.

CHAPTER 7

Diary of Dimitri

The boxing match also showed up the divisions within our ranks. In the eyes of the world we are the Red Army, one company of comrades resolved to one aim, the liberation of Russia. But within our company there are bloody factions, simmering vendettas and tribal feuds going back to antiquity.

The Ukrainians mistrust the Russians to varying degrees. As in all types of prejudice there are degrees. There are those who blame only the Tsars and Stalin for their countries woes and those, like comrade Gregor, who blame all the Russian people. And no wonder. In the 1930's whilst Soviet cinema churned out films showing well-fed peasants singing in golden wheat-fields I heard reports of millions of Ukrainians starving to death during the great famine. Stalin's disastrous implementation of collective farms was to blame. But I also know of reports of Ukrainians joining the Germans simply because they pay better!

Our training and uniform are meant to blend us into one cohesive fighting force but they barely conceal the harsh reality. Tartars hate Georgians who in turn hate Poles. Some of these men only fight for Russia because they were born within her borders but have no real allegiance to the Communist State. They have no choice. Fight or be executed.

The conquered lands of Georgia, Chechnya, Ukraine and Dagestan have always resented their forced adoption by 'Mother' Russia. There is an unholy mess of mercenary tendencies at one end of the scale and blind patriotism at the other. In such circumstance I understand the strict regulations imposed on the men. If the officers slacked off for a moment discipline would collapse and the war would be lost.

You have to see the bigger picture. In times of war a cruel tyrant is better than a benevolent king. Most men, it seems to me, equate kindness with weakness and do not respect it. And nothing focuses an advancing soldier's uncertain mind more than certain execution should he retreat.

In an abandoned barn we huddled in damp clothes before a make-shift fire. Shadows flickering across gaunt faces, vacant stares, rheumy breathing, savouring the precious warmth.

Oleg had unearthed a crate of Czech beer in a cellar. It was passed around the men. They beheld the bottles like prize trophies before supping hard and smacking their lips.

Vasily started up a refrain from a Russian folk song. I didn't know the words but a few of the men joined in, stiffening their backs with patriotic reverence. The words spoke of love for our native lands, of family and fighting for peace. The fire and candlelight gave us all a primal glow. Gregor the Ukrainian slept through the singing. Some men played cards. Others wrote letters home, more for themselves, of having at least tried, for there was no guarantee they'd be received.

I look around at the faces of my comrades.

Oleg, the muscleman from Astrakhan, plays chess with the cultured Vasily. An odd pairing, I'd have thought Oleg's intellect wouldn't take him beyond arm-wrestling.

Ivan is tall and clumsy, with large round glasses making him look like an overgrown schoolboy. His face has an expression of constant surprise. He is quite innocent (some would say dim) but Ivan has a good heart and should serve the Motherland well.

Fyodor the forger is a slippery character, sly and untrustworthy with slick-backed hair and dark moustache. As his nickname suggests he can fake anything, at a price. Black marketer, he is resourceful with more than a hint of Rasputin devilment behind his Mongol eyes.

Cerenkov is an enigma. Brooding and watchful, he can fall out with anyone over anything. Aloof with other soldiers, they tip-toe around him in case he explodes at them. He has an unspoken bond with Yuri, maybe because they both come from Georgia. Rumour has it Cerenkov was serving time for rape but was released early to fight in this war. Cerenkov has Lenin's Asiatic eyes, a thick head of unruly hair, Van Dyke beard and a deep scar above his right eyebrow. His whole demeanour reminds me of Ivan the Terrible.

Yuri is unremarkable, dark hair, slight build; he just tries, and succeeds, to blend into the background. He'd make a good spy. He's one of life's day-dreamers and carries around an illustrated book of birds. I've seen him sketching once or twice, architectural details or a bird on a rooftop. He doesn't seem cut out for fighting. But if anyone teases him they soon feel the wrath of his guardian angel, Cerenkov. It's as though Cerenkov can bully anyone but no one can bully Yuri... strange.

Any signs of the new *"Soviet man"* among my comrades are scarce. Avakov, a great bear of a man from beyond the Urals, comes nearest. Yet his Christian faith goes against Communism's aims at producing *a-religious* men.

The men all cling to and are proud of their own ethnicity, again contrary to the Soviet man's supposed rising up over such petty differences. The way they loot shows all efforts to bring forth *a-material* men - men who disdain private property - have failed spectacularly. Is Communism, as Ava suggested, a system ill-suited to the nature of man? Communism does recognise the brotherhood of man. But, at the same time, it denies the beauty of variety. We need both.

Vasily looks up thoughtfully from the chessboard.

"The French revolted to the cries of Liberty, Equality and Fraternity. We revolted to get what? Orthodoxy, Tyranny and Poverty?"

Oleg replies, *"Fuck the French."*

David J Robinson

CHAPTER 8

Moscow 1941

Ava's father, Stepan Antonova, was a stern-faced, buttoned-down, yet puffed up member of the Communist Party. Having been located abroad in foreign cities as part of his ambassadorial duties, he should have felt secure in his position. He should have sensed the respect of his colleagues back in Moscow. And yet, since those heady days after Stalin's accession, a time of optimism and of consolidation, a time when Russia's future looked bright, the atmosphere in the Party had now become mired in suspicion and mistrust. Like a fish that rots from the head, the emerging paranoia of Stalin had bled down into the ranks of every official, commissar and bureaucrat.

Everyone was watching their backs. They all felt the pressure of someone looking over their shoulder. All felt the anxiety of making a wrong decision, a misjudged remark, or even, God forbid, using one's initiative. Every single person feared becoming a non-person. Denounced, stripped of rank, career, housing, everything. This could happen in a blink of an eye to a clerk, a teacher or even the head of the NKVD himself.

No-one was safe from Stalin's withering assessments. A shuffle of papers, a glance at a charge sheet, a tick in a box and you were gone. Purged from the Party, interrogated, tortured then banished to the east, to slave in a camp until death or, now there was a war to fight, a reprieve. The chance to wash away your crimes against the Motherland with your blood.

Stepan Antonova now began to understand the full psychological impact of those huge portraits of Lenin, Stalin and Marx. Staring down impassively at the populace they say, *"We are watching your every move!"* It was the Soviet death stare that people feared could infiltrate the mind of anyone who held a subversive thought.

Tonight Stepan felt heavy, bloated by the Persian caviar from the southern Caspian followed by goulash and dumplings washed down with French wine. Then the pastries and cakes he'd finished off with a large brandy coffee. He'd finally topped it all off with a fine Panama cigar and Armenian cognac. Yet he still felt empty inside, a void no amount of gluttony could fill. A gluttony afforded by perks and paybacks, bribes and black market chicanery.

Everyone was doing it. Even the Government turned a blind eye to low-level criminality and petty frauds which they saw as short-term glitches. These glitches in the system were considered inevitable as human behaviour was remoulded to house the spirit of Marxism. Yet even Stepan was aware these corrupt means of shaping a perfect society did not bode well.

Stepan conjured with these thoughts on his way back to his apartment among the prestigious block of flats known as the House of Government. He was returning from the Stoleshnikov Hotel where he'd spent the evening with his latest mistress. Mistresses were a perk, he reasoned, for being in a position of power. He knew status was the ultimate aphrodisiac in any society. And it was his status that enabled him to bend the rules so his latest sweetheart got extra food coupons or a nicer apartment or even a better school for her children. Stepan liked to think he had some principles though. Preferring women with no male ties, he went for widows and divorcees. Women who for a bit of help in their domestic drudgery were willing to give up their body for his sexual needs.

There was Raisa, mature and full-bodied with red hair. She was dirt-poor yet had a taste for the finer things in life like caviar and champagne which he could easily supply. She was divorced, uncultured but sexually voracious.

Then there was Marya, young yet widowed with two infant boys who now attended an exclusive kindergarten thanks to Stepan's intervention. She was quiet, submissive and yet had a rare feminine grace that he found deeply attractive. She obviously didn't love him or the rough sex, but he saw this as a challenge. He wanted her to need him, to make him feel important. There was always sadness in Marya's eyes as though she knew this was as good as life was going to get. She had lost all self-confidence. Stepan liked that too.

Musing on these women and their social class, Stepan rationalised that people who expect a life of drudgery inevitably find their horizons shrink to meet their expectations, *'a serf-fulfilling prophecy'*, as he liked to call it. And as long as socialism encouraged the *'count-your-blessings'* mentality of the abject poor, Stepan knew people like him would always prosper.

He turned a corner and walked on beneath the black speakers strung out across the city from where Molotov had announced the outbreak of war only weeks ago. Even the prospect of war failed to lift Stepan out of his self-absorption.

He knew none of his mistresses loved him. Even his second wife, Katryn bore him scant affection. Why was he surprised? After all, he'd only remarried to conform to the Soviet model of being a devoted family man.

The State saw fit to give them a dacha in Peredelkino even though Stepan considered Katryn to be a writer of mediocre talent. Her biggest success was in writing magazine articles outlining the ideal attributes of the New Communist Woman.

Stepan thought she'd appreciated her birthday gift of Guerlain's 'Vol de Nuit' – a perfume named after the French author Antoine de Saint-Exupery's book called The Night Flight. Katryn thought this exotic perfume he'd brought back from Paris was exclusively for her. She imagined she was the only woman in Russia to wear such a scent. Yet when Stepan came home with traces of the fragrance on him she knew she was not only sharing her perfume, she was sharing her husband too.

Katryn was infuriated. Was there nothing she could call her own? These days she and Stepan rowed constantly. And for Stepan that was good a reason as any to stay at his city apartment when 'working late'.

Ava's real mother had died giving birth. Within a year Stepan had married Katryn. Unable to conceive, she became step-mother to Ava. She wanted to feel the maternal emotions, the bond of motherhood, but it had all been a horrible mistake. Having lived alone for two years before meeting Stepan, she'd grown used to solitude. With Stepan away at work most days and abroad for weeks on end, that was no problem. The problem was his wilful, precocious young daughter.

Katryn tried to exert control, to impose some discipline on this spirited girl. All attempts failed. Ava proved to be fiery, stubborn and contrary at every turn. That was how Katryn saw her, whereas Stepan preferred to think of Ava as passionate, tenacious and capable of looking after herself.

It was a marriage of convenience, a facade for Stepan who knew a good Stalinist was expected to be monogamous. It was this pursuit of reputation that had stripped him of self respect as he stubbornly gave value to the things he knew to be worthless. Like the writer forced to write what he does not feel, or the painter forbidden to paint what he really sees,

Stepan lived a life he really didn't want to live, and for what? A bit of comfort? A sliver of security?

Stepan walked down Denezhny Lane past random patrols of old men in scruffy uniforms who looked ill-equipped and ill-trained. *This bloody war!* He cursed, blaming it for his sudden recall from Paris. But he knew he couldn't just blame the war. After each trip abroad Stepan noticed his welcome home had got colder and colder. Gone was the easy-going familiarity with his fellow colleagues. The casual offer of a drink after work, even the usual dinner invitations between couples had dried up. His social circle was shrinking fast. Was he deliberately being frozen out? Or was it the same for everyone? All his peers carried the haunted look of silent persecution and, like the proverb of spooked crows, seemed afraid of their own shadows. Everyone in his office went about their work with grim determination. Determined to blend in and not be seen as 'agitators' in any sense of the word.

He now inhabited a grey world, a world of furrowed brows and lukewarm relations far removed from the life he had lived as an ambassador in Paris. As he walked in murky twilight past a giant department store, its exotic window display masking the bare shelves inside, he reminisced on his days in the French Capital.

Pre-war Paris had been a haven for film-makers, musicians, artists and writers. Artists called Cezanne, Picasso, Man Ray and Duchamp were pioneering the new art movements of Cubism and Surrealism. The open-heartedness of these visionary artists reflected the open-minded and fun-loving nature of the ordinary Parisians. How could his Communist beliefs not be disturbed by this carefree and colourful existence? How could he not long for those same pleasures in his own country where they were most absent? He knew he'd been infected by the ways of the West, seduced by the jazz clubs, intoxicated by the grand architectural shapes created by Le Corbusier on the modern buildings. His contempt for the bourgeoisie had also been softened by their love of risqué entertainers like Maurice Chevalier and Mistinguett at the Folies Bergére, and the enlightened hospitality they gave to a black singer called Josephine Baker. This was the Paris that mesmerised him and showed up the emptiness of Russia's state-funded artists who performed within a socialist strait-jacket.

He remembered with a shiver the day after his last return from Paris when he found a blank envelope on his desk. The message inside read,

"The scabby sheep spoils the whole flock".

Was it a warning? He'd told no-one of his admiration for the French way of life. And Stepan was truly convinced he'd long since mastered the art of saying one thing whilst thinking another.

He turned down old Arbat Street beneath another placard of Stalin, held aloft for veneration. But who would revere Stepan when he couldn't even look himself in the mirror? Integrity was something no amount of bribery money could buy. And yet where had integrity got anyone? A one way ticket to Siberia? In this society, Stepan had long since concluded, fewer scruples meant more roubles.

On the main streets all the buildings were now disguised with camouflage netting. On the rooftops anti-aircraft guns and searchlights were aimed in readiness towards the night sky.

From out of nowhere a gang of street-kids, ragged, barefoot and filthy, ran across his path and down a dark alley. For a moment Stepan counted his blessings that Ava was not one of them. They were the product of the State's purges which had ripped families apart. Thousands of these impoverished children formed street gangs, living rough in the cities, surviving off their wits and thieving from the very society that had robbed them of a future. There was no chance of reforming these feral beasts. They were Stalin's dirty secret, an embarrassing stain on the 'perfect' society.

Even the children from stable families fared little better being brought up in homes that were often grimy and overcrowded. Stepan knew too, from secret government statistics, that in the homes of the proletariat half the fathers were alcoholics and many mothers forced into prostitution to make ends meet. He knew the latter from firsthand experience.

He feared for the future. The Bolsheviks vision of a society wholly transformed by the revolution was not bearing fruit. They'd hoped they could remodel human nature so much that Soviet women would become maternal handmaids to all children, not just their own.

As always, even the best intentions - like the State's desire to rescue children from abusive and impoverished families - often had dire consequences. Funding for education and children's homes had been drastically cut ever since the civil war. Stepan deemed it tragic how the golden opportunity to overturn the old world and make real the grand utopian dream was undermined by a simple lack of funding. Instead of enterprise, reform and progress, the financial constraints on all sections of society only ensured cultural stagnation.

As he turned the corner into Arbatskaya Square the bright lights of the cinema houses and late night coffee bars gave him a feeling of normality. People behaved as if the war was never going to reach the Capital. Even now he marvelled at the shrewdness of the regime keeping open the theatres and dance halls as a means of bolstering morale.

As a crowd began to spill out of one movie theatre, showing the popular musical *Moya Lyubov*, Stepan hurried over to the other side of the road. Then, glancing across the street, he saw the face of the one person in the world who genuinely loved him. It was his only daughter, Ava. For a moment Stepan's heart leapt to see her face beaming with joy as she chatted excitedly whilst descending the crowded steps of the Khudozhestvenny Cinema theatre

Ava's prettiness made her stand out from the crowd. Indeed, Stepan thought, her beauty would hold its own amidst the glamour of the ladies of Paris. Since his return from France, the care-worn faces, pale skin and bulky overcoats covering the stout figures of most Muscovite women made him pine for Parisian elegance. Those immaculate women in slender outfits, fur stoles, silk chiffon with billowing sleeves and demure cloche hats.

He set off towards Ava. At first Stepan couldn't see who she was talking to behind the bobbing heads and jostling umbrellas. But when he caught sight of the laughing face of Dimitri Petrov he felt a chill throughout his body. Stopping dead in the middle of the road, a trolley-bus blasted its horn and Stepan withdrew hastily back into the shadows.

"Why can't the bastard keep away from her?" He thought to himself. *"Trouble seldom comes alone."* Although he'd never seen his daughter look so happy for a long time he dismissed it as the naivety of youth.

Why not confront them now?

He was still a bit drunk. And there were too many people around. He didn't want to cause a scene lest anybody recognise him.

Stepan watched them, hand in hand, disappearing into the crowded pavement. It was like a dagger in his heart. *Morning is wiser than evening*, his father used to say, and Stepan would take no chances where his daughter was concerned. Not many would know Ava was his daughter. But if anyone did, she could now be denounced for consorting with a child of enemies of the state.

CHAPTER 9

Diary of Dimitri

Fyodor the forger, Yuri and Cerenkov are plotting something. I can feel it in my bones. I've spotted them deep in conversation. Conspiratorial whispers which turn into ordinary barrack room banter when anyone gets within earshot. Or am I just getting paranoid?

Who can blame them? Maybe they're just letting off steam about the thousand and one petty bureaucracies getting in the way of the war. The carelessness of battle plans, the dearth of intelligent senior officers or the lack of decent clothes and ammunition. I share their concerns and it shows how much more Communism must do to make the system perfect.

Nevertheless, I shall not share my concerns with anybody. Even though the criticism is valid, it is seen as unpatriotic and met with serious punishment. I'll keep my head down and if the men feel they can't confide their criticism of the regime with me, so much the better. For if I did not report their grumblings I would be as unpatriotic as them!

When I signed up to fight in this war it was Uncle Leon, of all people, who pleaded with me to 'toe-the-line' and act as a fully-fledged Marxist. Along with Ava, Leon knew he'd planted seeds of doubt about Communism in my mind, yet he knew there might be spies within the army eager to root out any anti-communist sympathies.

"Your life is more valuable than any ideology." He'd said, before adding as enigmatically as only he could, *"Through war, generations are revered. But if being forgotten is the price of peace, I hope no-one visits your grave, Dimitri."*

We're across the Estonian Frontier.

I'm being genuinely vague with the dates and locations in case my diary falls into enemy hands. So I will keep the details to a minimum. I write in a concoction of scruffy English (Uncle Leon encouraged me to learn the language of the last great empire) and a dash of my own coded Cyrillic alphabet.

I write to Ava, telling her of our progress, of how strong we are as a unit. That the war will soon be over and those trips to the cinema and romantic walks in Peredelkino woods shall soon be ours again. As I read through the letter I realise I have expressed the exact opposite of what I really think. Is it to protect her feelings? Is it out of fear our letters will be vetted by Communist officials? Or is it just the stuff I want to believe myself?

We are billeted in an abandoned school. Vasily checks his rifle as scrupulously as ever. He closes one eye to spy down the barrel and, as another bomb blast shakes the building, he speaks a proverb of Isaiah. *"The earth shall lurch like a drunkard, the sins of men weigh it down..."* He puts his rifle down and turns to me.

"This is what we see now comrade, no?"

"It's not the kind of proverb Molotov has been broadcasting." I reply.

"Molotov speaks in clichés. *'The Germans are weak and have low morale.'* We knew nothing about what was happening at the front until we got here. He never said the German forces were over three million strong!"

"You speak too freely on the matter." I say trying to warn him of eavesdroppers.

"I speak with the freedom of a condemned man. We all saw the superior artillery the Germans left behind. That captured officer's leather greatcoat would cost more than a year's wages back home. It appears Hitler loves his people more than Stalin loves us."

Vasily is in full flow and has attracted the attention of Cerenkov and Gregor.

"Thanks to Stalin's farming programme millions starved in my Ukraine." Gregor adds to the air of dissent.

"I heard Ukrainian men welcomed the Germans with open arms and your women with open legs!" Cerenkov mocks.

"Some peasants did and is it any wonder?" Gregor becomes angry. "We know of parents so crazed by hunger they ate their own children! The Germans with their Christ–like crosses on their tanks were seen as liberators. They must treat us better than the Russians, we thought. But we soon realised they were even worse."

"We've all heard those rumours. It can't have been that bad." I counter, still trying to hold back the tide of mutiny.

"Rumours!" Vasily towers over me. "So tell me who these skeletal people are we see every day begging for a crust eh? That's not just come about through this war. That's our leader's legacy. They don't care about us. They are worse than the Tsars they replaced."

I can't believe my ears.

"You speak like an Imperialist. Do you want to see the return of the Tsars?"

Gregor stands up.

"I speak as a soldier. When you've served the Motherland for as long as I have you begin to see things as they really are. No Pravda bullshit or party slogan can blind me to our self-serving officers, the corruption of the NKVD and the deviousness of Stalin!"

A door slams and Gregor's words hang in the air.

Colonel Marchenko walks slowly out from the shadows, gun in hand.

"Bravo Comrade."

Gregor's face drains of all colour.

Marchenko orders Gregor to kneel down and points the gun at his head.

"Colonel Marchenko, I don't know what you heard but..."

"Silence," Marchenko shouts, "your own lips condemn you as the traitor I always knew you were."

"Colonel, we were just playing around. It's a play," Vasily pleads, "a play based on what the Germans think of us."

Marchenko keeps his gun trained on Gregor's head.

"A play?" Marchenko nods implausibly. "Well... actors in a play, as in life, have their entrances and..." he cocks his gun as Gregor trembles beneath him, "...their exits."

Marchenko's cold smile suddenly turns to fury. His outstretched arm presses the gun barrel hard into Gregor's skull.

"I know what you are, Gregor Nevsky, and you know what you are. I am arresting you as an enemy of the state. You will leave this unit immediately and be handed over to the NKVD with my instructions that you be shot by firing squad. The next person to speak will join you."

Marchenko stares at each of us in turn, daring us to utter a word.

"For all I know you are all guilty of treason. But I am a fair man and shall give you three the benefit of the doubt. Petrov, you will come with me to escort the prisoner."

I get up and stand guiltily behind Gregor.

"As for the rest of you, I suggest you find another play to perform. *'The Idiot'* perhaps?"

We escort an ashen-faced Gregor out into the cold night air. As Marchenko marched on ahead, these were the last words Gregor whispered to me,

"Don't worry about me, Dimitri. If I have not the truth of my own thoughts, I have nothing."

An hour later, from our barracks, we hear the gun crack of the firing squad and Gregor Nevsky becomes another hapless statistic of war.

CHAPTER 10

Berlin 1940-45

For as long as she remembered Violetta hated the Fuhrer. Long before he had taken the German nation to war she had seen a young Adolf Hitler giving a speech at her parent's Bierkellar in Cologne. Whipping up support for his Nationalist Party she had seen at first hand his ability to spellbind the audience with an oratorical and theatrical display of sheer brilliance. He began slowly, waiting for silence to descend upon the room. His opening words were quiet causing the listeners to strain to hear him. Then he would build up the pace and volume accompanied by dramatic gestures and poses that had everyone except the precocious Violetta in his thrall.

"In ourselves alone lies the future of the German people!"

This wasn't the polished, finished spectacle which Hitler perfected at Nuremberg but it did the job. He told the audience what they wanted to hear, that their failures and troubles in life were not their fault. No, it was the fault of having so many foreigners in Germany and so many constraints on German industry since the Great War.

The fault could not lie with the German people because the German people were a great people, the best of people. And therefore only German people themselves could save this once great nation by voting him and his Nazi party into power where they would unleash the shackles which bound Germany like a tethered Eagle. Violetta knew then what a dangerous man he was. Where others saw the passionate arguments of a true patriot, she recalled only his cruel eyes glinting with the zeal of a sociopath.

Violetta knew a good performance when she saw one. The theatre had been her lifelong passion ever since she saw "La Boheme" being staged as a young girl on a school trip. Drama class beckoned and her natural talent saw her excel rapidly onto amateur productions of The Tempest, Carmen and Gotterdammerung. As much as she enjoyed the high-brow operas, her blonde good looks and hour-glass figure combined with a love of a good time ensured her destiny lay in more earthy productions. Her talents turned towards Burlesque and erotic cabaret's in the seedy underworld of the late 1930's Berlin. By then Hitler and his entourage were in power and even in the fantasy enclave of theatre-land his force of will was being felt.

Orphan of the State

Violetta's best friend, singer and striptease artist Rula Hornski had been on the receiving end of harsh treatment by one German punter because of rumours about her Jewish ancestry. She'd been followed home once, and found graffiti daubed outside her door in the morning. Rula had become worried for her life and Violetta suggested she should come and live with her until this atmosphere of hostility had blown over. This suggestion did not go down well with Karl Hubresch, Violetta's husband. He was another man with a talent for hiding his true nature. Violetta should have seen through his personality charade as she saw through Hitler's. But she hadn't been in love with Hitler and that had made all the difference.

At the seedy Die Bosen Club, Violetta performed under the name *Viola L'Amour*. Onstage she was statuesque, and with her gymnastically-fit Aryan body, ticked all the boxes of the Nazi clientele's fantasies. One fateful night Karl Hubresch was sat in the audience watching spellbound from the shadows.

Viola knew how to put on a spectacle. *"Willkommen mein freunde!"* she purred before every performance beneath the crystal chandeliers. She went from tongue-in-cheek eroticism to downright raunchy, yet she managed to convey it all with a touch of class. Shimmying and writhing around to Debussy's *Claire de Lune*, she coaxed and teased the crowd by ever-so-slowly peeling off each article of clothing.

Back then Karl was a struggling bio-chemist being wined and dined by the Nazi elite. When he discreetly asked about Viola they insisted he meet her after the show. In her dressing room he was pleased to find her just as voluptuous and teasingly coy as onstage. She fulfilled his vision of the ideal German woman. Violetta fell for his manners and self-deprecating sense of humour, so unlike the brash German officers she usually met.

They married within the year. Twelve months later she gave birth to Maria. Karl and Violetta were so different and yet their relationship worked, initially. He was studious and heavily involved in his work. He had no time for shows and parties which suited Violetta's free-spiritedness. But although she appeared to be an unconventional mother she made sure she was always there for Maria.

Before she became a mother, Violetta had anxieties like everyone else. Not believing herself to be classically beautiful she found the heavy make-up of Burlesque a suitable mask for her insecurity. And, like anyone who dons a mask, she felt able to express herself more fully knowing she wouldn't be easily recognised apart from her stage persona.

This dual existence came in useful later when she joined the White Rose, a non-violent fascist resistance group. She joined to honour her father's memory. In later life he'd become a strident anti-fascist and had been killed in an unprovoked street attack by a gang of Hitler's drunken Storm troopers.

She'd joined the White Rose around the time her marriage to Karl was on the rocks. When they'd met he was just a young scientist at the Kaiser Wilhelm Institute. Now under Nazi patronage he was *somebody*, and he no longer wished to share his wife with the dregs of Berlin.

It was the little things at first. Karl would criticise her make-up or the way she'd cooked his breakfast. Then it was her job. He insisted she give up the stage to become a fulltime *hausfrau*. He wanted a big family and tormented her by saying what children would want a common actress – one who shows all her 'bits' to the people of Berlin – for a mother. He ignored the fact that it was this common actress and her 'bits' that had attracted him in the first place. She couldn't afford to leave him yet but she had a plan that her and Rula could maybe save up enough money to get an apartment together. In the meantime Karl was now in a constant rage. He'd hit Violetta many times and tried to rape her too when his drunken advances were shunned. She lived in fear of getting pregnant again and being tied to him even more.

While still married she began to play the part of the quisling Nazi seductress. A *Mata Hari* in feathers and lace. Her larger than life erotic image was a passport to meeting the higher ranks of the Nazi party. She found sex could propel one much further in life than hard work and good contacts ever could.

For the White Rose cause, Violetta seduced a small number of high-ranking officials. They fully swallowed her *whore in the bedroom/empty in the head* facade. Consequently the post-coital chit-chat about the way the war was going often drew more honest responses than they'd have given under interrogation. Here was a chance, in the manly glow of sexual conquest, to say what they truly thought. She expertly played on the vanity of these men. Along with the brandy and sexual fulfilment they became loose-tongued and let slip all manner of secrets in the vain belief that the doe-eyed plaything, who blinked and yawned and smoked beside them, wasn't really taking any of it in at all.

CHAPTER 11

Diary of Dimitri

At two in the morning there is banging on the door of our barracks. Oleg opens the door and the moaning figure of Gregor collapses into the room. Deathly pale and covered in soil and blood, Gregor had been buried alive. We found out later the firing squad had been drinking *denaturate* – an industrial alcohol. They were so pissed they couldn't see straight.

The sight of him haunts me still. How must he have felt regaining consciousness in a bitterly cold shallow grave, having been shot as a traitor by one's own comrades? Freezing, frightened and utterly alone. Where could he go?

What was his thought process? He came back so his friends could do the only decent thing they could. Finish him off.

How does death change a man? I don't mean his own death, not yet, but the death of his comrades, the death of his enemies and the death of all his ideals.

Death it seems is all around us now. But isn't it always? In times of peace one need only pick up a newspaper to read the countless deaths happening at all times all over the world.

Until this war, I had never seen a dead body, never known its stench of decay, never realised the indignity of a bomb-blasted corpse. In a strange way I'm glad to experience such proximity to death. It wakes me up, makes me realise just how little I have really lived up until now. Death shows us, and laughs at, our pettiness, our vanities and especially our ambitions. In that respect it comes close to its seeming opposite: love.

Since I fell in love with Ava, my previous self-absorption and self-conscious striving for achievement have seemed petty. Even my literary ambitions seem less fuelled by desperation and more buoyed by the energy of love. She was right; love is everything, all the rest are noises off.

Death reminds me of the fragility of life. I see the dead bodies of men. My mind separates the friend from the foe. Death makes no such distinctions.

I look at the lifeless body of a German soldier, *where is your cause now?* The same with the corpse of my comrade, *in death where is your revenge?* Their beliefs and ideals contain a force that carries beyond the grave to the next generation. War will continue as long as a generation hence believe that to venerate the dead they must continue with the wrong-headed values that took them to war in the first place.

Death again shows up our stupidity. All these men wanted to live in peace, to grow and be strong and healthy. To marry and have strong, healthy children in a society that was fair and compassionate with ever-improving standards of living.

Maybe it's the cordite or the constant shelling but all these thoughts make perfect sense out here. It's no grand philosophy but a realisation of a simple life based on humanitarian values and recognition of a shared brotherhood between all men and all nations.

David J Robinson

CHAPTER 12

Moscow 1941

W hy did Kariakin want to see him? Stepan Antonova wondered to himself. As he walked past anonymous offices down the stark corridors of the Prefecture of the Western Administrative District he felt sure someone had it in for him. Stepan had known Kariakin from when he was a minor diplomat at the Embassy. Always seen as capable and energetic, Kariakin had quit the Embassy and ascended to the rank of Vice-Chairman of the Prefecture.

This bland, concrete panelled building was a regimental maze of bureaucracy inhabited by Government informers. It was the frontline of Soviet Power where grey men and women imposed the Communist state infrastructure over the lives of the proletariat.

Stepan sat nervously waiting outside Kariakin's office. He didn't feel well. He was used to the insidious atmosphere these sorts of Governments buildings created; cold, functional and authoritarian. A nerve centre of the regime, he likened it to the brain of an octopus from which countless tentacles slithered out, guiding lives, moulding citizens and slowly sucking the life out of the masses.

Kariakin's secretary, stern and efficient, carried a huge box of files and dossiers out of his office. He wondered if his own denouncement lay somewhere among those papers filled out with forensic scrutiny.

Someone must have seen Ava, Stepan concluded, at the Moscow Cinema with the boy whose parents had been enemies of the state.

The thought of the Moscow Cinema triggered his memory of a hot July night in Paris. A recollection of the film he'd taken his French secretary to see, hoping to seduce her afterwards. The movie was called *L'Atlantide*. It could have been any movie to Stepan. A film was just the starter in his well used menu of seduction. Cocktails, caviar and oysters were the main course, followed by his secretary in his bed for dessert. Still, he remembered his disappointment; two out of three wasn't bad. His French secretary was immune to his advances. Seduction was an art he'd never had to learn in his native Motherland. Back here, threats and coercion replaced any need for romantic charm.

He'd failed to impress her, yet the film had made a lasting impression on him. If Stepan had thought his secretary, with her petite figure and Parisian-bobbed haircut was pretty, then the actress in the film was stunning. Brigitte Helm, all blonde curls and seductive eyes, dominated the screen as the Queen of Atlantis.

Looking back Stepan noticed how the film mirrored his life. He related to the lost men of the Foreign Legion crawling through the dry French Algerian desert only to come across a mirage. Whatever they desired, they saw. If they desired riches, they saw riches. If they desired water, they saw water.

Whatever it was remained tantalisingly out of reach.

Everything was an illusion. And now Stepan felt the same way, everything about Soviet society was an illusion. Utopia is always, *'Just over the horizon'* or *'After the next five-year plan.'*

The grand rhetoric of the party leaders glossed over the peasants' grim reality. The propaganda about the rural idylls of collective farms proved to be another mirage that vanished when he saw the famine starved farmers fleeing from the west.

"Comrade Stepan!" Kariakin greeted Stepan in that thick, throaty voice of his. "Come in, sit down. How are you?"

Inside his cramped office, Kariakin; bald head above broad shoulders, sat behind a table piled with papers on one side with a green-shaded table lamp on the other. The room was furnished with a Persian carpet, an antique Samovar, a leather couch and adorned with bronze figurines confiscated from houses of the old nobility.

"I'm fine thanks, Marshall Kariakin." Stepan took a seat facing him.

"And your family? The wife and child?"

"Not so much a child any more. She's now a precocious young lady who gives me sleepless nights."

Kariakin gave an empty laugh.

"That explains your appearance." His eyes swept over Stepan's crumpled face and clothes with a hint of disdain.

Kariakin rose from his chair and went over to the window clasping his hands behind his back.

"It is said a clear conscience sleeps soundly." Kariakin let the words hang.

That explained Stepan's insomnia. It explained the night terrors and sweat-soaked bed sheets as he suffered the nightmares of a split personality. He was the man whose lies and compromises fell little short of cowardice and treachery. He was the man who'd sold his soul for tickets to the Bolshoi's Imperial Box. He was the man who had cut short other people's lives by years so he could extend his living space by a few yards.

Stepan's conscience was far from clear.

"Are you still a believer, Stepan?" Kariakin turned to face him, his hulking figure encircled by light from the window.

"In what?"

"In what?" Kariakin huffed impatiently. "In the Party! Do you believe we are making progress? That all the harsh dik-tats and purges have been necessary for our new world to be born?"

"I still believe, yes," Stepan answered nervously, "but it's not proving to be an easy birth."

Kariakin gave a disappointed shake of the head.

"With ideas so bold and radical how could it be?"

"No, I mean yes." Stepan stammered. He could feel the pulse in the vein at his temples and wondered if Kariakin noticed. "I believe it shall be worth it in the end. When making omelettes eggs must be broken," Stepan blinked agitatedly, "and all that."

Kariakin walked towards his desk drawer and brought out a pipe and tobacco pouch. He began to fill his pipe and slowly returned to the window.

"I sometimes wonder how many out there," he gestured with his pipe towards the streets below. "How many really share our vision." He lit his pipe with a match, taking short puffs until the heavy aroma hit Stepan. "I'm convinced most of them just go through the motions, uttering platitudes, just to be seen as model citizens."

Where was this conversation going? Stepan puzzled. Was his fiefdom at stake? If his superiors knew his real feelings his career would be over in a flash along with the chauffeured limousine and the grace and favour apartments.

"I truly believe we are making progress in social welfare and we're certainly building more factories." Stepan asserted, but he wasn't even convincing himself, never mind Kariakin. He decided to shut up and stop digging himself into a hole.

In silence is strength, his deeply religious father had said to him on the rare occasions he said anything. Orthodox to the bone, he'd told Stepan to embrace silence. Told him that the journey into stillness is the greatest adventure a man can undertake. Stepan never got it. Silence made him fidgety. In silence all his crimes against his own soul appeared on a never-ending charge-sheet. In silence he found only cold oblivion. His father had also been a man who never rushed to judge anything, preferring to praise the day in the evening. From an early age he'd tried to drum into Stepan the old adage, *"Christ endured and told us to."* Now, more than ever, Stepan wished he'd inherited his father's virtue of patience.

Stepan abruptly stirred from his reverie to hear Kariakin, again facing the window, talking about how he used to love nothing more than to escape the city and hike up the Caucasus Mountains. It had been many years, Kariakin recounted, since those soul-nourishing walks that took him away from the petty bureaucracies of work.

"The granite outcrops, the magnificent cedar trees and the view!" He spread his arms as though he were seeing it right now. "The view of Sochi always took my breath away. Nature, in all her myriad ways, echoes the acts of man." He slowly turned to Stepan. "Or is man just a dull echo of nature?"

Stepan remained silent, unsure how to answer.

"Up on the Krasnaya Polyana Mountain there are ferns which grow in the cracks and crevices of rocks chastened by exposure to the elements." Kariakin slowly walked back to his chair. "Whilst the plants that stick up and stand out are blown to bits by the harsh winds."

Stepan furrowed his brow wondering where this was heading.

"In our line of work," Kariakin went on, "people who keep their head down and their opinions to themselves thrive like those ground-hugging plants." He sat down and fastened his eyes on Stepan, "Whilst those who stand out..." he added drily, "...don't last long."

He cricked his neck. Small talk was over. In an abrupt change of tack, he said,

"Now is the time for those with families to evacuate the city."

"What do you know?"

"I know the net is closing in." The muscle in Kariakin's jaw locked.

"But I've heard rumours of a counter offensive. Surely Stalin will not allow Moscow to fall?"

Kariakin looked gravely at Stepan.

"It's not the *Germans* you should be afraid of."

A silence followed.

"What?" Stepan felt the blood drain from his face, "you mean... NKVD?"

Kariakin puffed his cheeks and then exhaled slowly.

"There are people who see you as crooked timber, Antonova. The communist spirit does not rest easy in you."

"I'm not that way." Stepan noticed Kariakin had reverted to using his last name. The friendly preamble was long gone.

"I've been told you were watched, in Paris."

Stepan was overcome by a sickening rush of adrenaline. He could feel the sweat break out in tiny beads on his forehead.

"They put you on a long leash but, unlike an obedient dog, you ran like a pig towards the shit. You were called back because you'd become sloppy, an easy target for honey-traps and blackmail. I vouched for you before

Antonova, blamed your first wife's death for your erratic behaviour, but no more."

Kariakin and Stepan looked at each other. Just the ticking of a clock measured the silence between them.

"What should I do?" There was a gasp of desperation in Stepan's throat.

Kariakin stared back at him, inscrutable. Stepan never could make out what he was thinking. It was unnerving.

Kariakin leaned forward and said deliberately,

"Leave."

Stepan felt the room begin to swim.

"I can't just..."

"And you only have a few days." Kariakin's voice was matter-of-fact. "You're on a list of so-called political suspects." He tapped his pipe against the desk. "It's a long list," he sniffed, "but they'll come for you, be sure of that."

Stuck between the hammer and the anvil, Stepan tried to work out the ramifications. He could stay and argue his innocence but knew of no-one who, once accused, had their charges dropped. To flee could be seen as an admission of guilt yet Kariakin had thrown him a life-line; he'd no charge to answer, yet.

Stepan shifted uncomfortably in his seat and took a steadying breath.

"Where?"

Kariakin regarded him for a moment or two before retrieving a brown envelope from his desk drawer.

"There are regular trains for evacuees bound for Chistopol," he passed Stepan the envelope and nodded, "take your family, go." He got up and went back over to the window. "You know what risk I've taken telling you this. Do the right thing, Antonova. Don't hack the branch you are sitting on. Circumstances can always change." With his back to Stepan he muttered, "After the war..." he again cricked his neck, "...who knows who'll be in charge."

David J Robinson

CHAPTER 13

Diary of Dimitri

G lory is a fleeting thing. A General remarked after a great victory that all the glory heaped upon him meant nothing at all a few moments later. He had to start again and look for it in other places, in other battles.

Colonel Marchenko, his voice has an edge to it. Whatever he says sounds like an order. Even a request for someone to make a cup of tea carries threatening undertones. It is as though he feels the need to vocalise his high rank in every single utterance, never daring to let his guard drop as other officers do during breaks from the fighting. He is afraid to show an ounce of humanity to his soldiers lest it be mistaken for weakness.

He has so many petty rules on top of the official codes of conduct, so many fussy ways of going about things, and any slight mistake from a soldier is seized upon by him. His snarling, sneering voice gets right under our skin. It's hard to put into words the terror that man's voice instils in us, especially the new recruits. They tremble when around him for fear of doing something wrong. This fear itself causes them to make more mistakes as they try to second guess what he wants from them. His tone might be fierce but his articulation of orders are often lost and muffled by his heavy beard and habit of turning his back on us half way through an instruction.

He is a cunt.

Vasily digs a trench alongside Avakov.

Vasily says, *"They say the best leaders are the ones who don't want to lead."*

Avakov wipes the sweat from his brow and nods slowly.

"And maybe the best people are those who don't want to be led."

Vasily found that most amusing.

I am not supposed to keep a diary. No-one is. Only officially appointed journalists are allowed to report on the war. We're even forbidden to write about it in our letters home. Letters we know will be vetted for anti war sentiments and reports on "extraordinary events".

"Extraordinary events" is a euphemism for acts of cowardice, desertion, treason and anti-Soviet activities/sentiments. These extraordinary events are not to be written about or communicated beyond the army. Any naive complaint can see one branded as a defeatist or an "enemy agitator" and risks you being handed over to the Special Department.

Yesterday I helped a wounded Red Army soldier back to his unit. The soldier was in agony – his hand wrapped in blood-soaked bandages. We were apprehended by Colonel Marchenko and even as the chaos of war went on all around us – howling planes, explosions and distant gun-fire – he began to argue with us. All of a sudden Marchenko withdrew his pistol and shot the wounded soldier dead on the spot. I was stunned but after a dressing down from Marchenko, had to drag the soldier's body over to the burial ditch containing other dead comrades. Colonel Marchenko didn't believe he'd been wounded by enemy fire and the hand wound was self-inflicted to escape the front-line.

These on-the-spot executions are deemed necessary to instil fear and discipline among the troops. But to me, these spurious killings and the kangaroo court which condemned Gregor, only serve to lower morale even further. These punishments, rubber stamped and handed down by Stalin, put soldiers in a no-win situation. Attack the enemy, get wounded, retreat then get executed for cowardice! We all know discipline is the bedrock of all armed forces but the arbitrariness of these punishments makes a mockery of the word justice.

All the above - alongside petty bureaucratic edicts which mean vital supplies remain in warehouses and not on the front-line because someone didn't get round to stamping an invoice - make me despair.

We were ambushed on patrol today. Hidden within a misty forest the Germans took us by surprise killing two of our men instantly. They gave us no warning, no chance of surrender. Oleg, Cerenkov, Fyodor, Yuri, Ivan and I made a run for it and were soon pinned down in a hillside gully.

"Rus, uk vekh!" 'Rus, hands up!' One of them cried.

It was too late for that. We kept them at bay firing bursts from our sub-machine guns whilst radioing for back up. The Germans maintained constant fire with grenades falling short hitting the trees. Shards of screaming hot metal and deadly wooden splinters flew over our heads at hundreds of miles an hour.

Reinforcements arrived led by the hulking figure of Avakov. He led a full blooded charge towards the German lines. Hurtling into their storm of bullets he took their fire away from us. We broke through the burning pine trees, killing at least three Germans along the way. Avakov covered us by laying down his own barrage. Amazingly he returned with hardly a scratch. We all managed to flee before we realised Fyodor and Yuri were missing. We wanted to go back for them but Marchenko over-ruled us and ordered us back to camp. The Germans slipped away as quickly as they had appeared back into the forest.

Fyodor, though wounded, managed to make his way back. Yuri, he informed us, had been killed by a German grenade. All the men are saddened. Cerenkov, for all his protection of Yuri, hides his grief well. His face is a mask of stone.

I console myself that had Fyodor not witnessed Yuri's death, he would simply be described as missing-in-action, a catch-all phrase that even implied desertion. Any family of a soldier 'missing-in-action' got no recompense. Only those whose sons or daughters were proven to have been killed would receive financial support.

I wonder. Many comrades are left where they fall, many battlefields are left covered with dead Russian soldiers and we are not allowed to bury them.

We keep pushing on. *"They'll be buried later."* We are told. *"The units behind us will honour the fallen."*

But how will they be identified? Our I.D. tags are small capsules made from ivory. They're supposed to contain our personal details on a rolled up slip of paper. But many soldiers are superstitious and leave these slips blank. To fill them out, it is thought, is to sign your own death warrant.

Surely this promise of retrospective burials is not some cynical ruse to get out of paying recompense to their relatives? The more this war goes on the more cynical I become.

They call this the Great Patriotic War. Is patriotism a one-sided affair? Will my love of the Motherland prove unrequited? Is the state not loyal to the men dying to defend it? To hold these contradictory ideas in my mind is driving me mad.

David J Robinson

CHAPTER 14

Berlin 1945

V ioletta had a lover, a theatre-hand carpenter by the name of Josef Kane. He was conscripted to help in the munitions factories before the war started when Austria was annexed. Regarded as second class citizens these foreign conscripts were viewed with suspicion by Berliners. Their loyalty was questionable. If the wind of war changed direction they could easily swap sides. They were a visible Trojan horse right in the midst of Germany's capital city.

Now Josef worked at Die Bosen Club. It was the name a disparate bunch of actors, dancers and impresarios had given to their barely-legal takeover of an abandoned theatre. Josef, tall, handsome and honest, was set to work trying to restore the theatre to its former glory. The combination of its nineteenth century fittings and twentieth century exotic Burlesque lent the place an air of pure decadence. Die Bosen Club quickly became a favourite haunt of the SS and consequently the Gestapo left it alone but were always suspicious of it being a hotbed of reactionary activity.

Violetta was not initially interested in another man. She had enough on her plate at work and at home.

It was Josef who told her the rumours of Rula's Jewish heritage were true and that if the Nazis found out they could all be shot as co-conspirators. Backstage Josef and Violetta both confronted Rula who immediately burst into tears.

"I don't want to leave. The theatre is my home." In evident distress she began twisting the ends of her jet black hair. "You are my family. I've lasted this long, can't we just carry on?"

"We've got to get you out of Berlin or at least out of the theatre," Josef reasoned, "I've seen your identity papers and they wouldn't stand up to much scrutiny."

Rula began to tremble and shake her head. Josef glanced sidelong at Violetta, then turned to Rula, grabbed her shoulders and spoke deliberately.

"If they find you we will all pay the price. And the Gestapo would love any excuse to close us down."

"Let us help you, Rula." Violetta touched her cheek.

Rula's paleness was quite striking.

"Josef's right, we have the SS coming here every night. It's only a matter of time before they check you out."

"My make-up is my shield," Rula sniffed, "I'm a good actress, I've done this role for years."

Eventually, to buy some time, they persuaded her to leave the high profile stage and work behind the scenes. Unbeknown to the three of them, every word had been overheard by Monika Bauer. She was friends with them all but in these desperate days personal survival trumped ties of loyalty every time.

That afternoon, after her matinee performance, Violetta was getting changed in her dressing room when there was a ferocious banging on her door.

"Who is it?"

"Major Neumann. Let me in this instant."

Violetta's blood ran cold. She opened the door.

A stone-faced Major Neumann strode in and took a quick look round the room.

Violetta checked no-one was in the corridor then closed the door behind her. As she turned around, a blinding slap across her face sent her sprawling onto the floor.

"You scheming bitch!"

Neumann fumed, standing over her. He was tall and athletic with short blonde hair parted immaculately.

His eyes flashed icy blue.

"You scheming, lying, deceptive little tart."

He pulled her up by her dressing gown collar and pushed her hard backwards onto a wicker chair. Neumann was red-faced and agitatedly walked about the room.

"The oldest trick in the fucking book, and I fell for it. How many others have you fucked, eh? How many other party officials and generals?"

Violetta thought he had gone insane.

"Does your husband know?" He scorned.

"Does your wife know?" She replied.

"Bitch."

"You didn't think you were the only one, did you?" Violetta almost smirked despite her fear.

Neumann snatched the baton from his belt and smashed the dressing-table mirror. Violetta gasped loudly. Shards of glass showered onto the floor.

"The mirror lies, Viola, or is it Violetta? Who are you behind the mask?" He towered over Violetta, fastening his eyes on hers. "What secrets have you bled from your other conquests?"

"I don't know what you're talking about." Violetta tried to get up but Neumann pushed her back. He clenched his fists by his side, trying to control his rage.

"I told you, and only you, about the evacuation of priceless artefacts from Berlin by freight during the night of last Saturday. That train was held up, the crew butchered and the paintings, gold and other valuables all stolen." He tilted his head and frowned. "How did anyone know of such a train unless you told them?"

Violetta tried to reply but he went on.

"It was top secret." He was almost breathless with fury. "I couldn't believe it. But then it all fell into place. You're good at what you do my little Princess," Neumann withdrew his Walther KK. "But you fucked the wrong man this time."

Indeed it appeared she had. And although she had gained a reputation for having numerous affairs with Nazi officers, the truth was she only went as far as she needed with any of them. Most told her all she wanted to know upon first acquaintance. Violetta had an uncanny knack of weighing up the ones who would freely spill state secrets and those, usually the ones who didn't drink, who were as fastidious in their speech as in their sobriety.

Major Neumann fell between the two. Immaculate in his uniform, formal in his demeanour, he nevertheless had a roguish sense of mischief about him. In short he had an ego. And, knowing that ego loves an audience, it was this aspect of his character Violetta homed in on.

Violetta knew how to get a man to drop his guard. It usually coincided with the moment he dropped his trousers. With Neumann she had shown how impressed she was with his medals and stripes yet also questioned his real importance. *Could he prove how high ranking he really was?* 'Go on,' she had whispered, 'tell me how the war is truly going. I only hear rumours and gossip."

In the afterglow of their lovemaking back at his private quarters, Major Neumann had smoked French cigarettes, drank brandy and told Violetta of his frontline experiences during the invasion of Russia. He actually smiled when recounting the terrible acts both he and his men inflicted on the peasants.

"Once we had captured a village the lead infantry ploughed on towards Moscow. That is the essence of blitzkrieg. An unrelenting charge into the heart of whichever country we were invading. As commanding officer of Einsatzgruppe B, my orders were to stay behind and 'subdue' any uprising.

"The majority of the militia we had to control the village were ex-German policemen, older men not brainwashed by Nazi propaganda like our young soldiers. So we had to use psychology to get them to become cold-blooded killers." He took another slug of brandy and a heavy drag of his cigarette. "The masterstroke was our first order. *'Any man who has not the heart or stomach to carry out harsh penalties against these sub-humans can go home now. We are at war and in war we have to do things we would never dream of in peacetime.'*

"Of course they'd come so far and out of fear of being seen as cowards, and the bonds of loyalty they felt to each other, they all stayed. Then it was done in small steps. Round up the populace. Root out the agitators. Shoot them if they don't behave. Allow our soldiers to see how mistrustful these Slavs are. Hiding food, being uncooperative... shoot some more." Neumann's eyes gleamed with relish.

"They were only Jews, gypsies and the disabled, after all," he smiled sadistically. "Then I'd gently remind our men we know the addresses of their families back home. They'd be looked after... a veiled threat. Finally," he stubbed out his cigarette, "when our men are soaked in blood and guilty of many killings... it's not a big leap to murdering women and babies."

Violetta was wringing her hands and felt sick to the stomach. But she had to remain strong. She needed something more relevant, something the resistance could make use of. She poured more brandy.

"My daughter is so afraid... I don't know what to tell her." Violetta blinked, holding back the tears. "Please tell me what Hitler's plans are for us? I won't tell anyone else." She began to stroke his hair. "I promise..."

"The Fuhrer is a remarkable man." Neumann relaxed and lit another cigarette. "He has such, such... charisma. After speaking with him, just being in his presence, I am filled with belief once more. Since the attempts on his life he trusts no-one and tries to orchestrate every detail of the war himself. The strain... is too much for any man." Neumann spoke regrettably. After a moment's thought, he went on. "Hitler fears Berlin might be destroyed by the bombing. Goering and the Luftwaffe have badly let him down. Freight trains are being organised to evacuate priceless treasures from the capital to a safe place."

"Please believe me," Violetta was on her knees. "I never told anyone. Put the gun away we can..."

Violetta glimpsed something crash down with a sickening crack onto Neumann's head. He slumped, open-eyed onto the floor.

Josef stood behind with a long-stemmed chrome ashtray in his hands.

"It was bound to happen." Josef said breathlessly. "Give me a hand."

He began to pull the rug up around the body of the Major. Violetta was shaking and in tears.

"You've killed him!" her blood ran cold, "how do we explain that?"

"We don't." Josef answered, his voice matter of fact. "He seemed embarrassed. I don't think he'll have told anyone else about you and him."

"But what if he has?" Violetta cried feeling suddenly light-headed, almost dizzy.

"We'll worry about it later." He anchored her with his eyes and then added resolutely, "Let's get rid of the body first."

CHAPTER 15

Eastern Front 1944

Today Colonel Marchenko catches me writing in my journal and demands to know what I am writing about. We are billeted in temporary barracks near to an abandoned airstrip. The hum of chatter in our wooden hut falls silent. Only the floorboards creak as I stand to attention.

"I'm chronicling the day's progress by the heroes of the Soviet Union for our loved ones back...."

"Give it to me." He stretches out a gloved hand. I sense my comrades retreating into the shadows. After flicking through a few pages his face turns to anger.

"What is this scribbling?"

"It's in code, sir," I begin to sweat, "in case it fell into enemy hands."

"Or is it to hide your recording of extraordinary events?"

"No, no," I protest a bit too eagerly, "just the facts of..."

"I'll decide what the facts are."

He stuffs the journal inside his jacket. My perspiration starts to prickle my skin.

"I will have this looked at." He fixes me with his low-lidded eyes. "If, as you say, it promotes the heroism of your comrades you can have it back. Any malicious commenting of extraordinary events and this book will, along with its author, be terminated."

He takes my journal over to the Special Detachment office: NKVD military agents of counter intelligence. They shall recognise my code easily and I'll be facing a firing squad.

This is how easy it is to be denounced as a traitor. I have made nothing up in my reports, only told the truth. And it is a truth our leaders should know of if they care for the plight of the foot-soldiers. But every edict, every command, every trifling punishment showed they don't care. We must call it the Motherland, but no mother would treat her children with such contempt. Our experience in Stalingrad proved such a turning point. *Advance only. Not one step back.* If we retreated, our blocking detachment would shoot us dead. Any lingering naivety about love for the Motherland died in those bleak days amongst the rubble of Stalingrad.

Hours later, Marchenko bursts back into our barrack room shouting my name. My comrades go silent and again slink into the background. They had made their feelings known earlier.

"Pray for a miracle, comrade." Ivan had advised.

"No miracles happen in this world." Cerenkov had snorted. *"Dreams do not come true."*

As I come forward, Marchenko takes out his gun and, as with Gregor, orders me onto my knees. I remain quiet. Staring at the floor I await the inevitable. As the blood rushes from my face I feel his gun press into the back of my head. He throws my journal onto the floor in front of me.

"Do you know what the NKVD makes of your notebook?"

My hammering heart fills his pause.

"I know what you are, Petrov. Do you know what they say you are?"

He waits, letting silence fill the room.

Marchenko cocks his gun. I close my eyes. Feel I might pass out.

"Do you know what they say you are?" He repeats louder.

I am unable to speak, but even if I could, I have never seen anyone talk their way out of a situation as grave as this.

"They say..." he hesitates for a fraction of a second, "they say you are no Tolstoy!" Marchenko roars with laughter and removes the gun from my head. As I slump forward, I can hear his footsteps recede into the distance. I am shaking as I grab my journal and scurry back to my bunk bed. My comrades go back to their business. Ivan catches my eye and nods knowingly, as if my prayers had been answered. Oleg shakes his head in bewilderment.

I can't understand it either. Whoever has studied my journal must know what I wrote was treasonable. And, as they haven't reported me, if the truth ever comes out, be treated as an accomplice. I turn to my last page and find an entry I do not recognise. It is written to look like my writing but the pen is different.

Matthew 10:26

I borrow Vasily's battered bible. *"there is nothing covered, that shall not be revealed; and hid that shall not be known."*

I have an ally in the NKVD.

Oleg says, *"We'll win this war simply because we've got a bigger gang."*

My tough comrades have developed a certain zeal for the hard things in life, so much so, I cannot see any one of them sitting comfortably with a life of luxurious ease. I look at the strength and industry given in service to the destructive powers of war. If only we could learn to serve each other half as well, what a world we could build!

It is much more important to understand our history than to be proud or ashamed of it. And I reflect how the autocratic tyrannical Tsars of old have only been replaced by autocratic, tyrannical 'Party Leaders'. The rule by iron fist is the same – only the names have changed. I look around at this motley crew of Poles, Georgians, Lithuanians, and Siberians and wonder if indeed an iron fist is needed to create unity. Under what other system could men flourish, evolve and commune?

What is this Motherland for which we unquestionably lay down our lives?

It is the mysterious depths of Siberia. It is the old, almost democratic capital Kiev. It is the western-looking, open-minded St Petersburg. It is the haunting melodies of Borodin, the subversive strains of Shostakovich, the genius of Tolstoy and Pushkin. It is home. It is family and every single thing a man can care about and value in his life. All this is what *"they"* would have us think about when we march into battle, into the gaping pit of Hades.

In truth we're fighting for the Communist Party, for autocratic rule, to spread a political ideal to the world.

An ideal that is not even a reality in the Motherland.

David J Robinson

CHAPTER 16

Moscow 1941

The night air was raw yet the snow wet and squelchy underfoot. Stepan hurried down the street oblivious to the early evening stars glinting like jewels high above the barrage balloons and searchlight sweeps. With Kariakin's words of warning still ringing in his ears, he shivered and cursed the cold as he hurried past a paper-seller whose feet were wrapped in rags.

On his way to his luxury apartment in the House of the Government, Stepan evaded a group of drunken men drinking outside a corrugated iron stall on the corner of Gorky Street. But he caught a snippet of conversation.

"They can kiss my arse if they think I'm fighting for them."

"It doesn't matter if we fight or not. It's the end of days, comrade. It is foretold. The anti-Christ dwells in the Kremlin!"

Stepan paused by the roadside, pretending to be looking to cross the busy road in order to hear more.

"Hey, he's listening."

"So what?"

"Could be Cheka."

"So let him hear, he probably thinks the same as us anyway."

"Hey, comrade!"

Stepan turned slowly to see the men looking at him. The nearest wore a wet sheepskin jacket radiating that familiar rank odour Stepan could smell from yards away.

"Are you secret police?" he asked.

Stepan gave a faint shake of his head.

"Come and join us, comrade."

A grey bearded man reached out his hand to Stepan.

Why, he'll never know, but Stepan did join them, sharing their camaraderie and cheap vodka.

They huddled around a crackling brazier outside the make-shift stall selling black-market spirits and food. The stench of cheap tobacco and damp sheepskin almost turned Stepan's stomach. The men explained their factory had been shut down and their lathes and engineering machinery packed up onto trains bound for the east.

"That's where they want us to go too," Sheepskin man said, "but what fate awaits us there? We know only of labour camps and arctic gulags beyond the Urals. Are we to become slave labourers?"

"Go back to being serfs?" The man with the grey beard added.

"No," a small man in a cloth cap asserted, "we stay here and face our enemy."

"In the meantime," Greybeard raised a glass, "we drink!"

The owner of the stall, clean shaven with combed-over hair, served up a tray of black bread and pickles on the bar. Stepan began to see these people weren't beggars or state enemies, just ordinary men. They were simple men who, unlike him, weren't blessed with the cleverness or cunning to get on in life.

They treated Stepan like a brother and his insistence on buying more vodka only endeared him to them more. Deep down he knew he was being reckless but something authentic and primal overrode these concerns. Alcohol, the impending threat of his arrest, the possibility of torture, expulsion and now the prospect of obliteration at the hands of fascists proved the final straw.

He envied their genuine warmth which proved the old adage; *good brotherhood is the best wealth*. With their toothless laughter and red-eyed scorn they embodied the Russian trait of getting on with their lives when sober yet swinging to wild unpredictability when drunk.

This drinking session was the closest Stepan had got to how he'd felt in Paris. The conversation was less sophisticated perhaps and the arguments cruder in their way, but here was an oasis of freedom. He'd almost forgotten how the pleasures of drinking in company can smooth the rough edges of existence.

It was fascinating listening to these ordinary plain-speaking men. One had come from Berdichev to flee the Germans.

"The peasants I met say they will not fight for Stalin. They hate him and blame him for destroying their way of life, for making their lives miserable with forced labour and for ignoring the famine."

"It's the last judgement, I say," said another man who looked like a wild priest with black eyes and long white hair, "the end of days."

"Bad rumours fly on wings." Stepan retorted, although even he could sympathise with the peasants' plight.

"It's the day of judgement for the Bolsheviks," the wild priest went on, "half the population is against the Government."

The kiosk owner threw some wood chips over the brazier, stirring them into the coals with an iron rod.

"I think the Germans are civilised people," he put in, "we might be better off with them running the country."

"Or from fire to flame we go!" Stepan warned.

That half the men agreed with the kiosk owner didn't surprise Stepan. He had always assumed the ordinary Muscovites would be grateful for the welfare reforms and jobs created by the industrialisation programme. But he'd noticed in the restaurant and theatre that people seemed to be waking up from a stupor. Knowing the Soviet regime to be busy fighting the war they felt emboldened to laugh, voice dissent, and no longer in whispers. The silent bystander was silent no more.

These men, in their patched up clothes and flea-market shoes spoke with a rare, wise authority about the state of Moscow today. These men whose tongues had been tied to only utter Soviet-speak were venting thoughts and emotions the system was supposed to have purged.

Stepan saw the old Russia reflected in their faces and knew that the Communists constant battle against custom and habit was doomed to failure.

Yet their language was refreshing.

What these men voiced wasn't superstition, prejudice of ignorance. They spoke plainly of their hard-won experience and of the callous injustices they'd endured.

"At school they teach the children black is white and white is black!"

"It's nonsense. My son didn't know what a Tsar was. He asked me the other night, 'Papa, do the bourgeoisie eat children?"

"We can never be true Bolsheviks, my friend because we have families. Stalin said a true Bolshevik is wedded only to the Party."

They all expressed themselves differently, their native individualism shining through. Some frightened, wild-eyed and tearful, some defiant, others openly hateful of the regime and many spoke with a feral ferocity.

These subversive thoughts, now being spoken, proved again that the Party's control was far from absolute.

"If communism worked I would gladly welcome it," Greybeard said, "but while we scrape by on a pittance constantly looking over our shoulders, the party officials live like Tsars in their plush apartments, their country dachas and luxury holidays in Talinn. Hypocrisy? I share a kitchen with five families and they've just cut off our water and electric."

A military convoy passed by, young men in loose fitting uniforms carrying old French rifles.

"Cattle to slaughter!" shouted Sheepskin.

Stepan gulped heartily on the cheap vodka, wincing at its harshness. He tried to get a grip on himself but his disciplined ways were being dissipated by the minute as the alcohol flushed through his body.

He dug into his pockets and ordered the stall holder to crack open the Armenian brandy. He wasn't going anywhere yet. He felt emboldened both by the imminent threat of invasion and the cavalier attitudes of these common men.

Stepan hesitated, unsure whether to speak his mind or hold his tongue.

"Believe me comrades," Stepan found himself saying, "you think the Communists are bad but they're nothing like as bad as the Fascists. We're better in charge of our own fate."

"Fate? When your fate is decided upon the place of your birth there is no chance of freedom," said Greybeard.

"And as always it is the little thieves that are hanged whilst the great ones escape." Wild priest cursed.

"Anyway, what choice have we got under a one party system?" Sheepskin man asked.

"One party for now," Stepan continued, "but who knows... things seem to stay the same for a long time in this country. Mongols, Tsars – but when it comes, the wind of change comes fast. And remember, there are no bad winds, only bad captains. And we, the Russian people, need to step up to become good captains when the opportunity arises, not the Germans, Italians, Poles or anyone else, us! The proud descendents of Kievan Rus!"

Despite Kariakan's stark warning of his impending arrest, Stepan fell back on his default position of patriotic loyalty. He half believed what he was saying, or at least badly wanted to. As he spoke he realised he was treading the same fine line the Kremlin must take to get the people on board. First, admit the state's failings and then dismiss them as the inevitable stumbles of a society still learning to walk. Next, exploit the ancestral ties and latent patriotism that still beats in the heart of all red-blooded Russians.

In this hour, in the company of these men well lubricated with alcohol, Stepan reconnected to that sense of patriotism. If Stalin could also tap into that indefinable sentiment then Hitler would rue the day he invaded.

"If communism is good at anything, comrades, it is good at organising its people. I've spent time in France and marvelled at its diversity, but there lay its ruin. Their lack of unity caused their capitulation at the arrival of the Germans. They were too proud, too individual to unite against the enemy. The Germans, in my opinion, underestimate the collective strength we have with Britain and the United States. Together our three countries can out-produce Germany. We already have allied tanks and aeroplanes and more industrial supplies arrive every day."

"That won't stop us fearing the late night knock on the door, comrade," Greybeard's words were acknowledged by the others.

"Yezhov's corrupt reign is over," Stepan declared. "It was Stalin himself who had him arrested and shot. Beria is the new chief of the NKVD now, and since then over a million cases of wrongful arrests have been reviewed. Thousands of convictions quashed and many more released from jail. I think for all our criticism of our regime we forget, it is our regime and we will galvanise as a nation because we have been invaded. We did not start this war but, if you care anything for your women and children, it is surely down to us to finish it!"

At this there was much whooping and clinking of glasses.

"Rurik the Rus is in our blood!" the cloth-capped man cried, showering spittle over the hot coals.

It began to snow. There was a moments silence as Stepan gazed into the braziers smouldering depths. Then, from the nearby empty marketplace someone struck up a tune on an accordion, a jaunty, allegro march-like theme. Stepan recognised it as a crude rendering of Sibelius' *Karelia Suite*. Greybeard silently mouthed the words to this ancient folk song as he too stared wistfully into the burning coals.

He knew he might regret it, but he was drunk now and too far gone. Stepan's words began to flow like the river Don.

"Comrades!" he cried, "Russia is immense. It is six million square miles of immensity. We are the largest country on earth.

Orphan of the State

"The Russian emblem is a bear, and for good reason. The bear is the most formidable beast of the forest. It is solitary and mysterious. Asleep, it seems almost benign. But you prod it awake and all hell is let loose.

"Bears are strong. And throughout our history we have always venerated strength and despised weakness. Why do we admire it so much? Because it is an outward expression of our innate strength as a nation and as individuals. We are strengthened by our climate, by our political struggles and by adversity. Comrades," Stepan instinctively lowered his voice before mentioning the Great Leader, "you may hate Stalin and his policies but I've never met a man who doesn't admire his strength. Stalin's ruthlessness, which has sometimes been misused at home, will now be turned against our enemies abroad."

Some men nodded sagely. But the wild priest was still defiant.

"It's the end of days!" he repeated, as if he'd been waiting for them all his life.

Stepan ignored him and carried on.

"And strength is not only shown in action, my friends. In Russia's vastness lies her strength. As Napoleon discovered, invaders only get so far before their supply lines become overstretched, before the autumn quagmires and killer winters get to work.

"Aye comrades, there is strength too in tactical retreat. The farther we draw the bowstring, the faster the arrow will fly!"

As the accordionist's music reached its crescendo the men began to cheer and stamp their feet.

"If we die," Greybeard raised his glass, "we die as men, not cowards!"

"Moscow will not fall so easily this time," Sheepskin downed a shot, "we shall fight on with honour like the Cossacks of old!"

These men still had fire in their bellies, thought Stepan. How Russia had need of such men now. Men, who despite being downtrodden, belittled and exploited could still find something intangible to celebrate, honour and fight for.

"What was it?" he wondered, *"was it simple patriotism? Or a brainwashed sense of duty?"* His thoughts became blurry but he concluded that although they showed a fearless bravado regards their own lives, they would not, indeed could not, conceive of the annihilation of their culture.

Trucks rumbled by, delivering sand for sandbags throughout the city.

Amidst the defiant drinking salutations, Stepan felt a flicker of courage awaken inside him. So used to repressing his feelings, the excitement of getting drunk with these humble workers took him back to his youth. Innocent days before he had to filter every thought and feeling. A time when he was alive, living without fear. As the accordionist struck up another tune Stepan became enveloped in a warm fuzzy glow as he laughed and caroused like no time since Paris.

These few hours, huddled around this glowing charcoal brazier, were precious moments for these men. They all lived with their families in cramped communal apartments where there was no such thing as privacy. Paper-thin walls, nosy neighbours, shared bathrooms and kitchens meant one felt under constant scrutiny from one's housemates.

Although Stepan often heard it said that *'many sheep can be herded by few dogs'*, there simply weren't enough secret service men to go round. So the Bolsheviks created this communal population which, relying on the culture of envy, ensured citizens controlled each other through collective inspection. The controlling mantra was, *'What one person does can bring misfortune to all!'*

Stepan had grown up in one himself. It had been the house of a nobleman. Stepan's family were moved in and the rooms partitioned off for three other families. This was an old Bolshevik trick of using the proletariat to curb the ways of the bourgeoisie.

The gravitational pull of the most impoverished citizens drew everyone down into their orbit. Anybody seen to have more money, newer clothes or better food were soon the victim of whispered accusations. Equality and fairness in poverty meant one person's material gain must be at the expense of everyone else.

Here on the cold open street was a haven of freedom. These men, old enough to recall the old days, obviously trusted each other implicitly, displaying bonds of friendship the Bolsheviks were supposed to have crushed. Voicing their opinions was risky but a much needed escape-valve to liberate their real personalities from years of repression.

Stepan finally left the men around two in the morning. He was patted on the back, praised for his inspiring words and invited to join them again the following evening.

Stepan walked unsteadily back to the House of the Government. The things he'd told the men about the glories of Russia, the rousing speech, were all things he'd learnt to speak at Soviet Embassy meetings. He didn't really believe in all that patriotic clap-trap. But even he could feel himself carried away by his own rhetoric.

That's what a good ambassador I am! He vainly concluded as he swayed from one side of the pavement to the other.

Say one thing. Think another.

CHAPTER 17

Diary of Dimitri

We have retreated. It is to be a temporary respite amongst the isolated farms and villages of the bucolic East Belarusian landscape. This goes against Stalin's edict. *"Not one step back."* But sometimes we need to regroup, fall back when to go forward is futile. A good counter attack is more effective than blind advancement. Do the pen-pushers and strategists in Moscow not know the basics of war-craft? Have they even seen any action?

The seasons are changing. The sun gets lower in the sky and the temperature drops along with the glorious leaves of autumn. The scenery changes from the Volga to the Berezina

River. Scenes of destruction give way to Arcadian beauty. Oblivious to the drumbeat of war, nature marches to its own rhythm.

Many of us take shelter in the abandoned *Izby*. These simple log houses that dot the Belarusian countryside do a fine job of keeping the cold and rain out and the stove's life-giving warmth in. With their elaborately carved framework of interlocking logs they are charming remnants of a feudal past. But inside they are dark, impoverished and often squalid. They offer no sign of the peasants' paradise yet to come.

Today I am helping Avakov chop wood from the forest. Hailing from the Urals, Avakov has an inner strength hewn from the rugged landscape of Siberia's unending vastness. I don't think I have ever met a manlier man and yet, on occasions, he displays a simple sensitivity quite without shame or self-consciousness. Dark brown hair, dark eyes creased by much laughter, strong no-nonsense nose, and centre-stage of his weather-beaten face sits a bushy bulwark of a moustache. All combine to give the impression of a fit and vigorous man capable of much hard work. He always seems to be sure of himself, in command of his thoughts and emotions.

A crucifix hangs around his neck. I ask about his faith. He takes a break from swinging the axe. Leaning forward, resting on the axe handle, he mops his brow.

"I believe in God, but not the church," he looks around, "and certainly not the state."

Orphan of the State

Taking a step back he signals me to line up another log. He swings the axe over his head and brings it effortlessly down to cleave the log in two.

"I have faith in the sun rising every morning." I place another log down. "Faith in the seed that becomes the fruit." Again he swings the axe which this time only cuts halfway into the log. He then heaves both axe and log above his head.

"And," he strains, "I have faith in the good of mankind." The axe crashes down again and the log falls apart. He takes a deep breath and eyes me seriously.

"Faith that the good of mankind will outgrow the evils we see today."

I ask him how he feels about killing Germans. Aren't they members of mankind?

"At first it was hard. To shoot, knowing you're going to kill a man who probably wants this war just as much as we do. I'd rather shoot Hitler, the head of the beast. But I can't, so I kill these men who follow his orders. Because as far as I can see, his orders will lead to our graves and then onto the graves of my family and my loved ones, and that, as a member of mankind, I cannot and will not allow." His moustache quivers as he grins.

We take a break as the cook comes out of the Ibza with two steaming bowls of *shchi*, traditional Russian cabbage soup. Seated on a pile of logs, Avakov asks how I feel killing Hitler's men.

"Same as you at first, hesitant, guilty. But now I just think of what atrocities they did to our women and children and my blood boils."

"Ha ha, like a berserker!" Avakov wipes his mouth with the back of his huge hand.

"Save your rage for one-on-one combat," he shakes his head, "then the frenzy of hate can give you the strength of ten men, but it can also make you go blind, hence blind fury."

I listen intently. Avakov knows what he is talking about.

"Most fighting is done at its best when a soldier is even-tempered, prudent and resolute. Even tempered means you're cool under fire. Cool when the screechers dive towards you, unattached when your comrade is shot dead beside you. Rage, fury – save it for later. Prudent, don't take wild pot-shots or think you should always be doing something. Choose your moment. Each bullet is precious. Resolute, this means more to your comrades than anything. The knowledge that you will do your duty will strengthen all around you. Courage is contagious but so too alas is cowardice."

The wisdom Avakov conveys is also contagious. When he opens up I just listen. His words are like priceless rubies, his silence ubiquitous. It's like he has a vast well of knowledge deep within that can only be accessed by asking the right question. Most of the time he appears solemn, although that could just be the effect of his droopy moustache. He goes about his work with a quiet, efficient dignity. There is something kingly in his demeanour. Never rushed, agitated or sloppy. Quite simply Avakov is the man I would like to be.

"We Siberians are great men," he once said without a hint of boastfulness. "But how are we to know it, if fortune gives us no opportunity to show our greatness? A man cannot know himself without facing the wrath of misfortune."

I believe there is no refuge in this world, no place to rest my head. Even my inner landscape is changing. Cherished beliefs, rigid ways of seeing and interpreting the world are forever being undermined by the ruthless truth of war.

The extreme emotions of war. The adrenaline loaded, pumped-up blood lust of victory, of advancement, of beating the enemy. The lows of morale sapping boredom, retreat, death of comrades and death of ideals.

Now the peace and stillness of a Belarusian village seemingly untouched by the hand of war. Smoke steadily rising from the chimneys, the hypnotic swish of an old maid brushing the hearth, the bubbling cauldron of stew, fragrance of lavender blown across the fields prompting more Latin from Vasily.

"Et en Arcadia, ego." He tells me it means "I am in paradise." We stumble upon these havens of tranquillity every now and then. As if awakening from a nightmare, we glimpse Eden. Paradise lodged between victory and defeat. This simple life, to me right now, seems to be the essence of holiness.

This, I remembered, was what I was fighting for.

Who am I? Am I Dimitri the soldier? Will I ever again become Dimitri the Soviet citizen? I hope I make it to be Dimitri the old man one day.

With every comrade that dies, part of me dies also. But the part of me that remains wants to live more than ever.

For a brief moment of time, off-duty, helping on the farm, swimming in the river, playing with the children – I was free. Today I play as a child. Tomorrow I go back to killing people.

I try to make sense of the world. Ivan, whilst crushing the lice in his clothes, said this war is the end of the world. I know what he means. Civilisation rent asunder, depths of inhumanity plumbed, demolished city after demolished city. A huge dust cloud follows our bombardments, casting a deathly hue across the land. And yet I know somewhere in the world there will be sunshine and dancing, someone someplace will be swimming over coral reefs of spectacular beauty. And in some distant war-forgotten city two people will be falling in love. Birds will fly and swoop, bursting with life.

The life force that throbs throughout the world.

A beautiful world which we taint with our deeds of war.

CHAPTER 18

Berlin 1945

Monika Bauer worked as an assistant to both Rula and Violetta but she longed to be with them up on the stage. She had trained as an actress and indeed had the looks but not the body of a burlesque dancer. Curvaceous and voluptuous she was not.

Monika's husband had died in 1941 during the German surge towards Moscow. She was told he had frozen to death during the winter offensive. His body was never returned. Her husband had been a real man, a man's man. He had also been a simple man with simple tastes. Too simple for the artistic side of her, yet he had simply loved her. And though she never doubted his love, she had taken it for granted. That was until he was taken away from her. Now she knew how cold and cruel the world could be to one without love.

When Josef joined the theatre, although still grieving her husband, his strong hands and rugged good looks had lifted her spirits. Maybe she could find love again? That was until she came to realise it wasn't carpentry he was undertaking in Violetta's dressing room. It was a full blown love affair.

Now all alone and lonely, the bitter need to survive in the dark days of Berlin became all consuming. Monika had always wanted to be an actress yet she hated the role she now felt forced to play.

Her meagre earnings were hardly enough to get by. She survived on her wits. She stole liquor from the club and sold it on the black market. She traded illegal ration coupons for meat, coffee and sugar.

All her transactions were done in the dark. In the sleazy Die Bosen nightclub and in corners of dingy cafes and bars where the black market thrived in the shadows.

During her dealings she became friends with a homosexual prostitute called Franz who told her what the female prostitutes were earning. Monika had lost everything else. What matter now about dignity and morality in the moment by moment uncertainty of war?

So now, between time spent at the club and the black market, she more often found herself in the dark curtained room of her apartment performing dark deeds with strange men. And with the enemy getting nearer by the day, the fear of death acted like an aphrodisiac on the Berlin citizens.

Business was booming.

She couldn't understand Franz, with his dead eyes, pale skin and tell-tale bruising of his arms. He was the hollow eyed antithesis of the master race. She couldn't understand his wilful self-destruction while all around people would do anything to survive. And yet, through Franz, she learned that beyond prostitution the trade of information was even more lucrative.

When she overheard the conversation between Josef, Rula and Violetta she knew she had struck gold. With the net closing on Berlin, the SS were clamping down on insurgents and traitors. And what could be more treacherous than shielding a Jewess right under their noses? But Monika was streetwise enough to know if she went straight to the SS with this news she'd be lucky to get a *danke-schon*.

Rula had always been kind to her, yet Monika almost considered it her duty to give up a Jew. To give up Violetta for aiding and abetting was even easier. Easy because Monika had always been envious of Violetta's gilded lifestyle, her fancy house and beautiful daughter. And now she had Josef. Monika seethed to see him so enamoured by the gaudy charms of *Viola L'Amour*. How he turned a blind eye to her Nazi lovers and even her husband was beyond her comprehension.

She needed a middleman, someone who could trade her information for a high price.

She needed someone unscrupulous and with no sense of loyalty or kinship.

Someone like her.

When she told Franz of the hidden Jewess his greedy eyes lit up. He insisted on being given a ten percent cut for putting her in touch with a client of his, a homosexual with links to the Nazi party. Discretion was vital. His name was Otto.

It was arranged for Monika to meet Otto outside a run-down cafe in Wilhelmstrasse.

The few Berliners out on the streets seemed resigned to a fate beyond their control. All hope had gone. Hope that had sprung up around the time of Mussolini's removal in a bloodless coup. Hopes that were dashed with every ill-fated attempt to eliminate Hitler.

The weather was overcast. The clouds above Berlin were smudges of pinks and blues where the sun was burning away the heavy grey. It was as though last night's intense bombing, anti-aircraft fire and tracers had bruised the skies.

The restaurant carried on its act of surreal normality. Its green and white striped canopy was rolled back and the tables and chairs outside the cafe accommodated a handful of defiant customers. The 'menu' had been pared down to weak coffee, biscuits, black bread and whatever liquor it had.

Monika approached from across the street with her head held high. From her acting classes she knew appearances constituted reality, that fake confidence could take one a long way. But she had a tightness in her stomach like she used to get before a school exam.

Taking a deep breath she crossed the road. Her long, fitted Macintosh accentuated her slim figure and she attracted an admiring glance from an old man peering above the grim headlines of his outdated newspaper. She also caught the eye of a waiter who deftly pulled out a chair and motioned her towards a central table.

Monika glanced round for Otto. Her auburn hair was tied back with her grown-out fringe flopping either side of her furrowed brow. Across from her sat a fussily dressed fat woman with three spaniels panting for scraps beneath her table. Opposite were a young couple whose body language spoke of a recent argument now showing as uncomfortable silence. It could have been an ordinary day. Other attempts at normality included each table having a tall, thin ruby-red glass vase containing a single white rose.

Monika recalled when this place had buzzed with excitement, the days when waist-coated waiters and immaculate waitresses glided between restaurant and pavement tables with balletic grace. She could still remember the sweet aroma of fresh coffee, bagels and newly baked bread. But now all that hung in the air was the smell of smoke from last night's bombing.

After placing Monika's order of their strongest coffee on her table, the waiter moved aside and there, dressed as Franz said he would be, in a charcoal woollen suit, silver cufflinks and red tie stood Otto.

"Fraulein Bauer?" he held out his hand.

"Otto..." she half stood to shake his soft hand, "I wasn't told your last name, sorry."

"Otto will do, my dear."

Monika nodded as they both sat down. She could tell from those few words German wasn't his first language. He had an air of relaxed authority and the manners of an Englishman. Yet his skin had a slight olive tone suggesting to Monika nothing was as it appeared. He bowed his head to the waiter who acknowledged him and disappeared inside the restaurant.

"I've seen you before, Frau Bauer," he said, lighting a cigarette.

"Please, call me Monika."

"Monika."

He delicately unfolded the napkin and placed it on his knees.

"You have served me at Die Bosen Club."

"I have?"

She scrutinised his fine-lined, bland face but could not recall him.

Otto reclined, hands clasped and elbows on the arms of his chair. He regarded Monika carefully. She was appealing, he decided, in a sharp featured vulpine way.

"It's a dark place. You are always busy," he broke into a smile.

"That's true."

"Busy flirting with much younger men than me!"

She guessed he was in his early fifties. He didn't appear threatening but there was something about him which made her uncomfortable.

As he carried on with his well-rehearsed small talk she remembered Franz's warning that Otto could be manipulative and ruthless. As she held his gaze she could imagine herself being drawn through the windows of his soul into a moral abyss.

"....always the bridesmaid, never the bride?"

Monika snapped out of her thoughts. She hadn't been listening.

"Sorry?"

Otto smiled patiently as he stubbed out his cigarette.

"At the club, you are always in the shadows, never on stage."

"Huh, I don't think anyone wants to see me on stage."

She folded her arms defensively, hiding her ring-less fingers and red-chapped hands, signs that she'd more often scrubbed the stage than graced it.

"Why not? You're a pretty little thing, I'm sure..."

"Look," Monika politely cut in, "I'm sure you're a busy man and I have to be back at work soon."

He was giving her the creeps.

"The club?"

"No, my day job. I issue ration cards at the Town Hall."

"Ah, Franz mentioned that," he lit up another cigarette, "tell me, what do you do with the ration cards that go uncollected?"

Monika froze.

"It's amazing how many of them end up on the black market," he smiled at her knowingly.

There were always uncollected ration cards after every four-week rationing period and, though she needed her superior's permission to withhold them, she needed none to issue them. She couldn't believe Franz had told this stranger about her illicit sideline.

The waiter arrived and poured Otto a small glass of vodka and left the half-empty bottle. It was clear Otto held a tab here and was slowly making his way through the bottle.

How much more did this chain-smoking man, of whom she knew nothing, know about her? Monika felt at a disadvantage before their negotiations had even begun. Otto smiled as he raised his glass to his lips. Did he also know of her venture into prostitution? Coming from a known position of desperation was a poor starting point. Her mind started to wander as it always did when nervous.

Otto let out a small satisfied gasp,

"Go ahead," he put down his glass and relaxed in his chair, "what is it you want to tell me?"

Monika leant forward and lowered her voice.

"I know of a Jewess living right here in the centre of Berlin."

Otto's eyes narrowed.

"A full-blood Jewess or a mischling?"

"I'm not sure. Possibly half-Jew..."

"Half-breed." Otto interjected.

"She doesn't look obviously Jewish, if you know what I mean?"

Otto nodded. His arms formed a triangle on the table, hands together as if in prayer.

"Half-breed means half the value," he said.

Gone was the oily small talk. Monika now saw an edge to him. He realised how he appeared, forced a smile and absentmindedly rearranged their unused cutlery.

"Go on," he raised his eyebrows in a gesture that said *Trust me.*

He poured himself another glass and nodded to the waiter who came and removed the bottle.

"Will you ever finish that?" Monika asked.

"I get such pleasure from vodka, never more so than after my second drink. That is when I stop."

He savoured a sip.

"To let go of something at the point of greatest pleasure," he closed his eyes in ecstasy, "takes immense discipline, and discipline my dear, sets one free."

To Monika he was speaking utter nonsense. She found no pleasure in measure. The motto of Die Bosen Club, painted in gold letters on white alabaster above the stage read,

The road of excess leads to the palace of wisdom.

Monika saw freedom in having no political convictions. She sought peace by giving up any sense of responsibility. And she felt, from plenty of experience, that lust and passion were the highest of joys.

But right now she felt nauseated.

Was it the coffee?

Was it guilt?

Otto lit up another cigarette then took out a small notepad and pencil.

"Who shelters this Jew? The more names you give me, the more you will be rewarded."

"Violetta Hubresch, she's married to a scientist who works for the Nazi party," she looked to see if this extra information had impressed him. He looked unimpressed.

"And?" Otto cajoled her.

And," she struggled to say his name, "Josef Kane."

He scribbled in his book.

"And the Jew's name?"

Her lips tightened, turning down at the ends.

"You look pale my dear, are you feeling ill?"

Blinking back an unexpected tear, she regained her composure and took a deep breath.

"Promise me, if I give you the name of the Jew, she will not be sent to one of the death camps?"

Otto showed no surprise at her plea. He stubbed out his latest cigarette. Rumours of the Nazi extermination camps were now well established as terrible facts.

Otto placed his palms down on the table. They were smooth with manicured fingernails. His forehead furrowed turning his fine lines into deep grooves.

"Measures carried out against the Jews are beyond my control."

His words conveyed the banality of evil.

"However, there is a transit camp at Schulstrasse where many mischlinge are currently held. The way the war is going, I imagine they won't be getting transported anywhere soon."

Beneath the table Monika curled her nails tight into her hands.

"Rula Hornski. That's her stage name. I don't know her real name."

She lied, as if withholding this bit of information proved to herself she wasn't totally evil.

Otto wrote it down. Closed his notebook and nodded at Monika. He sat completely still, almost lifeless whilst Monika fidgeted, glanced around and slowly shred her napkin to pieces.

"How much will I get?"

Otto arched his eyebrows.

"For this information?" Monika hissed, "what are you paying me with?"

Otto drained the last dregs of vodka and put down his glass.

"With something the whole world needs right now, my dear."

He stood up and took out a brown envelope from his jacket pocket.

"Something more precious than diamonds, of more value than gold."

He passed her the envelope.

"Tomorrow, follow the instructions, use the key. Act as normal at the club. Goodbye Monika Bauer."

David J Robinson

CHAPTER 19

Diary of Dimitri

As our convoy loops back towards the front-line I stand up in the back of a lend-lease American Studebaker and survey our surreal rag-tag army. T-34 tanks plough doggedly across the land followed by Cossack cavalrymen on worn-out horses with booty strapped to their saddles, Dodges towing light artillery, Chevrolets carrying mortars and tractors dragging along great howitzers. Finally, horse-drawn carts and foot soldiers bring up the rear of this most ancient and modern procession.

I imagine we are returning home as conquering heroes. When, and if we do, I hope to feel more jubilant than now. Huddled masses of bewildered peasants shuffle up and down highways. Dirty and louse infested they are all going nowhere with nowhere to go.

As we pass through a town, on a crowded street corner, I spot a peasant who is the spitting image of Yuri. My blood runs cold. He sees me and looks away quickly. I've read Dostoevsky's *The Double* but this likeness is more incredible than any work of fiction.

"Yuri!" I cry.

But he keeps moving, mingling with the crowd, trying to get away.

"Yuri, you're alive!"

The men in the back of the truck stand up to see. He turns again. A scruffy balaclava frames his anguished face. I struggle to comprehend. How is he alive? Why is he running away?

I wince loudly as a punch to my rib-cage doubles me over.

"You fucking idiot!" Someone hisses into my ear.

I don't need to see to know it is Cerenkov.

We're back at the front-line, another garrison. I fear Cerenkov has broken one of my ribs.

Yuri has been arrested for desertion.

Fyodor arrested too for aiding him.

I am a pariah once more.

The men ignore me. My actions even went unrecognised by our officers as if they too couldn't acknowledge the merits of a snitch. I only did what I thought was right. I didn't mean any harm. If they had told me Yuri was going to desert would I have turned a deaf ear or told our commander?

To be honest, I don't know any more. Even though I'm disillusioned with the way the army is run I still believe we must unite to stop these fascist beasts. If we allow one man to desert where will it end? The fabric of brotherhood shall be weaker for the lost thread. We all need to pull together for the greater good.

Now we found Yuri alive it became clear Fyodor had lied to cover up Yuri's desertion. Before the subsequent 'show trial' I heard that Yuri had requested leave to return to his sick mother, who wrote to him that she was dying. Permission refused, he'd hatched up this plan with Fyodor. For deserting, Yuri was looking at the ultimate punishment; summary execution by an NKVD punitive detachment.

David J Robinson

CHAPTER 20

"**S**o, Yuri Mitrovic, in summation you are charged with deserting the Red Army, cowardice in the face of the enemy and resisting arrest. The court has heard the sworn statement of Colonel Marchenko. Do you have anything to say?"

The court setting is a large nursery classroom. The walls have held up to bomb blasts and mortar shelling but the white plaster has cracked badly and in places crumbled away altogether from the red brickwork beneath. Parts of the wall still hold display boards on which children's tattered drawings and paintings hang resolutely. What has become of these fledgling artists? The hand prints and smiling suns

149

remind us just how far we have fallen from the paradise of childhood.

Along with half a dozen non-commissioned officers, a random collection of troops have been selected to bear witness to this show trial. Cerenkov is stood to the left of me. I notice a faint swastika scratched into the plaster, faint because it has been scribbled over many times. At my feet a purple crayon lies wedged between the floorboards. A mound of rubble is piled up in the corner; remnants of studded partition walls, glass splinters and bits of wood.

There is an unnatural coldness to the room. Dismal light bulbs leave the outer corners in shadow and weak daylight barely penetrates the grimy cracked windows. Shorn of curtains, carpets and cushions it feels more like an asylum than kindergarten. It reminds me of the frozen garden in *The Selfish Giant* (another book of Uncle Leon's) yearning for the innocent laughter of children to bring it back to life. Through a broken window high up the outside wall, a lone brown linnet flits between the branches of a barren tree.

Seated behind a high desk at the front, the Troika, or military tribunal, is made up of three commissars. This trio of Communist party officials act simultaneously as prosecutor and judge to issue sentences on soldiers in summary proceedings. Puffed up with the self-importance such a role demands they are the antithesis of the compassionate, egalitarian men and women who started the revolution.

Or is that just a myth also?

Orphan of the State

The lead Commissar is a hard-faced little man. Wispy hair criss-crosses his balding head like the threadbare covering on a coconut.

"Are you deaf Mitrovic? Have you got *anything* to say?"

Yuri's eyes are bloodshot, his skin ash grey. When he'd walked into the courtroom it was with the bent shuffle of a geriatric. And when he talks his voice rarely rises above a whisper. We've seen it all before, symptoms of extreme stress culminating in a nervous breakdown. These men are of no use on the frontline.

"Not guilty, Commissar. I didn't know what..."

"Silence! I didn't ask how you wish to plead."

A seething Marchenko addresses Yuri.

"Do you not understand the gravity of the charge? Are you aware of the evidence stacked up against you? Even now at this late hour, don't you realise that to plead guilty is your only option?"

Marchenko is out of order. He's no right to address the accused yet not one of the commissars rebukes him. It is a stitch-up from the start. And we all know it.

The Commissar's voice cuts in again, high-pitched, almost whiny.

"Admit the truth of your moral cowardice and you may yet be granted a punishment that will at least save your pitiful little life."

Yuri glances behind at us as if looking for advice.

None comes.

"Mitrovic, face front! Do you really think your comrades are going to forgive you for abandoning your unit?"

Yuri bows his head. A broken man, his whole body trembles. If the NCO's know the meaning of compassion they'll find him an office job away from the fighting. Yet unlike physical wounds, mental scars are impossible to see. And some soldiers are good actors and feign delirium with all the psychological realism of a Chekov drama.

Exasperated, Marchenko can't help butting in again.

"He's giving you one last chance to explain yourself, damn it!"

Yuri sniffs and wipes his nose on the back of his hand.

"Stand to attention!" The Commissar barks. "At least try to bring a modicum of soldiery to that uniform you've so gravely desecrated."

Harangued on two fronts, Yuri tries to stand up straight. He looks like a little boy appearing before the headmaster; fearful, embarrassed and squirming under the attention.

"One last chance, Mitrovic. Explain your actions again and then I will take your final plea."

Yuri closes his eyes for a moment then slowly opens them.

"There were explosions." His voice is dry, hoarse even. "The blast from a German grenade knocked me off my feet." His eyes wander, unfocused. "I think I hit my head on a tree. When I came to, it was night. I'd gone deaf. I was disorientated. I didn't know who or where I was."

"Really? You expect us to believe this claptrap?" The Commissar said.

"I had amnesia."

"How convenient," the Commissar mutters whilst scribbling furiously on the paper in front of him.

"Of course, I recognised my uniform, presumed I was a soldier..."

"Presumed!" The Commissar gives a faint shake of the head. "I thought it was dark, pitch black in the forest at night? How could you see your bloody uniform?"

"I didn't at first. I just stumbled through the forest. The sky was so cloudy I couldn't get my bearings. I was in and out of consciousness."

"Why?" Asks the Commissar. "You've no signs of being shot or wounded."

"My head," Yuri mumbles a stream of excuses, "the pain from the bomb blast, I'd lost my memory. I survived off berries and water from streams. Eventually I came across a farmhouse. They took me in and helped me recover."

"And where was this farmhouse?"

"I can't say."

"Can't say or won't say? Who helped you there? Names, Mitrovic, we need names to add to this fairytale in the woods."

"Alexei."

"Alexei? Alexei what?"

"I only got his first name."

The Commissar slams down his pen and folds his arms.

"Good God! Must we go on with this farce?"

Marchenko, again ignoring protocol jumps in.

"What about his family?"

"He lived alone." Yuri begins to speak with more urgency. "My identity tag must have been ripped off my neck in the blast. By the time you found me in the village, certain memories had come back to me and I was searching for the Police station to hand myself in." He glances in Marchenko's direction. "I know what it must have looked like to you."

The Commissar signals Marchenko to sit down and he resumes the questioning.

"So why did you run away when," he glances at his notes, "Dimitri Petrov called out your name?"

Yuri shrugs, "I can't explain it."

His words sound feeble as they trail off into the silence.

Realising he isn't doing himself any favours, Yuri suddenly becomes more animated.

"I was scared. I was looking for a church. I needed to light a candle for my mother."

"A church? I thought you were looking for a police station a moment ago?"

Yuri pauses as though reflecting then raises a finger to his temple,

"You see? It's my mind, I still can't think straight."

"You mean you can't get your story straight." The Commissar dismissively shuffles his papers. "Let's pray your Mother doesn't pull through. At least then she'll die peacefully, not knowing her only son is a coward and a defector."

Cerenkov stiffens and mumbles *"Bastards!"* under his breath. It comes out louder than he probably intends. Either that or he just doesn't care anymore.

All three commissars look over at us.

"Silence in court!"

The chief Commissar turns back to the pitiful figure of Yuri.

"You're a bird-watcher I believe, a day-dreamer perhaps too? Indulging in flights of fancy thinking you're above us mere earthbound mortals."

The commissar's pasty face reminds me of a cadaver. His grey eyes seem to look inwards. His mouth thin and cruel, he sneers;

"Well, you know what they say, a bird maybe known by its song and your alibi is most hard on my ears."

Yuri swallows hard and frowns.

"Flying solo... abandoning the flock." The commissar speaks the words with relish. "You took flight with no regard for your honour, your comrades or your country." He stacks the papers on their ends like a pack of cards. "Last chance for you Mitrovic. How do you plead?"

Yuri closes his eyes for what seems an eternity. He sniffs, looks up to the exposed ceiling with its confusion of pipes, lagging, wires and cables. The courtroom becomes restless.

"Not guilty," he pronounces dryly.

The Commissar slams his papers on the desk. He turns to both men at his side, whispering and nodding.

They all stand up.

For a second, all the air seems to go out of the room.

"Yuri Mitrovic, the jury finds you guilty of all charges. The regulations of Orders 270 and 277 are clear-cut. But we are not going to waste the bullets of a firing squad on you."

Yuri takes a deep breath.

"You will be executed with a single shot in the back of the neck by one of the comrades you deserted."

The Commissar bangs his gavel on the desk.

The NCO's leap into a flurry of activity as noisy debate breaks out amongst the spectators.

"Bring out Fyodor Kuznetsov!"

"I meant *guilty* your honour!" Yuri shouts over the commotion.

"Too late!" The Commissar shoots Yuri a scathing glance.

There is a pause in the uproar.

"You're a *liar* Mitrovic. A stain on the honour of the Soviet Union. Even the schtraff unit has standards. Take him away."

Yuri pleads for mercy as he is dragged from the courtroom. He's no sooner been bundled out the doorway when Fyodor is roughly manhandled inside.

Fyodor stuck to the line that he genuinely thought Yuri had been killed and that he knew nothing about his desertion. He was a good liar. Not only an expert at forging documents but also able to forge his emotions to such an extent the tribunal was split. He was ordered to join the nearest schtraff unit as soon as possible. These units were an assortment of felons, deserters and cowards who were given a second chance to redeem themselves. They operated like mercenaries. Their missions involved highly risky manoeuvres behind enemy lines. If they survived they could be re-integrated into the army, though I had yet to meet one so fortunate.

Suicide squads didn't get their name for nothing.

Marchenko took charge of Yuri's execution. Cerenkov seemed like a broken man at this time. He still kept up his hard-boiled, Russian bear persona but it was shot through with sadness, as if his own flesh and blood was about to be put to death.

I was not alone in sensing this strange bond between Cerenkov and Yuri. Colonel Marchenko must have sensed it too. To test Cerenkov's loyalty to the cause he ordered *him* to execute Yuri.

Cerenkov had the audacity to refuse, saying he didn't join the Red Army to kill Russian soldiers. His logic is commendable but I see Marchenko going red with fury. If Cerenkov's not careful, he too will be up for treason.

"I will execute him." I find myself blurting out.

Marchenko hesitates.

Cerenkov glares at me.

"But I beg for the execution to take place away from here, over by the forest away from the troops."

Marchenko flares his nostrils like an angry bull.

"Yuri is so well liked," I continue, "his execution will badly affect the morale of the unit. Out of sight, out of mind."

Marchenko swallows hard and nods slowly.

"I shall be watching though," he growls.

For the first time ever, Marchenko has agreed to somebody else's terms – mine.

"And I shall watch also when you bury him."

Yuri was held overnight awaiting a dawn execution. By the window I lay awake watching fragmented clouds blowing across a bright moonlit sky. My guilt weighs me down like a physical force. I feel sick. Why did I volunteer to be executioner?

Yuri is hauled into the courtyard before us. Marchenko steps forward and nods in my direction.

"Take the traitor to the clearing before the woods. After you've executed him I want to see him buried out in the open ground."

Then the order is given to the men to move out. We are advancing again.

Yuri and I walk in silence across the bomb-scarred field towards the woods. The hoar frost makes the grass crunch beneath our boots. I can feel the pressure of Marchenko watching us through binoculars.

The murmuring of a flight of birds catches my eye.

All of a sudden, Yuri makes a run towards the trees. I am momentarily stunned before setting off after him, grappling to get my gun out of its holster. Marchenko shouts at me to shoot him there and then but Yuri gets to the woods first and disappears. Behind me the men strain above the sandbags to see the drama unfold. Marchenko curses and grimaces behind his binoculars.

Within moments of me following Yuri into the trees they hear my gunshots. Seconds later I reappear. Marchenko observes every move from across the wasteland as I drag Yuri's limp body out into the clearing. With the spade I have strapped across my back, I bury him in a shallow bomb crater in the ground.

Kneeling down to utter a silent prayer, I feel the peace of knowing I have done the right thing.

Maskirovka!

David J Robinson

CHAPTER 21

Moscow 1941

S tepan had awoken in a cold sweat, and it wasn't just a hangover. Was it the start of a fever, or a physical manifestation of his guilt? He was on a list of people to be arrested at a future date.

And now the saint-like figure of Beria was in charge of the secret police, people who questioned the methods of Yezhov were bound to feel that all upcoming arrests would be justified.

Including his.

Stepan always thought he had a talent for seeing the big picture, but right now he wasn't even sure what was going on right under his nose. He'd called Katryn upon awakening

161

to tell her and Ava to prepare for evacuation. Katryn had protested but he calmly assured her it was a blessing, an honour for someone so valued as Stepan was to the Party.

Stepan was one of the few who knew the catastrophic capitulation of the western defences had all been Stalin's fault. It was Stalin who ignored all warnings about an imminent German invasion. Furthermore, he knew it was Stalin's pre-war purging of the army's officer class which had left Russia's fighting force hopelessly weakened. As a result, the Soviet authorities tried to suppress all news of the disaster and there had been a surge in arrests in the first few months of the war.

Could the Germans really topple Moscow and render his imminent arrest obsolete? Would Stalin, in the aftermath of a Soviet victory, grant an amnesty for such as him? Kariakin was right, after the war who knows who'll be in charge.

As Stepan got washed and dressed for the last time in his plush suite in the House of Government, he vowed he would return to such privileged surroundings again one day.

The House of Government had been built on an island facing the Kremlin. It first opened its doors in the spring of 1931 to several hundred Bolshevik apparatchiks. It was originally intended to be a temporary home for these Government officials and ministers whilst the country transitioned into the egalitarian ideal of communal living. These huge, forbidding apartments formed the largest residential building in Europe. With its high ceilings, central heating and an array of luxury amenities such as cinema, subsidised cafeteria, library, gymnasium and grocery store, it was the embodiment of everything the revolution had sought to destroy.

These elite party members soon became attached to the comforts of their lavish apartments and saw them as just reward for their vital work within the Government machinery. Before long they soon forgot their original Bolshevik intentions and became a reincarnation of the old bourgeoisie. The House of the Government grew to be seen as a structure of rank hypocrisy where the orchestrators of the Communist project lorded over the rank and file.

When, during the mid 1930's, it became clear the Government had failed in its pledge to implement a fair and just society, Stalin began to look for scapegoats. Between the years 1937 to 1938 the purges began in earnest and the pampered denizens of Government House were ripe for the cull. During this time eight hundred residents, were arrested or evicted. Over three hundred were shot. They were an easy target. A human sacrifice, they were branded as saboteurs and blamed for not delivering on the utopian promises.

The persecution of these cosseted elites drew no pity from the ordinary workers. Food shortages and cramped housing throughout Moscow, plus the intrinsic belief that there were enemies everywhere, enabled these witch-hunts to go unhindered. It was basic class envy in a supposedly classless society.

Sitting in his stately room with its wall of wood and glass shelves, Stepan knew he would have to be patient and shoulder whatever hardships may await him in Chistopol. Despite Stepan's atheist sensibilities his father's words still echoed in his mind. *"Christ endured and told us to."*

By the time he'd lit the fire, heated a samovar for tea and opened up his typewriter, Stepan had formulated a plan.

Stepan would tell the authorities he had eavesdropped on a gang of workers conspiring against Soviet power. The things they had said about the peasants being unwilling to fight, the scaremongering priest with his ranting of it being the end of days and their criticisms of the system all crossed the line of heresy. Along with these treacherous remarks he would also add they'd bragged about being saboteurs and wreckers in their factories. He would say one talked openly of selling false papers.

Stepan would go on to say how he argued with them, warning them that bad rumours fly on wings. He would say he looked around for someone to arrest them for such talk but no-one from the NKVD was there. He would confess to being drunk and that he wasn't thinking straight and so waited until the sobriety of morning before filing this report. He couldn't admit to failings in the system so blamed their belligerence on tongues loosened by alcohol. It didn't lessen their crimes of defeatist talk and panic-mongering, but it explained their criticisms were not those of rational citizens.

His head was throbbing hard and he poured himself a large measure of vodka, the hair of the dog that bit him. Feeling queasy and with shaking hands he went on to describe the one with the long white hair as being an orthodox priest in proletariat clothing. He laid it on thick, describing some as class enemies, others as alien elements. His sentences were peppered with words like parasites, Jew's and kulaks.

Orphan of the State

As he wrote these words of denouncement, these sentences that would sentence those men to exile, hard labour or the firing squad, Stepan actually began to feel like the man he had always pretended to be. Whilst privately he hated the regime with all his heart and soul, he knew for his body to survive, publicly he must always be seen as an exemplary Communist.

"They meet every night at a corrugated iron stall on the corner of Gorky Street. Don't be fooled by their workers tunics and cloth caps." He wrote. *"Their forged papers and dressed up biographies are deceitful attempts to reinvent their social class."*

Stepan hoped this would reaffirm his credentials as a loyal, vigilant member of the party.

"I have every confidence in the Soviet system of justice."

He prayed this would wipe clean his name from the list and pave a way back to Moscow from Chistopol.

Yet, for all his rational logic, self-hatred was raging inside him. It was a real physical sensation, like an entity within. This entity he knew was his real personality, forever warring with his self-imposed public persona. Stepan even tried to reason with his inner self. If he didn't denounce those men, they could denounce him, and then what would happen to his family? They would become social pariahs. He knew countless stories of relatives of those arrested being shunned by their former friends. People would cross the road to avoid them, most would never talk to them again and some would even scratch out their faces from photographs. Where was the good in that?

But from the pit of his being the answer remained, better an honest death than a living lick-spittle, a cowering dog, and a traitor to everything he ever believed in.

Stepan poured himself more vodka, hoping to drown his conscience.

"No, no," he muttered to himself, "when you live amongst wolves, you must learn to live like a wolf!"

He knew the corruption in society came from the top. The men in the Kremlin were as devious as devils, as moral as Ivan III, yet, as the wild priest had rightly said, it is the little thieves that are hanged whilst the great ones escape.

He banged the empty glass on the table. The tightening in his chest was easing. His outer persona had won for now. But this war of attrition between the Party's truth and the truth of his own experience was tearing him apart.

"Rurik the Rus is in our blood!" the cloth-capped man had cried. Rurik was the legendary founder of the Russian state. And Stepan felt deep inside, the spirit of Rurik was suffering immeasurably. He was killing everything about himself that was once proud and noble.

When he'd finished writing the letter he went over to read it by the fireplace. As he finished reading, his cheeks streaming with tears, he scrunched up the letter and threw it onto the burning coals.

"No, there is another way out." He thought to himself as he walked unsteadily back to his desk by the large window.

"A way where only one person suffers, not many."

He took out his Government issued Nagent revolver from the side drawer.

166

Stepan thought only of Ava as he put the gun to his head. His only regret was not telling her it was Dimitri Petrov himself who had denounced his own parents. Maybe his hints about Pavlik Morozov and the newspaper cuttings would crystallise that notion in her mind. He consoled himself with his final thought that Petrov would surely meet his demise on the Eastern Front.

"Long live Stalin!" He cried.

The gunshot echoed around the apartment.

Then all was still again.

And in the cold silence, the imperious spires of the Kremlin reflected dimly in Stepan's glazed, open eyes.

David J Robinson

CHAPTER 22

Diary of Dimitri

W e lumber on through knee-high snow. The bleak, featureless frozen wasteland along with the monotonous trudge-trudge of marching numbs the brain. Intelligent thoughts become as scarce as food. It's a Long Way to Tipperary is being whistled rebelliously by somebody at the rear. Beneath my heavy boots and foot bandages blood blisters and fungal foot sores keep me awake.

It felt like we were marching forever. Each step a little closer to death, each breath a clinging to life. There were moments of utter clarity when I saw us through the lens of history. Another bunch of homo-sapiens involved in another stupid war.

I loved my country before the war. I loved the ideals of communism, equality and fairness. Now I felt conned, hoodwinked into a system of deception, a system that hijacked the ideas of Marx and twisted it to nefarious ends.

Oleg says, *"They say the most skilled leader is the most invisible."*

"Ah," Vasily nods. *"So is that why we never see Stalin?"*

It is cold. Snow lies on the frozen ground. The air is static and harsh on the lungs but there is a crystal clear clarity about everything. Objects clearly defined with sharp edges and glorious colours. Artists weather, where the eye can penetrate deep into the landscape. Sniper's weather for seeing – but not good for being seen! One can think and reason better in this weather but any movement is easily detected against this still, ice-covered background. Trees stand inert against a pure azure sky. Rubble, dust and masonry cleansed by a sheen of frost. No wind. This silent outer world frames my inner turmoil. After the tumult of war there is holiness amidst this quiet. All time is zeroed down to this moment. My shell-shocked mind recoils at the sublime peacefulness. It's hard to reconcile the blood-soaked memories with the optimism of a new day. The freshness of the moment is stale and contaminated by remembered misery. My past won't let me revel in the newness of life.

Orphan of the State

I am possessed by something. It is an emotion that refuses to be named. It weighs me down. It haunts my dreams. It blocks the light from my heart. It deadens my spirit and tells me nothing new. It is a carcass of death, a burden of war. Images obscene and perverse. An inbound imposter casting pale shadows over all joys, all hopes, all love. Then I re-read a letter from Ava and birds do sing and like a musical scale ascending, I am lifted, all too briefly into a higher realm of life, the domain of childhood, the kingdom of dreams.

As far as I can tell, war and adversity can do one of two things to a man. They can make him cling tighter to his beliefs even if they run contrary to his reality. He can hide in his mental landscape, evoking wonderful fantasies and tricks of the mind to take him away from the here and now. Or, he can let go of everything, know all he sees is just a part of one's life, a foot-note to a nation's narrative, a fragment of the world's history. We live in a chopped up storyline where the brave are also evil and the good can be cowards.

Vasily says, *"It took billions of years for the heat of the earth to cool down. How long will it take for mankind's hatred to burn itself out?"*

The Tsars have gone, my comrades have fallen, Berlin and Hitler and Fascism will fall soon. Of that I have no doubt. I also have no doubt the Bolsheviks who replaced the Tsars will be gone one day too. The new recruits will fall also. And what is built from the ashes of Germany, Hitler's replacement and Fascism's heir, will one day too be replaced. Because all is in flux. Since the planets and stars were set in motion we are all compelled to move, to change and evolve. It was this way always. To stand still is to die. To look back is to turn to stone. Onwards humanity! Onwards! But go forward with humility and understanding, aware of the past just enough as not to re-live it. Learn, change and evolve.

CHAPTER 23

Moscow 1941

I, Dimitri Petrov, had left the orphanage and was waiting at Kievsky station bound for Peredelkino and another stay at Uncle Leon's. Before the Metro this was considered the most beautiful train station in Moscow. I understood why. Built in the Byzantine style, to commemorate the defeat of Napoleon, the platform I waited upon was covered by a massive arched glass structure. After the confines of the orphanage it gave me an overwhelming sense of space.

I felt unworthy of such magnificence, sat there in my tatty cap and scruffy woollen jacket with my small bag which contained all I had of value in the world - precious little. The only thing of real value to me was my growing fondness of Ava.

"Love is all." She had said, quoting Tolstoy. As I gazed down the railway tracks, stretching off into oblivion in both directions, I realised it was true. A life without love, a life without Ava, would be colourless and cold. I could hear the sound of her voice, melodious and warm, her laughter, sparkling like a Chopin sonata. I knew no hardship in this world would be unbearable as long as Ava was by my side.

Then I realised, I *was* hearing her voice.

"Dimitri! Dimitri!"

Ava stood at the end of the platform. A Ushanka winter hat framed her face with fur.

She beckoned me.

"I knew you'd be going to Peredelkino today. Do you want to travel there in style, with me?"

Before I could answer, she grabbed my hand and guided me down the steps and through a subway back up to the street. A black snow was falling all around us. Ava explained these charred flakes were the ashes of official papers being burned. The imminent arrival of the Germans meant thousands of archives, files and documents were being incinerated by the Moscow authorities. These incriminating lists of purges, expulsions and denunciations were being set ablaze in a boiler house next to the Party archive building.

A horse drawn carriage was waiting for us amidst this sinister snowstorm and Ava gestured me to climb inside. The stern faced driver, in a battered sheepskin coat, complained about waiting, peppering his speech with vile profanities.

Ava fired back at him, saying how rudeness was a weak man's imitation of strength. He was a peasant, she told me. Farm peasants usually only came to the city in winter to earn money, but now he was one of the thousands fleeing the German onslaught in the west. No sooner had we settled into our cold seat when the driver gave a gruff cry, cracked his whip, and the horses began to pull us along.

"What's going on?" I asked as Ava threw a grey woollen blanket over our legs.

"There's panic all over the city, queues a mile long everywhere. No-one knows when the Germans will get here, no-one is telling us anything."

"A rumour going round the orphanage said there'd been a coup and Stalin has been arrested." I said.

"Who knows?" Ava glanced out the window.

"What I do know," she turned to me, "is factories have closed down, workers haven't been paid and fights have been breaking out in the food queues."

Considering our time together to be precious, I felt the urge to change the conversation.

"Where have you been Ava? I haven't heard from you since the night..." I tailed off.

"I know."

She dipped her eyes and toyed with the fur hat now resting on the blanket over her knees.

"We must have been spotted together the night we went to the cinema. Since then my step-mother hasn't let me out of her sight. Today she insisted I go shopping with her but I needed to see you. I pretended to faint and, as she didn't dare lose her place in the queue, sent me home in this."

"And you knew where I'd be?"

"You're very predictable, Dimitri." She tilted her head and smiled that wide, beautiful smile. "Actually I bumped into your Uncle Leon. He said you were arriving today by train. And I know only one train goes to Peredelkino on Sunday."

We were being jostled and jolted around the carriage. Ava leant out the window and ordered the driver to slow down. He protested he was trying to overtake the tidal rush of people fleeing the city. We could see them through the carriage window as we passed them by, ordinary Muscovites with what few belongings they could carry crammed into suitcases or tied up in bundles.

"There's real anger out there now, Dimitri," Ava said. "For years people have bit their tongue, suppressed their feelings out of fear. We all knew the real world wasn't anything like the one we were told it was. Pravda and the Kremlin have all told us how great our society is and we were browbeaten into believing it."

Her voice was dry and her lower lip trembled slightly.

"Now, the fear that Moscow will fall to the Germans has cut through our muddled thinking. Muscovites are starting to wake up and remember all the years of oppression and injustice. All that anger they suppressed just to survive is now coming to the surface."

As we trundled along, joining the exodus of evacuees on the highway, we could hear people voicing things that days ago would have seen them arrested. Some began singing anti-Communist songs. A florid-faced babushka, headscarf tied under her chin, stood up in the back of a flat wagon and pointed over to Red Square, shouting obscenities and accusations of betrayal. The sights of the ancient Moscow, the gold onion domes of the old Orthodox churches, the ravishing colours of St Basil's Cathedral were now shrouded by the smoky ashes. And, in the distance, the imperial majesty of the Kremlin stood aloof as always. Cold and remote from its fleeing citizens.

"Has Stalin and his cronies left us like rats from a sinking ship?"

The rumour mill ground on between peasant and worker.

"They played Hitler's storm troopers marching song over the speakers this morning. Did you not hear it?"

"It's every man for himself, comrade!"

Farther on, a lone standard bearing a simple crucifix swayed hypnotically above the tattered flow of humanity. A morose baritone chant came from a choir of retreating monks. Their incantation was deep and rich, resonating with the soul of this mighty yet desolate land. It sounded like a funeral march.

Being jostled side by side I suddenly felt nervous, intimidated by Ava's beauty. She seemed to see right through me. If she thought my politics naive did she see me as similarly child-like? I felt she always had the upper hand, guiding me down unknown paths both politically and literally. I wanted her to see me as a man of the world so I blurted out my bold statement.

"I'm joining the army. I'm signing up."

"Why?" Ava looked sidelong at me and raised her eyebrows.

"Why?" I spluttered. "To defend the Motherland of course!" I cringed at how that sounded, how predictable. "And to free Europe of fascism."

I hoped she would try to dissuade me, show me she didn't want me to leave.

"Or is it to spread Communism to the world?"

"Both... I mean all three!"

"But what if the world doesn't want Communism?"

I shrugged.

"Some people don't know what's best for them."

"Be wary of history, Dimitri. People who believe only they know how to create the perfect society usually do terrible things to get it."

I gave a faint shake of my head.

"When you chop down a forest, chips must fly."

Ava let out a deep breath.

"Tolstoy said the world always needs idealists, and although I don't agree with your politics at all, I think you believe what you do because you are an idealist." She dropped her eyes. "And while I don't agree with your reasons for going to war, I do admire your bravery."

"I don't feel brave, Ava. It's more out of a sense of duty why I'm doing this."

"Oh you are brave. Brave to climb the rooftop of Peredelkino Hall. Brave to come to my house, not once, but three times!"

"Brave to stand up for Communism?" I smiled.

"No, that's just foolhardy. Bravery is not recklessness."

A sudden lurch of the carriage pushed us closer together.

"I will miss you, Dimitri Petrov. But it's obvious we're not meant to be together." Ava breathed deeply. "We also have to leave Moscow." She rushed the words out. "My father knows the situation is bad. He rang two day ago telling us we have to evacuate to Chistopol for safety. We haven't heard from him since. A friend of father's, a man called Kariakin, called and told us to set off without him. He insisted Stepan will join us later. But to be honest, I've a feeling my father might be in some kind of trouble. I don't know who to trust anymore."

I held her hand and she looked at me so tenderly, I knew in that instant, I wanted to spend the rest of my life with her.

Instinctively, and surprising even myself, I leant across and kissed her on the lips.

Whether she pulled away prematurely, or it was the shaking of the carriage, it ended all too soon. I quickly turned my face away, pretending to look out the window. My cheeks burned with embarrassment.

"She'll think I'm an imbecile!" I cursed myself.

But beneath the blanket, Ava squeezed my hand and whispered.

"Do that again."

I turned to see her facing me, eyes closed, her lips ever so slightly parted in anticipation. This time I reached out my hand to cradle the side of her face. Nothing would shake us apart this time.

The kiss became more intense and our bodies closed together as we became wrapped in each other's arms. My heart was beating so hard I was sure she would hear it. We only stopped kissing when the carriage halted momentarily.

The end of the kiss felt like being forced to resurface, having swum luxuriantly in tropical waters, into cold air amidst all the jarring noises of the world. I wanted to dive deep again, immediately.

"I'd like to drink honey with your lips." Ava breathed, resting her head on my shoulder.

"What does that mean?" I asked.

"That this... us, meeting as we did... it feels too good to be true." She looked at me with sad eyes. "And now you're going west and I'm going east. How can fate be so cruel?"

"I'll be back, I promise."

"Don't make promises you cannot keep." Ava sat upright. "A white swan died in Moscow Zoo on New Year's Eve. I thought it was a bad omen for our production of Swan Lake. Now everyone thinks it was a doomsday prophesy for all of Moscow and beyond."

We fell silent for a moment.

"I'd like to have seen you perform again." I said.

Ava smiled.

"Do you know the story of Swan Lake?"

"Of course, it's about the doomed romance of Siegfried and Odette."

Ava became excited and held my hand again.

"There's a passage of music where the key changes to D sharp, I think. It's considered to be a cold, almost icy key. Tchaikovsky chose it to represent a moment of love frozen for all time." She looked into my eyes. "To me the music is all about the unresolved longing of two people who want to be together but circumstances don't allow it. It's an idealised love but surely one worth waiting for?"

"Worth waiting for? I thought it had a tragic ending!"

Ava didn't answer, but dug deep inside her pocket and brought out a small glass snow globe.

"Look at this, Dimitri. Isn't it beautiful? Father brought it back from Paris. Look, see there's a tiny couple walking towards the Eiffel tower. They're safe inside the snow globe like Siegfried and Odette's love, frozen in the ice of Tchaikovsky's wonderful music for all eternity."

She looked at me with eyes strong and calm yet obviously affectionate.

Our fingers touched as we held the snow globe together and I remember thinking how much I also wanted this moment, here now with Ava, to last forever.

David J Robinson

CHAPTER 24

Diary of Dimitri

J ust before I set off to war I decided to 'have it out' with Uncle Leon. He was bent over his desk writing beneath the dim daylight from the window. Pens, pencils and papers were laid out methodically. A crackling log fire the only luxury in his spartan chamber.

Why, I asked him, did he still cling to the old ways and not see that with every five year plan, whatever the short-term cost, we were travelling closer to a better socialist world?

Wearily he put down his pen, slid his notepad back on the desk, removed his glasses and sighed.

"All these years," he shook his head and looked at me earnestly, "I've provided you with all those books."

He gestured towards the bookcase hidden behind a false wooden panel.

"I've tried not to force my opinions on you, Dimitri, I really have."

He stood and walked towards the window.

"You couldn't escape being indoctrinated at the orphanage and by every aspect of life out there. I can't compete with such wall-to-wall propaganda, but I do try to make you think for yourself. I do try to access that God-given reason and innate goodness that they tried to suppress."

He came towards me placing his hands on my shoulders. I don't think he ever knew how much I needed those small familial gestures.

"I know that goodness is still inside you Dimitri, otherwise you would have denounced me by now."

He turned away.

"And that would have done wonders for your prospects in the party!"

"I would never betray you, uncle. Despite all your... unconventional ways, at heart you are a good man. I just wish you'd had the chance, like I have, to know only the times since the revolution. I don't remember the past, the aristocracy. It hasn't tainted me. But your ideas are too dyed in the wool for Russia today. I fear for you when I am gone unless you can change."

"Shush!" Leon stood back from the window as a large shiny black car cruised slowly by the front garden. He checked his watch, "Second one today. Well done Koba, keep the pen pushers on their toes."

Koba was a Georgian folk hero from a novel by Alexander Kazbegi; a satirical nickname Leon used when referring to Stalin. He began to draw the curtains together speaking softly as the agents' car disappeared behind the frozen pines.

"Ah yes, Koba, the socialist utopia. It's just over the horizon, is it?"

He turned to me.

"They've been saying that since 1917. The march of history! Do you not think I tried to adapt?"

All of a sudden Leon displayed an almost youthful enthusiasm. Striding back and forth, the floorboards creaked under his tall, sinewy frame. It was rare he acted so energetically unless he was under the influence of alcohol.

"I was as swept up as anyone by the Revolution and the future it promised. Indeed as a writer, Koba called us the engineers of the human soul! What a title. What an honour. And I strived to live up to that *exalted position*."

He just as quickly reverted back to his more dignified and cerebral ways. Sitting back down in his chair, facing me, his eyes narrowed in deliberation.

"I wrote a story of a young girl who grows up in the woods with backward parents. Cut off from society, she's brought up being told the glories of our Tsarist past; the happy lives and progressive culture of those halcyon days. In the forest one day she comes across a holy man and she tells him how she longs to see those Imperial glories. Using supernatural powers he transports her back in time and she sees the grim reality of the Old ways. She experiences serfdom, gross injustice, internal feuds and human misery on a scale she could never have imagined. She then comes across the holy man again but this time she recognises him as Lenin. He breaks the spell and when she returns, she sets off for the city, denounces her parents and joins the Komsomol."

"You never told me that story." I said.

"It was a fairytale, Dimitri, but it served a purpose. As well as securing my place here at Peredelkino I also received this award."

He delved into a small drawer on his writing bureau and picked out a gold medal on a white ribbon. I took it from him and held it in my hand. The image engraved was of children sat at the feet of a man holding an open book in his left hand. The index finger of his right hand is raised aloft as though making a point.

"But as you know, every medal has its reverse."

"I know the saying but never understood it."

"It means every good thing incorporates its opposite. Every pleasure contains the seed of pain. That after scaling the mountain there is the inevitable descent."

"And after every stay with you I have to return to the orphanage!" I said.

"It's no trivial matter!" Leon snatched the medal from my hand; another reminder that his temper could erupt at any given moment.

"Get your coat on, I need some air."

Minutes later we'd left the warmth of the smouldering logs and moved outside. The sky above Peredelkino was tombstone grey and the cold took my breath away. We followed an old path which, beneath a recent snowfall, had been pounded into the clay by generations long gone. The flaming reds, gold and orange of autumn were also a distant memory. All that was now brown, dead and ugly was coated by a thin layer of snow. As we approached Peredelkino woods Leon said,

"Why do you think so many myths and fairytales are set in forests, Dimitri?"

I struggled to find an answer before he put me out of my misery.

"Here, human time doesn't exist. It is always intensely *now* and yet incredibly ancient...much like old Russia."

We brushed past brambles and sycamore through a grove of regal pines towering up to the bare winter sky.

"The Bolsheviks may have hacked down the branches, felled the tree trunk and burned it to ashes." Leon strode on. "But the roots...the roots of White Russia still run deep through all of Russia's customs and institutions."

"But we also need to live in Russia as it is today." As I spoke I was reminded of Ava's words; *"Life is to be lived, Petrov, not postponed until the conditions are right."*

"It is true Dimitri, that we may live and breathe in the present but it is our past that allows us to do so."

I was still figuring out what he meant when he spoke again;

"Not long after being given that medal I was commissioned to write a book aimed at young adults and the sceptical older generation. It was to be all about Perekovka"

"What's Perekovka?"

"It is the remoulding of the human soul through hard labour. We had so many political prisoners going to work in penal labour battalions in the frozen north. The only way to soften the blow was to convince them, and their families left behind, that through intense labour their characters would be reformed into that of useful, valued Soviet citizens."

We tramped on beneath soaring coniferous trees, majestic and still.

"By taking part in collective work they would learn to become cooperative and beneficial to society. The philosophy was that hard physical labour was in fact liberating and provided its own redemption."

The path forked right past more brambles, hollies and bines of honeysuckle.

"I was sent, at no cost to myself, to see this great Perekovka in action. It made sense to me, having grown up with the proverb that *'work feeds a man and laziness spoils him'*. I wanted to believe this new doctrine that forced work can reforge character. It was exciting. However, when I saw the reality my scythe hit a stone."

"Your scythe...?"

"I found what I wasn't expecting."

I struggled to keep up with Leon's long, loping strides over the bitter hard ground. He was used to tramping this woodland, seeking poetic inspiration or respite from tending his garden.

"On my arrival I was given anything I wanted; comfortable accommodation, smoked sausages, caviar, wine, cognac – you name it. I should have been suspicious then. Oh there were doubts in my mind, big crushing doubts. And those doubts caused me so much anguish I could not immediately tell what was true and what was false."

We came to a clearing where the stillness echoed that of the graveyard.

"But I wanted to believe," Leon exhaled heavily, "I wanted to believe that I too could bury my own past and move into line with the new society."

There was a faint shake of his head.

"I see clearly now I was being forced to pen a new fable. Another fairytale, to justify the existence of our gulag labour camps."

We paused by the grassy bank of a frozen lake. Leon took a deep breath as he scanned the motionless, silent expanse. I'll never forget his expression at that moment. An inner nobility shone from his eyes. And, like a prophet, his whole demeanour emanated a humble wisdom.

"Wanting to believe is one thing, to see it in action is another."

We turned back towards the path. The forest floor was carpeted with frozen lichen, vegetation and icy reeds.

"Initially I saw what they wanted me to see; Potemkin villages like they used to persuade Catherine the Great that all was well with the peasantry."

Through the birch trees the snowy path lead us towards the thicket taking us deeper into the forest's dark interior.

"To fulfil the myth of Perekovka, I realised they were giving out bonuses and honours to those labourers suitably reformed. Even then, I thought, how easy to pretend one is a reformed character with carrots like freedom and material gain being dangled before one's incarcerated eyes!"

Two Siberian bullfinches perched on a young spruce appeared undisturbed by our sudden appearance.

"One day," he continued, "I got up at first light and whilst my official guide snored through his hangover I wandered off the authorized path and found myself outside a fence at a children's labour colony."

Leon was walking ahead of me but I could hear the emotion creeping into his voice.

"I saw beatings, abuse and deprivation no child of God should bear. And all in the name of reforming them into the Soviet spirit. I was appalled and most of all angry to be used as a mouthpiece for such barbarism."

The path had become hard like frozen iron. I shivered, chilled to the bone.

"So what became of the book?"

"I never finished it."

We'd reached the heart of the woodland and were now on our way back home.

He turned to me with glassy eyes and pulled out a handkerchief to blow his nose.

"I tried, but I can't put my name to a pack of lies. Even my most outlandish fairytales contain seeds of truth. My guiding principle when writing, and indeed in my life, is to live the genuineness that Shakespeare taught; *This above all, to thine own self be true..."*

"But who wanted to hear the truth? No-one, Dimitri. I got home, depressed. I couldn't speak to anyone about the suffering I witnessed. And you wonder why I drink so much? I went to get wool and returned sheared."

We passed a fallen birch tree nestled on dead leaves. In the evening twilight its frost-gilded bark bore a ghostly lustre.

"How could I have been so naive?" There was a quiver in his voice. "How can treating a man like a beast bring out his finest qualities? A good man cannot be forged by slavery; he can only be nurtured by love and discipline."

As we reached the forest periphery, the silver chimes of the Transfiguration Church rang out across the iron-grey sky.

"I'd been lying to myself. The stories I wrote only contained the state-supporting lies that would enable me to survive. I took part in the shabby compromises and evasions like everyone else. My worst act of cowardice was when I felt compelled to join in the condemnation of a fellow writer."

"Andrei Yudenovich? I asked.

Leon's stony silence answered my question.

When we reached Leon's dacha the sun was going down. The temperature had plummeted. And, in the tightening of winter's fist, the shadowy forest of Peredelkino again became frozen in time.

"It's a particularly human trait to venerate the dead and pass on stories of the past." Leon said whilst poking the fire's slumbering embers back into life. "These instincts can neither be removed surgically nor ideologically." He placed three seasoned pine logs onto the hearth. "Man can only go forward, yes; but his steps will always be guided by his past. All attempts to remould human behaviour will, at the most fundamental level, be doomed to failure."

I joined him warming our hands by the fire.

"But we can't live in the past either."

"Unless the future is seen and felt to be more glorious than what came before, man cannot help but look back. And when we look back, that rosy glow of nostalgia can be most hypnotic."

Uncle Leon told me of the new book he was writing called *The Magic Paintbrush*. In brief, a young boy discovers the very paintbrush Theophanes the Greek used to depict the glorious Icons that grace the Orthodox Churches throughout Russia. Through some mystical powers the paintbrush had been transformed into a talisman that can open portals into another world; the world of history.

The story begins one day whilst the boy is playing with the brush as its tip touches a painting by Andrei Rublev and immediately the boy is magically transported back to the time and place shown in the painting.

In due course, after numerous visits to the Tretyakov Gallery in Moscow, the boy goes back to the times of the Tsars, the early Russian capital of Kiev and the time of the Mongol invasion. After many adventures he comes to an understanding of the ways of man; how history is manipulated by the victors, of how the corruption of power and the greed of the few can never suppress the unfailing decency and love of the ordinary man.

Orphan of the State

Uncle Leon swore me to secrecy. He told me it would never be published in his lifetime... if ever. Yet it was something he felt compelled to write. He wanted to evoke the glories of a world he thought we had lost.

My grandfather was a Kulak and had worked hard on the land from dawn till dusk. Leon recalls his hands calloused and worn from the rigours of taming the soil. As a child he remembered the smell of the cattle in rickety barns, the biting wind that cut to the bone, the welcome warmth of the fire that burned all day in the Ibza.

I think he romanticised his father's rural life as being more ruggedly real than his calling as a writer. And through his words he wanted to bring that idealised, pre-Orthodox standard of living back to life. To show how our pagan ancestors had a hard life yet a wonderfully vibrant one. A life at one with the seasons, the land and the elements.

Leon despised all falsehoods and felt that the simple life was the best life. He missed going to church where he swore one could almost hear the echo of past generations singing along from the rafters.

As he read to me his first draft of The Magic Paintbrush his tone revealed this sad longing for Russia's lost medieval past.

"As the tip of the paintbrush touched the canvas a strange feeling overcame him. The brush seemed locked in place and try as he might, Ilya couldn't pull it away. As he heaved and hauled with all his weight a strange alchemy occurred; the painting began to bubble and hiss like methane gas escaping a boggy marsh. Then the paint travelled speedily up the shaft of the paintbrush. Ilya tried to let go before it reached his hand. But it was too late. Like warm molten lava the paint covered his fingers and hand and up along his arm. Ilya gasped. The feeling wasn't unpleasant. It wasn't wet or cold or sticky, it was like being bathed in warm sunlight. He struggled to catch his breath as the feeling consumed his whole body and Ilya felt himself being drawn into the painting like a speck of stardust into a black hole."

Ilya found himself transported via the painting of Novgorod by Appolinary Vasnetsov back to a time when Novgorod and Kiev carried the hopes of a Russian Golden Age. In the eleventh century a fledgling democracy was forming in Novgorod and the old capital Kiev. This was a time when autocracy was held in check by a measure of democratic participation. Nothing symbolised this better than the *veche* bell which would ring out to summon its citizens both young and old, from lord to merchant to gather and discuss proposals for governance and judicial matters. Novgorod had a sewage system and sturdy wooden pavements two hundred years before Paris and five hundred years before London. Uncle Leon's eyes sparkled with pride.

"What happened?" I asked.

"We had no unity." He sighed. "Feuding Princes and envious fiefdoms fought between themselves. The Song of Igor warns us of such perils; *"...Princes argued about trifles, calling them important matters, then brother said to brother, 'This is mine, and that also is mine.'*

Uncle Leon then paused, like the great storyteller he was before wistfully adding;

"And the infidels from the steppe came to conquer the Russian land."

194

"And come they did, the Mongol hordes that set Kiev ablaze, destroyed our chance of becoming a great European state. A culture of barbarism descended upon Russia. It cut us off from the rest of Europe. And just when Europe itself was advancing in terms of knowledge, freedom and civilisation the Motherland's progress was frozen in time."

David J Robinson

CHAPTER 25

Moscow 1941
Ava's horse drawn carriage on the way to Peredelkino.

We were now on the outskirts of the city, juddering past empty warehouses and abandoned sheds.

"Our time is precious." Ava turned to me. "And with you now going off to war, I feel you should know the truth."

"What truth?" My pulse quickened.

"You are a good friend, Dimitri and I don't want to see you getting hurt."

My heart sank. *'Good friend?'* is that how she sees me?

We both shook in our seats as the carriage rumbled over remnant cobblestones. It felt like we'd gone back in time. A young Tsar and Tsarina, rattling around in a royal rickshaw, suspended above the sludge and slurry of the street.

"Tell me again about the last time you saw your parents." Her eyes never left my face.

"What's that got to do with anything? " I protested.

"Shhh, trust me." She slipped her hand on my knee beneath the blanket.

I took a deep breath of the cold air. The memory I had of them was painful to recollect. Yet at the time - not knowing it would be the last I'd see of them - it struck me as no big deal.

"They were dressed smartly. I remember it was the best I'd seen them. Father wore a long black coat and tie, Mother had a fur stole and a beret on her head. They mentioned an important appointment but would be back before tea. Uncle Leon had come round to look after me. I said goodbye and went back to my den, just a table covered with an old curtain. I think I was playing with my wooden soldiers."

"How did they seem?" She fixed me with those emerald eyes. "Happy? sad?"

"Happy, I think."

I fell silent. I had never given it much thought before but now, in retrospect, there did seem to be an underlying tension behind the whole scenario, a strained smile on my mother's face, a look of resignation on my father.

"And Uncle Leon?" Ava pressed me.

"Oh he was in a foul mood. I heard him and father arguing in the kitchen not long before. Mother was initially upset by it too, but said it was nothing to worry about. If I'd had a brother, she said, I'd understand why it is they argued so much."

"And that was it? You never saw them again?"

"No."

"Did you see who they left with?"

Her question puzzled me.

"No, they left on their own."

There was a long silence as we rocked back and forth in the carriage which was getting chillier by the minute. Then, from nowhere, a new fragment of memory arose. A memory so non-descript that if it hadn't been for Ava's pressing would have remained a forgotten foot-note in my mind.

I had a faint recollection of Uncle Leon dragging me away from my soldiers and insisting I wave them off from the window. How could I have forgotten that? I should have known something was wrong then. Why did he force me to wave goodbye? The desperate edge to his voice? The twist of anguish in his face? As children we pick up on these things just as quickly as we forget them. As my parents pulled away I did wave but they never saw me. But now, deep in the shadows of my mind, I see a black car setting off at the same time behind them.

I relayed the memory to Ava.

"A black car?" Ava's smile vanished. "You mean a Black Raven, the standard issue secret police car. That would mean they were being tailed by NKVD officers."

"What?"

Ava let out a deep breath.

"Your parents weren't killed in a car accident, Dimitri. They were murdered."

"Think, Dimitri." Ava spoke as the carriage lurched and swayed around a bend. *"Like priest, like church... The apple never falls far from the tree..?* Why would my father say those things about you?"

I was at a loss what to say.

"You were told your parents were killed in a car accident and yet, coincidentally, it was at the height of Stalin's purges."

I roused myself at her insinuation.

"So you're saying during the time of the so-called purges, there were no accidents? That accidents ceased to exist?"

Ava raised her eyebrows ever so slightly and shifted in her seat.

"That behind every death," I went on, "there was an NKVD agent hiding in the shadows with a smoking gun?" I could feel the heat rising in my face. "Where's your proof?"

"I have none." Her shoulders dropped slightly. "But my father has forbidden me to see you and he won't tell me why."

"Purges." I say the word through gritted teeth. "You call them purges, Ava, but can't you see? There *are* dissidents out there. There are kulaks and White sympathisers everywhere."

"Shut up." Ava gave me a look of contempt. "I'm sick of hearing you parroting Stalin. I wonder who you really are,

Dimitri. If we ceased to be friends would you denounce me for my criticisms of the state?"

"You're no threat to the state." I replied. "You just have a wild imagination. I'm sure your father looks down on me simply because I'm an orphan. I understand that. What can I possibly offer his daughter?"

Ava gave me a sharp look.

"But I'll show him, one day."

"When you write for Pravda?"

I huffed at her sarcasm.

"Uncle Leon uses Pravda for toilet roll. He says that's all it is fit for!"

"Now that *is* a crime against the state!" Ava said deadpan.

I laughed uneasily. Ava smiled faintly.

The carriage was now moving uphill, the horses braying and snorting laboriously.

"Have you heard of Pavlik Morozov?" Ava suddenly asked. "The thirteen year-old schoolboy so brainwashed he even denounced his own father for fraternising with kulaks?"

I hesitated, unsure how to reply. Was now the time to tell her Pavlik had been a hero of mine? That I used to dream of emulating him by exposing someone as an enemy or a spy?

"Yes." I swallowed hard. "How could I not hear of him? There were posters of him on the orphanage walls. Morozov was set up as an example of how family loyalty must take second place to loyalty to the state."

Ava nodded slowly. I was sure she could sense I was holding something back.

"I suppose," Ava regarded me thoughtfully, "considering you were orphaned at such an early age, you have no real experience of a father. So the fact Morozov betrayed his own father would mean nothing to you. You wouldn't see it as a family tragedy, all you would see was a young hero."

I was now convinced she had a sixth sense.

"Father re-told me that story and showed me the news clippings of the widespread publicity." Ava paused, choosing her words carefully. "He showed me them on the evening of your second visit. I wondered later if he was trying to tell me something."

"Are you trying to tell me something too, Ava?" I glanced at her, not bothering to hide my annoyance. I could feel the blood pulsing in my neck. "I was a child for God's sake! At that age I thought a party worker was someone who organised birthdays and weddings. When I heard mention of 'the camps' I imagined families picnicking and singing songs round a fire in the woods. I wasn't aware of such concepts as treachery. I couldn't have even spelt 'denouncement'."

A cold draught blew through the gaps in the carriage as the horses began to pick up the pace. Ava shivered.

"But you're aware of such concepts now though, Dimitri." Her cool gaze swept over me. "I bet you know all the correct words of the Marxist script."

"There's no script. Socialism is completely natural to me."

"Socialists aren't born, they're made." Her tone was flat, cold. "And you, Dimitri, personify the whole revolutionary project. You were indoctrinated from an early age in the hot-house environment of the orphanage. What better place to raise the next generation of revolutionaries?" She gave a hollow laugh. "You were a blank page upon which they could write the future. Everything in your upbringing was guided by a strict socialist curriculum. You told me, even when playing outside, you were forced to build snow statues of the leaders of the October revolution."

"We weren't indoctrinated." I tried to sound calm although my throat was completely dry. "If anything we enforced our own discipline. Collective labour is natural. If no-one worked in the orphanage there would be no lunch, breakfast or firewood. It brought out the best in us. No community can tolerate parasites."

"You can't see it can you?" A faint shake of her head, then she spoke softly, almost patronising. "Your discipline wasn't self imposed it was quietly fostered. Your communal spirit was the socialist ideal in microcosm. Beyond their walls you would carry that spirit into society and overturn the old world."

"Would that be so bad?"

She fell silent for a moment as the carriage slowed to crawling pace. Through the condensation on the windows distant trees had become crude charcoal sticks. Hedges were now just blurred black lines across the steppe.

"Look, I'm not saying you're the only one to be manipulated. We all have. Nobody gets through the day without seeing a picture of Stalin or an image of Marx or reading about the revolution in books or newspapers." She gazed wistfully out into the darkening landscape. "He may be long gone but the embalmed fist of Lenin still holds us all in its grip."

The wheels were screeching as we rolled around another bend. Our driver's crude oaths and chastisement of his horses drifted in the wind.

Her mention of Lenin took me back in time to a visit to the mausoleum to see him lying in state. Even then, I struggled not to allow the frail, pale corpse I saw destroy my image of Lenin as a mythical hero.

Ava continued looking out of the window. The pine trees of Peredelkino were getting closer. Dusk was dissolving into darkness and the carriage now rattled on through folds of thick mist.

"We'll soon be there." Ava turned to me. "Look Dimitri, let's say you're right. But what if your parent's car crash wasn't murder or an accident? What if your mother and father knew they were under suspicion? That they were about to be separated by the purge, sent to different gulags?"

I could feel my brow knot in disbelief.

"Maybe... maybe they committed suicide so you, their only son wouldn't be implicated in their 'treason'."

My heart rate was rising again.

"Even as a child you would still be classed as a relative of enemies of the state and sent away. Maybe your parents thought that with their death any investigation into them would die also. A supreme sacrifice for the love of their only son."

I shook my head and exhaled slowly.

"What could they have been guilty of?"

"Why your parents were considered traitors I do not know." Her face was a blank. "But my father made out there was some rumour of anti-Soviet activity. If he knows it, so will others. You will be watched Dimitri..." She tailed off and then added quietly, "you probably always have."

David J Robinson

CHAPTER 26

Berlin 1945

Given patronage by the Nazi party, Karl and Violetta had been presented with a newly-built private house off a quiet tree-lined street in Dahlem, South West Berlin. It was Karl's reward for being one of the few German scientists capable of producing uranium.

That evening Violetta walked slowly towards the glazed brick facade of the house she never considered home. The incident with Major Neumann weighed heavily on her mind. Neumann was a man of ruthless cruelty. The world would not mourn his loss. He had been stationed at Smolensk and then Treblinka and she recalled the things he'd said, likening the mass murder of Jews to disinfecting a house to eradicate bugs and other pests. Thank god Josef had been there today to protect her. Unfortunately she knew Josef could not offer similar protection from her husband's violent mood swings.

Although today was Violetta's birthday she was in no mood to celebrate. Thankfully Karl never remembered any anniversary. A man of ambition, Karl was more interested in surpassing the milestones of science than remembering those of his wife.

Violetta entered the large reception hall and crossed the burnished parquet floor. The sound of a Bach piano concerto came from Karl's vast library. She prayed, as she opened the door, he hadn't started drinking yet.

Karl stood by the window. Glass in hand, his thousand-yard stare taking him way beyond the sash windows, far away from his surroundings of leather bound books and wall mounted hunting trophies. The sound of Violetta's footsteps curtailed his daydream.

As he spoke, Violetta knew he was already drunk.

"Enjoy your last day at the theatre, darling?"

"Last day? Why do you say that? I'll decide when I quit, not you."

"Believe me Violetta, today was your last day." Karl walked unsteadily towards her. "If you go back there tomorrow you will be arrested for sheltering a Jew, and then even my powers won't save you."

How did he know?

"A Jew? Don't be absurd. Who do you think..."

He slapped her hard across the face before she could utter another word.

"Don't ever lie to me!" He commanded, "I will not be made a fool of." He turned towards the mahogany drinks cabinet and poured himself another Schnapps in silence, downing a large measure in one go. Suddenly, he spun round and threw the empty glass at Violetta who ducked in time before it shattered against a portrait of Frederic the II.

"Today I had the head of the Nordland SS come to my door to tell me *my* wife is sheltering a Jewish whore *right here* in the centre of Berlin. Are you fucking crazy! This could end my career at a stroke. Where would you be then?"

"I....I don't know. I mean..."

"Shut up. I told you, no more lies." He poured another drink and walked over to the conservatory doors cricking his neck. "Thanks to my good standing in the party I was told they'd give you the benefit of the doubt, this once."

"Should I be grateful for that?"

"Should you be grateful for that? Of course you fucking should! Sometimes I'm sure I married an imbecile." Hubresch tipped more Schnapps down his throat, white knuckles gripping the glass. "This once great city has been destroyed by those Jews." He looked out of the window. "We Germans had strong moral values. The only way the Jews could take over was to destroy those values."

"That's Goebbels's propaganda talking, not you!"

He turned slowly to face Violetta as the music of Wagner replaced Bach on the teak wireless.

"That perverse Burlesque that you call art was unheard of before the Great War. The Jews introduced it. You see? They're destroying our society through degradation."

"And to think," Violetta shook her head in disbelief, "you're a man dedicated to rational science."

Karl returned to the window.

"Tomorrow you stay at home. The theatre will be raided by the Gestapo. The Jewess and her Austrian accomplice will be arrested and most likely sent to a labour camp."

"Josef?" Violetta asked.

Hubresch looked quizzically at his wife then snorted.

"Of course you know his name. I believe he's worked there long enough, damn Austrians. You can't trust them, Violetta. I've told you they're the enemy within, mark my words."

After his evening nap, Karl Hubresch went to his regular meeting of the *Werwolf* resistance organisation. This was Hitler's last throw of the dice. The Nazi leadership wanted the citizens of Berlin to become familiar with sabotage and subterfuge to fight the enemy even after defeat. Surrender, they were told meant death. Conquer or die was the *Werwolf* motto.

An hour later Josef crept through the backstreets of Dahlem under cover of darkness to meet with Violetta. She let him in through the conservatory doors and they kissed passionately.

Violetta slowly pulled away and searched his eyes.

"Major Neumann...?"

"I've taken care of it."

"How?"

"The less you know the better."

"Are you sure? Is there nothing to link him with us?"

"Soon there won't be."

"What have you done with him?"

Josef sighed.

"Look, I'm a carpenter; I work with axes and saws. What do you think I've done with him?"

Violetta put her hand to her mouth.

"Oh my god."

"Put it this way, the stray dogs of Berlin shall eat well tonight."

Violetta broke down in tears.

"Something else is wrong." Josef spoke. "Has he hit you again?"

"Yes." Violetta wiped her eyes. "A real body blow this time."

Josef grasped her shoulders looking into her eyes.

"What do you mean?"

"A body blow to all of us, Josef. He... they... know about Rula. They also know we've been hiding her. They're going..."

"Who Violetta? Who?" Josef shook her.

"The Gestapo... my husband! I don't know how they found out but Karl was tipped off by an SS officer."

"So how come you've not been arrested?" Josef loosened his grip.

She looked at him ashamedly.

"My husband's position protects me."

"I might have known." Josef looked around at the marble fireplace, the comfortable furnishings, a standard of living far beyond the dreams of ordinary Berliners. He turned and sat down on the sofa.

"Please don't say that." Violetta pleaded crouching in front of him. She took his hands. "If it wasn't for this lousy war..."

Josef bristled.

"If it wasn't for this lousy war... how many times have I heard people say that? As if it absolves us of blame, as if we have no say in our own destiny."

"We all do our best in the circumstances, Josef, but we're no good to each other dead, are we?"

Josef collapsed back onto the sofa and felt a bulge in his side pocket.

"I almost forgot." He pulled out a package wrapped in brown paper and tied with string. "Happy birthday."

Violetta opened it up to reveal a wooden musical box. She lifted the lid and, in front of a small mirror, a ballerina rotated slowly to the mechanised notes of a stirring melody. Also inside the box was a crucifix on a silver chain.

"It's beautiful." She held up the necklace. "What's the song?"

Josef carefully fastened the necklace around her neck.

"I think it's Russian. Not very appropriate, I know, given the circumstances."

Violetta laughed and felt the crucifix between her fingers. For a moment she wanted to forget their troubles. Lately these oases of happiness had seemed few and far between.

She admired her necklace through the music box mirror.

"Do you think it will ward off evil Russians?"

"Who knows?"

"I think it's a good omen." She closed the lid and placed the box down. "Do you believe in omens, Josef?"

"I don't know what I believe any more, but I know I need a drink now more than ever."

"I'll get you one." Violetta kissed his forehead and went over to the drinks cabinet.

"You must warn Rula tonight." Violetta's hand trembled slightly as she poured the wine. "You could call on your way from here."

"I will." Josef sat up straight as she passed his drink.

"And then you must both get as far away from Berlin as possible."

Josef took a long gulp.

"I knew this day would come." He sighed "But not this soon."

"We all knew. Perhaps it's better sooner than later. Unless Hitler surrenders or brokers some kind of deal, I think Berlin will fall by the end of the year."

"But I thought they still had a chance of..." Josef searched for the words.

"Winning the war? No. I've..." She hesitated... "talked with enough jaded Officers to know the war ended when we invaded Russia."

"Operation Barbarossa?" Josef raised his eyebrows. "And to think they nearly reached Moscow!"

"They awoke a sleeping giant." Violetta frowned. "I heard after Stalingrad was laid waste a Soviet colonel forced a group of German prisoners to look at the devastation. *"See that?"* He said. *"That is what will become of your beloved Berlin."*

"Not if the Americans get here first." Josef replied.

Violetta shook her head.

"Karl says the Russians will be here first. A de-coded message revealed they're desperate to strip Berlin of all its uranium before the British and Americans get here."

A distant siren began to wail.

"Come with me and Rula." Josef said. "We'll get a train out of Berlin at first light. We need to get as far away as possible before they get to the theatre and realise we've gone."

"We can't just leave like that!" Violetta stood up, her face flushed.

"Why not?" He said calmly. "It's better to leave the party before the lights go on."

She looked at him blankly.

"As soon as the Gestapo realise we've been tipped off they'll come for you." Josef paused as though reflecting. "Will Karl save you then?"

"We can't just *go*." Violetta was pacing to and fro, wringing her hands. "We'd need special permits to get out of Berlin."

"As I said, I knew this day would come. I've had passports and permits made for all four of us, me, you, Maria and Rula."

"How?"

"I used your promotional snapshots. I knew you wouldn't approve. And you know I have connections. It is damn risky yes, but less than staying here."

"Where do we go?"

"I have friends in Switzerland."

Violetta paused, almost lost for words.

"You did all this for me?"

Josef nodded and smiled grimly.

The siren got louder and shelling could be heard in the distance.

"I'd better stay." Josef stood up. "At least until the all clear."

Violetta shook her head.

"I wish you could but we can't risk being found here together. And you must warn Rula as soon as possible."

She stroked Josef's shoulder.

"Be careful out there."

They embraced tightly.

"I love you, Violetta."

"Are you sure it's me you love or Viola?" She asked abruptly.

"You, from the moment I saw you on stage."

They parted slightly and he looked into her tearful eyes.

"Then you fell in love with an image." Violetta's shoulders slumped with inexpressible sadness.

"No." He gripped her wrists. "I know the real you. Offstage you were still acting with Neumann and the others." Josef had a look of strange wonder on his face. "But even understanding *why* you slept with those fascists did not stop my jealousy."

"Oh Josef." Her lips and chin began to tremble as Josef held her close once more and whispered;

"*That* is how I know I love you."

CHAPTER 27

Berlin 1945

Josef Kane hurried through the dark streets of Berlin. A blackout had preceded the distant roar of bomber planes coming to visit yet more death upon the city. By the light of the stars alone Josef negotiated a route through the debris and rubble until a bomb-blast lit up the city in a blinding flash. In that brief burst of light Josef saw the silhouettes of men, women and children running towards a ferro-concrete bunker across the square. Another barrage of exploding shells, now only streets away, prompted Josef to join them. He slipped into the crowd of people pushing through the steel doors under the well-known initials LSR which stood for *Luftschutzraum* - air-raid

217

shelter. Black humoured Germans now said the initials stood for *Lernt Schnell Russisch!* or Learn Russian Quickly!

As a foreign worker, Josef was forbidden entry to the underground bunkers, but he was desperate. Explosion after explosion shook the air as the bombs rained down from the night sky.

Josef was breathing heavily as the steel door clanged shut behind him. The air was foul and the blue lights showed condensation already dripping from the ceiling. The lights dimmed with every bomb blast, often flickering off for seconds at a time. Candles barely lit up the gloom and the smell of sandwiches, sweet coffee and sweat added to his feeling of claustrophobia. Josef could make out couples in passionate embrace, some coupling eagerly in a dark corner. The imminent arrival of the Red Army saw any notions of innocence and inhibitions being desperately cast away. The overall atmosphere was one of restrained hysteria mixed with a palpable sense of doom.

From nowhere a warden shone a torch in Josef's face.

"Identify yourself!" He demanded.

Josef squinted and patted his pockets.

"I didn't have time to get my papers." He replied.

"Where are you from?"

Josef tried to squirm out of the torchlight to see his interrogator but the beam was kept on him.

"What does it matter?"

"It matters because I have never seen your face in this shelter before."

Josef turned away from the glare to see a huddled mass of people all looking at him.

"Anybody here recognise this man?" The warden asked.

The response was a mumbled negative.

Then a clipped German voice cut through.

"Answer the question, dummkopf! Where are you from?"

Karl Hubresch, in his camouflage *Werwolf* fatigues picked his way through the crowd.

"I confess, I am from a neighbouring district. I was visiting a friend and got caught in the air raid on my way home."

Another huge blast shook the walls of the shelter. Whimpers and prayers broke out amongst the people. Someone sarcastically shouted *"Heil Hitler!"* with undisguised contempt for the presence of Karl Hubresch and his paramilitary uniform.

His authority being undermined, Hubresch wiped the beads of sweat from his brow and tried to restore his status.

"Out! Out! There's barely enough room in here for legitimate citizens."

"Let him stay!" An old woman croaked.

Hubresch turned to see who else dared defy him. Josef, not wanting to cause more trouble spoke louder, bringing Hubresch's attention back to him.

"Please, it's carnage up there. No-one can survive outside this shelter."

Hubresch had heard enough, He grabbed the pistol from the belt of the warden whose torch still shone on Josef's face.

He pointed the gun at Josef.

"You're not even a Berliner, are you? That accent... are you Austrian?"

"Yes, but Berlin is my home now."

"Your name?"

"Josef Kane."

"Josef Kane?" Hubresch ruminated. "What are you doing in this part of Berlin after curfew?"

"As I said, I came to visit a friend."

"Who?"

"A woman."

"What woman?" Hubresch was sweating profusely.

Josef lowered his voice.

"Look, we're both men of the world. I need to be discreet. We wouldn't want her husband to find out." He gave Hubresch a sly wink. "Would we?"

The gun in Hubresch's hand trembled with fury.

"Open the doors." The warden ordered.

Another wave of explosions vibrated through the whole shelter, so intense, they seemed to come from below ground as well as above.

The warden snatched the gun back from Hubresch and waved it in Josef's face.

"Out!"

Josef left the bunker and emerged into a scene of utter desolation. The heat from the fires surrounding the square made him gasp. Buildings engulfed in flames, metal streetlights and cars melting in the inferno. A man leapt screaming from a blazing office block and landed with a sickening splat close by.

Josef took off his jacket to cover his nose and mouth from the smoke. He set off running but it seemed like the ring of fire had no exit. Through smarting eyes he saw the looming shadow of a dark building untouched by flames. His body was beginning to scorch from the furnace-like temperature as he lurched forward into the shelter of its arched doorway. Coughing violently he banged on the door. The intense heat was making him delirious as he slumped to the floor, crouching into a ball to escape the firestorm whirling across the square.

Josef didn't hear the faint whistle of a falling bomb above the roaring flames. He felt the blast though and the shrapnel that cut his skin to shreds. Badly wounded as he was, the survival instinct in him still remained. He thought of Violetta and Rula. *If he didn't survive this, what would be their fate?* No answer came then and none ever would. For Josef though, it was the falling masonry, the heavy stone blocks and tons of bomb-blasted bricks that finally sealed his fate.

David J Robinson

CHAPTER 28

German Border.

This bloody war of attrition is finally reaching its end-game. The Germans fight valiantly even though they know they can never win. It's a strange paradox that one can hate one's enemy with such passion and yet admire his courage. As Stalin has sacrificed some of Russia's finest men, the best of the best, so too has Hitler allowed a generation of stout-hearted Bismarks' to be slaughtered.

But then another paradox springs to mind. Is it the war that extracts these heroic qualities out of men who may otherwise have led quite unremarkable lives? Then it is man's situation that reveals his true stature.

These fine manly qualities, shown on all sides. Courage, comradeship, resolution, determination and sacrifice. If we could harness these virtues for the common good, what a world we could create!

I re-read a letter from Ava. I keep the dried blue petals that came with it in the envelope, but a faint odour of *Iris sibirica* still permeates the notepaper. She writes of her pride in helping the war effort by working in a missile factory East of Moscow. *"I'm making mortar bombs underneath a huge slogan; 'Our Energy, Our Strength, Our Life – All For The Motherland!"* Her sarcasm may have fooled the censors but not me. The image of her in overalls and with oil smeared over her face makes me laugh.

She says she worries for me and prays for me to return intact, both physically and mentally. Her Grandmother had told her of the disturbed minds of soldiers who'd returned from hellish battles in the past. Ava is convinced I must refrain from brooding on any horrors I witness. No matter what I see, hear or think about during this war I must remain true to myself. She has written a passage from Dostoyevsky and asks me to learn it by heart.

"...Above all, do not lie to yourself. A man who lies to himself and listens to his own lie comes to a point where he does not discern any truth either in himself or anywhere around him, and thus falls into disrespect towards himself and others. Not respecting anyone, he ceases to love, and having no love, he gives himself up to passions and coarse

pleasures, in order to occupy and amuse himself, and in vices reaches complete bestiality, and it all comes from lying continually to others and to himself."

"I know change is the essence of life, Dimitri, but I also know that fine principles and sound character remain the same in good times and bad. You are a good man, the best of the best. Create a firewall of love and pure thoughts to protect your true self. Let thoughts of our love sustain you during the dark days ahead. And most of all cherish the thought that whatever happens, I will always be here waiting for you."

Love Ava x

David J Robinson

CHAPTER 29

Diary of Dimitri

Marchenko, his thick beard blending into his Ushanka winter hat, gave a rousing eve of battle speech.

"One thing we can be sure of, we are living in an age of extremes, of unimaginable catastrophes. This is truly an age of heroes! Mark my words. Years from now, in more lukewarm times, men will envy our actions. Our battles will be glorified and our names revered by generations yet unborn. We sons of the Motherland, we Russians did not go through a bloody revolution just to be overthrown ourselves!

The blood we shed deposing the Tsars is to be shed again to stop the Fascists invading our Motherland."

Even those of us who despised the Motherland and its traitors to the Bolshevik cause were willing to be pumped up and inspired to go into battle. We needed to believe in something to get us through this day.

I fear dying. Fear of how I might die. That knotted tension in my guts is constant. I can't exorcise it any way except through drink or laughter. Black humour lightens the load. I couldn't survive this war without it. Germans frozen to death like shop mannequins, an armless man still trying to salute... awful humour, but funny nonetheless – in the context of war. And in sleep the dread disappears. It must do, because in the first moments of awaking I am born again, but despair soon returns as reality strangles my dreams.

One or two of the men aren't really 'here'. They go through the motions of soldiering, the drills, the digging of trenches. Even in the heat of battle these timid souls retreat into the mind, away from no-man's land into a dream world. They're back with their parents or home cosy in bed, wrapped in the arms of their wives.

There is a time for these reflections. The crucible of war isn't one of them. We need every soldier to be fully present alongside us, sensitive to the ebbs and flows of battle. When to wait, when to attack. There's more chance of surviving if one is fully tuned to the reality of our situation. The fantasies of life-after-war are soon silenced by a German bullet to the head.

Vasily, cleaning his spectacles, says, *"You could just as easily been born a German. Likewise, the German you're fighting could have been born a Russian. So, in reality, you're just at war with yourself."*

Oleg, lifting weights, replies, *"Don't fuck with my head!"*

Each man has his own attitude to the how's and whys of fighting. Some go into berserker mode, attacking every situation with a crazed look in their eyes, using up much precious energy, they are soon exhausted. Others have ice in their blood. They remain cool under extreme pressure and rarely make mistakes. They rarely take risks either, the risks that are needed to win a war.

The best are the bold. A line from Prospice, *for sudden, the worst brings the best to the brave.* These men prosper in adversity and thrive in hostile environments. They use hardship to fuel their courage. The fire in their belly devours and feeds off any danger the enemy throws at them.

Some men pray to the Gods to sustain them and make them strong. But I fear they have it the wrong way round. Be brave and greater Gods will come to your aid. Man is at his best when he throws himself fearlessly and passionately into the unknown. The blank page of the artist, the heat of battle, the unfathomed chambers of the human heart. One needs to summon up one's own courage, even acting brave and then it follows, *God helps those who help themselves.* We must help ourselves first!

Whether we win this war or not is secondary, it is the greatness of our deeds that count. There is such a thing as glorious defeat, even if the men who displayed great bravery are no more. What is the commemoration, the applause and admiration of generations hence when you are long gone from this wretched world?

I finally got to the bath house today. The women who run it are stern, disciplined Babushkas who are like Mother figures to us. They won't stand any nonsense and soon send us packing back to the front line with fresh clothing and clean uniforms. It is a great morale booster.

Fascism will not take over the world. I deep down know Communism has its limits too. Throughout all recorded history no empire, no tyranny, no political 'ism' has controlled the whole globe. It seems to be nature's way to allow something – anything – to grow so big and no more. No one thing can dominate. Night and day, the seasons – everything compliments each other. Good needs evil to define what good truly is. My heart sinks at such insights because it follows that peace also needs war to define it, to give it meaning.

I am too sentimental, as Vasily once said *'sentimentality is attaching more importance to life than God does.'*

My mind turns to thoughts of Ava. If we were to marry and have children, what kind of world will they grow up in? Without doubt the Romans, the Greeks and the Spartans must have had similar thoughts. Surely our time on earth should be used to leave a positive legacy for the next generation? Yet for all our advancements we seem unable to help ourselves. The barbarian inside comes alive and we pull down much of what our civilised selves built up.

That picture of Ava helped me through so much. I recite the poem by Simonov every night as I try to sleep. Her face the only thing my mind's eye wishes to see.

Wait for me and I'll come back,
Wait with all you've got,
Wait when yesterdays are past
And others are forgot,
Wait when from this hellish place
Letters don't arrive
Wait when those with whom you wait
Doubt if I'm alive.

I try to blot out the horrors I have seen and force my thoughts onto you. Your photograph has brought me so much solace Ava, that and your promise to wait for me. Our love echoes that of Konstantin and Valentines.

They will never understand
How amidst the strife,
By your waiting for me dear,
You had saved my life.
Only you and I will know
How you got me through,
Simply you knew how to wait –
No-one else but you.

I wish I could write like Simonov to you, Ava, but even if I could it would be wasted on our postal system. We regularly complain about the lack of post from home. We pray you are more fortunate in receiving ours.

Why do I love Ava? Is it the comforting smell of her clean skin? Is it her thoughtfulness, of how much she cares for other people – too much at times? Maybe I think that because it shows how far short my own feelings of empathy run. Ava has an almost saint-like virtue of selflessness. It is this big-heartedness, this vast magnanimity of spirit that humbles me. I am in awe of the power these simple virtues possess. She radiates the joy of life. And possibly her greatest attribute is her obliviousness to these qualities. They just flow effortlessly from the core of her being. My love goes beyond the draw of her emerald eyes, the softness of her skin and even the sensuous pull of her soft lips. I have placed her on a pedestal no doubt, but such a magnificent specimen of womanhood deserves worship.

I know in my heart she is the one. Only the cruel trick of time and fate stand between us. It seems spiteful to be separated for the duration of this war and dependent upon the will of God to survive it. Oh to be with Ava in a time of peace!

I try to rationalise my self-pity by recalling Russia's tumultuous past. From the early warring Slavic tribes, through the Mongol invasion up to the bloody revolution, many millions have lived and loved through the Motherland's long years of war.

Orphan of the State

By way of Yermak Timofeyevich, Boris Godunov, Ivan the Terrible and now Stalin, it seems as if all Russian history has been written by men of war.

David J Robinson

CHAPTER 30

Berlin 1945

The next day only Rula turned up at the theatre. By mid-morning Violetta and Josef had still not appeared. Monika couldn't understand why. She had no idea how long it would take Otto to inform the authorities but assumed once he had they'd all be arrested at the same time. Maybe Violetta and Josef had already been dealt with by coordinated Gestapo raids during the night? She shivered at the thought but it was too late for remorse.

Whilst restocking the foyer bar Monika reflected on the power she'd wielded. How just a few words from her lips could change lives forever.

As the morning wore on, the Die Bosen secretary began making phone-calls to try and locate Violetta and Josef. Meanwhile Klaus, the manager chain-smoked and paced around the theatre asking all the staff as to their whereabouts.

All of a sudden the secretary gave an anguished cry, slammed the phone down and began to sob. She had rung to check on her sister who lived in the suburbs of Berlin. A gruff Russian voice had answered the phone and taunted in broken German, *"Berlin ist kaput!"*

At that moment a car skidded to a halt outside the main entrance. Seconds later a frog-faced Gestapo officer and two tough looking militiamen carrying Bergman sub-machine guns rushed into the building.

"Rula Hornski and Josef Kane! We need to speak to a Miss Rula Hornski and a Mister Josef Kane right now!" He bellowed eyeing everyone suspiciously.

"She's in the dressing room," Klaus answered feebly, "Josef's not here."

"Show them," he gestured to his henchmen, "and get everybody in the building here this instant!" Within minutes all three bar staff together with two cleaners, four dancers and one carpenter had assembled in the entrance hall.

Screams of protest came from the corridor and Rula appeared shouting and cursing at the two militiamen restraining her arms. As they jostled her through the foyer, one of the henchmen kept glancing at Monika. She was horrified to recognise him as one of her sex clients. Her co-workers noticed the exchange of looks and, as she blushed slightly, began to wonder if she was behind the arrest.

Orphan of the State

The Gestapo officer barked further orders and everyone looked on helplessly as Rula was hustled outside and forced into the back seat of a small DKW car.

The frog-faced officer remained stock still and addressed them all with withering scrutiny.

"If any of you know the whereabouts of Josef Kane you must say so now." The cleaning ladies looked on aghast as he withdrew his Luger. "Anybody withholding such information shall be guilty of treason and face the consequences." In turn, each person found themselves staring down the gun-barrel as he aimed it slowly around the foyer. He went on a rant about how the Gestapo were "ever vigilant against subversive elements ready to rise up in opposition to the Reich." The implication being that they as artists all fell into that category.

After he had left, an atmosphere of despair descended upon the theatre. Conscious of the suspicious looks and cryptic mutterings of her colleagues, Monika took an early lunch and set about following Otto's instructions to retrieve her reward.

Outside, the air was laden with fumes, thick with ash and brick dust. Hurrying through her black market haunts of pubs, cafes and restaurants near Gesundbrunnen station, she tried to forget about Violetta and Josef and focussed on Otto. If he betrayed her with a worthless reward what could she do? What did she have over him? Knowing that homosexuality and macho National Socialism were incompatible bedfellows Monika entertained thoughts of blackmail. But she didn't know where he worked or what office or branch of the party he was involved with. Would

Franz know more? It was doubtful. Men like Otto were careful. She didn't even have his surname. How likely that Otto itself was a pseudonym? The more she thought about him the more she realised she had nothing on him.

Despite all this, Monika hoped beyond hope he would have left her something of real value. Hoping that, although they could not be more different, maybe he recognised in her a kindred spirit; a shameless survivor.

She passed only a few anonymous faces on the street. Rumours the Americans were joining in the battle against the Russians or that General Wenck's Twelfth Army was coming to the rescue had failed to convince an exodus of foreign workers, refugees and deserters. They don't believe the propaganda any more, she thought, they feel in their hearts the war is as good as over. But Monika still clung to the belief some divine intervention would save them all. She still had faith in Hitler.

She could hear indiscriminate shell-fire in the far distance as she negotiated her way past bomb-craters, shards of wire and trenches. Her route took her by the Schiller Theatre where she once worked with Violetta performing in Goethe's *Faust* twice a day. Then they'd rush across town to take part in illicit cabarets late at night. Even now show-business was one of the few businesses still going strong. The harsh reality of life in a besieged city is that apart from food and water what people craved most of all was escapism.

On she went, past the Berlin State Theatre, its peeling posters still advertising *A Winter's Tale*. The irony was not lost on Monika how it was the unique language and vision of

Shakespeare - the enemy's favourite playwright - that had helped Berliners transcend their hellish lives.

Monika strode on past an abandoned department store where only days earlier queuing shoppers had been strafed down by a Russian plane. Its walls were still peppered with bullets.

Sirens wailed. Monika picked up the pace. Explosions and the crackle of gunfire came from the east of the city.

Deep in her pocket she clung to her 'safe-conduct pass' for reassurance. It was one of many thousands of leaflets the Russians had air-dropped to reassure Berlin women they had nothing to be afraid of. No-one would touch them.

A shell exploded nearby, close enough for the blast to knock Monika to the ground. She quickly got to her feet and shook the debris from her. With strong determination she carried on into the Deutsche Reichspost ignoring the cries of the postmaster to get to a shelter, and through the back to where the safety deposit boxes were kept.

Inside, the immense thunder of artillery seemed to surround her. Surely the Russians were not so close?

She re-opened the envelope and held the key and a numbered code. Maybe not just an ordinary key after all but the key to her freedom. Free from a life of selling her body and losing her soul, of living off her wits yet dying slowly by the day.

She entered the code, put the key into the keyhole and turned it to the right. There was a satisfying clunk of the unlocking mechanism and the steel door sprang open. On the floor of the metal box was a bulky brown parcel. She picked it up and immediately the heaviness of the package matched the weight of her expectations.

"Something more precious than diamonds," he had said, *"of more value than gold."*

Monika placed the package in her satchel and became light-headed with excitement. She walked quickly to the nearby arbour by the entrance of Tiergarten urban park. It was a decaying cedar wood structure which now overlooked a ravaged landscape where all the trees had been hacked down for firewood. By night it was used by prostitutes and drug dealers.

The sun made an appearance, its rays barely penetrating the acrid dust hanging heavily in the air. The sun shines on the righteous, she thought as she made her way to the seated area within the arbour. She waited as a mother and child rushed by. "Find shelter!" the mother shouted to Monika. The boy stopped suddenly and picked up a used condom. His mother slapped it from his hand, scolded him, shot Monika a filthy look and hurried away.

With nervous anticipation she ripped open the package. Heart racing. Body trembling with excitement. The torn wrapping revealed a cardboard shoe box. Monika slipped her hand inside. Whatever it was felt like a book. Her fingers gripped its hard cover and pulled it out. It was a book. She shuddered with a sense of crushing disappointment and quickly flicked through the pages looking for a hidden compartment, a cheque, anything!

It was a book.

Monika's mind whirled. What sort of deception was this? With a deep breath she finally regarded the creased cover of the book itself. It showed a picture of a stern-faced bearded giant of a man striding above thousands of tiny peasants through the streets of Russia. He held aloft the scarlet banner of the Bolsheviks. The title read, "The Communist Manifesto."

"Something the whole world needs right now, my dear..."

At that precise moment a small civilian aeroplane, not long taken off from Tempelhof airport, flew west directly overhead. The plane juddered and bounced through the anti-aircraft fire like a tugboat on a rough sea. At his window seat Otto looked down on the bomb ravaged streets of Berlin. *Not a moment too soon*, he thought. It was time for home.

Once out of Berlin's airspace he breathed a sigh of relief. He was an important man and he knew the allies would have been ordered to ensure safe passage of this innocuous private plane.

The air stewardess leant beside him and smiled

"Ready for your vodka now, Herr...?"

"Please," he smiled back, "call me Sebastian."

David J Robinson

CHAPTER 31

Letter from Violetta.

Berlin, 28 April 1945

These will surely be the darkest days of this once great city. Now there remains but fragments of its former glory. A jagged citadel with mounds of rubble and bricks, electric cables and pylons in disarray. The air is contaminated with the dust of years. Dust from houses, plaster, asbestos, skin cells, dust from the earth and from incinerated trees and cars. The dust casts a grim shadow across the land and yet the humdrum of life goes on, trying to survive, trying to create some semblance of order. Women tackle mountains of debris with a brush and shovel, people queue for a tram. There is an air of resignation amongst the older citizens, defiant strutting from the Nazi youth but mostly panic from the majority of Berliners.

I have lost so much weight. My burlesque outfits would now shame my body. Potato and nettle soup, a scrap of bread and rancid butter counts as a feast these days.

We all pray for the British, with their sense of fair play, or Americans to arrive first. Not the dreaded Russians who seem blind with rage and bent on revenge at all costs.

Goebbels's slick propaganda machine – still trying to convince the Berliners of a glorious fight back – is reduced to a fat man with a loud hailer out of the window of a staff car. No-one believes a word any more. There are only rumours that contradict each other and make little sense. No-one knows whose planes now fly overhead. The explosions and gunfire get closer by the hour. The net closes in. Where is Hitler? He's not been seen for days.

Smog lies over the city like a widow's veil. The haze is pierced every now and then by artillery fire or the blaze of distant buildings. This dust with its mix of ash, soot and earth permeates everything. It's a taste of death, like being buried without a coffin and the peat and dirt are all you can taste, filling up your mouth, seeping up your nostrils, into your skin. It is claustrophobic.

Although surrounded by utter chaos, people just seem to focus on what they can do. I see a woman on ladders watering a hanging basket, a boy on a bike finds delight among the wreckage and people walk their dogs and exchange pleasantries as if this was all normal. The human being is an incredibly adaptable creature when it has to be.

Do I admire their stoicism and fortitude? Or do I despair of the inanity of their actions, at their inability to face reality? It is the former. At their core the German people are an exemplary race, tough, efficient and hard working. Betrayed by the Nazi party, swept up in a war they did not want, most Germans simply put up and got on with their lives. There lies the greatness of Germany. These straightforward, big hearted and determined people are the soul of the Fatherland. I have to believe that or else... History may consign us all in the same bracket but I hope not. Life is no simple affair. Between the black and white there are copious greys. I'm sure there are fascists and cowards in every nation, unfortunately ours became our leaders.

We rarely see Karl. His *Werwolf* group now assists the *Volkssturm* in defending the outskirts of the city. Karl fancies himself a master marksman, a lone sniper who will keep the enemy from entering the heart of the Reich. He's become mono-syllabic, shows no affection to Maria or myself and, when not out fighting he just sits and broods and drinks himself into a stupor.

Ps. I've not seen or heard from Josef since the night of the air-raid. I know he never got the message to Rula because the next day she was arrested and taken I know not where.

I wait here now, just me and Maria, hoping and praying the Americans get to us first.

David J Robinson

CHAPTER 32

Diary of Dimitri

Comrades including Oleg, Avakov and Vasily have returned from reconnaissance. I see them through the window of an abandoned German officers' mess alongside Marchenko and other senior officials poring over maps. There's a slow nodding of heads and rubbing of chins as they ruminate on a course of action.

The village we have surrounded is being guarded by geese on one side. The Germans pegged them out as an early warning system. They make an awful lot of noise. Under cover of mortars, Avakov and Oleg had implemented a fake attack in the early hours when they dropped poisoned pellets around the geese's area.

When we sneaked up at nightfall all the geese were comatose or dead. We stole quietly around the south-east side of the village. It was a starry moonlit night. Although exhausted my senses were on high alert. Oleg and Avakov snuck up behind two smoking sentries. Vasily, hidden behind a row of oil drums, distracted them by throwing a dead goose at their feet. Avakov stabbed one sentry through the neck and Oleg, with his meaty fists, bludgeoned the other to death with improvised bullet-shell knuckle-dusters.

The Germans were completely unprepared. Some of the German units had retreated and were yet to be replaced. The log bunkers, concrete pill boxes and dugouts were manned by a skeleton crew. Our reconnaissance party had timed our attack to perfection.

In the early hours Ivan and I burst through the door of a farmhouse in the deserted village. An old man sits alone by the fire. He smokes a pipe and looks at us with eyes that are at peace with the world. He welcomes us with the offer of coffee. Ivan is pent up and in no mood for courtesies.

"I could slit your lousy German throat right now and take all your coffee, your food and the clothes off your back if I want."

"And," the old man speaks in Russian, "if you choose to do that, Ivan, I can do nothing to stop you."

The Germans call us all *'Ivan'* but being addressed directly leaves Ivan stuck for words.

"You feel it is your duty?" The old man goes on. "Maybe in these circumstances it is."

"Circumstances?" Ivan mutters.

"Take away your uniform and in, let's say, two years time from now we could meet under different circumstances, we may become friends." He leans forward to poke the fire, his movements slow with age.

"In the last war," he eases back in his chair, "I was in your position. I had to fight. But I only fought soldiers. Old men, women and babies – which you were at the time no doubt – I left alone. The bible has it right. There is a time to kill and a time not to kill. Circumstances, dear *Rus'* dictate our actions."

As he speaks, Ivan and I slowly inspect the room. Equipped with brightly painted spindles, a loom, brass icons and cooking pots around a stove it radiated a humble charm.

"I am an old man, for me both the war and life itself will soon be over. You shall go on living. I talk of duty, Ivan, and as my country invaded your country it was your duty to fight back. Indeed I would hold your manhood cheap had you not! To be on the right side in a righteous war is a great boon. Don't undermine your moral superiority by shedding the blood of innocents."

"You talk fine, old man," Ivan replies as he takes out his gun, "a regular philosopher, aren't you?"

The old man shrugs.

"I want coffee anyway, so if you want to put some holes in this old body of mine please, do it afterwards."

I signal Ivan to put his gun away and watch the old man fill the copper kettle and swing it over the open fire.

Ivan scratches his head and settles on a stool.

"You're right, Fritz, you're at the end of your days, just like Hitler and his henchmen. Victory will be ours. Do you Krauts never learn?"

The old man stuffs his pipe. Remaining silent, he watches us with hawk-like eyes as he puffs on the earthy tobacco.

"The only real victory is a final victory, after which there can never be defeat. I think it was an American writer who wrote that man is not made for defeat. A man can be destroyed, but not defeated."

"Hemingway." I said, as I leaned back on a shelf made for sleeping.

He nods and pokes the fire beneath the steaming kettle.

"Until the individual leaders of society are at peace with themselves there can be no peace across the land. All the vices that disrupt peace such as anger, jealousy, fear, greed – if these are not conquered within an individual – especially those in a position of immense power like Hitler and Stalin, they then manifest through their orders and actions.

"They fear losing power so their grip on power becomes ever more tight. Jealousy of one's neighbours becomes jealousy of other nations. Fear of the unknown becomes fear of the Jew. Greed. Always wanting more, more power, more profit and more land. Go invade, build empires. It's taken me all these years to realise that all this," he spreads his arms to indicate the whole world, "all this will pass away, not just for me, but for you both. Pass away as did Catherine the Great, the Romanovs and the Kaiser himself. All hail the glorious dead!"

The whistle outside signalled it was time to clear out. As we stood to leave, Ivan spotted something hidden among the brooms and brushes stacked together in the far corner of the room. He went and retrieved an old Russian rifle. He held it up and raised his eyebrows at the old man, "What's this Fritz? A relic from the last war?"

"Indeed. One can't be too careful with all these *Russkis* on the loose." He smiled.

"Not been fired for years." Ivan said as he checked the bolt action. "A Mosin-Nagent 1891 model, if I'm not mistaken."

"Let him keep it." I said. "On our way back from Berlin I'll give you good money for it, if you're selling that is?"

The old man laughed.

"If I knew it would be used to depose Hitler, you could take it now."

"You're not the only German to speak that way." Ivan propped the gun back against the brooms. "When did you people go from loving your Fuhrer, to hating him?"

"I can only speak for myself." The old man became serious. "About two years ago three Jewish women were on the run from Hitler's men. They came here." He closed his eyes in recollection. "I gave them food but I could not shelter them. My late wife was still loyal to the Nazi's back then. To escape the Germans they hid in the pine forest across the river. It was freezing cold and that night they were savaged and killed by wolves." He gazed into the fire, shaking his head. "The sound of their cries, rising and falling on the wind have haunted me ever since."

The door burst open. Cerenkov stood on the threshold blocking out the light.

"You two deaf? We're out of here, get your shit together."

We bade the old man farewell and joined the exodus of our comrades through the village. As we reached the main road we heard two distant gunshots from back inside one of the farmhouses.

"Keep moving!" Marchenko barked before we could look back. "Not far now to the lair of the fascist beast!"

That night there was a commotion in our barrack room. I pushed my way through the crowd and there was Cerenkov showing off a looted rifle. It was the old man's. I suddenly remembered the gunshots after we had left him. My blood boiled.

"Did it feel good killing a geriatric to get your prize loot, Cerenkov?"

The men looked at me as if I had just blasphemed Lenin himself.

Cerenkov's cruel Asiatic eyes smouldered with contempt.

"You fail all these men." He pointed the rifle in my direction. "When you leave good weapons, indeed *Russian* weapons, in enemy hands, virgin." The *virgin* jibe still got a few sniggers. "Frightened of women *and* old men are you now?" More guffaws from Cerenkov's cronies. "Go fuck yourself, if you know how." The men laughed along with him and I was pushed backwards. I saw red and went for my gun. Luckily, Ivan read my mind and restrained my arm before anyone saw what I was about to do.

"Wait," he hissed.

Ivan led me away and whispered, "Circumstances. Remember? Kill Cerenkov here and you'll be killed yourself. Bide your time."

I brood over Cerenkov night and day. The man gets right under my skin. Circumstances.... the old man was right. There is a time to kill and a time not to kill. My time to kill Cerenkov shall come. But will I be up to the task?

David J Robinson

CHAPTER 33

Diary of Dimitri

Avakov and I wandered into the ruins of an old church. The steeple had a huge hole right through it. A charred fresco of seraph angels and pink cherubs gazed in adoration towards the gaping void. The side chapel had been blasted to rubble and a bomb damaged Christmas tree and various Icons lay in collapsed states of repose. The smell of incense and lighted candles in the alcoves showed it was still in use.

I sat on a dusty pew and bent forward to pray for Ava and her family. I could hear Avakov's boots crushing broken glass as he scanned around for booby traps.

From my pocket I took out my snow globe, a keepsake from Ava. Inside the glass sphere was a miniature scene of Paris, I shook it once to stir up the snow and held it in my hands like a sacred object. From outside came a drunken hymn from a passing soldier. An old refrain, he had swapped the word Caucasus for Berlin.

"So shall I sing that glorious hour when the Russian eagle rose above Berlin and Russian drums did beat in combat bloody?

All to the Russian sword do now bow down!"

The words trailed away into the gloom.

"Pushkin," Avakov smiled, *"A Captor for the Caucasus.* Nothing changes it would seem, apart from the enemy." He picked up a candle to light his cigar. "Do you know, comrade," he spoke between puffs, "a revolution, in the literal sense of the word, takes us back to where we originally were?"

"So we always return to the same point?"

"So it appears."

Avakov turned towards the shrapnel-scarred pulpit. Above us the old oak beams, roughly carved, glowed in the candlelight.

I looked down at Ava's snow globe again.

Entranced by the swirling snowflakes it pulled me into its own little world. A world sans hunger, sans sadness, sans war.

Then it took me way back.

Back to the last precious moments I had spent with Ava...

Orphan of the State

Peredelkino 1941

Dimitri waited. Surrounded by towering birch and pine trees, those whispering sentinels of the forest, he stood silent and alone. Through the high branches, the late October breeze gently caressed their fading leaves. Beyond them the first full autumn moon illumined their swaying motion against the darkening sky of Peredelkino.

Dimitri checked his watch. It was almost midnight. Way past the curfew. He looked around and strained to see beyond the immediate tangled undergrowth into the dusky woods beyond. Out of the darkness came the sounds of crickets and the trickle of water from a nearby spring. There was a growing chill in the air and the earthy smell of peat and damp ferns pervaded his senses.

Dimitri shivered involuntarily. He quickly assured himself it was instinctive, not out of fear or trepidation, but because of the cold. He'd have a lot more to fear in the coming weeks and months. In his mind he conjured up the sacred verse Uncle Leon had impressed upon him; *'Let my soul be like a lamp whose flame is steady, for it burns in a shelter where no winds come.'*

He looked at his watch again. She was late. Maybe she wasn't going to come. Why would she? After all she couldn't possibly know their time together was about to end tonight.

He thought he heard a faint rustling in the bushes. A twig snapped close by and a female voice cursed.

257

"Ava, is that you?" Dimitri asked.

"Who else is it going to be?" She hissed coming into view through the gloom. "Who else in their right mind would want to be crawling through here at this time of night?"

Ava brushed herself down whilst shaking her head. He'd never seen her look less than immaculate. But now she looked like she'd been dragged feet first through the bushes.

Dimitri stifled a laugh.

"You got my message then?"

"I'm here aren't I?" A flash of anger passed through her eyes as she dragged her fingers through her hair. "There is a curfew you know? And if Katryn checks in my bedroom..."

"So you did climb out of the window, well done!"

"Don't patronise me." She scowled. "This had better be worth it."

As she continued to brush herself down, Dimitri stepped forward to remove a small twig entangled in her long hair.

"Ow!"

"There." He looked her up and down. "That's better."

"Well?" She addressed him directly. The force of her bright eyes unnerved him. Yet again he felt pierced by their strength.

"I leave for basic training tomorrow. They only gave us a day to get ready." He looked at her regretfully. "After two weeks we'll be fast-tracked to the frontline. They're desperate for men, Ava."

"Tomorrow?" She looked shocked. "I never thought it would be so soon."

"Things must be bad." Dimitri shrugged. "Rumour has it that frontline soldiers have only one rifle between two of them, and they're the old French and Polish rifles at that!"

Unconsciously her lips parted, trembling ever-so-slightly like a butterfly's wings preparing for takeoff. For the first time since he'd known her, Dimitri realised, she was practically speechless.

"So," she said eventually, "we might never see each other again."

"Don't say never. I won't promise anything to you Ava, save this," he took a steadying breath. "I want you to be my girl. I want you to promise that you'll wait for me. No matter how long."

Ava betrayed no sense of emotion as she stayed silent and lowered her gaze. She knew what he'd just said had taken tremendous courage. And although Ava knew her own boldness was often regarded as unfeminine, Dimitri's sudden bluntness had taken her completely by surprise.

A most pleasing surprise.

"The thought of you waiting for me, wanting me to return..." Dimitri continued, undaunted by her silence. "It's probably the only thing that will keep me going."

His words dissolved into the darkness and still Ava said nothing. Beneath the starred and leafy sky the chilly air was only slightly disturbed by the baleful hooting of a barn owl from deep within the forest

After what seemed an age, Ava straightened herself up and met his gaze. He noticed the faint moonbeams picking out the subtle crimson of her lips.

"Are you sure that's what you want?" She said suddenly, breaking the oppressive silence. "You hardly know me, really."

"I am certain." He replied, his decisiveness still surprising himself.

"I mean." She hesitated, not used to being on the back foot. "For a start my father will be furious if he found out."

"Your father is a hypocrite."

"Pardon?" Again, Ava was taken aback by his audacity. Yet there was no mistaking the glint of forthrightness in his eyes.

"He has a mistress. I've seen them together hand in hand. Whatever you think of your stepmother, no-one deserves that."

Ava didn't look particularly surprised by this revelation.

"I think Katryn knows about the other woman, or women in his life. God, I've heard them arguing about it often enough." She sighed and softened her gaze. "My Grandmother, on my real mother's side, she had Stepan weighed up. She'd tell me, 'Ava you must love your father but don't put him on a pedestal. In fact don't put anybody on a pedestal, especially yourself. We all have flaws. Stepan is a weak man, not wicked, just weak."

"He's had many affairs?"

"Oh yes." She said. "And I'm not surprised. Just to survive in high office he had to adopt a necessary schizophrenia. It's hard enough to live a moral life with a clear head. Impossible I'd say with a personality split in two." A distant look came to her eyes as she reflected. "I've often thought that if I could work out the riddle that is my father, I would finally understand the times we are living in."

"But my point is," Dimitri said, "I'm not like your father."

"I know you're not like my father. Not now. I'm sure he was once idealistic. I just worry that you might change when you've really experienced life." She took a deep breath. "Will you bend to the ways of the world Dimitri? Or shall the world bend to the way of your will?"

"You and your riddles!" He huffed. "I'm as you find me, Ava. What you see is all there is."

A trickle of moonlight ran down her blonde hair, flowing over her shoulders, and a mischievous twinkle came to her eyes.

"Oh, and there was I, hoping for *much* more!"

Dimitri laughed. Her carefree ways had surfaced yet again. Unlike the other girls he knew whose stoic reserve gave them an ice-like aura, Ava's soul was not buried deep. Never far beneath her glowing skin, it sought ways to burst out, shining through her eyes, animating her demure smile.

"Maybe this war is your destiny." She looked attentively at him. "A hero's journey if you will, to uncover the real Dimitri. Maybe," She warmed to the subject. "This adventure you're embarking upon will open your eyes. And the belief structure that the orphanage and Komsomol imposed upon you will come crashing down."

"Look, can we skip the politics this time?" There was weariness in his voice. He waited a moment or two and said; "I'm just a soldier going off to war, standing in the woods with a girl, asking her to wait for him."

261

"Well I'm not going anywhere." She said hurriedly before dropping her eyes adding, "Katryn says we're not going to Chistopol, not without Stepan."

"No," Dimitri impatiently pushed on, "I mean wait for me as your..." before his voice dried up.

"As my what?"

"As your boyfriend."

"Oh, is that what you are?" She searched his eyes. "I don't recall you asking *me* about that."

"I suppose I'm asking you now."

"I suppose you are."

"And your answer is?"

"Will *you* wait for me?" She tilted her head and raised her right eyebrow slightly.

"I will."

A hush descended upon the forest. The tracery of silver birch swayed silently overhead.

Ava looked up thoughtfully into the clear night sky bedecked with uncountable stars. As her eyes roamed the heavens their celestial light washed over the graceful contours of her face. Her lips gently parted in wonder and Dimitri noticed the white brilliance of her teeth. "Where the snow falls," she spoke with a look of strange wonder on her face, "that's where you'll find me."

"What's that supposed to mean?"

"Nothing." She said, looking brightly at him. "Just thinking out loud."

They were silent again.

"Come on," she said, holding out her hand, "let's go to the bridge."

Orphan of the State

Dimitri held her hand as they walked through the path of birch trees, their footsteps softened by the dark turf. In the distance the gilded turrets and golden cupola of the Church of the Transfiguration shimmered eerily in the starlight. This was the Ava he couldn't fathom, her sudden flights of fancy, her enigmatic ways. His lantern-jawed resolve had proved to be a blunt instrument with which to unravel the puzzle that was Ava. He glanced at her sidelong; Ava's eyes, iridescent in the moonlight showed no sign of devilment, just serene candour as they proceeded slowly to the sound of the running stream.

"Can I trust you?" She hesitated for a fraction of a second. "If you really are my boyfriend, that you will be loyal to me? No matter where you go or who you meet?"

"I promise."

"I have high standards, don't you know?"

"Yes, and I have high ideals as you well know!"

"You live up to my standards and I'll live up to your ideals. Deal?

"Deal."

Dimitri's spirits soared. Now he could face anything.

The bridge came into view. The lichen and moss on its heavy stone structure glistening with early morning dew.

"You're bound to come back anyway?" Ava said.

"Why do you say that?"

"Because Russia," she turned and playfully dug him in the ribs, "is the best place to live in the world!" She laughed like a schoolgirl and ran off towards the stone bridge.

Had he really said that? Yes, Dimitri remembered, he had. And the reproachful words of St Benedict came to mind; *'A wise man is known by the fewness of his words.'*

In this moment, watching Ava running sylph-like through the trees into the clearing that led to the bridge, a moment he would somehow remember until his dying day, a sense of enchantment filled the forest. Was it the lateness of the hour, a trick of the light, or the simple feeling of love which gave rise to this wonderful atmosphere?

Dimitri knew the answer.

Ava sat breathless on the wall of the bridge as Dimitri caught up with her.

She looked up at him smiling that wide, beautiful smile.

"What other Marxist would allow me," she gasped, "to taunt them so much without denouncing me?"

"Only one who loved you."

"Love?" She raised her eyebrows. "Is it not too soon to be saying things like that?"

"No." Dimitri spoke resolutely. "All my life I've been..." He hesitated. "Well... hesitant! I've left too much unspoken. And from my experience of life, it's the things you don't say that make all the difference. Good and bad."

"Now who's speaking in riddles?"

"Going to the front has focussed my mind." He fixed her with his eyes." I do love you Ava." Dimitri moved closer until her intense green eyes were disconcertingly close to his own. "From the moment I saw you beneath the skylight. The moment my life changed for the better."

Ava looked startled, speechless again. Then her actions spoke for her as she leant forward and flung her arms around him.

"I feel it too."

"What do you feel?"

"Love."

She pulled away brushing a tear from her cheek with the back of her hand. "I feel it every time I think of you." She snuffled, blinking back more tears. "It drives me mad, but there you go."

He passed her a handkerchief and held her tenderly by the shoulders.

"When did you realise?" He searched her eyes.

"Oh," she sniffed dismissively, "it took a long time."

"A long time?" Dimitri raised his eyebrows. "By my reckoning we've only had one proper date."

Ava blew her nose and replied in a rapid whisper.

"It was the flowers that clinched it."

"Really?" Dimitri laughed.

"Really."

Then they came together, like the petals of *Iris Sibirica* at sunset, and began to kiss.

An hour later, they strolled hand in hand past the familiar fallen tree trunk surrounded by a cluster of mushrooms.

"I'll have to be back soon." Ava echoed her own words from their very first meeting. "But there's something I want to give you before you go."

"I'm not really into flowers." Dimitri smiled as they both gazed at the scattering of Iris Sibirica frozen in starlight near the base of the trunk.

"No, not flowers." She frowned. "Something else to remember me by." Ava cast a wary glance through the thinning trees towards her parent's dacha. The house was in darkness. "Come with me as far as the road. I'll have to sneak back in to get it."

As they walked down the wooded path to the main road, Dimitri told her what time he was leaving and where he was catching the train.

"I won't be able to see you off, Dimitri." Ava gave a faint shake of her head. "I'm sorry but there's no way I'll get past Katryn during the day."

They stepped out into the road.

"You will write to me though won't you?"

Before she could reply, a black car sped around the corner catching them full on in its headlights. It screeched to a halt just a few yards in front of them. Their guilty faces froze in the intense beam.

Blinded by the light they couldn't see who got out but heard the sound of car doors opening and then slamming shut.

Two government agents, their long black trench coats and hats silhouetted in the dazzling headlights, walked towards them.

"Well well," said agent Pavlov. "It looks like pigs will find mud anywhere." He cut a gaunt figure, pale and sinewy with a cold hard face.

Dimitri quickly recognised the second agent who was coming towards him at some speed.

"I know you," Dimitri gasped, "you're the man from the Cheka!"

"Shut your mouth!" He commanded before lashing out with a hefty right fist, punching Dimitri in the face, harder than he'd ever been hit before.

The pain was intense and he stumbled backwards, his lip bleeding. Dimitri heard Ava let out a scream. And when he looked up again a Nagent revolver was pointing in his face.

"You don't know me and you have never seen me before." The man from the Cheka whispered sternly to Dimitri.

"Get up." He said in a raised voice. "I want to see your papers." This was the closest he'd been to Dimitri, and in the half-glare of the headlights there was a strange familiarity beneath his rugged features.

"It doesn't matter who they are." Pavlov said. "They've both broken curfew."

Pavlov had Ava in an arm-lock. She struggled and kicked backward against his shin. "Bitch!" He cursed in pain, letting go of his grip.

"You idiots!" Ava said as she ran towards Dimitri. "This man is going off to fight for the Motherland tomorrow." She passed him a tissue for his cut lip. "And you want to arrest us?" Her eyes were ablaze. "Damn you."

"You have broken curfew." Pavlov said, limping forward, fumbling inside his leather trench coat. "Assaulted an officer of the NKVD and now tell lies to get you out of trouble?" He pulled out his revolver and waved it threateningly. "Keep digging, bitch."

"It's not a lie." Cheka man said, turning to his colleague. "It's all here amongst his documents. He's got orders to report at Belorussky Station," he glanced at his watch, "this afternoon."

"Well that is a crying shame." Pavlov said. "Because I believe they've both got an appointment at the Lubyanka at the same time."

Dimitri's blood ran cold.

"A word." Cheka man's voice took on a steely note as he gestured to his colleague to join him at the side of the road. Then as an aside to Dimitri, "Don't even think about running."

Both men were soon locked in intense conversation. Ava held on tight to Dimitri. She was trying to compose herself but panic was jolting through her with sickening force. Dimitri's features registered confusion as he strained to hear them.

The man from the Cheka mumbled a few hushed words in his cohort's ear.

"Most irregular, most irregular..." Pavlov could be heard replying, shaking his head and looking at the ground. There was an obvious difference of opinion over what action to take.

Dimitri and Ava shivered like deer in headlights on the cold tarmac.

Cheka man was holding firm with his argument. Glancing back and forth to Ava and Dimitri, some of his words carried on the night air. "They're just kids after all." Something about his low-lidded eyes, smouldering with defiance, reminded Dimitri of his father. "You think they'll reward us for depriving the frontline of conscripts?"

Pavlov's low voice exuded quiet menace throughout their exchange.

"It will all go in my report," he murmured.

His words faded into silence.

Light was starting to make its presence felt, etching out the branches of the trees lining the roadside. In this pale first-light Pavlov looked a little cowed, his cheeks darkened with shame. It seemed that the man from the Cheka had put him in his place. Then Dimitri realised it wasn't a look of shame at all but the glow of rage.

"Do it your way." Pavlov spoke at last. "But I've a feeling we..." he paused, glancing sidelong at his co-officer, "or should I say *you*, might regret this."

They made their way back to Dimitri and Ava.

"You," the man from the Cheka addressed Dimitri, "get in the car." He then turned towards Pavlov. "And you better make sure he gets home."

"As for you young lady," he observed Ava impassively, "you're coming with me."

Moscow's Belorussky Station

269

Ava had to barge her way through the vast crowd, making her way slowly towards the packed locomotive. On her way to the station she had spotted a firestorm on the horizon. Was it the advancing German army she wondered, or the handiwork of native saboteurs undermining the war effort?

She soon found herself caught up in a stream of young Russian men, and a few women, shuffling along the platform with all the gloominess of condemned prisoners. They all formed parts of volunteer battalions, sub-units from the regular army and VoenKomats conscripts. The sky above was lead grey capturing the time-worn faces of babushkas, fathers and mothers of these soon to be departed. She saw the look of anguish on a tearful grandma's face, the proud resignation of a middle-aged man. They were being jostled and cheered on by an even larger crowd of civilians. She witnessed tearful farewells, clasped handshakes and comradely embraces. A sea of flat caps and headscarves seemed to overwhelm this narrow current of conscripts and volunteers.

Regimental banners and flags of the Soviet Union were everywhere but the forage-capped soldiers going directly to the frontline had faces that already looked battle-hardened. Unfamiliar faces with all-too-familiar expressions. Yet that was the look of most Soviet men and women these days, she thought. A life of struggle, a life of strenuous work, creases the faces of the most handsome of people. Their mannerisms conveyed a hard-boiled, no-nonsense masculinity, devoid of affectation. On the other hand, she noted that those in the officer class displayed a more refined bearing, their bodies looked more used to the luxury of the sauna than the coalmine; more at home in the warmth of an office than in the heat of the steelworks.

A strong smell of coffee wafting from the station canteen brought Ava back to her senses.

Suddenly, from the end of platform the Red Army Choir, resplendent in spotless uniforms, peaked hats and red and gold epaulets, struck up *'Holy War'* - a song specially written in response to the German invasion.

"Arise vast country, Arise for a fight to the death, Against the dark fascist forces, Against the cursed hordes, Let noble wrath, boil over like a wave! This is a people's war! A sacred war!"

Seated in front of the tiered rows of the male choir were accordion and balalaika players and even a couple of trumpeters. The conductor urged them on with great gusto as the choir swayed from side to side as if marching.

Then, as though Stalin had ordered it himself, the sun appeared driving away the atmosphere of oppression that had hung over the station like a shroud. This sudden glare, along with the rich harmonies and soul stirring melodies, soon had feet tapping and bodies rocking back and forth in time to the rhythm. It was hypnotic, and an immediate alchemy took place within the people. Ava could see the wide smiles reflecting the swelling hearts this blood-pumping music had aroused. The amalgamation of tenors, baritones and basses were evoking memories of deep Russia, conveying the sense of power and the wide-open spaces of the steppes.

When the song finished there was silence all around the station.

271

Then thunderous applause.

The soldiers loved it and shouted out for more. The choir then launched into *"Let's Go!"* and in front of them a young soldier began doing mid-air splits in time to the music.

"The path we'll take is a long one, Cheer up soldier, look! In the wind our regiment's flag is high, Commanders lead the way, Soldiers let's go, let's go, let's go!"

The choir sang with such pride, such enthusiasm that a whole group of recruits began squat-kicking, competing against each other with intense expressions etched across their faces.

"Brothers we are one in glory, Glory we have earned in battle!"

This music was a bridge; a link between the raw youth of today and their proud Scythian ancestry. The solemnity and pure emotion of the singing blew away any lingering notions of cynicism. It evoked the dormant patriotism that was in the soul of all Russian people. It created a feeling of unity and togetherness, harking back to a time more sacred and noble. The military precision of the beating drums symbolised the discipline needed in wartime. The magnificent melodies embodied the civic romanticism of Russia's Imperial past; ideas of beauty, dignity and integrity.

The stationary train was well worn by arctic blasts and blazing suns. Ava ran down the platform looking into every carriage window. At times the steam from the engine blew into her eyes and the smell of oil and diesel was almost overpowering.

In one carriage men played cards for cigarettes, their artillery belts discarded casually on the floor.

The next carriage contained a rowdy crew swapping bottles of vodka, their hands clapping as they sung along with the choir outside.

Next along had a stocky man stood stripped to his waist dropping a whole pickled herring down his throat like a seal, much to the delight to his shot-drinking comrades.

She eventually saw him in the last carriage, head down reading a book. Ava banged hard on the condensed window.

Dimitri glanced up and a look of pure amazement crossed his face. The other soldiers in the carriage paid scant attention as he picked his way through the kitbags and cases.

He slid open the topmost window.

"Ava, what happened to you last night?" He shouted to be heard amongst the shouts and whistles coming from the platform.

"You'll never believe it." She shouted up to him. "That man from the Cheka escorted me home. He let me climb back in through the window. Katryn doesn't know I ever went out!"

Dimitri's face was a picture of bewilderment.

"But how did you mange to come here?"

"He came back today."

"The man from the Cheka?"

"Yes. He took Katryn in for questioning about Dad's disappearance. After she'd got in the car he came back and said to me, "You've got two hours!""

273

The whistle of the train pierced the air. Guards urged people to get further back on the platform. Dimitri could feel the mighty engine beginning to churn.

"I'll write to you Ava. As soon as I know where we're staying."

The train hissed and groaned laboriously as it started to slowly move forward.

Ava walked alongside.

"Here, take this." She passed him a brown paper parcel tied up with string.

"Get back! Move away from the train!" A flag-waving guard was coming towards her.

"Something to remember me by."

The guard caught her by the arm as the train moved steadily forward.

"Where the snow falls, Dimitri!" Ava cried.

A look of faint recollection passed over Dimitri's face.

"That's where I'll find you?"

Ava laughed whilst being admonished by the guard.

"My letter explains everything. Bye my love!"

"Bye, Ava."

The train guard was still berating Ava as the train picked up speed, passing the flag waving well wishers, past the saluting Red Army Choir, bound for a destination unknown. Dimitri pressed his face up against the cold glass until he last saw Ava's slight figure shrinking smaller and smaller until eventually she became just one of a thousand anonymous faces stood waiting on a platform.

That was the last time I saw her.

But what revolution could take me back to my first sighting of Ava? What offering, what sacrifice would I not make to turn back time?

Avakov, as if he read my thoughts, spoke down from the wooden podium.

"Good to see you praying, comrade. But remember, a selfish desire is still a selfish desire whether or not we enlist God's help."

Avakov stood with the nonchalance of Michelangelo's *David*. Rifle hung over his shoulder, cigar smoke trailing up into the sacred space. Uncle Leon once quoted me St Irenaeus. *The glory of god is a man fully alive!* I'd never met a man as fully alive as Avakov. So competent and self assured he is actually graceful in his manner. Stoic in nature, he is above pettiness and the vices of the weak. After a long time spent gazing at the fallen Icons and stained glass windows he said,

"So much for German Christian values," he paused, "they produced a generation of very unchristian soldiers!"

I nodded acknowledgment, but my mind was back in the enchanted world of childhood. The smell of the pine floorboards had taken me back to my days in a Moscow kindergarten. I remembered the tactile pleasure in using my first wooden abacus, the outings to the woods, hunting for mushrooms and berries. I could almost taste the semolina pudding, milk kasha with macaroni. I fleetingly re-felt the awe I had then of the Young Pioneers who came to visit us.

"Back home they raised us to be gullible agents of the state," I belatedly replied.

"And here they raised a generation of fascists," Avakov retorted. "But at least they were allowed to celebrate Christmas, eh comrade, not like us."

"We had a Christmas tree in junior school," I answered.

"Oh yes, we all did, but do you not remember?" Avakov looked amused, "we were not allowed to associate them with Christmas! Christmas trees were banned in 1929. Fir trees were allowed but only to symbolise trees that did not shed pines in winter. And we were only allowed to call them New Years Trees. Much like when Christmas was renamed the Winter Holidays. Religion was taken out of everything."

Avakov went on, "my family did celebrate Christmas though," he whispered. Even now the fear of denouncement ran deep in our subconscious. "In the evenings Mother brought out the icons from their secret hiding place and we all lit votive lamps. My parents made me swear never to tell anyone we had a Christmas tree. *'Tell people that,"* my mother warned us, *"and we'll all be sent to the camps!"* He gave a shake of his head.

My heart rate quickened and my mouth became completely dry. My nervous system pre-empted my memories as a fresh recollection, one lost in my childhood paradise, resurfaced now in my adult hell.

I was still at school, nine years old and naively oblivious to the purges going on outside our school walls. There was an atmosphere of blissful anticipation of the Winter Holidays.

Orphan of the State

"Who has a Christmas tree at home?" Our newly arrived classroom assistant asked innocuously.

At the time we were making a collage for the winter festival, sticking scrunched up tissue paper onto cardboard swans. I can still smell the cheap glue. Feel the rough wooden floor beneath my bare knees.

My hand shot up excitedly. Then I looked around and saw I was the only one. I felt sorry for my classmates. Yet some of them looked sorry for me.

The man looked at me like he was in a trance. There was a long silence. Doubt passed over his face like a shadow. Then his lips twisted into a sneer.

"And what is your name, boy?" His voice was cold.

As soon as I rushed out my name the bell rang and in the chaos of going home-time I quickly forgot his strange demeanour. The Winter Holidays had begun and I ran home as fast as my legs could carry me.

"Let's go, comrade." Avakov kicked the long bench. He saw me slip the snow globe into my greatcoat pocket. "Miracles happen in this world. Dreams do come true." His eyes glistened as he stroked his moustache, "I have to believe that. I dream of seeing my son still as a baby, his strong toes treading the earth."

David J Robinson

CHAPTER 34

Diary of Dimitri

W e're getting closer to Berlin by the day. As a consequence we are a day nearer to home. The thought of home fills me with as much anxiety as happiness. I'm not the man who left Moscow. He's gone. All naivety burnt away by the searing heat of war. The value of life has plummeted. The shock of death, of seeing disfigured German and Russian corpses' is replaced by a sickening apathy. Another hum-drum atrocity. It's as if living or dying doesn't matter anymore. I don't feel dead inside, more like hollowed out, empty of joy. I fear returning home as a shadow of the man who left.

Has Ava waited? Is this brutal effigy of a man what she deserves after waiting so long? I feel like I've lived so many lifetimes and am ready to die, but one emotion dominates, hatred – hatred of Hitler's men. They plead for mercy but we show them none. They saw and treated us as sub humans, destroyed Russian farms, killed, raped and plundered. It is they who fall far below any standard of human behaviour.

My heart is cold. I hope Ava has found someone else. The wait has been too long. I will not bring her happiness. I am no bringer of light. What will I do when the killing stops?

Comrades still tease my virgin status. They say I must rape some German bitch to bring me back to life. When I resist they tell me the final push for Berlin will bring many casualties. Do I want to die a virgin? They say I owe it to Mother Russia to conquer these people as they tried to conquer us, through rape and humiliation. Crush the bastards. No mercy.

At times I get carried away with their macho bluster, other times I recall the man I once was and am ashamed to feel such affinity with these brutes of men. But, I am quick to remind myself, it's not their fault. Stalin himself says we deserve the fruits of war. My mind is in torment. We are on a route uncharted. Fire and blood erase our tracks. I will not die having never fucked a woman. And whether Ava has waited or not, maybe even she would understand my feelings of frustration after all I've seen and been through.

I know of a reconnaissance party who found some German girls hiding in a basement. They found vodka and raped the girls in a manner I found shocking. But part of me was aroused. I would draw the line at forcing a woman to have sex with me but surely I'd find a willing Fraulein. After all we are liberating the ungrateful wenches!

As I read back over my diary I am shocked at my change. Truth is I vacillate between man and beast. The civilised Dimitri and the bestial Dimitri vie for dominance. After the guns have stopped I hope my former self is victorious. I hope the peacemakers will be able to piece together my shattered nerves. But for now, for pure survival I give way to the beast. The evils I've witnessed have poked and prodded this demon within. The demon has awoken and, as he rises, he makes me feel strong and virile. Pulsing through me, these intense emotions charge my being. I feel alive.... bad, but alive!

I fear the peace more than I fear the war now. I have become institutionalised. An uncaring, self-preserving, killing machine. What job in civilian life warrants such skills? Maybe my future lies with the NKVD. But I couldn't stomach the hypocrisy and deception. I may be broken but I'm pleased to see, in my revulsion of the NKVD, that I'm not yet without principles!

You see, for all its failings, war can reveal the unceasing freshness of eternity. By that I mean cities fall, soldiers die, the rivers run red with blood, but tomorrow dawns anew. Cities rise from ashes, future soldiers are being cradled, while the rivers run afresh from the mountain streams. Nature, in spite of our personal hell, goes on regardless. If we do not see its beauty amidst our toil, if in our haste to kill we aren't aware of the seasons unfurling around us, she does not care. We are sand grains in infinity.

In conversation with Avakov I remark that whichever army fights with the most passion will surely win the war. He shakes his head sadly. "One must strive to be free of passion," he makes it sound like a dirty word. "Remember, the ancient meaning of passion was anguish and suffering, that is passively reacting to external events."

In an instant I understood why Avakov said this. He is indifferent to external vagaries. His stoicism is marked by inner-serenity, stern self-discipline and a conscientious undertaking of duty.

"Follow where reason leads," he added smiling enigmatically. Avakov then lit his pipe, signalling the end of our conversation.

"But I don't know where reason leads." I confessed. "In that sense I am lost."

Avakov regarded me thoughtfully.

"The wisdom of God can be perceived in silence only."

I remained silent but none the wiser.

"Have you heard of the art of Hesychasm, my friend?"

I shook my head.

Avakov smiled broadly.

"Then let me enlighten you!"

CHAPTER 35

Diary of Dimitri

The German women thrust hand-picked flowers upon us. With their blonde curls and bare naked calves they are a sight for sore eyes. I share the feeling seen in my comrades' eyes as they cast their gaze over these smiling, ripe-for-the-plucking Deutsche girls.

For all we know their husbands and boyfriends were responsible for the raping and killing of our people. I know the words of Christ, but it's hard to turn the other cheek when sexual desire and wilful revenge combine forces.

To the victor the spoils! Rumours circulate that more advanced units have gang-raped these whores of Hitler. That is what Cerenkov calls them, *"They should be flattered and grateful for our Russian cocks now we've slaughtered their men-folk!"* He says in his usual pithy way. Cerenkov dismisses Vasily's warning that the way we make love to women is how God will be with us.

"God helps those that help themselves," he snarls.

The farther away from Stalin's clutches we get, the bolder and more reckless we become. And when out of sight of officer's eyes our platoon embodies a raw form of manhood. The men become primitive, stripped of chivalry and human decency. The facade of civilised living becomes barbarous existence. The inner beast unleashed.

The Motherland owes us so much now. We've blazed a trail to Berlin, a trail steeped in blood, sweat and tears. The men are optimistic about life after war. They can see the sun rising on glorious days back home.

It shall be as heroes we return. Our exploits standing tall among past exemplars of Russian patriotism. They will erect monuments in our honour. They shall carve statues in our image! We will have power to change society for the better because the people will respect and listen to us. Stalin and his men must bow down to our bravery and our demands that conditions, pay and justice are improved. That our peasants can enjoy more freedoms of the like we saw among the Austrians and the Germans.

I don't want to undermine the men's soaring morale but I fear they are mistaken. Dictators are not so easily coerced, they know - as the rare well-meaning Tsars of old found to their cost - any concession is seized upon as weakness.

The soldiers returning to Russia after the Bonaparte campaign contained the seeds of revolution having seen the greater progress, enterprise and freedoms of other lands. If that is my true understanding of history then the parallels with today's returning heroes, won't have escaped Stalin's mind. He'll be plotting ways even now to root out potential troublemakers, ways of besmirching the reputations of honest soldiers, silencing any cries of dissent far away in the depths of a Siberian gulag.

I'm fighting to keep my soul intact. Nothing seems new and fresh any more. Like a child who finds no pleasure in toys and games when his innocence is opened up to a bigger reality. How can the banality of 'normal' life satisfy a mind corrupted by such depravity that would even make Ivan the Terrible squirm?

Apart from my good comrades, Vasily and Avakov, I have no real friends here. Everyone else seems closer than brothers. And I know it is Cerenkov who has poisoned their minds against me.

The paranoia of Stalin knows no limits. A rumour has it that Stalin was enraged over news that Rudolph Hess had parachuted into Scotland. Our psychotic leader saw this as signs of an Anglo/German pact to turn on Russia. Apart from during formal talks with Officers the men rarely mention Stalin's name anymore, and when it is uttered it is with treasonable irreverence.

The men are terribly confused. When we see the ordered lives of the ordinary German people we are struck by their lavishness compared with our own.

"I was told the workers of the Soviet Union had the best living standards in the world!" cried Vasily as he raided a larder filled with racks of vegetables, tinned food and salted meats. As a former member of the Komsomol these contradictions also blew my mind.

I too had been led to believe Russia was the best place to live, that Communism is the best system. But my eyes now tell me otherwise. I see the quality and amount of food these ordinary Germans have in their homes. I see the superiority of their clothes and utensils, of books and pictures. I see every kind of comfort a man could want.

Hitler is evil, of that I have no doubt, but his people live under a system of kindness and plenitude. Our troops become more merciless as a result of such revelations. Revelations that expose the lies of propaganda back home.

Years of misinformation had imbued us with real hatred and convinced us that all Germans were ravening beasts. Now we couldn't understand why such a prosperous people, such an advanced, seemingly civilised society should want to invade our comparatively poor country. Or how they could see and treat us as sub-human and indulge in an orgy of violence against our women and children. It was just wanton greed.

I have always blamed Hitler and referred to the German army, navy and Luftwaffe as Hitler's men, but surely the German population as a whole are also responsible for supporting and voting for such a monster.

Orphan of the State

Marchenko addresses the troops outside Berlin.

"Comrades, I know how you are feeling right now. Exhausted, drained, a feeling of 'job done'. Well the job isn't done. An army is never more in danger than when it becomes complacent. It is a fine line between complacency and confidence. I'm confident we will finish off Hitler's men before long. I'm complacent if I think these fascists, with nothing left to lose, are going to roll over and die.

"So remember, all the struggles and sacrifices and sheer bloody hell we've all been through have won us nothing. They've just paved the way for us to reach this point and unless we redouble our efforts, our vigilance and our ruthlessness from this point onwards, the rest has all been in vain.

"To get to heaven, we have to go through hell... so we *know* we're on the right track!" The men laughed.

"To start a war is easy, any fool can do it, and many have! To sustain a conflict is easy when you have no choice but to fight to preserve your way of life. But to end a war, to show no mercy and pummel our enemy into complete submission... well, that's why we're here today.

"We're going to hit Berlin hard. We're going to beat the Americans and the British to the prize – Hitler himself. To do that you're going to have to dig deep and scrap like hell for every yard, every house, every brick of Berlin. The rats are cornered, they'll hiss and bare their teeth and pounce on you. Do not be afraid, whilst they have their backs to the wall, you have the might of the Motherland behind you. We need to crush them into the dust. Rout them so completely they will never again dare to contemplate invading Mother Russia.

"Dig deep into your souls, men. Yours are the souls of the proletariat. These lands we've conquered will be future colonies of the Communist utopia. It is a utopia you and your children shall all see. But, should you die fighting for that future, or die of old age in that future, you shall all die equally as warriors and heroes of the Soviet Union!"

A sign says "You are Entering The Lair of The Fascist Beast!"

Vasily says, *"We are entering the city of Nietzsche, Goethe and the Brothers Grimm. I wonder if they ever foresaw its bloody demise."*

"Wasn't it Nietzsche who said, 'God is dead?" I replied, proud of my memory.

"Yes", Vasily glances at me, *"but he went on to say that it was we who killed him!"*

The men's bloodlust is up. The scent of victory is in the air. The talk is of reaping the spoils of war, in other words - rape and pillage. Edicts are read out half-heartedly that looting will not be tolerated and women must be left untouched. But these are accompanied by a tacit understanding that there will be no real punishment. The men nod and wink to each other when told to "be magnanimous in victory" followed by a pumping of the hips and crude barrack-room remarks. These edicts are purely perfunctory. They'll be used to excuse Stalin's tactics when the post-war dust settles and word gets out of our atrocious sins committed in the Fatherland. Our most recent propaganda is the opposite.

"Kill them! Nobody in Germany is innocent. Neither the living nor the unborn. Heed the words of comrade Stalin and crush the Fascist beast in its cave! Break down the racial pride of the German woman! Take her as your legitimate spoils of war! Kill them you brave soldiers of the victorious Red Army!"

Finally, I get a letter from home. Six months it took to travel from Moscow through the desecrated Russian landscape, past innumerable, unnamed fallen soldiers, through scenes of horror, places of despair and battlegrounds of victory. Now my fingers tremble as I begin to tear open the battered envelope. I wonder if an NKVD agent had already done so, to censure or deem it 'suitable' reading for a *frontski* - frontline soldier. I could imagine the type, detached, clinical, scanning the words for signs of dissent or coded messages.

The news is devastating.

Ava is dead.

The letter offers a short report of an explosion in the munitions factory where she worked. No dried flowers, no poems, just '*Deepest Sympathies*' from an illegible scrawl on official Soviet notepaper.

Tears obscure my sight and my heart pounds as if it's about to explode.

David J Robinson

CHAPTER 36

Diary of Dimitri

I feel I have nothing to lose. No-one to remain faithful to. No country to honour. I fear for the German people, for I know not what I am about to do.

We are in the suburbs of Berlin, a blazing, shell-shocked city. The Germans fight like rats. They know that after the atrocities they committed in Russia there is no future for them. They do not fight for the Fatherland any more nor the Third Reich or their families. They fight us out of fear, fear of being caught alive.

Street fighting and house to house skirmishes go on with Hitler's rag-tag army of school boys and old men. The

German dead lie unburied on the street. The smell of raw sewerage and rotting corpses is overpowering.

I am lost. There are no new and fresh mornings in my life. I have become robotic. Cold, dead behind the eyes, I stalk the enemy through a city of dust.

I tell Colonel Marchenko about the letter. I ask for leave but am flatly refused.

"We need all the men we can muster for the final attack." He speaks on auto-pilot.

"Can you make sure my condolences will be sent to her parents immediately?" I plead.

He looks at me emotionlessly and nods.

"I shall address the matter when," he spreads his trembling hands, "all *this* is over."

"I demand you send word..."

"No comrade." Marchenko takes off his reading glasses and rubs the bridge of his nose. His eyes are bloodshot. He looks exhausted. "Wait until the final shot is fired and then we will clear this up."

Night.

March of the machines. The night sky hums with the roar of aeroplanes, the whirr of caterpillar tracks and throbbing engines, machine-gun blasts and distant mortars, anti-aircraft fire and tracers. Why don't we all go home and leave the machines to it? But we built these killing machines. They would idle and rust without men to will them into deadly action. Oh how far we've advanced from battling with slings and arrows to now waging war on this industrial scale.

I reflect on the past. My inspirational teacher, Oska who taught me about Marxism and the ideology of Socialism yet seemed to be cynical of Stalin's policies. Everyone thought he sailed too close to the wind with his anti-communist slurs. One day he was reprimanded by the head teacher. A week later he disappeared and no other teacher ever mentioned him again.

Having once borrowed a book from Oska I knew his address. Peering through his apartment window, I saw it had been ransacked. I asked his neighbours if they knew anything but I was met with a wall of silence. Oska's wife and children were also never seen again.

Uncle Leon scolded me for having gone. "He'll be lucky to make it to the gulag," he shook his head.

"But surely if Stalin is made aware of what happened he would intervene? Parts of the Police and security service are corrupt but..." I blathered.

"Don't you see?" He gripped my collar. I could smell the alcohol on his breath. "The whole system's corrupt. Koba's the puppeteer and the Cheka does his bidding."

"But if Communism means that every man is of equal stature...." Even now I wince at my idealism.

"Shut up, shut up." My quick-tempered uncle covered his ears. "You are too naive to see. Communism is like an icicle in the sunlight, glistening luminously even as it melts. Your teacher saw the rottenness at the core of Russian society and now he pays the price. Close your eyes to it, Dimitri or we too, the last of our family, will go the same way."

Later, just after my carriage conversation with Ava who had cast doubt on my parents' death, I broached the subject again with Uncle Leon.

"I've told you a dozen times." Leon removed his glasses and rubbed his eyes. "Why rake over the past, Dimitri. God gave, God took back. Let it be."

"No, and I'll tell you why. The black cars we see cruising the streets; Cheka, secret service... whatever. I remembered seeing one follow my parents' car on that day. You even insisted that I wave them off from the window. Did you know then that would be the last I would see of them?"

"You must have been imagining things."

"Was I? Or did I witness them being escorted to the Lubyanka to be interrogated?"

"What's the saying?" Leon reflected. "Ah, the less you know the more soundly you will sleep."

"I'm not that naive orphan boy any more. I just want the truth."

"If you're no longer naive you'll know that telling the truth in this society can get yourself and one's family wiped off the face of the earth." Suddenly that harsh edge was back in his voice. "Expunged from history!" Leon got up and started pacing to and fro. "Scattered to the camps... separated by thousands of miles of forests, tundra and swamps."

"So there is a truth to be told?"

"Oh you're suddenly a man of the world eh, Dimitri?"

"It never added up... hardly anyone at the funeral. No visitors *after* the funeral!"

"Cats die of curiosity, don't you know?"

"I remember you taking me down to the bridge and the priest saying prayers across the frozen river. But I don't recall seeing their bodies lying in open coffins in the orthodox way. None of it adds up. And you won't tell me the truth."

Leon shook his head and lowered his tone.

"Because the truth is Dimitri... there were no bodies to bury."

David J Robinson

CHAPTER 37

Diary of Dimitri

L eon was in full flow. "Someone, we will probably never know who, denounced your parents, Dimitri. Cheka men burst into their apartment and caught them red-handed listening to an illegal short wave radio set. For that alone, my brother and your mother were looking at a ten year minimum sentence. Your mother wasn't well, she had mental problems, she kept forgetting names, where she lived. She began talking to statues for God's sake! Your father and I tried to cover for her fragility. No-one is allowed to be psychologically ill in the Soviet Union. Koba redefined psychological illness as deviant thinking and equated it to political disobedience. Mental illness reflected badly on the state. Better to deny it even exists." I hung on every word, fighting back the tears.

"The thought of her alone and vulnerable in the Gulag system terrified your father."

"Why had the two of you argued that day?"

"I think I still had faith in justice back then. I told him to be brave and endure whatever sentence fate threw at him. I was sure the state prosecutors would take pity on your mother, that maybe they wouldn't be separated." He looked at me earnestly. "Back then I too was naive."

"So was their crash an accident or not?"

"An accident I'm afraid. Your father was stressed and I do believe from the testimony of witnesses that he was driving far too fast when he came to the bridge."

"Could it have been... I mean, could he possibly have driven off the bridge on purpose?"

"What are you saying?" Leon asked gravely.

"Suicide." I said.

"Good God, Dimitri, never ever suggest that! And why would they? They didn't realise short wave radios had been banned. I was sure that they were going to clear their names at the Lubyanka. There had been a mistake. They would set things straight and be home in time for tea. I convinced them that they could prove their denouncement false. At least they were spared the terrifying sounds of jack boots approaching and the night-time banging on the door. They weren't torn from their beds dazed and half asleep with government agents hurrying them to pack."

"So we should be grateful for that!" I said through gritted teeth.

"In many ways we were all lucky, Dimitri. One, it saved them from interrogation. And two, because their death was a tragic accident, they died as free citizens. Given that they hadn't been formally arrested, merely escorted to be questioned, they were never officially charged. If they had been then eventually all their acquaintances, relatives and indeed you, their only son, would have been rounded up as friends or family of enemies of the state."

"So when you said there were no bodies to bury, what exactly did you mean?"

"Moscow River is their resting place, Dimitri." Leon held me by the shoulders. "We never told you because you were too young. The authorities said they'd send divers to the wreckage in the spring. They promised to dredge the river bed if need be. The sad truth is Dimitri," he looked at me blankly, "they never bothered."

David J Robinson

CHAPTER 38

Diary of Dimitri

Does the Motherland know whose feet trample across her earth? Is she aware of the difference between goose-stepping Nazis, galloping Cossacks and the tracks of us native Russians counter-attacking across her plains? Does she give a damn? And who is "Mother Russia" anyway? An ideal of nationhood? A fairy tale?

I knew about the history of Russia from my disappeared teacher, Oska. He spoke passionately about the roots of our country, how unfortunate it was that the fledgling sparks of democracy in early Kiev were snuffed out too soon.

Oska taught us the legend of the perpetually warring Slavic tribes around 800AD who sought the aid of a Viking Prince to rule over and bind them together with a rule of law. Rurik the Rus was the Viking Prince who came across to Novgorod and founded the embryonic nation named after our Slavic word for Viking – Rus. His descendents became known as *Rus-sians*. So goes the legend. True or not – one can easily see the evolution of small warring tribes joining together to fight bigger warring tribes culminating in the tribe of Russia fighting this Germanic tribe. Sadly, the only evolution seems to be one of scale, the size of tribe and sophistication of weaponry.

Having been well nourished with the blood, bones and entrails of our eternally warring ancestors - from Rurik the Rus and the wild Slavic tribes, to the Palovtsian invasion, Tartars and Mongols, Teutonic knights, the famine and time of troubles, rebellious Poles and border states, wars with Prussia, the peasant revolts and Napoleon's men - this land of ours should be a most bounteous land.

Those democratic nations such as Austria, Belgium and France soon capitulated to the might of the German war machine. The soft underbelly of democracy was laid bare, an inability to perform quick, decisive action. Weighted down by the rule of law, of time-consuming debate and the need for a consensus of opinion before a bullet is fired, they are like rabbits dazzled in the spotlights of a Panzer.

Although Stalin was caught on the hop and totally unprepared for war it was the "iron fist" of autocratic rule, of one man at the helm of power that swung the tide of war back in our favour, that and a seeming inexhaustible supply of cannon fodder.

I heard what happened to the newly mobilised recruits in the early days of the war. They were sent into already disorganised units creating more confusion. Many were sent like a human wave straight into German guns. These were the most primitive and stereotypical tactics. It was a human sacrifice.

While rebellions and their quashing are the stuff of every nation, the overriding notion of Russianness was that the State comes first. The individual must be prepared to sacrifice his own life to uphold the status quo. Before Rurik there was just warring tribes. His was the first dynasty. All the Tsars after him followed his example of ruling with *silnaya ruka*, the iron fist of centralised power. History shows that from the very beginning we craved a strong leader to bring order and unity to our volatile land. It is a mindset and belief that has endured down the centuries.

One of the other stories we first learnt at school was the sacrifice of the brothers Boris and Gleb, two brothers who became the most venerated of early Russian martyrs. Victims of a power struggle with their brother, Svyatopolk, they offered no resistance to the soldiers he sent to kill them lest it lead to a civil war. The Tsars taught this as an example of Christian humility. But the Communists used it to symbolise the nobility of sacrifice in the cause of Russian unity. Throughout our lessons on Russian history the same theme arose. That ultimate self-sacrifice is justified if done for the supreme good of the State.

The doomed venture of Prince Igor and his small band of men came to mind. His valiant but ill-fated mission against Polovtsian raiders from the Steppe is entrenched in the Russian psyche just as the heroism of the Charge of the Light Brigade is lodged in the consciousness of the British Empire. As schoolchildren we had to memorise and recite the Song of Igor's Campaign.

Then Igor gazed upon the sun and said, "Brothers! Better it would be to be slain than to be a slave. So let us mount our swift horses that we may look upon the blue waters of the Don. I want to break a lance at the limit of the Polovtsian steppe. With you O Russians, I will lay down my life, or else drink of the Don from my helmet."

We had to understand its dark, disturbing images unaware of the subtle patriotic propaganda at play, working on our open minds at such a tender age. I now see clearly how the ruling elite use the past to justify their methods of control, as if to say – *"See? We've always needed an iron fist!"*

These thoughts weighed me down during the next day's reconnaissance in part of Berlin the Germans were thought to have fled. Newly promoted, Avakov led our four man team through the shelled factories and mortar-bombed housing that seemed devoid of life. The sky was grey above the rubble and desolation on the ground. I stepped over a smashed mosaic tile and wondered how many millenniums of art, culture and architecture were reduced to dust beneath our feet. The going was slow. Buildings could collapse at any moment. Avakov pointed out a solid paving stone wedged perilously over a gaping hole. Our senses were on high alert for such booby traps as we picked and scrambled our way through craters and debris of bombed-out roads.

Avakov was about twenty yards ahead when he stopped by a burnt out tram. The doors were open and he sat on the footstep. He removed his helmet, scratched his head and signalled me to follow. At that moment a single gunshot rang out in the square and Avakov slumped forward, the back of his skull blown clean off. His legs kicked blindly as the last bit of life-force went into spasm. Ivan and I dived for cover behind a low wall.

"Sniper in clock tower!" Vasily shouted from the rear.

I attempted to peer out as another gunshot ricocheted of the corner of the wall. The dust blinded me momentarily. Pinned down, the three of us hung tight until back-up arrived in the shape of a T-34 tank. The sniper in the clock tower tried to fend off the inevitable with pot-shots ricocheting off the armour plating. As we carefully advanced behind it, the T-34 began blasting the tower to bits.

Hours later we found the body of a German soldier among the fallen masonry. He was dressed in *Werwolf* combat fatigues. We know the German army are down to their last dregs but this amateur has ended the life of one of our best. It looked like he'd shot himself in the mouth rather than risk being taken alive. Word has obviously got round as to how pitiless we Russians can be when it comes to torture.

Evil begets evil. Now they have killed Avakov, I too feel drained of all compassion. I too want to be callous and cruel to all Germans. I fear the last of my humanity has fled along with the soul of my great comrade.

David J Robinson

CHAPTER 39

Letter from Violetta

Morning.

I wake up to that familiar smell, a cross between a steelworks and an abattoir. The sky is Armageddon grey, dust and soot and ash hinder the sun. Trees are black and smouldering and dead as they stand.

Gnarled metal street signs are twisted and melted beyond recognition. Smoke still rising from last night's shell-holes like portals of the underworld. A mangled pram, a settee carcass and a regal looking tin bath have been torn out of

307

these wrecked buildings by the Katyusha rockets last night. Those rockets were so loud they must still be echoing around the world.

As I write, the low rumbling of distant bombers cut through the silence. The familiar roar of their engines now elicits little emotion. The noise that once sowed terror into my heart no longer does so. It's amazing how soon a sense of normality pervades one's attitude to these harbingers of destruction. Even the women and children outside my window seem inured to the danger as they walk without urgency to the shelter or basement. Across the road two old men play chess beneath a shredded canopy. They eye the sky with derision, in two minds whether to finish the game or pack up and make their way to the nearest cellar. No panic, no drama. This is the leavening effect of a long drawn out war.

Maria and I have moved into an apartment nearer the centre of Berlin. For all I know Dahlem is now in the hands of the Russians. What will become of us? If civilisations like ours can be brought to its knees by a foe many thought beneath us what hope is there for the future? I was convinced my actions would go a small way in helping us lose the war. I expected a full surrender, not fighting on until every last soldier, building and hope is gone.

This morning I saw a neighbour, who used to be a postman, strung up from a lamppost by SS officers for daring to drape a white flag in his window.

The Russians are here! You can smell their horses and hear their gruff voices in the streets below. They are ill-disciplined. They don't appear to know the value of anything yet they are obsessed with watches. They are a disparate bunch. Not the conquering heroes I expected. Their brown uniforms are scruffy and stained. Their boots are falling to pieces. Some are respectful, others aggressive. One or two seem quite debonair but most seem uneducated and coarse in their behaviour.

Since they got here, Maria and I spend more time in the communal basement. The Russians have been in and taken girls out to have their way with them.

They ask every woman, *"Are you married?"* There is no correct answer. Say no, and they will see you as fair game. Say yes, and they'll say it could have been your husband who butchered women and children in the Motherland. Either way, you are fucked. One young soldier, who reeked of onions, tried to drag me out but when he saw Maria clinging to my leg he let me go.

I will be strong. If I am to be raped by the Slavic hordes, be that as it may, but I will protect Maria with my last breath.

Since then I try to make myself look old. I stoop with a scarf over my blonde hair. The Russians seem particularly keen on blondes. I rub soot into my face. I black out my front teeth, anything to put the beasts off me.

At the other extreme I've seen women practically throw themselves at the Soviet officers. They offer to be their 'girlfriends' in exchange for protection from the sexual predators that roam the streets at night. Monika Bauer, an assistant from our Burlesque days, gave herself up so readily to the Russian soldiers that even they became fed up of her submissiveness and began to ignore her. It seems even rapists like the thrill of the chase.

With their arrival death is no longer an abstract thought. Death now breathes down my neck, spikes my dreams, haunts my waking hours. It's always there.

I've started to read the bible. First time I've opened its pages since school. I want words of solace but find only echoes of this Godless land.

Isaiah 24:10

The towers of disorder are broken up: all houses are shuttered, that none may enter.

Outside is heard the clamour for wine, although all joy has become gloom: the earth's vitality is gone.

Havoc remains in the city: The gates lie battered to ruin.

I'm grieving for Josef. He must not have survived the bombing raid. I blame myself for sending him out into that maelstrom. This grief is like an illness but I must be strong for Maria.

I haven't seen Karl for days now. He went to fight the enemy. He still thinks amateur guerrilla tactics can turn the tide for Germany. Mankind's capacity for self delusion knows no bounds.

I know of one couple who hide their daughter in a false room at the end of their attic.

The old men of the Volkssturm are exhausted.

A young woman, being chased by two drunken soldiers leapt to her death rather than give in to her attackers. It made me feel sick.

Maria has gone missing. A member of the Volkssturm saw her heading back to our apartment. She's been asking for her toys and I fear she has returned there to save them.

I must go and bring her back

David J Robinson

CHAPTER 40

First-floor apartment in a suburb of Berlin, 1945.

A drunken cry, "Make way for the virgin!" and I am pushed into a room where my comrades are gathered. Head to toe we are all caked in grey dust, a mixture of plaster, soot and ash. Like ghost soldiers, it's hard to see where our skin ends and our uniforms begin. The huge dust clouds we kicked up crossing the endless Russian plains seem to have followed us here, casting a Biblical cloud of doom across all of Berlin.

We are in a stranger's bedroom, once a place of sanctity for a married couple. But for us, nothing is sacred anymore and only the profane remains. The room is filled with the acrid fog of war. As though seeing through a shroud, we now occupy a murky underworld devoid of light and love.

There is a feeling of dread in the pit of my stomach, a slow churning of anxiety and fear. I don't notice the gaping shell-holes in the walls, the snatched glimpses of a city in its death throes. I am oblivious to the flashes of bombardment and the distant glow of blazing buildings through shattered windows. I have become a zombie soldier, unaware of the bullet-holed walls and the shards of glass being crushed under every footstep.

The men part and there, face down, tied and spread-eagled on the bed with a pillow under her hips, is my sacrificial victim. This is my first sight of a real naked woman. A woman I'm expected to rape. The men jeer as my belt is ripped off and my trousers dragged down to my ankles.

Sirens wail in the distance.

"We've warmed her up for you, Petrov." Oleg raises an empty bottle in the air, followed by the sadistic hint of a smile.

"She's fucked many SS Officers, Petrov." Cerenkov shouts over the din of artillery. His dark hooded eyes penetrate deep into mine. "Don't you dare let the Motherland down."

My mind is in torment. Is this what we've become? Sons of the Motherland avenging the sins of the Fatherland?

How will the history books remember us? Liberators, rapists, heroes or villains? Right now, we are a mixture of them all.

Discipline has broken down. Commanders allow our men to roam the streets unsupervised. Moral codes are non-existent. No women are safe. From as young as twelve to eighty, some of our men think it is acceptable to gang-rape them. Not only is it acceptable, it is practically encouraged through propaganda which places the blame for the war at the door of every German civilian for not resisting the Nazis.

I feel both shame and pride. Shame for what I am about to do, yet proud my impulses can still respond to a sight so cruelly erotic. I'm embarrassed to say the more she squirms and thrashes about, the more aroused I become.

For a brief moment I think of Ava. What if she could see me now?

How far I've fallen from her standards.

How far from my ideals.

Goaded on by the war-weary veterans, I now feel compelled to rape just to fit in. War-weary, battle-hardened and life-destroying; we are all these and more. A gallows humoured, cold-blooded army of the damned.

I am drunk but not too much. My longing for sex competes with revulsion for what I am about to do. Then the bombing starts again and the building shakes. Some of the men run out. My instincts take over. Kicking off my boots, I step out of my trousers and grab the woman by the hips. She screams and curses in German.

"Get on with it!" Cerenkov shouts.

A nearby explosion shatters the remaining windows. Colonel Marchenko barks orders from the street below and the rest of my comrades hurry out of the bedroom and down the stairs.

The woman struggles valiantly against the ropes tying her wrists. I freeze as another huge blast close-by sends glass, furniture and masonry crashing to the floor.

Cerenkov is the only person left and he is losing patience. He grabs the woman by her long blonde hair, places his gun in her mouth and looks at me.

"Now, fuck her!"

From out of nowhere the most beautiful music fills my head. The unmistakeable melody of *The Gates of Kiev* plays from a jewellery box that has fallen on the floor. On its side, lid ajar, a tiny ballerina rotates innocently amidst all the madness.

This music is gentler than the piano crashing grandeur of my memories, but no less powerful.

I am in rapture.

For a moment I am back on the Communal Hall roof in Peredelkino watching my beloved Ava pirouetting below.

For a moment I am myself once more, untouched by the brutalising hand of war.

It matters not how many times you hit the deck but how often you get back up again.

I have hit rock bottom.

I step back.

Cerenkov pulls the gun from her mouth and points it at me.

"Don't you fucking dare stop!"

I ignore him and buckle up my trousers.

Cerenkov gets up, knocks me out of the way and starts loosening his belt. He is just going to take my place. Dazed, I stagger past him and pick up the gun. He looks at me with cold dead eyes, like he really doesn't give a fuck anymore. A missile whistles towards us and, as I pull the trigger, the whole world seems to explode.

David J Robinson

CHAPTER 41

Diary of Dimitri

I ask the woman her name. We are in a side-street in Berlin. She seems to be struck mute by the ordeal she's just undergone. She appears startled, as if awakening from a nightmare and for a brief instance believing it to be true. Only this time there will be no wave of relief for this wretched woman. Her worst nightmare was as real as the chaos all around us.

She looks how I felt. In those mind-scrambled moments after the blast I had managed to untie her and wrap a fallen curtain around her shoulders. Parts of the house were ablaze.

It was only a matter of time before the whole building collapsed. Cerenkov was nowhere to be seen.

"Maria, Maria!" The woman cried and pointed to a cupboard blocked by debris. I clawed away the rubble with my bare hands and dragged open the door to see a sobbing, wide-eyed little girl. I carried her over my shoulder and guided her mother down the all-but-destroyed staircase and out into the street.

I now grip the woman by her shoulders. Her petrified daughter clings to her legs. The smoking ruins of Berlin reflect in her eyes. I shake her hard. She slowly begins to focus on me. What can I possibly say to her? Her hair lies lank around her pale white face. Her lips are trembling. I hold her tight in my outstretched arms and make eye contact at last.

A line from Rumi arises from somewhere within me,

"Where there is ruin, there is hope for treasure."

She hears me, of that I have no doubt, but she's hardly receptive to anything outside of her violated body. Her shaking hand reaches up for the crucifix hanging around her neck. She looks to the sky.

"Lord, why hast thou forsaken me?"

"God does not take sides," I shout over the noise. "If you had marched in those men's shoes, those shadows of men, their humanity crushed by this war, if you had to fight with death moment by moment you may understand that it, this, what they did to you, was not personal. They didn't even see you as a human being. Socialism? They betray the very idea.

Believe me they shall suffer for what they've done to you. The whole of Russia will tremble when I lay bare the truth of Communism to the rest of the world."

I stagger away from the woman and child, away from the direction of my unit and farther away from my once cherished homeland. I know the allies are closing in on West Berlin. I have to get to them before I am reported missing. My head throbs and my ears are muffled amidst a high-pitched whine that won't go away. I can no longer envisage normality. My nerves are shot at.

I stumble through a nightmarish landscape. I fear I'll meet the four horsemen of the apocalypse just over the next ridge or riding out of some bomb-blasted crater. But I understand with utmost shame that this desecration wasn't visited upon humanity by some outside deity. This isn't the result of God's wrath. All this death and destruction is the work of mankind itself. A Pandora's Box of evil has infected our souls. Good is bad, right is wrong, we have gorged on wicked appetites, feasted on vices and spewed out the resulting bile, destroying the very civilisation our forefathers had built.

I see the check-point up ahead. Upon seeing me, uniformed soldiers take up position, rifles trained on me.

"Comrades!" I cry, "I am a soldier of the Soviet Union. I have papers..." I reach inside my greatcoat.

"Keep your hands where we can see them, Rus." An English voice demands.

I raise my hands and keep walking.

"Turn around, Ivan." Another voice orders from behind the barriers. "Your men are back there, behind you."

"Yes." I nod, "but my future, I hope, lies behind you!"

CHAPTER FORTY-TWO

North Russia, 2015

Julia Stirling, now 23 years old, had been on a long journey. She had travelled on the Eurostar from London to Paris and then the Paris-Moscow Express and was now onboard the Trans-Siberian Express sending her deep into the old Soviet interior. The earlier part of her journey from Moscow saw her mingle with more cosmopolitan passengers. They were a generation removed from the iron fist of centralised control that had squeezed all initiative and enterprise out of the Russian people. This generation had moved on. And they now embraced liberty and technology with all the free-spiritedness of the Cossacks of old.

Julia gazed out of the window of the restaurant car as the red and grey Rossiya express train carved its way through the bitter Russian steppe. She'd finished her ham and eggs long ago and now nursed an iced tea. Primarily she'd gone into the restaurant car to get away from the vodka-swilling, hyper-active Russian computer geek who'd joined her in the 2-berth compartment from Nizhni-Novgorod. Thankfully, she knew he would soon be getting off at Perm to attend a coding conference at its State University.

Looking out at the seemingly endless Russian landscape Julia soon became lost in thought. But at least she no longer felt lost in the world, no longer cut adrift in a sea of confusion. It was reading Dimitri's diary that helped put her life in perspective. The depth of suffering, the deprivation; all provided a yardstick to measure against her own existence. Her insecurities regarding her looks and her body now seemed so vain and petty when pitted against the real life and death worries of her grandmother Violetta and her mother, Maria.

Even as a child, Julia had always thought her mother Maria had a strange relationship with her father. She never saw any signs of affection between them and found it odd they had separate bedrooms. The fact they conceived Julia proved they had at least shared one intimate moment.

Julia grew up in a family almost devoid of displays of love. Even a peck on the forehead at bedtime was rare. If, on the unusual occasion, they watched television together, Mum would *"tut"* loudly signalling Dad to switch channels if there was a hint of rudeness. Wildlife documentaries were a no-no. It was as if sex, intimacy or even the most innocent show of affection were taboo. No wonder her father, Robert, had eventually walked out on them.

Maria then continued to bring Julia up in a straight-jacket of moral prudishness. Sex was a dirty word. When conversation with friends turned to topics of a sexual nature, her cheeks reddened, her heart raced and she felt an awkwardness and alienation from what everyone else took as normal.

The rhythmic rumbling of the train brought Julia out of her daydream just as smoothly as it had lulled her into it. Between the miles of rolling, treeless terrain isolated stations passed by in a blur. Sombre faces on platforms. The more remote the station, the more these faces seemed pinched with poverty. Faces that said life is still hard. Hard too for the raven she saw gnawing at a frozen carcass on the windswept plains. An old Christmas carol played in her head. *In the Bleak Mid-Winter*, conjured up by the sight of snow falling on snow, snow on snow.

Julia had grown-up envious of the relationships her female friends had with their mothers. They were often like best friends, sharing intimacies, being open and honest with each other. Yet her mother, Maria, seemed to come from another generation altogether. And Julia had felt that the fear of physical intimacy had been passed on to her along with Maria's unspoken hatred of men. But now having read the diary of Dimitri, understanding what bitter experiences both her mother and grandmother had been through, she began to see Maria's maternal failings in a different light.

A small, rabbit-like mammal sped across the steppe and into a sprawling pine forest. The snow-covered trees looked cold and forbidding under the leaden sky. And, looking around at her grim faced co-passengers, Julia saw a populace whose very souls seemed to have been carved from this icebound landscape.

"You're a Westerner."

Julia turned in her seat. Across the aisle a stout, traditionally dressed old woman stared at her with dark feline eyes.

"Yes," Julia smiled, "how can you tell?"

"You smile too easily," she scrutinised Julia with perplexity, "it's not normal."

"Sorry."

"Smiling, apologising..." the woman cackled, "you'll never last out here."

"It must be a cultural thing," Julia murmured as she turned away and began to flick through her travel guide.

The weight of history showed in the old woman's face. Her words still coated with the bitterness of oppression. It seemed that deepest Russia, unlike Moscow, still bore the scars of yesteryear.

Julia was two days into her three day journey east. Upon departing Perm, along with the departure of her permanently sozzled travelling companion, she returned to her first-class, sleeper wagon. As the train cut through the barren plains of the tundra, blasted by the icy north wind, Julia rocked in her bunk and her thoughts turned to the last conversation she'd had with her mother.

Maria Stirling was suffering the onset of Alzheimer's and wanted to put her affairs in order before the inevitable decline. Laid up in her bed she showed Julia an old, battered notebook.

"Remember all those years ago when we went to that graveyard in St Petersburg to find the disgraced Russian soldier?" Her mother asked.

"I remember." Julia answered.

"Mysteriously, this diary came into my possession not long afterwards. It is the war diary of Dimitri Petrov."

"The soldier who..."

"The soldier who your grandma, Violetta, asked me to forgive."

"I'm not a child any more. I know what awful things the Russians did to German women. Did this man, this Dimitri Petrov, rape Grandmother?"

"You always jump to conclusions," Maria shook her head.

"Conclusions?" Julia said, "It seems pretty obvious."

Her mother sighed.

"I thought the same as you until I came across Violetta's letters. She never said much. The war changed her."

"Rape would change any woman," Julia folded her arms.

"I don't know if it was that." Maria's eyes searched Julia's. "She never married again. There was sadness, a melancholy that accompanied her throughout her life. Only when she knew she was dying did she come alive again. I lived in Bonn back then. By the time I reached her bedside she could hardly talk. She whispered she loved me, the first time she'd said that since I was a child.

"Find Dimitri Petrov. Ask Dimitri to forgive me as I have forgiven him and his comrades. She then pressed a Russian

identity tag into my hand. I was shocked. It awoke long buried memories."

Julia watched her mother's blank gaze shift to fear as though she was reliving the past.

"I was five years old when the Russians arrived in Berlin. I had gone back to our apartment to get my dolls. I was unaware of the danger. But mother followed me. I was at the window looking at the soldiers in the street below. Mother tried to pull me away but a woman across the road looked up and pointed us out to the Russians."

Maria took a sip of water from the glass on the bedside cabinet. Her hands were trembling slightly.

"We quickly barricaded the bedroom door with furniture but it was futile. My mother hid me in a cupboard as they broke in," Maria became more agitated. "I could hear my mother's screams but I promised I'd stay hidden. I covered my ears and tried to stifle my crying. A stray bomb must have hit our house because the next thing I knew the walls collapsed, the ceiling caved in and I could see nothing but smoke."

She took a deep breath to compose herself.

"This," she held out an ivory capsule, "this is the identity tag of Dimitri Petrov, the man who saved me from burning to death. It came off in my hand as I clung to him, a terrified five-year old girl. My mother took it off me and I never saw it again," Maria sighed with exhaustion. "His name and regiment were written on a slip of paper inside. After Violetta died I also found a small box of newspaper cuttings and a love-letter from someone called Josef. I never found out the truth, Julia, but I pray you do. It's the only thing that matters in the whole world."

Julia had packed her belongings and was now wearing thermals beneath her jeans, woollen layers and padded black Parka. She was back in the restaurant car where the landscape had changed from snowy meadows and frozen streams to the rolling hills within the boreal forests of spruce, pine and larch trees of Eastern Siberia. Again she was struck by the sheer size of Russia. This immense space through which she travelled reflected the opening up of her own mind, providing her with the mental space in which to think.

There had always been a sadness and melancholy surrounding Maria too, thought Julia. They say the sins of the father can be passed down to their sons, is it true for women too? Can a mother's lifelong hatred of men be inherited by her daughter? As soon as she was old enough, Maria had rushed into marrying Robert Stirling, a colonel in the British Army Intelligence Corps. They relocated to England where Julia was born soon after. Within a few years they had separated and divorced.

Maria always kept her emotions in check and never showed Julia much maternal love. She seemed weighed down by the guilt of what happened to her mother, Violetta. But this revelation never came from Maria's lips. This was Julia's conclusion from years of trying to break down the walls of silence, years of wanting to give her mother a good shaking. Then she saw it happening to herself. The lingering death of her mother triggered off this introspection in Julia. First grief, and then depression descended on her, and the only way out was by digging up the past and by doing so, understanding it and exorcising the ghosts of family secrets.

The whistle of the train and the hiss and squeal of brakes brought her back to her surroundings

Irkutsk station was the end of the line for Julia. As the train slowed down she could see the massive grey domed roof above the turquoise and alabaster-white station building. Julia was one of many to disembark onto its busy platform where hawkers and babushkas were selling everything from woollen shawls and cuddly toys to porn magazines and smoked fish. The train set off immediately as though it couldn't get away fast enough. The snow fell steadily and a freezing cold wind whipped down the platform. It was so cold she could see everyone breathing misty clouds of air from their mouths and nostrils. Icicles hung at the edge of the long canopy, glistening like rabid fangs in the late afternoon light. She hurried inside where an old man in a balaclava and ill-fitting uniform tore her ticket in two.

"Welcome to Paris of Siberia." He said.

"It doesn't feel like the Paris I left." She shivered.

"You go far?" he asked, revealing bad dentistry.

"To Angarsk."

"Ah," he closed his eyes briefly, "Home of Russia's most violent serial killer." He made the sign of the cross over his chest before adding, "Good luck." Whether he was joking or not it was an ominous welcome.

Julia crossed through to the exit which opened onto a large promenade filled with cars, mini-buses and taxis. The distant mountaintops, looming in the fading light lent a rugged beauty to the place. It was a brutal charm. Julia felt she was in a wilderness at the end of the world. She was staying for one night in the Angara hotel which was two and a half miles from the train station. A tram passed in front of her. Through its windows, thick with condensation, she could see people wearing winter hats and heavy clothing crammed tight inside.

She made her way to the taxi rank.

Her guide book stated that many distinguished Russians had been banished to Irkutsk for their part in the Decembrist Revolt of 1825. That revolt was spurred by the harsh indignities suffered by Russian Army Officers during the Napoleonic war. Their protest against the repression of Tsar Alexander the Ist was also inspired by news of the American Revolution and the freedoms expressed in the US Constitution. Later, under Communism, even more prominent political prisoners were exiled to Irkutsk. The Guide book made the case that having so many intellectuals living in the city raised the average IQ level of its inhabitants.

"If you like to hunt and fish then you will be like a pig in the shit!" The taxi driver said in reply to Julia's question of what passed for entertainment in Irkutsk.

"We have television and sporadic internet," he rolled his eyes as he turned the radio down a notch. "I'm Vladimir by the way." His craggy, Slavic face was pock-marked and he smoked and talked excitedly. "And no," he raised his eyebrows and gave a lop-sided grin, "my surname is not

Putin, though I sometimes wish it was. Great man, Putin. Great man."

Julia was seated in the back of an old *Lada* taxi. Vladimir's eyes darted rapidly from the road to rear view and side mirrors as if ascertaining that they weren't being followed. He looked like he was on something illegal.

"There are places to dance and get drunk but not places where a woman should go by herself," he nodded at her through the rear view mirror from which hung a pennant of the Irkutsk coat of arms; a Siberian tiger with a sable in its mouth. "There is little crime here, but there are drugs available, if you should want them..."

"No thanks."

Julia had read about the AIDS epidemic that came to Irkutsk at the end of the 1990's. Heroin had come to Siberia from Afghanistan and Tajikistan and, through the sharing of needles, many ethnic Russians began testing positive for HIV during the early 2000's

"Why you here?" He asked.

"I'm researching for a book."

"A novel?"

"Not exactly. More a collection of old soldiers memories of the Second World War."

"History," he glanced at her again and then shook his head, "a past that has passed, let it pass."

Julia nodded.

"But to be ignorant of the past is to be doomed to repeat it."

They pulled up at a set of traffic lights.

"Speaking of the past," Vladimir said with one hand on the wheel, "there," he leant over and pointed through the passenger window, "can you see the Church of the Cross?"

"Ah yes," Julia replied, "a pinnacle of Siberian baroque architecture."

"Umnaya zadnitsa," he mumbled, putting his foot down again as the lights changed.

"I'm not a smart arse."

Vladimir glanced back at her in surprise.

"When in a foreign country it pays to learn a few phrases." Julia coolly gazed out the window. "Suss out places of interest," she said watching the snowflakes swirling and glinting in the traffic headlights, "and find out what local taxi drivers *should* be charging."

Julia met his gaze in the rear view mirror.

Vladimir smiled disarmingly.

"What can I say?" he shrugged, "he is dead who is faultless."

Julia rummaged in her bag and asked him if he knew the whereabouts of an address she had written on a card.

"You've come to see the Beast of Berlin?" His eyes opened wide with surprise.

"You know him?"

"Hardly, he keeps to himself. The beast lives with his Ukrainian wife on the outskirts of Angarsk." Then he added, almost boastfully, "It's the same place Russia's most prolific serial killer came from!"

"Yes, so I've heard."

"He's not friendly, this Beast of Berlin. Does he know you're coming to see him?"

"No, but I trust he will see me."

"Aha, trust indeed, but one must also verify."

Julia watched the quaint wooden houses passing them by.

"That's all I am looking for Vladimir, the truth."

"In Russia they say the truth is written with pitchfork on running water. Good luck finding that."

"I believe they also say it's better to be slapped with the truth than kissed with a lie."

"Hey, you know our proverbs!"

"Guide books are full of trivia."

"Here's one for you," he shuffled upright in his seat, "if you fear wolves, stay away from the forest. May be good advice for you not to go to Angarsk, no?"

"No." Julia replied deadpan. She looked out through her own reflection at the Soviet tower blocks in the distance. They loomed ominously in stark contrast to the nearby ornate, hand-carved timber homes that bore testament to the cultural heritage of Irkutsk's adopted exiles.

"Could you take me there tomorrow?"

"The arse-end of nowhere?" Vladimir huffed. He screwed his eyes and scratched his chin.

"I can take you part way there. You shall have to walk a short distance. The side roads are blocked. I will get you a map."

"Why did you call him the Beast of Berlin just then?"

"I'll let him tell you," a flash of impatience. His fingers tapped fretfully on the steering wheel as the tinny melody of a Russian pop song wafted from the car radio.

"War is a savage occupation," he sniffed. "I served for two years fighting the Chechens, which was nothing compared with World War Two, but even then I came to see that war," a faint shake of the head, "makes beasts of us all."

Vladimir pulled up outside the Angara hotel in Kirov Square and arranged to pick Julia up at ten o'clock the following morning.

The hotel appeared to be designed for corporate functions rather than tourists but that didn't matter to Julia. All she wanted was solitude and a good night's sleep. In the foyer two smart suited businessmen and a couple of women, who might have been prostitutes, were hunched over their drinks preoccupied with their smart phones. Dressed to impress but expressionless, their eyes were transfixed by the little screens, tapping, swiping and staring. The crisply uniformed receptionist was equally blank-faced and unsociable. Indeed the whole place still felt imbued with the atmosphere of Soviet-era conformity. But once in her small but spotlessly clean hotel room, Julia settled back on the firm bed and read an extract from a letter her grandmother Violetta had written to Maria.

Letter from Violetta

"I want you to know the truth about me, Maria. I have to write it down for even if I survive physically, mentally I am already 'missing in action'.

I could have settled for a comfortable, even privileged existence as the wife of a Nazi scientist. That is what your father was. I could have, yet something inside wouldn't let me. I realised that a gilded cage is still a cage. I'd tasted the

335

freedom of the stage, of expressing my innermost self, and was determined to remain true to that self.

It was the war that changed all that. It has taken my best friend and killed my lover, Josef. It's a shame you never knew Josef. He was a greater man than your father ever was. I'm using the past tense to describe your father because I believe he died in a street battle just outside Berlin in the final days of the war. I've been told he was holed up in a clock tower when a Russian tank blasted it from close range.

You must know too that I aided the fascist resistance. I engaged in sexual acts with top-ranking Nazi's to glean important information from them. Do not be ashamed of that. I'm not. One must use whatever talent one has when serving a higher cause.

I say I am not ashamed, but the strain of living a double life has taken its toll. As was the injustice of being accused of being a Nazi-lover by the hypocrites who will never know how many lives I've saved.

It was Monika, a girl from the theatre who betrayed us. I had gone back to our apartment to find you. At the window I saw Monika across the street drinking with Russian soldiers. She pointed to me and the soldiers looked up instantly. I later found out she'd told them I was a whore who had slept with many German officers. Before I could get us away from the window the biggest soldier threw his cigarette into the gutter and walked resolutely towards our apartment. The others must have followed...

My life has been a constant blurring of morality, of compromise and deceit, of pretending to be one thing, whilst trying to maintain my true identity. Could I assume a vice and expect my soul to remain unstained just because I knew it to be a vice?

The habit of doing evil things makes it easier to do more evil things. Learn from my mistakes, Maria. Small acts of evil, even when done for the greater good, can snare the unwary."

Julia's eyes were beginning to droop with exhaustion. She lay back on the bed and allowed the letter's contents to wash over her. It seemed Violetta was always being pulled in opposite directions. Violetta; the good operatic girl turning burlesque bad. Violetta; torn between a safe but loveless marriage and her dangerous love for Josef. Violetta; who made love to German officers whilst wanting to slit their throats.

Eventually, when pulled and twisted in opposite directions, even the strongest metal snaps. Violetta snapped. She disappeared from Germany and took Maria with her. They moved to Belgium. Maria and Robert Stirling eventually ending up in England years later.

Violetta never tried to justify her actions but she didn't need to live with the rumours either. All she'd lived and loved for had died in the hell-hole of Berlin. No, Julia reflected, it wasn't the brutality of any one man that broke Violetta's spirit. It was the brutality of all men of war.

David J Robinson

CHAPTER 43

"Why do Stasi officers make such good taxi drivers?" Vladimir asked, flicking his ash out the car window as they sped past the frozen fountain in Kirov Square. "You get in the car and they already know your name and where you live!"

He threw back his head and laughed a throaty laugh. In that instant his gurning face reminded Julia of a painting of Zaporozhian Cassocks seen in her guide book.

Julia could only muster a less-than-genuine laugh in reply. It wasn't the worst joke she'd heard but she wasn't in the mood. She hadn't slept well. Her mind had been beset by many images, thoughts and doubts as to why she was here at all. Images of those strange days in Berlin 1945, imagining her grandmother wanting to help in the clean-up operation and finding her offer shunned because of her reputation. Wondering why Violetta and then Maria would keep the identity tag of a soldier who, although he rescued her, had probably been part of that group of rapists?

Now, being rocked about by pot-holes in the back of an old, battered *Lada* taxi, she was on her way to find answers. She had tracked down a former comrade of Dimitri Petrov now living in this God-forsaken outpost of Russia. He would be an old man now but maybe, she hoped, he would remember enough to fill in the gaps.

Angarsk was the quintessential one horse town, a back-water of the old USSR frozen in ice and time. A town south of Irkutsk, it had the largest industrial zone in Asia. Full of old Soviet style apartments, the whole place seemed grey and drab. Angarsk's monochrome cityscape was punctuated with garish advertisement hoardings proffering pre-packed cold meats or jars of pickled herring. There was no comparison to the elaborate, hand-decorated wooden houses she'd left behind in Irkutsk. That's how Irkutsk got its nickname the Paris of Siberia, Vladimir had told her.

He dropped her off at the end of a dual carriageway by a row of buildings with dilapidated shop fronts.

"Visiting is good," he said poignantly, "but home is better."

He promised to be back in two hours.

Julia then had to trudge through knee high snow to reach the address. On her feet she wore a pair of Kamusi fur boots bought that morning from the souvenir stall in the hotel lobby. A low moaning came from the Sayan Mountains, at first she thought it was a dying creature, but it was just the sound of the wind rushing through the forest of the Angarsk pass. This suburb of Angarsk was full of wooden houses all groaning under the weight of snow and the sub-zero temperature. With their distinctive carvings on the wall and window frames she imagined this was what a typical Russian village would have looked like pre-industrialisation.

A grey owl swooped from the eaves of the small wooden dacha she was heading towards. It plunged its talons deep into the snow and took flight carrying off a struggling vole.

An inconspicuous silver haired, plump woman answered the door of the ramshackle home. Julia explained who she was. The old woman then went back inside. She returned a minute later and beckoned Julia inside. The woman, who she assumed was her would-be host's wife, then gestured Julia towards a door at the end of a narrow vestibule.

Cerenkov had his back to Julia when she entered the room. Empty bottles were on the floor beside him. An ashtray overflowed on his armrest. As she slowly walked towards him he turned and she saw his war ravaged face in the firelight. She knew now why they called him the Beast of Berlin.

Without a hint of surprise, in a deep Russian growl, he spoke.

"You took your time."

"You were expecting me? I only..."

"I was expecting someone from your generation," he spoke over her, "I knew one day my illustrious past would be dug up and brought steaming like shit to my door."

Cerenkov laughed loudly which turned into a catarrh-ridden cough.

"So, you're the Beast of Berlin?" She leant forward to shake his hand, "I'm Julia by the way."

He didn't respond.

Cerenkov motioned her to sit in the worn green armchair opposite his. An old Mosin-Nagent rifle hung on the wall. Threadbare rugs covered the floor. Grey lace curtains hung limply over windows thick with condensation. A musty damp smell permeated everything. On a crooked wooden mantelpiece over the fireplace stood a Matryoshka nesting doll. Next to that was a brass picture frame. Inside was a black and white photograph that showed the Russian flag flying over the smouldering ruins of Berlin.

"When you meet an old man it is like seeing an iceberg," Cerenkov caught her gazing at the photograph, "the bit you see, the feeble body, the slow moving mind, all is just above the water. The main body of his life lies beneath the surface of history. Not unfathomable, but are you sure you want to dive in and see his past? Swimming in icy waters can be dangerous and you might not like what you see."

She knew he was toying with her. His barely concealed disdain for this nosy western woman echoed the male-chauvinism of old Soviet society.

She asked him about the war.

"I too made it to the top of the Reichstag," he gestured towards the mantelpiece, "we flew the Red flag like we were saviours, liberators with pockets full of booty. Looking round at the destruction of Berlin, I felt like a conquering giant. I would return home as a hero to a life of luxury and ease..." Cerenkov cleared his throat. "Alas, the glimpse from the mountaintop is soon forgotten in the valley of ordinary life."

Julia could hear the wind wrapping itself around the dacha. It howled against the walls, doors and windows barring its route down the mountains to the bitter hard fields and open plains.

"I believe you and Dimitri Petrov were comrades back then. Do you remember?"

Cerenkov stiffened.

"I remember him. We weren't comrades."

"Do you remember what happened to him after the war?"

"I know he deserted."

"Was he a rapist?"

Cerenkov grunted.

"Who the fuck are you to ask these questions? To come here and examine our lives?"

"The unexamined life is not worth living," Julia replied.

"And the unlived life is not worth examining," Cerenkov growled.

"I'm only interested in Dimitri Petrov," Julia asserted "there was some connection between him and my grandmother."

"Ava?" He raised a bushy eyebrow.

"No, my grandmother who was an innocent citizen of Berlin. She was there when your army arrived."

"No-one was innocent."

Cerenkov breathed deeply. Like a snake before the strike, there was a malevolent stillness about him.

"It comes back to the same old question," he sighed, "why did the Red Army rape and pillage the *innocent* people of Berlin?"

"Go on then, why?"

Cerenkov's hooded eyes glistened with relish.

"The spoils of war. I fucked girls around your age. If I was not an old man I'd do the same again and you know what?" He gave a reptilian smile, "you'd enjoy it!"

"You're disgusting."

Cerenkov grimaced.

"That's it. Put your modern, western morality on a period of history you would never have survived. A time you know nothing about."

"Of course I know..."

"Oh you've read the history books and seen the films, yes very good. You've read a menu but you haven't tasted a damn thing!"

Julia understood his ravaged features now. Apart from the scars his was a face sculpted by years of bitterness and regret.

Cerenkov went on.

"I was ten years into a twenty-five year jail stretch. In a prison, in the heart of Russia, surrounded by a forest the size of Germany. Hundreds of miles from the nearest city.

"Wrongly convicted of rape, they let me out to fight in the war. To fight for the system that had incarcerated me. I was convinced after the war they would put me back there. I thought I might as well be a rapist as be condemned as one."

Cerenkov sat back in his chair and was silent for a few moments.

"In a way they kept their word. But Stalin's paranoia knew no limits back then. After the war I, along with many others, was accused of *counter-revolutionary crimes*. Condemned by a military tribunal I was deported along with the limbless samovars to the far north. You see my face, scarred and burned? Stalin thought the people of Moscow shouldn't be reminded of the cost of war. No-one wanted to be reminded of our losses and see thousands of wounded veterans on the streets."

He sighed deeply then took a deep breath.

"Years later, thanks to Khrushchev, I was allowed to live here in the back of beyond," he stroked his grey Van Dyke beard. "We have a saying, *that song is sweetest whose melody still takes us by surprise.*"

"That doesn't absolve you from your actions in Berlin." Cerenkov fumed.

"You dare to judge and condemn the allies who helped you win the war? We, who sacrificed millions of lives to defeat fascism, should heed the moral lectures from the world's great imperialists? Britain? A country with the shame of slavery and the guilt of empire around its neck? A country who themselves raped and pillaged their way through the Crusades and beyond?"

He slowly shook his head.

"All you talk of is rape. You have made too much of all that. As soon as the war was over, we Russians became your enemy. But your people knew we were heroes! How *did* you sully our name? By the kind of propaganda of which *Pravda* would be proud!"

"You now defend Communism?"

"I defend nothing. But," he breathed heavily, "if an ideal is hijacked by a tyrant, does that invalidate the ideal?"

"You admit Stalin was a tyrant?"

"Of course. In a way he had to be. Stalin was from Georgia. We Georgians love to drink, but when you're drunk you don't really see what's in front of you. When you're drunk on power, you see even less. *Silnaya ruka*, it's in our blood."

They were interrupted by Cerenkov's wife putting her head around the door. She addressed her husband sourly, mentioning something about hospitality and food, but Cerenkov dismissed her in a slur of angry Russian.

He went on.

"Stalin, after the war, wanted to promote the positive. Show that Communism, having beaten Fascism, would go on to conquer the world."

"But it didn't."

"That is the world's loss. Look at Russia now. Weak leaders like Gorbachev and Yeltsin were seduced by the West. They killed our economy. Before glasnost we were looked after from the cradle to the grave, given housing and enough food. It wasn't perfect but there was little crime because we all had the same.

"Now we are in no-man's land between communism and capitalism. Between lies about the past and corruption in the present. We have beggars on the roadside as the oligarchs drive by in their Jaguars. The mafia run things now, protection rackets, you name it. Thank you for civilising us backward barbarians."

Julia gazed out the window where a windswept cloud revealed a thin sickle moon high above the mountains.

"I didn't come for a lecture about Russia today."

"You mean you didn't come for the truth."

"Okay, truth," Julia sat up straight, "I've read Petrov's diary. After Ava died he seemed to lose his way..."

"Ava never died," Cerenkov said.

Julia was shocked.

"What?"

For a brief moment silence fell upon the room.

"The letter that told him she'd died was a fake."

"I don't understand," Julia was confused, trying to work out the implications.

"Fyodor the forger could turn his hand to anything."

"Why would he do that?"

Cerenkov hesitated for a fraction of a second, then said, "Because I told him to."

Julia's pretty features registered hurt and bafflement.

"You hated a man so much you stooped to that?"

"I blamed him for the death of my brother, Yuri."

"Yuri was your brother? You mean flesh and blood?"

"Yes. Brothers weren't allowed to serve alongside each other. It was seen as a distraction. We had to be fully committed to Stalin and the Motherland. Amidst the confusion of enlisting, Yuri used our mother's maiden name. I promised her I'd look after him."

"But Yuri would have been executed anyway. According to Petrov's diary Marchenko ordered you to kill your brother. At least Petrov saved you that ordeal."

"I never said I had no regrets."

"What happened to Ava?"

"After the war I did try to find her, to tell her what we'd done. But she had disappeared. Her family said she was devastated to hear Petrov had gone missing-in-action. She went to find him."

"Did she?"

"You tell me. He was in your country."

"England?"

Cerenkov nodded.

"I saw him walk over to the British lines. Marchenko denounced my failure to stop him as a counter-revolutionary action. For that, I was sent to that frozen wasteland *Belaya Zemlya* for years. It was kept secret he'd defected but, to dishonour his name, missing-in-action became deserter, traitor and coward."

"He came to England? Are you sure?"

"It's true."

There was a moments silence as she took it all in.

"I was sorry for your brother."

Cerenkov's lizard smile returned.

"You don't know much, do you?" He looked at Julia scornfully, "Yuri survived the war."

"What?" Julia shook her head in disbelief.

"When Petrov took him to the woods, he whispered to Yuri to make a run for it. Yuri thought he was going to shoot him in the back. No, it was to give him more time. Petrov must have known there were German corpses in that forest. He fired three shots into the trees and dragged a dead German out to the clearing and into a shallow grave. Yuri was on his own again, but this time he made it back. He saw our mother before she died. So now you understand my regret over the fake letter about Ava? We could see Petrov was a ghost of the man who joined up. That letter was intended to crush the only thing he had left – hope."

"Is Yuri still alive?"

"No. Back in Georgia he went working in the mines. He laboured for many years until a landslide collapsed the pit and killed him. He left a young wife and child. But at least he'd lived longer than the Motherland decreed, thanks to Petrov."

"So now you forgive Petrov? You should pray he forgave you."

Cerenkov sighed and lit his pipe.

"Another comrade, Vasily, once said, *to understand all is to forgive all,*" he nodded sagely, "I don't understand all, but I can forgive a little."

"Vasily was mentioned a lot in Dimitri's diary. What became of him?"

"I never saw Vasily again. After the war I heard he married a Jewish woman called Rula."

"Rula!" Julia exclaimed, remembering the name from Violetta's letters.

"Yes. He was in one of the units that liberated a transit camp in Berlin. He was always a gentleman, Vasily. I believe he protected her from the likes of me and they ended up falling in love. They settled in East Berlin if memory serves me well. At least he met a better fate than the rest."

"What do you mean?"

"Colonel Marchenko was shot and killed by Fyodor just after Germany's surrender. Against all odds Fyodor made it to Berlin. But he knew there was no way back to civilian life from a schtraff unit. So he took the life of his nemesis... then he took his own."

"That's terrible," Julia frowned.

"Worse was what happened to Oleg and Ivan. Thinking it was alcohol, they celebrated our hard won victory by drinking from metal barrels containing industrial solvent. From that moment they were dead men walking. It poisoned them. They died in agony within days."

Silence fell between them as the fire crackled and spat beneath that picture of their historic victory.

Julia stood to leave.

"Why don't you to go back to Georgia? You don't have to stay banished here forever?"

"I'm not banished from my homeland," he replied coldly. "When you love a place or a person with all your heart there is no such thing as separation." Cerenkov leaned back in his chair as if exhausted, "I pray Petrov found this to be true."

The wind had died down and the afternoon light fading as Julia left Cerenkov's dacha ruminating on his complex character. One minute castigating the communist regime, the next defending it. His indifference was typically Russian. Yet his permanently etched grimace was for the world to see how bravely he suffered. Julia compared this contrived stoicism to the tough zeal of a man like Avakov. Dimitri's diary showed his was no self-conscious hardiness. Avakov's quiet strength emerged from the virtue of infinite patience.

Orphan of the State

Dimitri's diary had been an account of one man's slow descent into a psychological hell. *'To understand all is to forgive all'*, Cerenkov had said. Would Dimitri have been able to forgive Cerenkov and Fyodor for making him believe Ava was dead? Julia wondered.

What became of him in England? Did Ava ever find out that is where he had gone? Would she ever understand why?

As Julia walked away down the snow-covered lane leading away from Cerenkov's dacha she was suddenly accosted by his wife. Wrapped in a beige shawl and a red headscarf she introduced herself in broken English as Tatiana.

"You in the liberal west must understand." She said forcefully. "Power is a virtue; strength is a quality of God. Without Stalin's strength of will we would still be in the dark ages. For sure, we made mistakes along the way because we were so eager to catch up with the industrial West. But I doubt any other worker in the world felt as proud as we did." She spoke quickly, breathlessly. "We workers were the heroes of the Soviet Union. The hardest workers were rewarded – a bigger house, a car. Born in Ukraine, my family moved to Moscow where I went to work on the metro. On your way home go look at it. What a legacy to Stalin and the workers."

Julia was surprised at her eloquence.

"For a brief moment in time we, the workers, were the shooting stars of the revolution. Poetry praised us, artists painted us as gods, taming nature to glorious ends. Whether true or not, we believed in what we were doing; building the workers' paradise."

"But do you not now feel betrayed?" Julia said.

"Were we betrayed? Were we deluded? It matters not. What a man or woman believes themselves to be... they are!"

Julia stamped her feet to get warm yet Tatiana seemed oblivious to the cold.

"But here's a simple truth, my husband is not like me. As cynical as a magpie, he claims he didn't go to war for anyone. But I believe deep down – subconsciously maybe – he fought for the Russian land and all the Russian people; the souls of the living and memories of the dead."

"What a patriot," Julia huffed, "you must be so proud."

"The word *patriotism* covers all we did and died for." Tatiana picked up on the sarcasm. "In your world patriotism is seen as antiquated, racist even. Yet without it we would never have defeated fascism. Patriotism goes beyond leaders, beyond politics and ideals; it is the very core of our being."

"Forgive me, but it's also the last refuge of the scoundrel." Julia said.

"No no, you misunderstand." Tatiana shook her head and gripped tighter on her shawl. "We may have been suppressed, we may have been treated badly by Stalin, but we never stopped loving each other, the peasantry, our sacred land, our achievements and *that*, to me, is patriotism. We may not be perfect but we'll defend our imperfections with our last drop of blood."

She started to walk away.

"One more thing," Julia called after her. "I'm curious. How the hell did you manage to tame your beast of a husband?"

Tatiana turned back to Julia and shrugged,

"The same way you tame any man," she scowled, "by filling his belly and emptying his balls."

Two hours later a cold wind scoured the platform as Julia boarded a train bound for Moscow Airport. She left Irkutsk knowing there was more forgiveness to be sought and a lot more of Dimitri Petrov's actions to understand.

David J Robinson

CHAPTER 44

Secret Service Offices

West Berlin 1945

Dimitri Petrov squinted at the brightness of the interrogation room and shuffled towards the three-legged stool. He caught sight of his wretched state in the wall mirror. His wrists and ankles were in chains. His nose and throat were still raw from the dust and smoke of Berlin. He'd no idea where he was. Insomnia and headaches had fragmented his memories of the last few days.

Dimitri only recalled one recurring dream.

It was dusk and he was alone in Paris walking round and round the base perimeter of the Eiffel tower. He was dressed as a soldier and thick snow crunched beneath his boots. Then he saw a figure shimmering in the Parisian gloom. She walked slowly towards him with all the grace and poise of a dancer. It was Ava. The gap between them was shorter than at any time since he'd left for the war, yet Dimitri feared his experiences there had opened up an insurmountable gulf between them.

Like the fixed course of the stars above, they didn't run but walked slowly towards each other. Fate, and an iron will forged in the furnace of true love, ensured their destiny lay in each other's arms.

"I waited," Ava spoke, searching his eyes.

"I knew you would."

"I knew you would come back to me."

They kissed, lost in a world of their own.

"I don't think I'm the same man who left Moscow. There's been so much...."

"Shhh," Ava gently brought her finger to his lips, "the past cannot touch us here."

Suddenly the ground seemed to tremble beneath Dimitri's feet. He looked around, horrified to see the Eiffel Tower and buildings all made of plastic and the fake snow lying all about. Ava, as if she read his mind, held him close and placed her hand on his heart.

"Only this is real. Only love is real...My love."

The sky darkened as the ground shook violently sending the snowflakes billowing up into the air, swirling fantastically before Dimitri's eyes.

When the snow settled, Ava was gone.

Mary Sinclair sat writing notes at a small table opposite. Hair scraped into a bun, her whole look was austere and no-nonsense. She glanced up at the 'defector'. He struggled to sit down.

"What's with the limp?" she frowned.

"Shrapnel wound, Berlin," Dimitri croaked. He then coughed to clear his throat. "Doing my bit for the allied cause." Dimitri subtly pressed home the point that they were supposed to be on the same side.

Sinclair returned to her notes.

"We'll get the doctor to take a look at it."

Feign concern. Let the detainee think he has some worth, and that these are decent, civilised people dealing with him.

She recalled Rudy's briefing comments.

If we want to turn agents we must convince them to the core that we are better people than the Communists, that we're moral people. They must believe in the Capitalist system.

"On the other hand, a limp can be used by a spy to send a signal to other spies. A warning perhaps?"

"Well, unless you're a spy, or my prison guard is a spy, then I guess I'm wasting my time. But as long as I don't forget which leg I'm supposed to limp with I'll be fine."

His sarcasm noted, Sinclair played a straight bat.

"You put a small pebble in the shoe to remind you. It's a basic form of spy-craft, Mr Petrov, up there with sticking a cushion up your jumper to appear fat, or using your semen as invisible ink."

"Charming." Dimitri looked up and met her flatly hostile gaze.

"Charming, exactly. That's what you want us to think of you, the charming idealistic young Russian who's had enough of Communist hypocrisy and undergoes a Damascus-like conversion to Western ideology."

"That is an accurate description, yes," Dimitri coughed, "but you don't believe me do you?"

"Put it this way, I need a lot more convincing of your bona-fides as a defector. Disillusion with your Kremlin masters is not strong enough reason to leave everything you love behind, family, friends, sweetheart...?"

Dimitri sighed.

"Have you not read my diary?"

"I want to hear it from your lips, Mr Petrov."

"I was orphaned and raised by the state. Sure, I'll miss my uncle but he always loved the bottle more than he loved me. My sweetheart, you will recall if you've actually *read* the diary, died whilst I was fighting my way into Berlin. I have left nothing behind but a broken dream and a corrupt society."

Sinclair put her pen down and looked at Dimitri.

"I'm sure there are Tommies out there who have similar sob stories, who feel let down by King and Country. But we're not seeing any defections to Russia."

"Maybe they've all read *Brave New World*," he gave a ghost of a smile.

Sinclair checked her notes.

"You studied English language and history. What perfect grounding for a spy. Know your enemy indeed."

Dimitri looked heavenwards and saw only a grey plastered ceiling above him.

"It was an orphanage education for God's sake, hardly Eton. Look, I enjoy Dickens almost as much as I enjoy Dostoevsky. Elgar is good, but I actually prefer Mussorgsky." His voice became hoarser and he cleared his throat again. "I feel Peter the Great was a better monarch than Richard the III, but that is the past. That is the Russia I romanticised, not the Russia of today. A place I cannot bear to return to."

"Are you sure you've not romanticised the West too, Petrov? This is no longer the land of chivalrous knights, fair maidens and fair play. It never was. So, cut the bullshit. What do you want from us?"

"Us?"

"England, Great Britain... the state? You yourself mentioned our being allies with Russia. Privately we have our misgivings but the public must see us as allies. It helps promote stability within society. If we revealed your diary today it will send Anglo-Soviet relations back years."

"Yes, but it will advance the Russian people by years. All the hypocrisy of Stalin and the Politburo shall be revealed one day, the truth will come out. Together we can speed up the process, maybe save thousands of lives."

Sinclair shook her head and gathered her papers.

"You're no use to us. Your diary is patchy at best." She shouted over her shoulder, "Guard!"

"Wait!" Dimitri breathed heavily. "I have a friend in the NKVD."

Sinclair regarded him for a second then dismissed the guard who'd just come into the room.

A sheen of sweat began to spread out across Dimitri's back.

I can't go back.

A feeling of dread in his gut.

He coughed again then spoke slowly, hesitantly, "I only mentioned him once in my diary but I actually met him and he told me of classified secrets I have committed to memory."

Sinclair was still shaking her head.

He could feel the perspiration on his scalp.

"He gave me information. Secrets the West needs to know." Dimitri's breathing became shallower. "Have you heard about the Katyn Forest massacre?"

Sinclair looked blank.

"Lenin's Testament?"

He couldn't hide the desperation in his voice.

"The gulags?"

The sweat started to trickle down his back.

"The show-trials?"

Sinclair pursed her lips and looked down at her notes.

"I didn't think so," Dimitri gasped.

Sinclair sat back and looked at Dimitri as if she'd just had an idea.

"There is a way you could save thousands of lives."

360

He took a deep breath.

"How?"

"By going back to Russia. By claiming it was shell-shock that made you leave. We could say we treated you for both that and the shrapnel wound and send you back."

Dimitri's blood ran cold.

"Why would I want to go back?"

"To show you care, to get us to believe in you, to become our spy."

"You think *I'm* a Soviet spy and you're trying to turn me?"

"Yes."

"That's not going to happen."

Sinclair shrugged.

"I didn't expect you to say yes straight away. You think it over," she shuffled her papers and nodded to the guard through the one way mirror.

"*We* have all the time in the world."

David J Robinson

CHAPTER 45

London 2015

T he Gentleman's club was just off Pall Mall. After the frantic pace of city life, the flashing neon, ceaseless traffic, tourists and shoppers, it was an oasis of tranquillity. The elaborately carved stone archway ensured those passing through knew they were entering a world of privacy, privilege and meretricious respectability. A mosaic tiled lobby stretched off into various corridors and rooms. An old caged elevator smoothly lifted Julia up to her awaiting host.

It had been a month since her encounter with Cerenkov. After extensive enquiries and use of the freedom of information act, Julia had been allowed to meet with a retired foreign office diplomat called John Hodgkinson.

Hodgkinson greeted her in the coffee room and warmly guided her towards two high wing-backed leather chairs either side of a wood burning fireplace. Dust motes floated in the afternoon's fading sunlight streaming in through huge Georgian windows with tied-back royal blue curtains. A fresco of the battle of Waterloo took up the far wall and a portrait of the Duke of Marlborough hung over the fireplace. Over the years, Julia mused, this bastion of colonial Englishness must have borne witness to crucial discussions of state, conspiracy-fuelled gossip and off-the-record secrets whispered by the upper echelons of society. It was the social hub of business, commerce, intrigue and scandal.

"All of history is dead." John Hodgkinson took in the room with a sweep of his arms. "But all the consequences of history are alive in this very moment."

Hodgkinson was a convivial little man, with razor wit belying his portly demeanour. He spoke with the dark warm voice of a broadcaster.

"Don't patronise me and don't be obsequious and we'll get on fine," he assured Julia. "I've acquired special dispensation to get you in here today."

Julia settled into her chair and studied his features. Half moon glasses accentuated his wide eyes which seemed younger than the translucent skin around them. His sagging jowl and age-spots contrasted sharply with the starched white collar, pristine tie and bespoke tailoring. He reminded her of a character from the Pickwick Papers.

"The sad thing about all this," he spread his fingers like a cat's cradle, "is that I really liked him."

"Dimitri?"

"No. Rudy. We'll get onto the Russian later."

"Who's Rudy?"

"Good question? I've asked myself that a lot over the years. Coffee?"

"Tea please."

Hodgkinson ordered off a passing waiter.

"This, er... Rudy? Is that a pseudonym?" Julia asked.

"You know," he smiled, "it could well have been. No doubt his real name was something similar. Keep a lie as close to the truth as possible, don't they say?"

"Do they?" Julia looked at him blankly.

"Well, officially, his father named him Rudyard, after his fondness for the work of Rudyard Kipling. You know Kipling, he wrote the poem 'If'?"

"Now who's patronising who?" Julia answered.

"Yes quite," Hodgkinson chuckled. "Well, although Rudy had the knack of walking with kings without losing the common touch, he ignored the most important part of the poem. Rudy most definitely dealt in lies. In fact, you could say that lying defined him."

"No disrespect," Julia shuffled in her seat, "but who the hell is Rudy?"

Somewhat offended by her tone, Hodgkinson fixed her with his eyes.

"Leonardo da Vinci stated that the noblest pleasure is the joy of understanding," he replied, "if you want to understand what happened to the Russian, you need to hear Rudy's story

365

first. I'll tell you all I can but, be aware young lady, even today I am still bound by the official secrets act."

Feeling admonished, Julia sat up straight and set her attention on every word Hodgkinson was saying.

"Working at the foreign office, Rudy was diligent, hardworking and focussed. He rose quietly through the ranks, never gossiped and never got involved in office politics. Like a ghost he moved seamlessly through all the positions of officialdom without anyone really knowing him, apart from me. I was the nearest he had to a friend. I admired his intellect and ferocious work ethic.

"Born in India to an English father and an Indian mother, he was educated at Cambridge but extremely naive, or so I thought. I felt sorry for his lack of social skills and, as a good Christian, went out of my way to befriend him and open him up to the delights of London society. My wife, Phyllis, had me invite him for dinner where she tried to fix him up with her friend Lucy from the W.I. My word," Hodgkinson shook his head, "that was the most awkward dinner I've ever had to sit through. The conversation was so stilted and strained, Rudy made no pretence of cordiality. He positively raged at me afterwards, saying I had no right to manipulate him in that way."

"Good God, man! Lucy's a real looker." I told him. *"I'd be interested myself if I wasn't already married."*

"Since then my wife was convinced he was a homosexual. Rudy was always dapper, with manicured nails but I couldn't believe it. Until an incident on Hampstead Heath late one night. He was found in a distressed state. Claimed to have been mugged. His wallet, shoes and, even more intriguingly, his trousers had been stolen. We managed to keep it out of the papers but he never received an invite from my wife again."

The waiter returned carrying a tray with a small teapot and a glass cafetiére alongside two china cups. He placed it down gently on a table besides Hodgkinson.

"So where does Dimitri fit in here?" Julia slightly narrowed her eyes, looking attentively at him.

Hodgkinson tapped his fingers on the armrest and gazed into the middle distance.

"I remember the day well," he began, gravely. "I knocked on his office door. Rudy was sitting in his leather chair smoking a pipe, pen in hand, scanning over a document."

"We've got a defection, Rudy," I said.

"A what?" His pipe nearly fell from his mouth.

"A Russian soldier. Handed himself over in Berlin two days ago."

Rudy himself had just got back from Berlin where he'd been working undercover for months.

"Now why would he do that?" Rudy was up on his feet pacing the room as he always did when mulling over problems. "He could return home as a war hero. Was he in one of the units to liberate Berlin?"

"Looking back," Hodgkinson blinked agitatedly as he poured his coffee, "that was the most animated I'd seen Rudy in a long time. I thought he was as excited as I was at getting a new 'tongue' on our side."

I nodded. "In exchange for a new life in Blighty he's offering us his diary and classified Soviet secrets from an NKVD source. He also claims to know the whereabouts of Russian spies in the upper reaches of the establishment... as if!"

"Huh," Rudy grunted tapping the base of his pipe, "as if."

Hodgkinson fell into a dreamy silence and took a sip of his coffee.

"With hindsight," he went on, "I see Rudy had the uncanny knack of sensing where the mood was. He identified the most powerful person on whom his future depended then worked his way into their intimate circle. By now he'd inveigled his way into the inner sanctum of the Secret Intelligence Service, MI6."

They were briefly interrupted by a small group of men entering the room and crossing the floor. Julia caught snippets of their murmuring;

"Didn't know the old boy still had it in him!"

"John always was a charmer."

"I wonder if Phyllis knows!"

Laughing quietly to themselves they disappeared through an adjacent doorway.

"Where was I?" Hodgkinson resumed. "Ah yes, Rudy. Shadowy and secretive, I never saw his talent for running with the hare whilst hunting with the hounds. He was known to have flirted with communism at university, but," Hodgkinson smiled faintly, "who hadn't?"

Julia was becoming restless. She sipped her tea though and let him carry on.

"Rudy always had a chip on his shoulder. Maybe because he was born in India and was taunted as a foreigner at school, maybe it was his latent homosexuality, who knows what makes a man feel inferior to his peers?" He asked rhetorically. "Perhaps it was this feeling of inferiority, itching and writhing inside Rudy that led him to Marxism and from there onto full-blown Communism."

"He was a communist?" Julia scrutinised him with perplexity, "working in MI6?"

"I know," Hodgkinson shifted uneasily in his chair, "embarrassment is not the word. Not the first time though and probably not the last, eternal vigilance and all that, what?"

Hodgkinson cleared his throat.

"Have you read the Communist Manifesto?"

Julia was about to answer but Hodgkinson rattled on.

"Great bedtime reading, it had me snoring in seconds. Dry, dull and repetitive, I fail to see how it inspired anyone to take up arms for its 'cause'. One passage stood out to me though. Something about the Communists knowing better than the Proles what's good for them. Can you believe that? It's saying they represent the people but the people cannot be trusted. Those sentiments could have come from any one of their long line of Tsars and despots."

"Please!" Julia interrupted with a flash of impatience in her voice, "can we get back to his connection with Dimitri?"

Hodgkinson gazed intently into the poor girls face.

"Ah yes, the Russian." Hodgkinson leant forward rubbing his hands together. "The British establishment didn't know what to do with him. There had been no publicity of his

369

arrival. And although we were keen to hear what he had to say about Soviet secrets, we had no intention of embarrassing Russia, or ourselves for that matter, not now in the afterglow of our greatest triumph." Hodgkinson glanced briefly out of the darkening window as rain began to fall.

"And what about the Russian side of the story?" Julia pressed him. "Surely any defection was bad for them?"

"Well they played it down too. It forces a nation to search its soul when their bravest and best seek a better life elsewhere. Only a few knew about Dimitri's defection, some members of his platoon, a few NKVD, and a small cabal within the Politburo. In their eyes he was a traitor – pure and simple. Officially they let it be known he'd brought disgrace to the Red Army with his *acts of immorality,* Soviet-speak for *rapings,* and that in the death throes of the war had simply gone missing-in-action. They blackened his name and covered their bloody arses in case we tried to use him in some propaganda war."

His descent into crudity brought Julia to attention.

"So let me get this straight," she asserted, "Dimitri was stranded in a no-man's land between both countries?"

"Ha ha, yes, that's a good way to put it!" Hodgkinson blinked. "But you have to remember the times we were living in back then. We, in Britain," he stressed, "had many prominent people vouching for the Communist system. Poets, writers, influential people, all believed in the Communist utopia. This diary would have sent shock-waves both East and West."

He cleared his throat and leant in towards Julia.

"And, nasty as the cold war was, it never became full-blown, all-out-war which would have cost us, them and the world dearly. We thought it better to let Communism wither on the vine, be exposed slowly, bit-by-bit to reveal its true hypocrisy. The words Khrushchev used to describe Capitalism as *'a dead herring in the moonlight, gleaming brilliantly as it rots'* – were actually more appropriate to Communism."

Hodgkinson summoned a waiter and persuaded him to bring them two small whiskies. Darkness had descended upon the London skyline and the rain began to hammer hard against the high windows.

"And Dimitri?" Julia gently pressed him.

"Rudy had personally taken on Dimitri Petrov's case and, after several interviews, wrote a report to the effect that he was a vegetable, shell-shocked. Post-traumatic stress as we call it these days. That, plus the fact there were no official dates or locations in his diary, made it impossible to corroborate his claims."

With an effort of will Julia kept her expression neutral but inside she was starting to feel nauseous.

Hodgkinson sighed.

"Rudy reported to me. His opinion was that Petrov's worth as an informant was negligible. He even suggested Petrov might be a spy."

"The Russians say he went missing in action," I told him.
"Well they would, wouldn't they?" Rudy fired back.
"That is also a euphemism for a deserter," I replied.

371

"Better for them to label him a deserter, with connotations of cowardice, than a hero who wants nothing more to do with his homeland."

"Hmm," I pondered, "it is suitably vague for the Communists, 'missing-in-action'."

"They know where he is and what he's doing here," Rudy scoffed, "they bloody sent him!"

"How can you be so sure?" I asked.

Rudy relaxed back into his chair. Hands behind his head, he shrugged.

"You get a feel for these things. This diary for instance," his arm swept over the heavily redacted photo-copies on his desk, "it's too good to be true. It chronicles the slow disenchantment of a former Soviet devotee. If he was an ordinary soldier like he claims, and not a spy, there is no way he'd be allowed to keep such a diary."

"You give too much credence to Soviet discipline," I countered.

Rudy ignored that.

"There are no dates, no accurate place descriptions. He didn't even have a dog-tag for Christ's sake. I think it has all been made up to get us to believe his story. There's a Russian name for this kind of set-up, Maskirovka. It means a little masquerade."

"As usual," Hodgkinson gave a shake of the head, "I was taken aback by his grasp of detail when it came to the Russians. Rudy went on,"

"Sun-Tzu described warfare as the path of eternal cunning. The Russians have, more than anyone, perfected these techniques over the centuries. Techniques to wrong foot the enemy, sow seeds of confusion and to hide the truth behind a phalanx of lies."

"I was out of my depth." Hodgkinson raised his hands, "Rudy was persuasive."

"Anyway, it matters not. Mentally he's a bloody mess. I've had him secured at Holloway Sanatorium. He's under the best Doctor who will alert me to any improvement in his condition. But he doesn't hold out too much hope."

"What are you saying? Is he permanently insane or just temporarily deranged?"

Rudy smiled glibly.

"The former I'm afraid, old boy. It's a shame. We could have used him in the war against Russia."

"But we're not at war with Russia. Hopefully we never will be!"

"Aren't we?" Rudy lit another cigarette. "What about Operation Unthinkable? Churchill talks about an iron curtain descending across Eastern Europe. We may have beaten fascism but we now face the creeping dangers of communism."

Julia intervened.

"Operation Unthinkable? What the hell was that?"

Hodgkinson shifted uncomfortably in his chair.

"Operation Unspeakable more like," he took out a handkerchief and blew his nose loudly. "It was some crazy plan for Britain and the United States to make a pre-emptive strike on Russia immediately after the war. As you can imagine it was top secret. For Joint Planning Staff only. The fact Rudy knew about it set off alarm bells in my head."

Julia considered the situation.

"So by now did you not suspect Rudy was a Russian spy?"

Hodgkinson took a large gulp of whisky and shivered slightly.

"Rudy *was* partial to vodka," he gazed at the fire and smiled to himself, "and I once caught him whistling Tchaikovsky's Swan Lake, but apart from that.... We all thought him an oddball, but a brilliant oddball and anyway, aren't we Brits supposed to love a great eccentric?"

Julia shrugged knowing he didn't actually expect an answer. What tiny flame of hope she'd had was fading inside her. As she took a sip of her whisky, Hodgkinson went on.

"But looking back I always sensed Rudy despised the class system of the time, the right school tie, the old boy network. The foreign office, like all Government offices, was manned by the upper classes who thought themselves 'better' in every way than the rest of society. Rudy hated all that and he obviously thought the Empire was in terminal decline and that Communism was the only hope for mankind."

Julia gazed up at the Corinthian columns around the exterior walls. "Well he was right about the Empire at least." On the mantelpiece she observed a bust of Sir Humphry

Davy and one of Michael Faraday. Opposite was a painting of Cecil Rhodes. Valued remnants from the days of the Realm.

"Nonetheless, a few months later there were solid allegations of betrayal." Hodgkinson became animated once more. "We had a mole working for us in the Polish Intelligence Service – a satellite department of the NKVD. Our mole found lots of British Secret Service documents in their possession which they of course would share with the Russians. We had all the Polish material re-evaluated many times, painstakingly cross-referenced and cross-checked with every report that had landed on Rudy's desk over the years. Access to these papers had been highly restricted but Rudy had been on the distribution list every time. Typically, Rudy dismissed it out of hand."

"How can we trust this 'source' in Poland? And anyway I'm not the only agent who had access to those documents."

"But, as I mentioned before, Rudy, using the codename *Sebastian*, had also spent time working for us undercover in Berlin during the war. Soon, another allegation emerged that on the sly he'd been trading information with the Germans. He'd been accused of giving up the names of remnant Jews and anti-fascist members still active in Berlin. For these activities we found he used yet another alias, *Otto*."

Julia's brow furrowed in concentration.

"He rebuffed that charge with real aplomb," Hodgkinson smiled. "I could see why he'd got so far up the ladder, but it was all a bit too slick, a bit too mechanical. I'd be apoplectic if I'd been accused of betraying my country. Rudy was calm. In retrospect it was as if he'd expected to be caught out one day."

"When was all this?" She asked.

"This was eighteen months after the war. I even brought up the subject of our forgotten Russian soldier, left to rot in a secure sanatorium, suspended in a morass of bureaucratic aspic."

"There are things coming to light, Rudy. Things like the Katyn Forest massacre, the Testament of Lenin, things that Dimitri Petrov warned us of before he became incarcerated. The Home Secretary wants a second opinion on his state." Rudy glanced up at me but said nothing. "There's a lot we can do now with mental traumas, shock therapy for example."

Julia shivered at the thought.

"Why *had* Rudy insisted on taking over his case?" Hodgkinson narrowed his eyes and pursed his lips. "Because Rudy *himself* was a spy and a genuine defector may have pointed him out to us. But Rudy just chain-smoked, sipped his vodka and gave the impression he had loftier things on his mind than being worried what his peers thought of him."

Julia was transfixed as she distractedly finished her whisky. Hodgkinson was quick to notice and immediately ordered two more.

"Before I left him," Hodgkinson went on, "I told him an SIS tribunal wanted to grill him on the Secret Service leaks. He also faced questions about being spotted and photographed with a minor diplomat from the Russian embassy. They'd give him a harder time than I did. I was his friend and still wanted to believe him, even if only to save face for not having rooted him out earlier!"

Julia sat pale and motionless.

"But Rudy didn't answer me," Hodgkinson looked down sadly, "he just blew smoke rings towards the ceiling as he stared into the distance."

"Rudy, if you don't attend this tribunal you'll be arrested, it won't look good you know?"

He gave a non-committal shrug, downed his glass and closed his eyes.

"Of course I'll be there, old boy," he brightened, "what have I got to hide?"

"He flashed me that winning smile of his, but whether it was the vodka or the lateness of the hour, even that trade-mark Rudy-ism now seemed as sincere as a Judas kiss. I never saw him again."

Julia took it all in as she gazed over Hodgkinson's shoulder at the rain-blurred glass frontage.

"What happened to him?" She asked, swirling her newly served whisky around her glass.

"He disappeared into thin air," Hodgkinson raised his eyebrows. "Was he a Russian spy? Absolutely! A later search of his Dolphin Square apartment found an expertly concealed Praktina document-copying camera. But Rudy wouldn't face his allegations and fled when he realised the game was up. Officially he became just another missing person. Thousands of people disappear each year and it was most convenient, to save the embarrassment of the British Government, that Rudy was one of them."

Julia met his gaze.

"And what became of Dimitri?"

"I'm afraid that's where this story ends."

Julia's shoulders slumped despondently.

"Around the same time, Dimitri suffered a massive heart-attack in the sanatorium and died. For once in this whole sordid affair the Foreign Office did the decent thing and had his ashes sent back to Russia. They only buried the ashes after the fall of Communism. I am told what remains of Dimitri are laid to rest in a cemetery just outside St Petersburg."

"That's it?" Julia had tears in her eyes.

"I can see you wanted a 'happy ever after' my dear."

"It just seems I've come this far for nothing. The story comes to a dead end."

Hodgkinson paused momentarily then leant forward smiling.

"I said that's where *this* story ends," he tapped his nose, "official secrets act, remember?"

Julia nodded.

"You want to know more? I can point you to a lady who isn't bound by such an act."

"Is there more to know?"

Hodgkinson leant back and clasped his hands over his chest.

"You know how Churchill described Russia as a riddle wrapped in a mystery inside an enigma? Well,"

Hodgkinson's eyes twinkled mischievously. "This Russian doll has yet more layers to reveal."

David J Robinson

CHAPTER 46

Green Park Court

North London 2015

Hodgkinson had given Julia an address of sheltered accommodation apartments in North London. She was to meet a woman there who knew the rest of Dimitri's story. Julia wondered what more she could reveal now she knew the details of his death.

After escorting her to the lift doors at the Gentleman's Club, Hodgkinson had helped her with one other piece of the puzzle.

"By the way, in his diary, the person Dimitri called 'the man from the Cheka' turned out to be Dimitri's second uncle, Sergei Petrov. The Cheka had long since been taken over by the NKVD but the term was still used for anyone involved with the secret service.

"Once a Kulak, Dimitri's second uncle left Moscow before the purges and forged a new identity for himself. Dimitri was only a baby when he left and grew up knowing nothing about this subterfuge. When he returned, using the pseudonym Feliks Kozlov, Dimitri's father and his other uncle, Leon, never let on he was their brother. They hoped his position inside the secret police could protect them all. Nevertheless, an anonymous tip-off led to the NKVD raiding Dimitri's parent's home.

"Afterwards Kozlov - the man from the Cheka - managed to get Dimitri sent to an ordinary orphanage and not a home for children of enemies of the people. If he'd been sent to one of those he would, once he'd turned eighteen, have been arrested and sent to the camps. Unfortunately Kozlov was later detained for not being vigilant enough with the neighbours under his watch. And, like the proverbial domino, he was the next to fall."

Julia keyed in the apartment number. There was a slight pause followed by the buzz of the doors being unlocked. As far as sheltered accommodation went, Green Park Court did not seem such a bad place to see out one's days. The ambience was more akin to a hotel than an old folk's home.

The furnishing looked new and modern. The air was fresh and there was an orderly cleanliness about the place.

On the second floor she knocked on the door of room 31 and an elderly lady's voice bade her to enter. Julia went through a small vestibule leading to a doorway into the main living room. An old lady stood leaning on a walking stick.

Sarah Collins's skin was like soft parchment. Her hair was a shock of white yet her features still conveyed the beauty of her yesteryears. And her eyes were a pale watery blue. Eyes that even after a lifetime retained a childlike innocence.

"So, you're the young lady intent on digging up the past?" She regarded Julia carefully over the top of her spectacles. "You're as pretty as Hodgkinson described. I wasn't bad myself at your age." Her fingers moved with the elegance of an artist as she picked up a framed, sun-faded image off a bookshelf. "That's me," she passed Julia the picture, "outside Holloway Sanatorium."

It was a photograph of a shy-looking young nurse wearing a white smock over a navy blue uniform. Auburn hair swept back behind a white band, head tilted coyly against the sun, a smile wide with endless possibilities.

Sarah walked awkwardly and talked to Julia about her recent hip operation. The room was a collection of chintz. There was a drinks cabinet filled with more crystal glass than spirits, pastoral prints on the walls, an assortment of vases and ornaments on every surface.

"I believe you want me to fill in a few gaps of the Russian story." She carefully removed her spectacles and let them hang on the chain around her neck. "It seems a lifetime ago."

Minutes later Julia had made them both a pot of tea and sat across from Sarah.

"Can I start by asking about the day you first became involved with Dimitri Petrov?"

"I'll never forget that day," Sarah toyed with her walking stick whilst gazing out of the window in recollection. "It was just towards the end of the war when I'd served as a nurse to the allies in North Africa. I returned home and found work at the Holloway Sanatorium," she slowly took a sip of tea.

"After the miseries we suffered during the war, Holloway Sanatorium seemed like a palace." Sarah's face lit up. "Everywhere was a blaze of colour and light. Every surface of wood and stone was painted or gilt finished. Portraits of distinguished people hung on the walls, Queen Victoria, Alfred the Great, Nelson, Shakespeare, Isaac Newton. It was Holloway's aim to show his patients flesh and blood examples of people who embodied a cultured mind.

"The book-cases provided only the best quality literature to help those confused patients develop a more ordered intellect. Holloway wanted to stimulate their brains and raise their spirits. He did not want them to feel like helpless inmates as previous cold-walled asylums often did.

"We could accommodate two hundred patients. Typically we had overworked barristers, mentally exhausted government officials or extreme sufferers of bereavement.

"That is why the latest arrival to our sanatorium was so unusual," Sarah frowned, narrowing her eyes as though reliving her confusion. "He didn't tick any of those boxes. One day, as I was sorting the laundry outside the red brick houses where we lived, an ambulance and black car came speeding up the driveway. I was surprised, as we weren't expecting any arrivals and assumed one of our patients must have fallen ill. I left the pile of washing and slipped back into the sanatorium through a side door. Hiding behind one of the pillars in the entrance hall, I spotted Doctor Walsh waiting nervously at the bottom of the wide staircase. Two porters carrying a heavily bandaged patient on a stretcher were guided in through the entrance by a bowler-hatted, officious looking man. Doctor Walsh held out a clipboard and the man nodded curtly and quickly signed the form. Dr Walsh then took a case from the man and beckoned the porters to follow him up the stairway.

"Doctor Walsh was the staff member I liked least. He was rude, impatient and laughed at the most offensive of things. Matron told me not to be too hard on him as he'd never been the same since his stint in the First World War. I did try not to judge him but when he lost patience with our patients I'm sure he did them more harm than good. An asylum should be a cheerful place." Sarah gripped hard on the handle of her walking stick. "Not the fearful one I saw reflected in their eyes when Dr Walsh did his rounds.

"I was curious to know who this new arrival was. When I asked Matron, I was told to mind my own business and get on with my duties. A stolen glance at our patient register proved just as unhelpful with no mention of our latest guest. If he was a casualty of the war he'd be our first as we usually only dealt with civilian patients."

"What about soldiers?" Julia asked.

"Well yes, a soldier suffering from shell-shock I could understand but I saw the bandages covering this unfortunate man's face. Physical injuries were for general hospitals not a sanatorium."

Sarah sighed deeply and raised herself up in her chair.

"In the weeks that followed I tried to put all thoughts of the patient out of my mind. He had no visitors and was attended only by Doctor Walsh and his senior nurse. He was being treated in a third-storey single room in the north-east section of the sanatorium. Cut off from the rest of the patients.

"One day I had duties to perform on the third floor and my curiosity got the better of me. I tip-toed towards the door of our mystery patient and listened for any noise. The room was silent. I tried the handle and to my surprise it was locked. This went against our open door policy. Our patients were to be cared for not treat like criminals."

"Nurse! What are you doing?"

Matron caught me red-handed rattling the door handle.

"I thought I heard a noise coming from inside."

"That room is out of bounds for all members of staff apart from Doctor Walsh. I suggest you get back downstairs and I don't want to see you anywhere near this room again. Is that clear?"

"Yes, matron."

She nodded stiffly as though that was the end of the matter. I bit my lip.

"But why all the mystery? Who is this man? Don't we have a right to know who we're treating?"

"A right to know? Who do you think you are?" Matron stood to one side and pointed me back down the stairs. She followed me down to the basement.

I turned on the bottom step.

"If he's a soldier and its top secret I understand, but how can we help someone if we're not allowed to get near him?"

Matron glanced around to be sure we were alone.

"Even I don't know who he is," she hissed, "no-one on the board has informed me about any of this. It's all highly irregular. We just have to trust our superiors and not let this side-show of Dr Walsh's get in the way of our duties."

She nodded brusquely and left me none the wiser.

Dimitri woke with a start. Where was he? Sunlight streamed over his bed through Georgian sash windows. The bandages that had covered his face were gone. Or had they also been part of his dream? He was weak and he struggled to remember all that had happened to him since Berlin.

Interrogations.

Injections.

Incarceration.

He couldn't think straight at all. It was as if some hallucinogen was clouding his thoughts. He stared round the room. It was like the study of an aristocratic English gentleman. Antique architraves, oak writing bureau, fine tapestries and rugs with leather wing-back chairs, and he, absurdly, in the centre in a four poster bed, stripped back of curtains. He was hooked up to a drip-feed surrounded by trolleys and stands full of medical equipment, phials and medicines.

387

The mental effort exerted in trying to make sense of all this drained him. His head fell back on the pillow. He gazed blankly at the white carvings etched into the ceiling; angels, cherubs and arabesque ornamental arrangements. Even God and all the angels, Dimitri thought, would struggle to unravel the truth of recent events.

As his eyes closed his shell-shocked mind prised open. From nowhere, forgotten memories began floating to the surface like oxygen bubbles from the bottom of a lake.

'It was the second week of the Winter Holidays. Me and my friends had just played a game of Reds versus Whites with snowballs for ammunition and broom sticks for swords. I'd returned home soaked to the skin expecting a telling-off from my mother. As I rushed into the apartment foyer three stern-faced men in long black trench coats came out of the lift. I slipped on the wet floor. One of them caught me.

"Better to trip with the feet than with the tongue, little comrade," he said with a malignant grin.

They all laughed, as though it was some private joke.

I thought I knew him. His face looked familiar.

As I burst through the door of our apartment I saw my mother sat weeping at the table with her arm around my father. On the table lay broken pieces of our radio; coils, springs and wires. Father was holding the twisted aerial. He gave a faint shake of his head and slammed it down. Then he turned to me, his face full of grief.

"What happened?" I asked.

Mother got up quickly, wiping her eyes with her apron.

"Nothing," she forced a smile, "look at you! You're wet through. Let's get you out of those clothes right away."

My mother could be as garrulous as a magpie when trying to cover up any misery we might be going through. Father remained quiet at the table. His head was in his hands. I'd never seen him look so defeated.

"What happened to the radio?" I protested. Mother started fussing round me, roughly pulling my jumper off over my head.

"We need to get you out of these clothes before you catch your death. The radio," she looked over at father, "it fell on the floor. That's all. We'll get it repaired."

"Why were you crying?"

She let out a long sigh.

"I've had a long day, Dimitri. I was upset about it at first but everything's going to be fine. Your dad will sort it out."

"Can he mend it?"

"Yes," she murmured.

"No," snapped father.

They both spoke at the same time.

"Dry yourself off by the stove." Mother wrapped a thin towel around my shoulders.

"Please try to mend it, Dad."

"No, I said!" He boomed at me as his arm swept across the table sending all the wireless parts crashing to the floor.

I literally jumped with shock. I'd never seen him so angry before.

He got up and grabbed his long coat off the hook. He gave me a severe look.

"I'm going to see... someone," he nodded knowingly to mother, "see if they can sort this mess out."

Mother nodded submissively. Father slammed the door.

"Who dropped the radio?" I asked.

"Never mind," her lips and chin began to tremble, "it was an accident. We should never have got it in the first place."

"But I thought you loved listening to..."

"Come on," she spoke over me, "get changed quickly. I want you in bed before your father gets back."

"But he said he's gone to see someone who can fix it, hasn't he?"

"Oh, Dimitri!" She looked as if she was about to cry again. Fighting back tears she sniffed and stiffened as she helped me dress.

"I don't need help," I protested.

"Listen, Dimitri," she spoke sternly, eyes fixed on mine, "did you tell any of your friends about our radio?"

"You told me not to."

"Did you tell anyone at school? A teacher perhaps?"

"No, I didn't tell anyone, even though you told me never to lie."

"It's not a lie if you just don't talk about a thing," she huffed, "you have a lot to learn my son. We've been too soft with you. There are some nasty people out there. Jealous people. That's why it's best to say nothing about our business."

The heat from the stove was making my face hot. Yet Mother right beside me, looked pale, lost in her own thoughts. I'd never seen her look so worried.

"Come on," she held my hand when I was clothed, "a little Kasha before bedtime?"

I protested it was still the holidays and too early for bed. Then I noticed that our Christmas Tree by the window had fallen over, tinsel and baubles scattered everywhere. I was about to ask about that when she shook me hard and, for the first time ever, I saw fear and anger in her eyes.

"You're going to bed when I say so young man. From now on you will do as you're told!"

Dimitri's eyes shot wide open.

"Who has a Christmas Tree at home?"

Dimitri saw the face of his inquisitor. It seemed an innocuous question. Then,

"Better to trip with the feet than with the tongue, little comrade."

It was the same voice!

Unmistakeable.

How strange that his hallucinations should reveal the blinding truth?

He remembered him now. He was the man at his school. The one who Dimitri thought was a new classroom assistant. The one who asked strange questions about what books they had read or did they know what a Kulak was. Every totalitarian state knew that an innocent child was the best informer. They knew over time a child would let slip something incriminating, something they had overheard their parent's say. Now Dimitri knew why his parent's apartment had been raided. Not only had they caught them with a Christmas tree but also an illegal short-wave radio. That was enough to condemn anybody in a society where one could be imprisoned on no more than an accusation.

And he was to blame.

It became obvious that the last time Dimitri saw his parents they were on their way to be interrogated. They were even escorted by the secret police. Yet he knew they never reached the Lubyanka for questioning or any other prison or labour camp. Uncle Leon swore they had crashed through the Borodinsky Bridge and into the Moscow River.

He replayed the memory of a conversation he'd had with Ava. A conversation in which she'd conveyed an intuition that now made perfect sense.

Ava continued looking out of the window. The pine trees of Peredelkino were getting closer. Dusk was dissolving into darkness and the carriage now rattled on through folds of thick mist.

"We'll soon be there." Ava turned to me. "Look Dimitri, let's say you're right. But what if your parent's car crash wasn't murder or an accident? What if your mother and father knew they were under suspicion? That they were about to be separated by the purge, sent to different gulags?" I could feel my brow knot in disbelief. "Maybe... maybe they committed suicide so you, their only son wouldn't be implicated in their 'treason'." My heart rate was rising again. "Even as a child you would still be classed as a relative of an enemy of the state and sent away. Maybe your parents thought that with their death any investigation

into them would die also. A supreme sacrifice for the love of their only son."

Dimitri cried out.

A cry that echoed loudly around the corridors of Holloway Sanatorium.

David J Robinson

CHAPTER 47

Sarah Collins finished her tea and asked Julia to fetch a glass of water. It was time for her medication. When she returned she took a pill and swallowed it down. She then continued the story.

"One day I was halfway up the staircase when I heard a man cry out. A horrible, anguished cry. It stopped me in my tracks and sent a chill through my body. I dropped the bedding and leant out over the banister just in time to see Dr Walsh rushing from his third floor office towards the locked room. His senior nurse, who we called the Ice Queen, followed him brandishing a cluster of keys that she fumbled and dropped. Picking them, up she saw me watching her from below. Our eyes met for a brief moment. I smiled. She didn't.

"Be quick with that key!" Walsh shouted. And with that she was gone.

"Almost a year went by before I got to meet our 'new' inmate. Dr Walsh's senior nurse, her real name was Katherine, sat next to me in the canteen one day. I don't know who first called her the Ice Queen but it suited her.... gorgeous cheekbones and immaculate make-up... she could be intimidating."

"Can you keep a secret?" She said outright.

"Of course."

"I'm trusting you on instinct alone. You seem well bred, and good breeding produces women of integrity and discernment."

"I nearly burst out laughing but I could tell she was deadly serious."

"Go on," I stifled my amusement.

"Dr Walsh is not well. He's going to take some time off. It should only be for a few weeks at most. I need somebody to help me care for his patient. I can't tell you anything about him but as long as he is kept strictly on the prescribed medication then he is of no danger to anyone."

"Danger?" I shook my head. "This is no place for dangerous patients. In fact he should be discharged soon."

"He's going nowhere unless Dr Walsh decides he is."

"But," I had a good memory for the small print, "the Sanatorium's rules state no patient will be allowed to remain an inmate for longer than twelve months."

"So you won't help."

"I never said that."

"Good," she smiled coldly. "You'll be called to Dr Walsh's office in the next few days."

Julia refilled their teacups and Sarah Collins settled back in her armchair.

Dr Walsh's office was a mess. There were papers piled high everywhere. Books were crammed onto shelves and stacked up on the floor. A smell of damp plaster emanated from the bare fireplace. Dr Walsh sat at a grand oak writing bureau. The walls around him were lined by tall dark oak cabinets, cupboards and wardrobes. If it wasn't for the high ceiling and big light window it would have been claustrophobic.

"Come in, do sit down."

I stood looking for a space to sit.

He looked up at me in an exasperated donnish way.

"The papers," his fingers waved agitatedly at a chair to my left, "dump the papers on the floor, there's a good girl."

There was something of the mad professor about Dr Walsh. Although he often wore a suit beneath his white coat he always looked scruffy. Above his bloated, tired looking face his greying hair was parted severely and a short greasy fringe drooped over his forehead. His eyes were never still, always distracted like he was thinking two days ahead.

He took a drink out of a tin cup. I could smell the brandy from across the room. Walsh could talk. He was a raconteur of puffed up self importance.

"Now," he scratched his neck and looked at me dubiously through half-rimmed glasses. "Nurse Katherine has vouched for your credentials," he began rifling through a drawer by his left. "I have business elsewhere to attend to," he produced a note book and flicked through it. "Your discretion is paramount," he held the book up by its spine and a single stamp fluttered from between its pages onto the desk.

"Aha," he licked the stamp and held it delicately between thumb and forefinger whilst rummaging with his other hand through the papers on his desk. "It is often said the first casualty of war is the truth. But the first truth of war," he picked up an envelope and proceeded to place the stamp on it, "is that there will be casualties, lots of casualties." He scribbled an address on the envelope. "We have a casualty of war in our care. Your care now Nurse. Oh, and he's a Russian by the way, name of Petrov." He folded a sheet of already typed paper into the envelope. "His presence here is at the bequest of state security." He licked the envelope and stuck it down. "But whilst he's in our care, and we keep him sedated, he's of no danger to himself or anyone else for that matter."

He held out the envelope and started patting his pockets with his other hand. The man couldn't keep still.

"Nurse Katherine will give you details of his regime. Post this for me on your way out, there's a good girl."

I leant forward to take the envelope and noticed it had a Whitehall address on it.

"I don't like the word danger, Dr Walsh. Mr Holloway stated..."

"Mr Holloway died a long time ago. In medicine we have to move with the times."

He stood up and began to amble towards me, shooing me out of the room.

"I can't tell you anything else about this patient," he tapped the side of his nose conspiratorially, "top secret, old girl."

I was only nineteen.

Opening the door, he whispered as I passed by.

"You must tell no-one of Petrov's existence and he must remain in his room at all times."

"For how long?" I whispered back.

"As long as it takes," he turned and slammed the door. The smell of alcohol on his breath undermined all his assurances.

"I can't remember exactly how it happened. But the Ice Queen had messed up the rota between us. For two days we both thought each other was administering Petrov's sedatives. In those two days he became more lucid and began to ramble. It was all in Russian and I could only make out one word, a name... Ava. Back in Dr Walsh's office I re-checked his chart and realised our mistake.

"Immediately I went to put him back on the sedative. I walked into his room and his bed was empty. I couldn't believe it. Then the door slammed shut and Petrov grabbed me from behind. I thought he was going to kill me. He pushed me up against the wall."

"What are you doing to me? Who are you people?"

"His English surprised me. But back then I was strong and I pushed back against him. He was obviously weak and almost fell, coughing violently as he staggered back to his bed."
"You are safe," I tried to reason with him.
"Where am I?" He looked at me, "am I in England yet?"

"He was so confused I felt sorry for him. I got him back in bed and prepared his medication. He stretched out his arm and pushed away my hand holding the needle."

"No more. Please, no more."

"What can I say?" Sarah's eyes became tearful, "I felt such pity for this man. No matter what he'd done he didn't deserve to be kept in limbo like that. I'm a Christian and truly believe in treating others as I would like to be treated. Call it stupidity or just a gut feeling but I felt I could trust this man. He had some innocence about him. I wanted to find out from his own lips what he'd done and why he was here."

"So what did you find out?" Julia asked.

Sarah, with a coy tilt of her head, smiled just like in the photograph.

Orphan of the State

"As luck would have it, Nurse Katherine had to leave for a few days to visit a sick relative. And, with Dr Walsh still absent I had the patient all to myself. I fed him nourishing food and fresh strawberries from the garden in place of the drip-feed that barely kept him alive. He spoke to me of the war, that he was a Russian soldier who came to us, to England to tell us the truth about Stalin. I was a believer in socialism myself back then and I was shocked at what he told me."

"If the Russian people knew about the true Stalin, his war crimes and purges, then I think a real revolution would sweep the land and kick all the grim-faced betrayers of socialism out of the Kremlin. But most people are so loyal to the State ideal and the righteousness of Stalin they refuse to believe he is responsible when things go wrong in the system, when people disappear in the middle of the night."

"When Nurse Katherine returned she didn't object to me taking over all drug administrative duties. Actually she seemed quite relieved. Dimitri was quite the actor. Through his comrade, Avakov, he'd learnt the Russian Orthodox art of '*hesychasm*', the ability to be completely still and contemplate God. It came in handy. When Nurse Katherine was present he played the comatose invalid with real aplomb. And, on her days off, I took him out into the grounds for fresh air. I disguised him as best I could and kept out of view of Matron. I felt alive again and as I wheeled him round the rose-garden he'd tell me more of his story. Those days were heavenly. I had no idea they were soon to be cut short."

"Have you heard of Lenin's Testament?" He asked me.

"No."

"I have a friend in the NKVD. He told me it's a document in which Lenin assessed the merits of his potential successors. Put briefly, he admired Bukharin, was dubious of Trotsky but was most damning about Stalin. After Lenin's death Stalin suppressed it. If that document had seen the light of day our history would have been very different.

"Stalin's record within the Bolsheviks was low-life criminal activity. He ran bank raids, kidnapping and murders for the party in his native Georgia. His disastrous collective farm policy resulted in the death and starvation of millions of peasants. All this is kept quiet. The whole world needs to know this!"

"We call him Uncle Joe." I said, "I thought he was a decent man."

"People all over the world see the Soviet Union under Stalin as some wonderful utopia. The Western intellectuals admire Stalin and denounce those who flee from Russia.

"Many Russians are so brainwashed they still shout, "Long live Stalin!" just before they are executed. They cannot believe their great leader is aware of the gross injustices carried out in his name."

"Petrov warned me that future generations will probably say Stalin's Communism wasn't true communism." Sarah leant over to pick up a tattered old book on the table beside her. "That the ideal was hideously distorted by a paranoid despot." She donned her spectacles again. "But for Karl Marx," she raised the book in her hands, "violence and bloodshed was always part of the plan." After flicking back and forth through the pages she cleared her throat and began to read to Julia.

"There is only one way in which the murderous death agonies of the old society and the bloody birth throes of the new society can be shortened, simplified and concentrated," she paused and peered above her glasses at Julia, "Marx wrote this in 1848." She looked back down and finished the sentence, *"and that way is revolutionary terror."*

"Petrov believed Stalin was a genuinely faithful Marxist. But, like Lenin before him, Stalin believed the price of building a new world by sacrificing millions of his own people was worth it. Petrov was adamant it was the ideal that was monstrous, not just the man."

Julia was at a loss what to say. She knew many people still held a torch for communism today. And that socialism, as an ideological alternative to capitalism, was again finding favour amongst the intellectual elite.

"I found our conversations stimulating." Sarah went on. "Here was a man who had lived through hell. He answered all of my questions, especially about what had gone on in the downfall of Berlin."

"There was a conspiracy of silence about the rapings. How could I know if anyone else felt like me, ashamed and disgusted when everyone was as silent on the subject as I was. But it was," he insisted, *"just a minority.*

"The majority of my comrades were helpful to the German people. As comrade Vasily said, 'we beat our enemies by not becoming like them.' I saw many of our soldiers sharing food, handing out clothing. Those little acts of kindness shown to our enemy were, to me, beacons along the dark road, guiding us back to our humanity. However dim the fire; however faint the flame, the glow of man's innate goodness can never be fully extinguished."

"I got Petrov to do exercises to build up his strength. I knew I'd be dismissed if I got caught but," Sarah hesitated, searching for the words, "I don't know, it just felt right, to help this man. I was sure it was the right thing to do. I remember we became more daring."

Her eyes flashed mischievously.

"One day we left his wheelchair behind the ice house and spent time roaming through the yew maze. As we talked under a blue sky, I knew I was getting more attracted to this man."

Sarah, still in obvious discomfort, shifted in her chair.

"Not just physically attracted, I mean, it was his soul I began to love. He didn't appear to hold any hatred towards anyone. After all he'd been through. That's when I asked him about Ava. He seemed shocked upon hearing me say her name, but I reminded him he'd repeated the name many times in his sleep."

"Ava?" He gazed into the middle distance, "she was my saviour. No matter what depth of depravity we as soldiers

plunged to, she was my North Star, guiding me back to my humanity."

"Was your saviour?"

"She died during the war."

"I'm sorry to hear that," I didn't know what to say, "but at least you survived."

"Yes, but only because I held her in my heart. That feeling of love... it gave me the strength of a thousand men."

He looked at me earnestly.

"The thought has stayed with me ever since, if I can feel this way, so can all mankind."

"And yet the notes I've found in Walsh's office say you are a traitor," I told him.

"What makes a traitor?" He asked. "What makes another man sacrifice his life for a patch of earth? We need to learn, to empathise with all men. Not to condone or condemn but to understand."

"He spoke with the heart of a poet."

"I sensed I belonged to a unique generation. But I now see it was a coincidence. Being in that moment of childhood when the world appears magical and equating that magic with Communism. We all experience freedom as a child. Even the most wretched, down-at-heel childhood cannot totally blot out the pure radiance of a child's heart. And once freedom is experienced it is never forgotten. All those social confines, of trying to purge our 'bad selves' was destined to fail."

"But he was unflinching in his assessment of the Germans."

"To have carried out such atrocities on my people Hitler's men must have had souls as black as night."

"Yet he equally criticised his own side's failings."

"Terrible rumours circulated that the Germans did not raze a particular village to the ground. It was done by our men under Stalin's orders whilst our people still lived there! Stalin's intent was not to allow the Germans anywhere to shelter or find food. If it won us the war was it a price worth paying? Or is it further proof Stalin and Hitler are just different sides of the same coin?"

"Dimitri wanted me to help him escape." Sarah fixed Julia with her eyes.

"Where could you go?" I asked.
He shrugged. "I could go anywhere. It's obvious the British Government don't want me. And I presume I am a disgrace to the Motherland. I have lost everything, so what stands in my way? I can't let what happened define me. After all, what is identity other than a collection of memories? My old life died in the chaos of Berlin. The rest of my life I dedicate to living well."

Sarah struggled to get to her feet and Julia rushed over to help her.

"He told me I had brought him back to life in more ways than I'd ever know. "

"I loved Ava. I put her on a pedestal and thought no-one could possibly match up to her. But the qualities you've shown me, your care and patience, your personality, the way you blush when I compliment you... like now. All our hours together have proved to me I can love again. In that respect my incarceration here has not been wasted."

"Indeed I did blush. If the times had been different... well, who knows?" She smiled in recollection as she hobbled across the room. "I was incredibly touched when Dimitri gave me this though." She reached over to a snow globe on top of the bureau. Returning to her armchair she passed it to Julia.

"This travelled with me," Dimitri said, "all the way from Moscow to Berlin. It's a keepsake from Ava.

This snow-globe of Paris was our link. When she was a child, Ava's father worked in the Russian Embassy in Paris.

Ava was only a young girl but that miniature world with its Eiffel Tower, Sacre Coeur and Arc de Triomphe was like an exotic dream brought to life by shimmering snowflakes.

That small memento, probably smuggled in illegally by her father, ignited Ava's desire to travel beyond our borders.

We knew little of the outside world except what we'd been told. That it was backward, corrupt and immoral. Ava also knew that was probably just Communist propaganda. I thought her cynicism was a shield to preserve her innocence.

The snow globe along with her father's description of chic Parisian women, gourmet food beyond anything the Tsars would have tasted, the artists quarter packed with poets, playwrights and painters, the marvels of Montmartre, the smells of freshly ground coffee and bustling cafe culture. To Ava it sounded like paradise.

When shaken, the snowflakes in the globe sprinkled magic onto her youthful imaginings. To be in love, in Paris... that was Ava's dream."

Sarah Collins expression suddenly changed.

"A hand up, please."

Julia helped her to her feet.

"Are you okay?"

"These days," she straightened herself, "I find that tea goes right through me. Don't get old Julia." She said as she shuffled out of the room.

Upon her return Sarah leant back in her chair and that distant look glazed her eyes again. Julia had the impression that she was reliving the past in incredible detail.

"Inevitably," she sighed, "the Ice Queen found out. She walked in on us playing cards on the bed. There was no use pretending. I told her the truth. She couldn't believe he hadn't assaulted me or tried to escape.

"Walsh was due back soon. Nurse Katherine confided in me that he'd actually gone to a clinic to dry out. She panicked over Petrov and wanted to tell the Holloway governors. I persuaded her to give me more time.

"Everything happens for a reason. Bless that girl. Whilst walking with Dimitri in the rose garden she came to warn us of the arrival of a Whitehall civil servant. That civil servant, I now know as Rudy, had often dropped by at irregular intervals.

"Progress report," he'd say and go and visit Dimitri for a few minutes.

"What happened next? Well you'll be the first to hear it from me..."

David J Robinson

CHAPTER 48

Rudy's hands gripped tightly on the steering wheel of his Kremlin funded Aston Martin as he careered down the country lanes leading to Holloway Sanatorium. This time next week, he realised with a sickening dread, he could be driving a Trabant.

As trees and hedges flew past in a blur he checked his racing mind. He'd been burned, his cover completely blown. That bloody fool, Hodgkinson, who'd been Rudy's very own *'useful idiot'*, had thankfully given him the heads-up about the impending tribunal.

Damn that mole in Poland! How had his handler not known about that?

As he screeched around the narrow bends cutting through the Surrey heath-land, he knew the game was up. The Foreign Office, that haven of bumbling upper-class idiots, had checkmated him. He'd been a knight in London, a prime square on the global chessboard. Now he was simply a pawn, soon to go back in the box whilst the great game continued without him.

He could be caught at any moment. Anxious glances in his rear-view mirror assured him there was no-one following. He lit a cigarette.

That morning, at the drop, he'd found the unequivocal message from his handler. It was a diagram of the Bear constellation. A code, nobody but Rudy knew what it meant.

"Odysseus trekked east by keeping the Bear constellation to his left."

Rudy was going east.

After the drop, he'd called at the safe house in Hounslow and received fake documents and a passport that would enable him to flee via Dover to a rendezvous in Calais. From there he'd be hidden in a specially adapted camper van bound for Moscow. To Russia, the homeland he'd never stepped foot in but on whose altar had sacrificed the lives of countless British agents and soldiers.

What had it all been for?

Rudy now knew all about the purges and gulags. If Stalin saw his own people as untrustworthy and expendable what trust would he give to a foreigner with delusions of the socialist paradise? It suddenly became clear Rudy himself had been Stalin's *'useful idiot'*. And maybe not now or next year or even the next decade - once his usefulness had been snuffed from the collective memory - he'd be a liability, untrustworthy and expendable too.

Mother Russia was beckoning him. A land of permafrost and brutal industrialisation. A place of corruption and betrayal. A life of struggle and waiting.

But waiting for what?

If you can wait, and not be tired by waiting...

The poem *If* came to mind, imprinted on his childhood brain by a father so enamoured by the author he named his only son after him. Rudy had been the knave in MI6 who'd twisted the truth to make traps for fools.

If you can bear to see the things you've given your life to broken and stoop and build them up with worn out tools...

Rudy couldn't see a way of building anything up from this mess, with tools worn-out or otherwise. All he'd ever known were the tools of spy-craft.

As an outsider, born in India, he felt able to view British life more objectively than his peers. Rudy could observe impartially and question the way things are. He was shy and insecure as a young man and not particularly interested in politics. But at Cambridge his ears had been pricked by the news that after the revolution homosexuality had been legalised in Russia.

His own father, cold and distant no matter how Rudy tried to please him, seemed a metaphor for the whole English class structure. He hated the veneer of respectability among the aristocracy and their denial of class division. Yet he strived to become one of them with his first-class appearance and impeccable manners. Despite that, he believed his olive skin, bequeathed by his Indian mother,

413

had been a hindrance to his social and professional career. He felt sure from glib remarks of *'More char, Sahib!'* that people were laughing behind his back. He detected undertones of racism everywhere he went. This burning sense of injustice raged inside Rudy until a college friend took him along to a talk about Marxism and The Social Contract. It was an epiphany.

After that illuminating lecture, which clarified Rudy's wayward mind, he saw the world in a different light. Russia was now humanity's beacon. Liberal and egalitarian, it sounded like paradise to the sensitive homosexual with a chip on his shoulder. Rudy tried reading the socialist pamphlets and the Communist Manifesto but, apart from the bullet points of 'workers freedom, emancipation of women and abolition of the old aristocracy', the minutiae of Marxist theory left him cold. One sentence though he did learn by heart. *"Labour is the source of all wealth, therefore to the labourers all wealth is due!"* The nursery rhyme logic, the common sense ideology, Rudy lapped it up. It didn't require too much brain power. It sounded true, therefore it must be true!

Besides, studying languages and photography left no time for learning about socialist theory. French, German and Russian were all on his agenda, but now learning Russian took on a whole new sense of importance.

It was around this time, December 1935 when Rudy was approached to work as a Soviet spy. Attending a Christmas party near Cambridge it was just after midnight when Rudy went outside for a cigarette. The party was held in a large maisonette with a sweeping drive surrounded by trees. He'd stepped out onto the porch. It had been snowing heavily and most guests were planning on staying the night. He stood alone, taking measured drags of his cigarette. Then, like in a film, a man came into view across the driveway. He was wearing a black fedora and dark Mac and was staring at Rudy. As soon as he realised he'd been seen he began to walk towards Rudy and asked in fluent Russian, *"Have you a light, comrade?"*

It was the start of his indoctrination.

They spoke together throughout the night sharing ideas of equality and fairness, lambasting capitalism, Britain and all its corrupt lords. The man, who introduced himself simply as Fenrir, said he'd been recommended by a friend. They talked about George Bernard Shaw who was a great champion of socialism in all his writings. Fenrir said he recognised a kindred spirit when he saw one. He then went on to diagnose Rudy's mental state by paraphrasing Shaw's own words, *"In Britain you are still a foreigner and you shall die one."* It was true. Rudy hadn't lived long enough in India to feel that was home, yet still felt an outsider in England after all these years. Russia was home in his imagination only. Would it match the reality?

On their second meeting, they walked through Hyde Park where Fenrir talked about Russia and what it wanted from Rudy.

After a while Fenrir pointed to the night sky.

"Did you know, comrade, Odysseus trekked east by keeping the Bear constellation to his left?"

Rudy shook his head.

415

"One day, not too soon I hope, you too will make the journey east. It's your Motherland now."

"If you are ever in danger here, compromised or if they find out you are a homosexual, they shall hang you. But in Russia you will be lauded."

Rudy was almost convinced, and then Fenrir recited another passage from Man and Superman by Bernard Shaw. *'The more things a man is ashamed of the more respectable he is.'* He smiled knowingly at Rudy. "That sums up the aristocracy over here."

He went on to point Rudy to an opening at the Foreign Office where languages, especially Russian was essential. Apart from that, all one needed to blend into Whitehall's priestly caste was a public education, Saville Row suit and a bowler hat.

Rudy realised this was his chance to put a bomb under it all. To undermine the British class system, the society he lived in. That realisation - allied to his romanticism about the revolution, of working for a higher cause and the thrill of secret meetings with his handler, Fenrir - proved highly addictive. Before long he was going under the radar at MI6.

The road wound upwards, tyres screeching in protest at his speed. Out of the wooded highway, Rudy gasped on another cigarette and drove through open fields divided by ancient stone walls. He passed isolated farmhouses, a medieval church, and a country pub close to the railway tracks. In the distance, plumes of steam from a south-bound train drifted up into the cloudless sky.

Orphan of the State

Would these be the last sights he had of this green and pleasant land?

He cringed at his sentiments, how naive, how pitiable. Yet if he truly believed in the Communist way over all others why did he feel so sick? He knew this day would come sometime but the thought of giving up his 'freedom' as a double agent terrified him. Where would he find fulfilment in the USSR, never fully trusted by the Soviets, always a potential target for British retribution? But, when it came down to it, he'd choose a wood-wormed dacha over Wormwood Scrubs any day.

On he drove, through coppice and over vale. A solitary car appeared in his rear view mirror. Rudy's heart rate quickened. *Was he getting paranoid?* If he was, it was no wonder. He'd been a grey man, working alone in the shadows for far too long.

He realised he was a stranger to himself and to his unchecked assumptions. Did he really hate the British Empire so much? All of a sudden the benefits of his life in the West flooded his mind. Memories of sun drenched afternoons at Lords Cricket Ground, seated in the best box with fine wines and sumptuous lunches. Squirming slightly in his car seat, he recalled his two-faced pleasure at mixing with the great and the good at Royal Ascot. The Gentleman's Club. Rainy afternoons spent playing chess and sipping Scotch with his old chum, Hodgkinson. He realised he'd also miss the free press, gambling on the stock market and the freedom to trawl around Soho at night.

Rudy had justified his bourgeois lifestyle by reminding himself of the apocryphal story of Lenin returning from

Finland to Russia in a first class carriage to begin the revolution. When asked to justify this lavishness, how it wasn't symbolic and didn't convey the ideas of equity and fairness, Lenin replied,

"After the revolution there will only be first class carriages."

What such pleasures awaited Rudy in the state controlled uniformity of the Soviet Union? The dawn of this dreaded realisation hit him like a hammer. He didn't believe in any of it. It had all been a game for him. His resentment of not being born an Englishman had contorted his sense of right and wrong. Had it all been one big ego trip? His thoughts turned to the wretched German girl he'd fobbed off with a copy of the Communist Manifesto.

"Something the whole world needs now!"

Had he ever truly believed that? Rudy felt the blood drain from his face.

Speeding along muddied roads, through verdant pastures and looming hilltops, a strange feeling of nostalgia crept over him. The quote from Samuel Johnson came to mind.

"When a man knows he is to be hanged in a fortnight, it concentrates his mind wonderfully."

Rudy was entering the death throes of his old life and beginning to see everything with glowing clarity.

Although he was more at home in the city with its clubs and restaurants, this tinge of affection for rural England gave him an eleventh hour consolation.

This countryside of rolling chalk hills and rich grasslands was the living, deep marrow of Englishness. Leafy Surrey was close to the capital yet a world away from London's hustle and bustle. A landscape of such beauty, it provided solace to the weary and inspiration to the poet. Reminded of his love of ancient history, he thought of Stonehenge, Roman fortifications, Kings and Queens, the sweat of the labourer, the fox-hunting squire, the bloodied battlefields and the spirit of Empire. For the first time ever in Rudy's colourful life, he felt at home. He felt it, but would never admit it. He couldn't live with that thought. It would destroy him.

On he drove, foot down on the accelerator, zig-zagging and chain-smoking through a mosaic of woodland. Despite Hodgkinson's hapless incompetence, he had been his friend. Perhaps the only true friend he had in the world. Rudy had no friendships to count on in Russia. Who would give a damn about him back there? An ex-spy?

He could see it now. After the debriefings, the medal ceremony, maybe even a meeting with Stalin himself. When the applause of uncaring apparatchiks had died down... what then? What friendships could he make to see him through the dark winter months? The loneliness would kill him. What perks could be offered to compensate for the loss of his respected status within the fraternity of London's elite?

A large central tower and spire came into sight above the ancient woodland. As he got nearer, the imposing skyline of Holloway Sanatorium came into resplendent view. The silhouette was accentuated by countless mansards, conical roofs, domes, pinnacle towers and elaborate chimneys. The central hall was built in the style of the Cloth Hall at Ypres. The rest of the sprawling structure owed more to early

French renaissance style with a dash of Italian and Belgian gothic.

Oh yes, Rudy mused, *he hadn't sent the Russian defector to any old asylum.* Although Holloway Sanatorium was an institution for the treatment of the insane, it was also a truly magnificent building set in a place known as Virginia Waters in Surrey. Built well over a hundred years ago by the millionaire philanthropist Thomas Holloway, its purpose then was to provide mental healthcare for the forgotten middle class.

Rudy only chose this place because he was acquainted with one of its leading physicians, Doctor Walsh. Their paths had crossed years ago at a lavish party held in Dolphin Square. Walsh was a homosexual too, and when Rudy later learned about his gambling habit and addiction to morphine, Walsh proved all too ripe for blackmail. Rudy soothed his conscience with a wad of Kremlin money. And before he could say *maskirovka!* - Rudy had the Doctor in the palm of his hand.

Rudy turned the car into the open driveway of the sanatorium. As he sped past the tall beech trees, the strobing sunlight made him feel he was in an old motion picture. It gave a flickering animation to his pale, bleak face. Driving past still images flashing by in rapid sequence, time appeared to slow down. He parked in front of the entrance hall, twelve stone steps leading up to an ivy covered portico. Slamming the car door, Rudy took a steadying breath and prayed to God he'd make it to the climactic scene before the final reel played out.

Climbing the steps up to the red brick and stone dressed building, Rudy thought he could hear a car engine coming up the drive. It stopped abruptly behind the trees. All was quiet again, and he swiftly became aware of his tranquil surroundings. Off to the right, where the sun was setting, birds swooped over the golden colours of the landscape reflected in the lake. Dappled sunlight revealed the chapel's splendid stained glass windows. It was an oasis of calm.

Rudy entered the hallway, briefcase in hand. Across the polished parquet floor were three vast archways, brightly painted and gilt finished. The middle arch framed the wide carpeted staircase and the others led off down radial corridors. A monogram of Thomas Holloway's initials formed the centre of the ceiling panels. Rudy didn't need to look up to see Holloway's *Nil Desperandum* motto high above his head. Holloway's initials and coat of arms were copied over and over throughout the building.

"Do not despair, never despair."

Their meaning was lost on Rudy, his mind fogged and whirling with desperation.

Desperate to escape the clutches of MI6.

Desperate to be rid of Petrov.

Although he'd been responsible for God-knows how many deaths, Rudy had never done the dirty work himself. *It will be easy,* Fenrir had said. *Petrov's practically dead already. Just inject the serum into his arm like I told you. Within minutes he'll die of a massive heart-attack. Leave the rest to Walsh.*

Rudy started climbing the staircase where a portrait of a fresh-faced Thomas Holloway, strong nose, dimpled chin and dark hair curling onto his cheeks, gazed down at him.

"Where do you think you're going?"

Rudy froze then turned around to face Nurse Katherine who'd appeared from a downstairs side office.

"Progress report," he answered and proceeded up the stairs.

"You can't see him yet."

"Why not?"

"There's a nurse in there administering his medication right now."

"I won't disturb her," he continued up the stairs, "I'll wait outside"

"But," she hesitated for a fraction of a second, "you need to sign some paperwork first."

Rudy sighed impatiently.

"Dr Walsh having been absent, the board need some documentation going over."

"What?" He screwed up his eyes in disbelief.

"Please," she motioned to her office, "it will only take a few minutes."

Reluctantly, casting a weary glance at the arabesque figures and designs above the marble balustrade, he slowly made his way back down. Katherine watched him closely.

"One should never underestimate the effect of surroundings on the mind."

Rudy glowered at her.

"Thomas Holloway said that." Nurse Katherine chatted eagerly, ushering him into the office. "Speaking of his patients, he said if these men live an interior life of morbid, dark thoughts, then let their outer life be one of splendour, light and beauty to show them the way back to life."

"Look young lady, I don't have a lot of time. Where's this paperwork?"

"Wait here. I'll only be a moment or two," she stepped out pulling the door behind her. "The papers are in Walsh's office."

"This better not take long," he called after her.

Rudy sat there, ruminating agitatedly. Even the office wasn't immune to Holloway's ethos of splendid decor. It was more befitting the room of a Belgian town hall than of an asylum for the insane. The wall paper was an expensive mural of decorative patterns of curling foliage on which hung gold framed pictures of the sanatorium down the years. There was a black and white photograph showing the seven bay pseudo medieval hall complete with hammer beam roof. Pictures of the Winter Gardens, Gentlemen's terrace and cricket pavilion were interspersed with mounted Doctor's certificates and Nursing diplomas.

Where was she? Rudy fumed. Unable to sit still, he got to his feet and looked out of the window across the bowling green. Patients in dressing gowns, some in wheelchairs with nurses in attendance, were playing a high-spirited version of the game. He patted his pockets but knew he had run out of cigarettes.

What type of cigarettes did they have in Russia?

He gazed absentmindedly for a moment into the middle distance then caught sight of Nurse Katherine walking quickly, almost breaking into a run, from the garden's high-hedged lower walk and around the bowling green towards him. There were no papers in her hands.

What the hell!

She was playing him. Playing for time. But why? Rudy decided not to wait a moment longer. He walked out into the hallway as Nurse Katherine entered breathlessly.

"I thought you were getting some important documents?"

"In a minute," she gasped, "there was an emergency."

"Emergency? I don't think so. I'm not waiting a moment longer," he started for the staircase.

"Wait," Katherine raised her voice. "I'm in charge here," she placed her hands on her hips, "you will get to see the patient when I say so. Now, kindly go back and wait in my office."

Rudy was partial to a bit of sternness in a woman but this was not the time.

"You think you're in charge? Do you?" Rudy was losing his cool. "I am here on behalf of the Government. Do you know who's paying for all of this patient's treatment?" He fell silent as a male patient, head slumped forward in a wheelchair, was pushed by a nurse in through a side door and across to the corridor by the service lift. A look of horror passed over Katherine's face. Rudy mistook it for indignation.

"I'll tell you who's paying for it," Rudy continued, "the Government." He took a step backwards up the stairs and raised a finger of caution. "So keep out of this, there's a good girl."

"As far as our system of democracy works," Katherine countered, "the 'Government' has no money of its own."

She marched quickly up the stairs and Rudy sensed this could get nasty. She was soon alongside him, halfway up the stairs, red faced and physically jabbing him in the shoulder. "It's funded by the taxpayer like me," *Jab.* "Matron," *Jab* "and everybody else who works here." *Final hard jab.* Rudy was incandescent. He'd never hit a woman, yet.

"So in effect," she grabbed his wrist like a scolded boy, "you're working for us." She started to pull him back down the stairs. "And we need you to come down here and sign these forms."

The ping of the service lift stopped Rudy in his tracks.

What's going on here? Today of all days?

Katherine couldn't get him to budge. She tried a calmer approach as Rudy backed away with a vacant look in his eyes. "Look," she reasoned, "the nurse will be a while yet so," she shrugged her shoulders, "you might as well make yourself useful while you wait." As she turned around, Rudy swung his briefcase as hard as he could. It hit her on the side of the head sending her sprawling to the bottom of the stairs. He heard the crack of her skull hitting the marble balustrade. She lay motionless.

Damn! Bad move.

Rudy rushed down and dragged Katherine's limp body across the polished floor into the office. Her head was cut but she was still breathing.

No turning back now.

He hurried up the stairs and along the corridor to Petrov's room. As he approached the door, the nurse and wheelchair patient exited the service lift and proceeded to enter the room next door. Rudy, desperately trying to not look

425

desperate, nodded to the Nurse. She also looked highly stressed as she rushed the patient into the room.

Rudy tried the handle on Petrov's door. It was locked. Rudy couldn't believe it. Then he remembered, Petrov was supposed to be having his medication.

"Nurse", Nurse?"

He rattled the handle and banged on the door. No reply. Rudy ran back down the stairs. No-one was around. In the office he knelt over the prostrate figure of Nurse Katherine. Finding the keys on her belt he quickly yanked them free. By the time he'd run back upstairs, tried numerous keys and gained entrance to Petrov's room, he was seriously out of breath and sweating profusely.

There, in his usual comatose position, lay the rapist, coward and traitor to the Motherland. Thinking of him in those terms would make the job so much easier for Rudy. He sat on the bed breathing heavily as he fumbled inside his briefcase. Yet something didn't feel quite right.

Rudy noticed a wheelchair in the corner of the room. *What was that doing there? Petrov was never to be moved out of this room.*

He tried to ignore it and concentrate on the job at hand when he then spotted the curtains by Petrov's bed. They'd always been there but now they were parted slightly. He went over to investigate. The curtains hid an adjoining door to the next room. Rudy smelt a rat. Nurse Katherine had tried to delay him, but why? Her conversational tone had been unnatural, false from the start. He couldn't fathom what was going on. Nor had he the time. Petrov was as sedated as ever, that's all that mattered.

It was time to make it permanent.

David J Robinson

CHAPTER 49

Ensconced with a fresh pot of tea, Sarah reassured Julia that Nurse Katherine had only suffered concussion and made a full recovery from her 'fall'.

"I'm sure Hodgkinson with all his careful ways missed out parts of the story." Sarah's raised eyebrows conveyed a hint of mischief. "He is still bound by the law to keep state secrets. But, along with me, he also kept certain things secret from the state."

Julia nodded, intrigued. That tiny flame of hope was beginning to flare again inside her.

"In his briefcase Rudy carried a syringe containing a deadly serum of potassium chloride recently developed by the Soviets. It would leave no trace and cause the victim to die of a massive heart-attack within minutes."

Julia felt a pang. She knew where this was heading. Rudy disappearing, Petrov murdered.

"It was a win-win situation as far as Rudy was concerned. Dimitri was an embarrassment to the British Government and the Kremlin. Every day he remained alive on British soil was a potential foreign-relations disaster.

"Anyway, Rudy could not help boasting to this motionless Dimitri, hoping he could hear, but never expecting a reaction to his taunts."

"You could have been a hero, but back home, you're only known as a coward, deserter and rapist. Your name, if it is remembered at all, is toxic. Anyone interested will find you tarnished the reputation of the Red Army by raping German women. You deserted your comrades by going to the West rather than face Stalin for your crimes. No-one weeps for you Dimitri Petrov. No-one tends your grave because you haven't got one. Erased from our history, you are an embarrassment to the Russian people."

Rudy sat on the edge of the bed watching for any sign Dimitri was registering any of this. Apart from a faint flicker behind his eyelids he reckoned he was wasting his breath. He picked up the syringe, held it up to the light and gently tapped the side.

"Apart from Ava, of course."

Rudy was too entranced with the droplet of poison seeping onto the needle point to see the change on Dimitri's face or notice his breathing speed up.

"She's still alive. She waited for you and you broke her heart. The only person in the world who cared anything about you and you even fucked that up."

Dimitri lunged forward and grabbed Rudy by the throat. Rudy was in shock. There was a struggle. Dimitri was still weak but rage is a powerful energy.

"I rushed in as Dimitri plunged the syringe into Rudy's neck," Sarah looked at the wide-eyed Julia, "within minutes he was dead. We had to act swiftly. Rifling through his briefcase I found a death certificate, already signed by Doctor Walsh, stating that Dimitri Petrov had died of a sudden cardiac arrest. Also another document stating he was to be cremated at once and the ashes sent back to Russia."

Sarah paused.

"We had a dead body and, let's be honest, one man's ashes look much like another's...."

"You didn't?" Julia gasped.

"We did. We being Dr Walsh and myself." Sarah sighed. "Walsh was looking at a long sentence for faking a death certificate plus it also suited him now to be rid of Rudy.

"It seemed Walsh had a weakness. He was hooked on morphine. Rudy had used this knowledge to blackmail him to administer Dimitri with those mind-numbing drugs. For eighteen months Rudy had Dimitri exactly where he wanted him."

"What happened to Dimitri?" Julia's face was a picture of confusion.

"Now the establishment thought him dead, it was relatively easy to smuggle him out of the country."

"How?" Asked Julia.

"Hodgkinson, of course. He'd been suspicious of Rudy for quite a while and had followed him to Holloway. He walked in and found Dr Walsh and I zipping up Rudy's body. He helped us. Diplomatic immunity goes a long way in this world. New identity for Dimitri. No questions asked."

"But where did Dimitri go?"

Sarah gave out a long sigh.

"When he heard Rudy say Ava was still alive he knew where she would be. He told me that as he set off for war, Ava gave him a parcel containing the snow globe and a letter. In it she suggested that if they ever became separated they should attempt to meet up again in Paris.

"At twelve noon on either of their birthdays they would walk for an hour around the base of the Eiffel tower. Ava would walk clockwise, Dimitri anti-clockwise. For however long it took. Now he knew she was alive there was no question in Dimitri's mind she wouldn't have waited for him."

"And did they ever meet?"

"No-one knows. I'd love to think they did, but really?" Sarah arched her eyebrows and waved her hand airily, "a pair of émigrés living out their days in the City of Lights?" She gently shook her head.

Julia's mind flashed back to the burial ceremony in St Petersburg. The old couple they'd met at Dimitri's grave. What had the old man said?

"If it wasn't for love, I could have been in a grave like that."

It was his love for Ava that had given Dimitri the strength to overcome Rudy, which in turn saved him from the grave.

Were Rudy's ashes in that grave?

She thought hard and remembered the old man's scar.

"You said Dimitri's head was covered in bandages when he arrived at the Sanatorium. Was there any damage to his face? Anything that could leave a scar?"

"No, those bandages were just a security measure. For Rudy, the fewer people who saw Dimitri's face the better. But, now I think about it, during the struggle with Rudy the drip-feed stand came crashing onto Dimitri's head. It left a cut just above his right eye. I told him he'd need stitches or be left with a nasty scar. But he laughed and said it was nothing compared to the wounds he'd seen during the war."

Julia shivered.

The enigmatic words, the scar and the trip they'd made all the way from France. The fact her mother had anonymously received the diary of Dimitri just days later.

Julia picked up the snow globe, shook it and watched the flakes all falling into place like pieces of a puzzle, coating the city of Paris with a virginal innocence.

In her mind she saw the old couple suddenly becoming young again, walking in the snow, past the Sacre Coeur and into a boulevard of mended dreams.

"Living life is not like crossing a meadow." Julia recalled the old lady, Ava, quoting a line from Peredelkino's very own poet, Boris Pasternak.

Was this the happy ever after Julia wanted?

She thought of the pain of Violetta, Josef and Rula. The treachery of Monika and Rudy, or was it Otto? – now buried in a traitors grave. She thought of the Communist state and a vicious ideology which, along with many millions of people, had led to the death of Dimitri's parents.

Could she forgive them?

Wasn't that the highest virtue?

The voice of a ghost soldier echoed from the past.

Second only to love.

Orphan of the State

David J Robinson

Primary Sources and Select Bibliography

RUSSIA; A 1,000-Year Chronicle of the Wild East by Martin Sixsmith

BERLIN; The Downfall 1945 by Antony Beevor

A WRITER AT WAR; Vasily Grossman with the Red Army 1941-1945 Edited and Translated by Antony Beevor and Luba Vinogradova

MOSCOW 1941; A City and its People at War by Rodric Braithwaite

THE WHISPERERS; Private Life in Stalin's Russia by Orlando Figes

CHILD 44 and THE SECRET SPEECH by Tom Rob Smith

THE SECRET LIFE OF BLETCHLEY PARK by Sinclair McKay

RUSSKA by Edward Rutherford

A SPY AMONG FRIENDS; Kim Philby and the Great Betrayal by Ben Macintyre

PRISONERS OF GEOGRAPHY by Tim Marshall

436

Orphan of the State

ARCHANGEL by Robert Harris

PALACES, PATRONAGE and PILLS; Thomas Holloway; His Sanatorium by John Elliott

SMALL COMRADES; Revolutionising Childhood in Soviet Russia by Lisa Kirschenbaum

David J Robinson

ACKNOWLEDGEMENTS

I'd like to give a big thank you to the following people who offered advice and encouragement during the writing of Orphan Of The State.

They are, in no particular order:

Ian Ward, Lesley Ward, Dave Snazell, Mick Buckley, Maureen Lofthouse, Paul Harrison, David Belshaw, Mavis Newell, Marilyn and John Rushton, Rita and Harry Hornby, Allan Poyner, David and Doreen Woods, Anne Cort, Lisa Atkinson, Tom Rob Smith, Anthony Walton, David Holden, Joanne Geldard, Chris and Adam Hawra, Doug Watson, Nick Leyland, Katie Birks, Marianne Faithful, Graham Brindley, Lyndon Sumner, Frank and Nora Boswell, Ian Coogan, Julie Hitchens, Julie Croston, Tom Rawstorne, Olga Ivshina, Lucy Ash and Tim Marshall.

Special thanks to Mum and Dad, Pauline, Alexandra and Lauren, Julie, Dave and Hannah.
And finally, special thanks also to Victoria, Jessica and Emma for their patience and encouragement.

Printed in Great Britain
by Amazon